MONSTERS & ANGELS

Monsters & Angels

ONE TRAGIC DEATH, TWO HAUNTED LOVERS...THE DAWN OF AN IMMORTAL DYNASTY.

ANNE MARIE ANDRUS

ISBN: 0998415510
ISBN 13: 9780998415512

ALSO BY ANNE MARIE ANDRUS

RAIMOND

The Monsters & Angels Series

This book is dedicated to The Mothers;
To Rosemarie, and her unshakable faith,
To June, and her insatiable passion for New
Orleans,
&
To the spirits of the Crescent City,
All who grace the heavens, wander the streets,
and dance behind walls of stone,
Your footsteps fall next to mine,
Your voices whisper in my ear,
Your stories flow from my soul,
Vive la magie!

Chapter 1

NEW YORK, 1935

"A NURSE IS the Lord's fiercest angel."

Sorcha recited script painted over the double doors as she plucked hairpins from her handed-down nursing cap. *Malarkey. We're much too exhausted.*

The hum of voices giving orders and answers swirled down the hall behind her like invisible fog.

"No more exams." Sorcha let one hand fall on the worn door handle, drew a long breath and followed with the deliberate grasp of her other hand. "No more school." She burst through the hospital entrance, and shook her hair free to warm in the sun. "I've done it."

"So, you're gainfully employed?" The security guard tipped his cap.

"Starting tomorrow, I'll help put food on our table." Sorcha turned her face to the sky and savored the last of the brilliant, late October air. The streets of her neighborhood were crowded with residents dragging themselves home from work. On a whim, she stopped at a bodega to splurge on a few flowers.

"Congratulations on your graduation." The shop owner's eyes crinkled as he added extra blooms to her bouquet. "Nurse Alden."

Sorcha waved her hands in front of her face. "No, no. Nurse Alden is my mother. Though, perhaps I'll get used to it." She plunged her nose into the petals and jogged the last block to her grey apartment building.

"Mum, I'm home." Sorcha kicked the peeling front door shut. She pulled black and white portraits from her bag before she tossed it on the floor. "Need your opinion on my yearbook pictures. I don't love any of them, but you've always said my smile is my best feature. There are a few here…"

A teakettle's shrill whistle beckoned from the kitchen. Stepping around the corner, Sorcha tripped over a crumpled figure. "Mum!" Photographs and flowers tumbled to the floor as she knelt and shook the motionless woman's shoulder, staring into her blank eyes.

"Mum, are you…? Oh, God!" She brushed panic aside as instinct and training took over. *Pulse check, present, but weak. Breathing, shallow.* Her hand splashed in an expanding pool of blood and black fire seared behind her eyelids. *Damn, calm down. You know what to do. Now do it.*

Two steps at a time strained the muscles in her legs, but today Sorcha skipped more stairs than she hit. She pounded on the caretaker's door until his wife answered. "What's wrong?"

"Frannie! Mum fell—she's bleeding—can't wake her up."

"Take a deep breath, go to your mother. I'll be right there." Frannie dialed the operator while Sorcha raced back to her apartment.

Careful not to move her mother's neck, Sorcha sunk to the kitchen floor and cradled the limp body in her arms. "I'm here now." She dabbed blood from the back of her head with a pristine kitchen towel and winced as her fingers found a telltale squish at the base of the skull. "I'll buy you some new linens, don't worry. A few sutures in the emergency room will fix you right up."

She stared in disbelief as the bloody cloth turned from crimson to black in her hands. *Pull yourself together.* Sorcha squeezed her eyes closed, touched her forehead to her mother's, and prayed. *Please, God, I realize I'm a lousy Catholic, but my mother devoted her whole life to serving you, to helping the sick and dying. She needs you. I need you. I'll do anything. Please!*

Fingers tapped Sorcha's shoulders and tugged at her sleeves.

"The police will follow the ambulance." Frannie steered her away from the kitchen as the apartment filled with uniformed strangers. "You can ride with them, dear."

"Can they take her to St. Margaret's?" Sorcha asked. "We both work there."

"This way, Miss." An officer with gentle eyes guided her to his car. "Do you have family in New York?"

"No, it's just the two of us. My father was killed in the war." Sorcha stared at a stray drop of blood on her sleeve that bloomed in front of her eyes and shot up her arm like roots. She squished her eyelids shut to drive the illusion away.

The turmoil of lights and sirens gave way to the bustle of the emergency department and finally the forced tranquility of a private room. Sorcha sat motionless while an endless parade of doctors examined her mother and left without a diagnosis. The clock on the wall ticked, the shifts changed, and she lost all sense of day and night. She woke to a nurse with red hair, rubbing her shoulders. Doris, her mother's closest friend and co-worker, had taken over the room.

"So sorry. I must have dozed."

Doris shooed off-duty nurses out the door and clicked it closed. She dropped her voice to a whisper. "We have news, dear."

When the doctor spoke, his voice sounded familiar but his face was a blur. "Sorcha, we aren't sure whether it's apoplexy or bleeding inside her brain, but the damage is catastrophic. Adelaide is part of our family and this is a tragedy for all at St. Margaret's."

"Whatever you need, we'll help you," Doris said.

"Peace and dignity is all she ever wanted." Sorcha clutched her mother's hand and watched her shallow breathing falter. "Mum, please, I don't know what to do. Remember that new job I applied for, the Labor and Delivery position in Manhattan? I still need your advice. I may not be ready."

Doris squeezed Sorcha's arm. "I know you aren't ready, but it's time."

Only a priest and a small circle of close friends were present when the doctor pronounced time of death. No heroics, no strangers, no chaos.

Sorcha's hands trembled. *Remember Mum's secret.* Treading lightly to the window, she cracked it, then flung it wide open to set a beautiful soul free.

On a flat grey November morning, Adelaide's funeral took place in a cemetery overlooking the Hudson River and Palisades. Sorcha slipped graduation pictures into her mother's hand before the casket was closed. "You never got to see these, but I'll make something of myself. Promise."

"She was so very proud of you, dear. Always." Doris tucked tissues into Sorcha's pocket. "Being one of the top three nursing graduates in New York City is quite an honor."

"I'll do more." Sorcha waited for the last of the mourners to drift away before she plucked a pink rose from a bouquet beside the chapel's altar. "Like building the legacy she and Dad deserve."

As she placed the flower on the coffin, her hand brushed polished rosewood and a vision knocked her to her knees: a body alone in a dark forest, drenched in blood.

Is that me? This isn't happening. Sorcha wiped cold sweat off her forehead. *I do not see things.*

A priest ushered Sorcha to a pew. "Child, you're pale as a ghost. Your signature is required on one last paper, and then you should rest before the burial."

Sorcha willed her trembling hand to sign, but froze as she finished the *n* in Alden. *No, not again.* Blank faces danced against blinding white. Blood trickled down her fingers and oozed through the letters. *That's my name, written in blood, black as tar.* She whipped her hand back and flung the pen across the stone floor.

"What in the world?" The funeral director furiously motioned for help.

"A stranger was holding my hand." Sorcha stared at her fingers. "I swear, I saw it."

"Enough of this." Doris elbowed everyone away and crushed her in a hug. "There's no shame in crying, you know?"

"Wish I could." Sorcha dabbed dry eyes with her sleeve. "I'm fine, really. Just overwhelmed.

I'm not dying in a pool of blood or signing my life away in someone else's.

Extra night shifts at the bustling hospital provided Sorcha an escape from her lonely apartment and the first Thanksgiving without her mother.

"Sorcha, eat something." Doris tossed her nursing cap on the counter. "You're wasting away. And, don't be surprised when your peers start asking you to cover their holiday shifts. Heard them plotting."

"No one to be running home to, plus some of them are lousy…"

"Go ahead and say it." Doris crossed her arms. "Be honest."

"They're not, em, grandly ambitious."

"I hear the melody of your mother's voice in you, lassie."

"She made me practice and practice, until it was nearly gone." Sorcha's lip trembled.

"Not the easiest task, surrounded by us Irish folk," Doris said. "She wanted the best life for you."

"My accent still comes bubbling up when I'm tired or nervous. I want to hang on to it a wee bit. I've lost so much of Mum."

"You have her rebel instinct and shrewd judge of character." Doris patted her shoulder. "Miss her every day."

"Me too. Every minute."

"I know you had plans to work in maternity, but you should reconsider. These elderly patients' eyes light up when they see you."

"I'll think about it." Sorcha glanced at her watch. "Half five to start morning baths?"

Doris nodded. "Send your co-workers out here. Their break was over ten minutes ago."

A young nurse crept around the corner and poked Sorcha's shoulder. "Sorry to bother, but would you consider covering for me on Christmas Day?"

"Sure. Spend time with your family." *I should remember her name. The instructors yelled at her every day for making stupid mistakes.*

Another nurse followed with her fingers crossed. "How about my night shift on Saturday?"

"I'll do that too, don't worry." The girl's face exploded in a grin and forced one on Sorcha, too. *Don't know her name either, but the only thing worse than stupid is lazy.*

There wasn't much to do on her break except eat stale pastries and leaf through magazines in the tiny nurse's lounge. Sorcha held up a copy of *International Medicine,* wondering if it was current. She flipped the journal back to its cover. February 1935. Not bad for the rubbish pile. A full page advertisement pictured a young nurse with a radiant smile and a handful of maps. The organization provided training, housing, meals and travel.

How lovely would it be to escape all this and run away to an exotic land? *Not much left for me in New York.* Sorcha glanced around—the place was a ghost town. She tore the page out of the magazine and stuffed it in her pocket.

Chapter 2

THE CRESCENT

SORCHA'S HEAD SWIVELED as she navigated the train station, struggling to decipher the signs. She hurried down several hallways and trudged back again when she wound up at dead ends. She finally ducked behind a post and brushed the hood of her cape off her face. *If someone recognizes me, I'm sunk.* Scanning the crowd, she backed up until her shoes bumped the edge of the platform and steam hissed around her ankles.

"May I help you, ma'am?"

Sorcha whirled toward the voice and flailed her arms for balance before the conductor hauled her onto The Crescent. "Thank you, I'm—oh golly, my ticket." She dug into her pockets.

"First, your bag." The conductor plucked Sorcha's luggage off the platform.

"Got it!" Sorcha presented a creased document, printed with her new beginning.

"Miss Sor...hmm...Alden, cabin forty-two is this way. Good choice."

"Spent most of my savings on it." Sorcha followed her through the narrow passage and collapsed into a seat. Her grip on the armrest turned her fingernails dusky gray.

"You're anxious?"

"I am, a little." *Try petrified.*

"Well, relax. I'll make sure you enjoy the ride."

"Thank you..." She studied the conductor's nametag as The Crescent rolled out of the station. "Alexa." *Since when do women work on trains?*

Sorcha leaned her head back against the seat and let the pulse of the rails permeate her body. *Hope this journey isn't a mistake, because there's no back-up plan.* She watched small towns and fields zip past in the pre-dawn light and dozed off until bright sun forced her awake. Her legs wobbled when she stood to adjust her slate-blue skirt and white blouse. The graduation gift from her mother gave the illusion that she actually had a figure.

"Looks custom-made." Alexa leaned in the compartment door.

"Bit loose. I forget to eat. No wonder men don't give me a second glance. Why can't I look like Greta Garbo?"

"Garbo probably wishes she had your hair." Alexa smirked. "Long waves with auburn highlights. We should all be so lucky."

"Please don't be offended, but how did you get your job?"

"I needed to hide this frizz." Alexa removed her hat to unleash unruly curls. "I really want to be the engineer. You know, drive the train. Only reason they let me work here at all is my father owns part of the railroad." The conductor offered her hand. "Alexa St. James. Think I'm about to mangle your name but, Sorka?"

"That's the true Gaelic pronunciation, but my mum preferred Sor-sha."

Alexa nodded. "Got it."

Sorcha's lips twitched into a smile before she remembered to shake hands. "Sorry, I'm jittery around people."

Alexa slid the compartment door shut. "Not that there's anything wrong with it, but why are you traveling alone?"

"For a new job, as a nurse."

"Impressive."

Sorcha shook her head. "Salary's not."

"Never is for us girls. Where?"

Sorcha produced the official letter from her satchel and read the final line. "We are eagerly awaiting confirmation of your arrival. The

Sisters of the Peace."

"Ah, New Orleans."

"Corner of Gravier and Magazine Streets. Sounds so exotic."

"Been there." Alexa rubbed a smudge off the window. "I mean, to see friends. It's the best hospital in the city, but they have strict visiting hours."

"I've never been out of New York. Not sure what to expect." Sorcha held up a yellow pamphlet. "These travel essays are mostly maps and pictures of the Mississippi River."

"I've visited New Orleans more times than I can count. My father says it's the land of sinners and devil parades."

"Devils?"

"Not exactly, but every inch of the place is haunted. I've seen odd things like people who move so fast, my eyes can't catch up with them."

"I don't believe in any of that." Sorcha forced herself to breathe.

"You may change your mind."

"Tell me something less, em, scary?" Sorcha stretched cramps out of her fingers.

"Musicians play in the street in every corner and doorway. You'll always hear them in the distance, even in your bed at night."

"I like that."

"The smells are strong—some not so great. Outside the bars at night it smells like a barnyard."

"Ugh." Sorcha wrinkled her nose.

"But," Alexa held up her finger, "in the morning, after everything is clean, the aroma of fresh baking and coffee takes over. Strong, chicory coffee. You've never tasted anything like it."

"Can't believe I'm saying this." Sorcha rubbed her belly. "I'm hungry."

Alexa cracked the door open to the sound of clinking dishes. "Ooo, I need to get back to work. I'll show you to the dining car."

"If it wasn't included in the ticket, I can't afford it." Sorcha dropped her eyes.

"You're eating." Alexa pointed down the passage. "I'll take care of it."

Sorcha returned to her cabin after lunch and unpacked a box from her New York apartment. *Where's that locket?* She sifted through pictures, letters and a pair of ticket stubs from the 1932 World Series. *Mum's guilty pleasure—the Yankees. What was I, nineteen years old? I can't believe that was only three years ago.* Sorcha didn't realize she was holding her breath until her nose began to burn with the scent of roses. She expected her mother to walk through the door any minute.

"Everything all right?"

"Mum?" Sorcha grabbed the locket and slammed the box shut. "Oh, Alexa."

"What are you running from?"

"Pardon?"

"I saw that look in your eyes, back in Penn Station." Alexa handed her a bottle of soda-pop. "Come on, you can talk to me."

"I was worried someone would scare me out of this whole trip. I'm not known for courage." Sorcha wilted into her seat and sipped the soda. "I lost my mother last autumn."

"Oh, dear. I'm so sorry for your loss."

"It was an accident." The air thickened in Sorcha's throat. Tears threatened, but didn't flow. "The doctors couldn't save her."

"And this New Orleans job?"

"Pretty much a volunteer position that I accepted without thinking. I forgot I even mailed the application." Sorcha's eyes wandered to the window. "I'm after honoring Mum's life and work. Her legacy."

"I think it's admirable."

"Running away from home?"

Alexa placed a hand on Sorcha's shoulder. "Maybe you're running toward a new home. Get some rest. Seven o'clock will be here before you know it."

Sorcha slipped the locket over her neck, buried the chain under her blouse and focused on the hypnotic thrum of the rails. *It's almost time.*

Alexa tapped Sorcha's shoulder as the train slowed. "Wake up. It's six-thirty."

Sorcha's stomach flipped.

"Remember what you're here for—to make your mother proud."

"Thank you for your kindness." Sorcha's gaze followed the train tracks as they curled along the Mississippi River. Even in the fading light of the March evening, vicious swirls and eddies roiled the brown water. *Doesn't look great for swimming.*

"We received a telegram that a porter from the church will meet you at the station." Alexa crossed her arms. "Listen, as much as I love New Orleans, it's not a place to walk alone at night."

Sorcha's knees buckled when she stepped onto the station's platform. She looked down to see tremoring wooden planks under her shoes.

Alexa grabbed her elbow. "Whoa, are you okay?"

"Yes, grand." Sorcha glanced around the frenzy of passengers, all standing firmly on stable ground. "Too many hours on the train, is all."

"I think this is yours." Alexa held out the cape. "May not need it in the South."

"Oh my, thank you." Sorcha folded the navy fabric and tucked it under her arm. "It was a gift from nursing school on the night of my pinning ceremony. My security blanket."

"There's your porter."

Sorcha glanced back at The Crescent. The shiny silver and chrome was now cloaked in grime. *I'm a long way from New York.*

"*Bienvenue*, Miss Alden, I'm Joseph." The stout man tipped his cap. "Follow me. Take care you don't twist an ankle on the banquette."

"The bank-what?" Sorcha watched Joseph point to the pitted

sidewalk. "Ah, got it."

"Folks 'round here will help you pick up New Orleans lingo in no time."

Sorcha trailed the porter from Southern Railway Terminal, navigating uneven banquettes and endless turns on the way to the convent. The New Orleans air clung to her skin like soggy paper. *New York is humid in the summer. This is dripping-down-my-face muggy.* She dabbed her forehead with her sleeve and stared straight ahead, glad to have Joseph to walk her past the unsavory characters on the crooked curbs. *Quite sure I look like an out-of-towner.*

Gas street lamps flickered on as dusk surrendered to darkness. Sorcha ran her hand along block after block of whitewashed stone. *Everything here is behind a wall.* She gasped at her first glimpse into a courtyard. A lush, candlelit garden was tucked behind the scrolled gate. Sounds of bubbling water hinted at a secret fountain amongst the flowers.

"Come along, Miss. I thought I'd lost you."

"Yes of course, Joseph. I'm sorry."

"Long trip?"

"Yes, very, very long." Instinctively, she touched her locket and followed him to the threshold of a weathered building.

Massive doors creaked on their hinges and a girl in a flowing, white habit tumbled off her bench in the foyer. "Miss Alden—I was afraid you'd changed your mind about coming."

Sorcha touched her hair and tamed stray ends with her fingers.

"Oh, where are my manners? I'm Sister Ann. I made up a little room where you can get a good night's rest. Nurses live in the barracks, but they're settled in for the night, so you can meet them tomorrow. I'll send dinner—you must be ready to drop."

"Thank you, Sister." Sorcha followed her up the winding stairs.

After almost nodding off in the small bathtub, Sorcha slipped on her nightgown and paused at a keyhole window, drawn to the same garden sanctuary she glimpsed from the street. The steamy air lent a shimmering gloss to the foliage. *I smell flowers.* Every spring, blossoms sprouted in the tiny gardens of her neighborhood, but nothing this intoxicating. The spicy bowl of soup sent up by Sister Ann stopped her stomach's growling. She drifted to sleep with her fingers wrapped around her polished locket, as the breeze of a mysterious city blew straight in her window.

Chapter 3

ZELIA

SORCHA WOKE TO a rap on her door.

Where am I?

Memories of yesterday's journey flooded back and her mouth watered as the aroma of coffee and baking bread wafted into the room. Certain she would be issued a nursing uniform later, Sorcha pinned her hair back and dressed in the plainest clothes she owned. Making her way down the stairs, she followed the unmistakable clink of silverware on dishes.

Sister Ann rose to greet her. "Mother Superior and Sisters of the Peace, this is Sorcha Alden. Her train from New York arrived late last night."

The sisters murmured their hellos and welcomes. Mother Superior stood, towering over Sister Ann. She introduced herself and grasped both of the newcomer's hands. "Thank you for your sacrifice to aid our patients in these times of desperation and poverty."

"I'm anxious to meet the team and begin my training," Sorcha said.

"Very soon, but first you must eat. You'll need your strength." Mother Superior pointed to a seat, and retook hers as the entire table resumed their meal.

Sorcha assumed a convent would have simple food, but these nuns could teach New York a thing or two about serving breakfast—there were plates of croissants, sweet rolls and bacon. She took a bite of poached eggs on a biscuit and her fork froze in mid-air.

Sister Ann nudged her shoulder. "Good?"

Sorcha swallowed and nodded. "I've never had…" She lifted a forkful of eggs draped with ham and drizzled with creamy sauce. "So extravagant."

"Eggs Benedict. Served every morning." Sister Ann leaned over and whispered, "Our medical director makes sure we never go hungry."

Sorcha ate until she was stuffed and took full advantage of the bottomless pot of coffee. Alexa had been right. Nothing on the East Coast prepared her for the taste of New Orleans coffee.

Back in her room, Sorcha discovered a little note folded and tucked in the pocket of her cape. Perfect handwriting on Crescent letterhead gave an address in Nashville, Tennessee.

In case you need a friend,
Alexa St. James

My first friend. Sorcha hid the paper behind the pictures in her locket and followed Joseph to the nurse's barracks. Spanish-style buildings lined a courtyard, featuring ornate porches and a scaled-down version of the convent garden. Everything looked well cared for and smelled fresh. Painters had even worked around vines crawling up the walls. The sag in the roof looked built in. The porter had barely handed Sorcha over to Sister Ann when a slim nurse ran up and grabbed her sleeve.

"I'll take it from here." The young woman's mahogany eyes lit up. "I'm your lonely roommate, Zelia Pavet, who's been dying to meet you."

"Is this our room?" Sorcha peeked through the French doors.

"Yes, but unpack later, let's walk to the hospital—can't let you get lost on your first day."

"You must have heard about my lousy sense of direction." Sorcha couldn't help but smile, though sweat trickled down her back. "Is it always so hot here?"

"We're having a warm snap for March, but during the summer nobody steps outside during the middle of the day. You either go out early in the morning or after dark, unless you're a tourist." Zelia winked and held the hospital door open to a spacious lobby cooled by fans. The nursing office provided short-sleeved, cotton uniforms.

"What's this three-petal gold design?" Sorcha pointed to the front of her blouse. "It's everywhere."

"*Mais chère*, that's our *fleur-de-lis*, brought here in 1718 when explorers claimed *La Nouvelle Orleans* for King Louis of France."

"It's beautiful."

"We're a diverse city with unified pride." Zelia pointed to each petal in order. "Past, present, future."

The façade of the Sisters of the Peace hospital resembled its name—smooth and austere. On the inside, it couldn't have been more opposite. Patients crowded the corridors, leaned against walls and slept on cots in the corners.

Sorcha blinked hard. "Did I mention I wanted to be a Labor and Delivery nurse?"

"Not as bad as it looks." Zelia swept another door open and nodded as Sorcha passed through. "When you get to know the doctors and nurses, you'll see."

Sorcha pretended to believe her. *So many new faces. Thank God for name tags.*

The patients were sicker than she expected, diagnosed with fevers and tropical diseases rarely seen in New York. Ten nurses had answered the magazine advertisement and joined the international team. Being Zelia's roommate kept Sorcha in the inner circle and up-to-date with all the gossip. During the first chaotic days of orientation, she worked alongside Angela from California and Ivori, a nurse from Plaquemines Parish just outside the city.

"Can I help you finish up, Ivori? Take some vital signs, maybe?" Sorcha asked. "You look exhausted."

"Pfft." Ivori turned her back.

"Does she have a problem with me?" Sorcha pulled Zelia aside. "Ivori's work is meticulous, but she refuses to make eye contact, no matter how professional the conversation."

"Don't mind her. She comes from an old family with lots of history." Zelia snorted. "There's plenty of peculiar in this town—and she sees things."

"Things?"

"Ghosts, angels, spirits…different rubbish every day."

Angela whirled around the corner and grabbed Sorcha's hands. "Are you coming out with us tonight? Hope you didn't forget. Zelia's been planning this French Quarter outing all week."

"It's Friday already?" Sorcha slumped against the wall.

"Come on, it's a celebration! We have tomorrow off—you can sleep in," Angela begged. "Everyone's telling me tall tales, even the patients. I need adventure."

"Okay, sounds fun and I'm dying of curiosity." On her way to the lounge full of giggling nurses, a distinguished man in a long, white lab coat caught Sorcha's eye. She'd seen him before, but always in the evening when they were gathering their things to leave. Senior staff worked during the daytime—nights were reserved for residents. She poked Zelia's shoulder. "Is that doctor with the dark hair new?"

"No, dingy. That's Dr. Banitierre. Patients need care after dark too—that's what he says. The man is sent from God, working the graveyard shift all the time." Zelia looked Sorcha up and down. "How have you not met the director of our mission?"

Sorcha rolled her shoulder and winced.

"What is wrong with your arm, *chère?*"

"Fingers keep falling asleep." Sorcha shook her tingling hand. "Why do I smell cookies?"

Chapter 4

THE WATCHERS

THE PARTY KICKED off in the barracks as nurses changed clothes and primped for their first excursion in the Crescent City. Sorcha's only summer outfit was a flowing lavender dress with gossamer sleeves. After a week of jamming her hair into a nursing cap, loose waves were a simple treat. She tucked her precious locket under the ribbon collar.

They dodged the Canal Streetcar and filed down Decatur Street, close enough to the river to smell wet tobacco and rotten eggs. Ivori held her nose and dragged her feet. After a few blocks, cramped warehouse rows opened up into an expansive square surrounding a bronze statue.

Zelia poked Sorcha's arm. "That's Andrew Jackson on his horse."

"Got it—Jackson Square." Sorcha caught her first glimpse of St. Louis Cathedral against the pink and purple backdrop of a late winter sky. She stopped so abruptly on the flagstones, Zelia nearly knocked her over. Three spires soared above the white façade; she craned her neck to see the top of the middle one. Pictures on postcards had done no justice to this castle from another world.

"We can go to mass here, if you'd like."

"I'm not all that religious, but I'd love to see this church," Sorcha said. "I know this sounds stupid, but what is *Rue* on some of the street signs?"

"That's French for street. The city is finally getting serious about preserving the *Vieux Carré's* history, and there's plenty more to see." Zelia dragged her roommate past apartment houses decorated with tropical flowers overflowing their ornate galleries.

"Who lives there?"

"Lucky people. *Chère*, pay attention to your surroundings and don't trust strangers."

"*Rue Royale*." Sorcha pointed to a street sign on the next block. "Using the French word will help me remember which streets I've walked on."

Sorcha stumbled forward on the cobblestones. Her eyes were glued to iron lacework, potted gardens and treasures displayed in lit windows. She stared at painted lead soldiers, iridescent jewelry and chandeliers of stained glass. The single element of the *fleur-de-lis* was the thread that spun it all together—in every color and size.

Zelia chose a cozy restaurant with gas lamps on the walls and flickering candles on each table. Rich-sounding items that Sorcha couldn't even pronounce filled the menu. "Em, my paycheck."

"Stop squinting, *chère*. I'll help you order. Hospital employees don't pay full price here, anyway."

Sorcha sat on her shaking fingers and studied her options. Oysters, shrimp remoulade, and turtle soup. *Turtle anything sounds disgusting.*

When the waiter arrived, Zelia ordered her roommate a Garnet Martini, pecan-crusted gulf fish and turtle soup.

"Turtle? No way."

"It's delicious," Zelia said. "Trust me."

Sorcha nodded to the waiter. *Probably not eating the soup.* The martini went down easily, but made the room tilt.

"If y'all want to poison your bodies, it's not me you'll be answering to." Ivori sipped water and glared at her co-workers.

Not a stitch of jewelry. Not a wisp of make-up. Real party girl, that one. Sorcha surprised herself by trying the turtle soup, and devouring it. *Tastes like…pepper steak.* She took charge of her own dessert, ordered the bread pudding and was stuffed by the time the group wandered into the music-filled street.

While the nurses window-shopped, Ivori paced the center of the street. "Y'all can't hide from the watchers."

"The who, now?" Sorcha leaned closer and was met with the back of Ivori's tightly twisted bun. "Why did you come out with us if you didn't want to have fun?"

Ivori flicked her hand in dismissal.

Never mind her. Behind the cathedral, Sorcha was drawn to a lighted figure whose shadow covered the entire back wall of the building. Dramatic, stunning and beautiful in its simplicity.

"That's the Statue of the Sacred Heart, and this is St. Anthony's Garden," Zelia said.

"I could stare at this all night." Sorcha stalled in the street again.

"Unfortunately, we still have a curfew."

Sorcha stared at the clock above the shadow. "Midnight, already?" As they scurried toward home, her companions froze in front of a dark alley.

Angela jumped back like a frightened cat. "Ghost!"

"Don't be ridiculous. There are no ghosts." Sorcha crept up and peered over shoulders, waiting for a ghoul to spring from the dark. *Are they making fun of Ivori or playing a joke on me?* "All I see is a pile of old furniture."

Charged silence was followed by the footsteps of fleeing girls. Everyone except Ivori, who had disappeared.

"Jayz, wait!" Sorcha forced herself not to chase them. *No running on the banquette.* A faint noise made her backtrack and peek into the murky alley. *A hiss or a drip?* Invisible fingers of ice skimmed her cheeks, sending her scampering down the block to the safety of her friends. "Just a pile of garbage."

"Yes, of course," the nurses mumbled in unison.

Alexa did say the city was haunted.

Back at the barracks, Sorcha lingered at the dressing mirror, brushing her hair and replaying the evening in her mind. "Zel, what's that fragrance I only smell after dark?"

"Night jasmine. You don't have it in New York?"

"We do not. It's enchanting—one of my first, strongest

impressions of New Orleans along with the oppressive humidity."

"You never really escape the heat." Zelia chuckled.

"It was simply junk in that alley, right?" Sorcha checked the lock on the shutters. "Maybe I was dreaming, but I'm sure I heard people whispering."

"*Chère*, in this city, nothing is simple and anything is possible."

The French Quarter's top bartender was still shaking his head long after the pack of giggling nurses left the restaurant. His jaw dropped as regular customers tossed large bills on the bar and vacated seats they occupied until closing every night. Before he brandished a bar rag, the coveted chairs were filled with a party of three, dressed in the latest fashions and flashing another impressive amount of cash.

"You almost got us caught, fool." A tall blonde flicked away the crumbs and napkins in front of her. "Dropping that ridiculous handkerchief."

"Oh, please." The only man in the trio flagged down the bartender with a twirl of his finger. "The usual, Jeffrey."

"You got it, Steven." Jeffrey grabbed two bottles at a time and began to pour.

"Julia, you forced us to spy on those girls. I was perfectly fine perusing the options in here." Steven's eyes wandered over the patrons.

"Stop the bickering, both of you. It's tiresome."

"See, you're even giving Lily a headache." Julia grabbed a glass out of the bartender's hand.

"Murder." Steven sipped his martini. "Julia, you need something stronger than anemic white wine. Or just drink more."

"You and the ridiculous slang," Julia said. "Are you gate-crashing college hops again?"

"Go head and shrivel into an old bird. I'm the eternal live wire."

Steven swiped a full bottle from the bar and shoved it at Julia. "Let me guess. We're snooping on silly nurses to protect Raimond from the grave danger of a redhead."

"Really?" Lily tossed her long black hair aside to stare at Julia. "Raimond is in love with the redhead?"

"No. Shut up." Julia slammed the bottle on the bar, her eyes shooting daggers at anyone who turned around. "He referred to someone a few times and I was curious. The brunette—who is in dire need of a map."

"Hmm… she's much more his type," Lily said.

Julia groaned and stared at the crowds trudging up and down Royal.

"She was the least stupid of the bunch." Steven snapped the cuffs of his dress shirt. "Saw the alley was full of trash, not ghosts."

"Only because she didn't look up." Julia pointed at her companions. "At you two, clinging to the walls."

"And if she did, we would have erased her memory. No harm done." Steven zeroed in on a tourist sipping cheap bourbon and teetering on his bar stool. "If you ladies will excuse me, I see someone tasty."

"Make it quick." Julia finished another glass of wine. "We're meeting Raimond at midnight."

"Still need instructions on how to babysit the kingdom?" Steven looked at both girls. "Come on, that was funny."

"I hate these hospital trips. They drag on forever." Lily dropped her forehead onto the bar. "Without him, our family is…"

"Don't even talk like that." Steven squeezed Lily's shoulders. "And Julia, we'll keep an eye on the nurse situation."

"We'd better," Julia mumbled. "Because the girls Raimond falls for—these sweet, innocent flowers—tend to cause incredible damage."

Chapter 5

MARION

FOLLOWING THEIR ADVENTURE in the French Quarter, the nurses-in-training spent Saturday sitting in the convent courtyard, chasing the shade and sipping lemonade. Sorcha refused to acknowledge Ivori glowering from behind the porch columns. *Don't care where she went last night or what time she got home.* Angela shoved a letter under her nose, and interrupted her daydream.

"Someone slid this through the front door. Who's it from?"

Sorcha unfolded the paper. "Alexa. I met her on the train. She wants to have coffee." She spent the rest of her day wondering how to sneak out of the hospital on Tuesday and getting talked into working a few extra hours.

Maybe I'll catch another glimpse of the mysterious Dr. Banitierre.

"I appreciate your help, Nurse Alden." Sister Ann slumped her shoulders and stared at the pile of charts on her desk. "Not many of your colleagues take extra shifts on this ward."

"It's no problem. I enjoy working here. I'll get Miss Marion ready for bed."

"Such a tragic case. Marion was a proper southern lady before she fell ill."

"She still is." Sorcha tied the strings of her uniform behind her back. "She communicates with her eyes, but it takes patience to decipher what she's saying."

"It's a blessing to have you with us." Sister Ann returned to her mountain of work, leaving the young nurse in charge of the fifth floor.

Sorcha stuffed her pockets with medication and piled linens so high in her arms that she couldn't see past them. *Why on earth is Marion's door shut?* She juggled the stack and nudged the door open with her elbow.

"What the—" Sorcha dropped crisp sheets on the floor and gawked at a stranger. "What are you doing to my patient? I wasn't informed of any procedures tonight."

"I'm practicing, nurse."

"Practicing what?" Sorcha grabbed the sterile drape off Marion's face. "You're suffocating her."

"Listen little miss, this is a teaching hospital, and I'm here to learn. Fluff the pillows in the next room."

"Excuse me, Dr. Winters." Sorcha read from his name tag before reaching across the bed and grabbing the bloody syringe from his hand. "You're hurting her. Did she give consent for this torture?"

"Nobody cares." The doctor opened a new needle. "Stand back, I'm busy."

"Over my dead body." Sorcha knew she should take deep breaths and calm down, but before she had time to think, she found herself on the opposite side of the bed, knocking Dr. Winters on his backside.

"Your dead body, nurse? Try fired body." The man scrambled to his feet. "You little bitch. I hope this vegetable was worth it because you'll be unemployed in an hour."

"Get out." Sorcha shoved the doctor to the ground again. "Get the hell out!" She followed him as he crawled to the door, kicking it shut behind him.

Sorcha squeezed Marion's hand and nodded as she blinked her eyes furiously. "Never mind that eejit, he's not coming back. Let's get you ready for bed."

Sorcha trudged down the hall, peeked around the wall of the nursing station and listened to her co-workers pepper Zelia with questions.

"What happened again?" Angela asked.

"I told you." Zelia placed her palms on the desk. "She knocked Dr. Winters on the floor."

"Sorcha really did that?" Angela shook her head. "So unlike her."

"Didn't think she had it in her," Ivori said.

"I hope she doesn't get fired," Angela whispered. "Dr. Winters is mean to everyone, even the patients."

"She looked terrible when I saw her," Zelia said. "Been awake all night."

Sorcha took a deep breath and stepped around the corner to face a sea of blank faces.

Zelia pushed past the gawking nurses. "What happened?"

"Fired."

Angela gasped.

"No, no. I'm sorry." Sorcha waved both hands in front of her face. "Not me. They fired Dr. Winters."

"Oh, thank God," Zelia said.

"What a shame." Ivori's eyes never budged from her paperwork. "I was betting you'd quit."

"Shut your miserable mouth." Zelia glared at Ivori, steered Sorcha away and gathered her in a hug. "Ignore her, *chère*. You need sleep."

"I'm headed back to our room right now." Sorcha squeezed her hand and shuffled down the hall. Lost in her bleary world, she turned a corner and smashed into a stranger.

"Hi. I, em, I'm sorry, sir. I wasn't looking." A hint of cinnamon swirled in the air around her.

"No harm done, Nurse Alden. You've made quite a name for yourself. I'm Raimond Banitierre."

"Dr. Banitierre..." Sorcha's eyes followed the chiseled curve of his profile. Her spine tingled when she met his gaze.

Raimond lifted Sorcha's hand and held it still. "You must be exhausted."

"I am." Sorcha took half a step back from his firm grasp and cool skin. *He's just being polite.* "Thank you for not firing me."

"Dr. Winters was already on probation for poor ethical judgment. Tonight was the final straw."

"He was so awful to Miss Marion." Sorcha swallowed hard. "I couldn't..."

"Not many nurses have the courage to defend a patient as you did. Assaulting other employees, however, is not acceptable."

"I know that, sir. Won't happen again." *Don't know how it happened this time.*

He flashed a smile, more on one side of his mouth than the other. "I look forward to working with you."

After he walked away, Sorcha rubbed the throbbing at the base of her neck. *Almost made a complete fool of myself.*

"You're supposed to be resting in the barracks." Huddled in a supply closet, Zelia peeked into the hall and repeated her answer despite Sorcha's badgering. "There's no deep, dark story about Banitierre. He's been a respected doctor here for as long as anyone can remember."

"I'm just curious. I mean, he's the reason I still have my job."

"He's got a reputation for being fair and level-headed. Saw through that resident's garbage story."

"How old is he anyway?" Sorcha touched her forehead and winced.

"*Chère*, I don't know. Too old for you, but the city is full of eligible and acceptable suitors."

"Not interested in men."

"That's hard to believe. A beautiful girl like you?"

"I had one boyfriend—it didn't end well." Sorcha closed her eyes against the past. She leaned on the wall and committed every inch of Dr. Banitierre's face to memory.

Raimond ignored the glare of bar lights, along with the villains and drunks that made Bourbon Street their playground. His commanding stride propelled him to a decaying house, just past the point where the street turned dangerously dark.

Dangling gutters and crippled railings blended one home into the next for blocks at a time. He found the decline of the *Vieux Carré* tragic, yet still beautiful with its lace ironwork and stained glass...if one looked past the ruined surface, into the elegant disrepair.

Black doctor's bag in hand, Raimond rapped an ancient knocker against the warped oak door. Tonight's mission was an act of compassion in sharp contrast to the excess and debauchery that made the city famous, and the first step in his recommitment to an oath taken decades ago. Complacency and apathy had derailed him for long enough.

If he was completely honest with himself, his motive was selfish. The endurance of his own kind was directly linked to humanity's survival, but his faith in mortals had been rekindled by the actions of one fledgling nurse.

Chapter 6

CLOVES

EARLY TUESDAY MORNING, a hush of suspense fell over the hospital staff as they waited for an emergency announcement.

Sorcha nudged Zelia's elbow and pointed to a line of photographs set up on easels across the stage. "What are all those?"

"Medical teams from past missions." Zelia swiveled around. "I see the photographer waiting in the back."

Dr. Banitierre strode to the front of the auditorium and took the podium. "Welcome. I know you've all made personal sacrifices to be here, committed to our humanitarian work. Word has arrived from our affiliate hospital in Nepal. They're prepared to host our team next month."

Dr. Banitierre paused while the Sisters shushed the crowd.

"The trip will take approximately ten days by steamship and overland. Our departure date is scheduled for two weeks from today. Everyone will need preventative vaccinations. The hospital will issue uniforms, hats, trekking gear and boots. This is a different environment than you're used to, with uncommon diseases, and you'll be provided materials to study before we arrive. Good luck and may our Lord bless this mission!"

Everyone in the room rose and applauded as the lead doctor accepted handshakes from his senior staff. Team members brimmed with questions.

"Can you believe we're leaving?" Angela asked.

"I hope it's not too much new information to learn," Zelia said.

"How many shots do we need to get?" Sorcha slumped in her chair. "And do we really need boots?"

After the group and individual pictures, Zelia found Sorcha hiding in the restroom. "Why so quiet?"

"Just overwhelmed. Wish Mum could see me now." Sorcha turned on the sink and splashed cold water on her face. "How much would it cost to get a copy of that group picture?"

"About a week's pay, for a small one."

"Oh." Sorcha's face fell. "Mum had a dear friend, Doris. I left without saying good-bye. I'd love to send her a picture and tell her I'm all right."

"I'll spot you the money."

"You'd do that?"

"Of course. You're part of our family here. Everyone looks out for everyone else. Even Ivori. And I'll cover for you today so you can meet your friend."

Sorcha hugged Zelia and exhaled. "Let's get these shots over with. I want to see this trekking gear. How far do we have to hike anyway?"

In only five minutes outside in early May, Sorcha was sweating through her underwear. *Feels like the Fourth of July in New York.* Before her eyes adjusted to the dim light of the corner diner, someone grabbed her hand.

"Glad you could sneak away." Alexa rubbed the hem of Sorcha's blouse. "Pretty official."

Sorcha gasped as Alexa dragged her out the side door. "You look so different out of uniform."

"We'll eat in the courtyard."

"Stinks back here." Sorcha sat at a lopsided table and scratched candle wax off a piece of worn wood. "Is this…a spirit board?"

"For the séances." Alexa pulled out a brown cigarette and lit it. "What's new with you?"

"You smoke?" Sorcha shifted back in her chair.

"Just cloves—take a whiff."

"Smells like the voodoo shop."

"I thought you didn't believe in all that?" Alexa tilted her head.

"I do not. But my friends might."

"Want a drag?" Alexa held the cigarette out. "Nobody's watching."

"We're leaving for Nepal in two weeks." Sorcha leaned across the table and wrapped her lips around the cigarette. Tingling in her throat escalated to a blaze in her chest. She gulped two glasses of water before she stopped coughing. "Never done that before."

"I wouldn't have guessed." Alexa pushed a plate of toast across the table. "You need to get out more. Tell me about Nepal."

An hour flew by as the friends updated each other on their adventures, picking up right where they left off on the train.

"I'm pushing my luck, being gone so long." Sorcha brushed crumbs off her skirt.

"Where can I write to you?" Alexa asked. With Sorcha's address in her pocket, she disappeared, swallowed up by the New Orleans streets as if she were never there.

Luckily I can see the hospital tower from here, or I'd be hopelessly lost. On her walk back, Sorcha shook off visions of a body crumpled in a gutter. *No more smoking.* She started to imagine the consequences if the scent of cloves lingered on her hair or uniform. She peeked in a side door before tiptoeing into the hospital.

"Don't think you're getting away scot-free."

Sorcha whirled at the unexpected voice.

Ivori stepped from the shadows. "You have the boneyard eyes."

"There you go again," Sorcha hissed, "spouting craziness."

"Mark my words, Miss New York." Ivori pointed to Sorcha. "You will bring nothing but disaster."

Sorcha was shocked by the amount of supplies required for a trip to the far side of the world. She expected to bring new technology and penicillin, but bandages and stretchers? *We take all that for granted. The place might be in bad shape.*

When time allowed, the nurses slipped into town to stock up on items they couldn't live without. For Sorcha, that thing was lipstick. She and Zelia always stopped for refreshments across the street from St. Louis Cathedral, where the riverboat whistles serenaded them as they sipped café-au-lait.

"I'm going to miss this." In the boutiques lining Jackson Square, Sorcha found the perfect plum shade of lipstick before turning her attention to combs and barrettes. Her thick hair hung halfway down her back, a handful in the southern humidity. "Who needs fancy hair accessories in a rural hospital village?"

"But?" Zelia plunked a hand on her hip.

Sorcha held up a sapphire comb with tiny purple and green beads glued in intricate swirls. "Have to have it."

"*Chére*, New Orleans is finally getting to you."

"This weather sure is." Sorcha fanned herself with a restaurant menu. "I'm not breathing the air, I'm wearing it."

"I think it's hot where we're going too," Zelia said. "Good training."

"Can we walk past the back of the cathedral on the way home?"

"Yes, just remember to steer clear of strangers. If you get a bad feeling, follow your gut. Never know who's lurking about."

Sorcha watched through the wrought-iron fence as the small statue grew into a giant at dusk. Jasmine, oak and magnolia laced every breath she took.

Once they were safely home in their room, Sorcha tapped Zelia's shoulder before she dozed off. "Do you think it's okay if I keep my locket on during our trip? I feel lost without it."

"You're not one for jewelry." Zelia propped herself up on one elbow. "I've been meaning to ask you about that little charm."

"It has two black and white pictures." Sorcha pulled the chain over her head and clicked the locket open. "One is me and Mum, and the other is my parents' wedding day. Adelaide and Captain Robert Alden." Sorcha's heart swelled with pride and her eyes brimmed with sadness. "British Royal Navy."

"So regal, Adelaide and Robert. You never talk about them."

"Mum was a nurse in Ireland in 1914."

"The mystery of the Irish accent, solved," Zelia said.

"Don't hide it very well, do I?" Sorcha nodded when Zelia shook her head. "Mum met a British sailor on the hospital ward, after he was injured in a firing drill. A minor wound, according to her, but he kept making up reasons to return. I think it was love at first sight for him, but Mum made him chase her—hard."

"Did they elope?" Zelia whispered.

"Not really, they got married on an emergency pass my dad begged from the admiral. But her parents were a doctor and nurse, so marrying a military man was not what they envisioned. Mum realized she was pregnant after Dad's ship was already at sea. When she got word to him, he insisted she stay with family friends in Manhattan."

"He sent her to America?"

"To flee the war. My very pregnant mother told my grandparents nothing, got on a steamer and headed west. She became a mother, and then a widow—all in about four months."

"*Chère*, don't you dare take that locket off. Is it gold?"

Sorcha shrugged. "So, I've been meaning to ask you what the **R** on your name tag stands for."

"An old family name, Roussel. It's not used much anymore. A long story for another night." Zelia rolled over and back again. "Do you know about the Bon Voyage party?"

"What party? When?"

"This Sunday night. Dr. Banitierre is hosting dinner at a private French Quarter club in honor of our mission and—well—us."

"Same restaurant we had dinner in last time?" Sorcha asked.

"No, this one's a little deeper into the Quarter."

Everything Banitierre does is a surprise. Of course I'm in the dark. "Are you sure I'm invited?"

"Um—yes. Why would you ask that?"

"Because, I have no idea what to wear."

"How about the skirt you wore on the train? I can lend you my sleeveless white blouse and you can wear that comb that you spent a month's pay on."

"Good thinking. Is Ivori going?"

Zelia flopped back into her pillow. "We need someone to protect us from the ghosts, right?"

Sorcha tossed and turned for hours, twisting bed sheets into knots from nightmares that whipped her through the uneven streets of the city. Screams filled her sleep as she clawed at the cobblestones. She kicked hard against the monster, but nothing freed her legs from the fierce grip of giant fangs. She looked at her hands, sticky with her own blood. *I'm done—killer's winning.*

Dripping with sweat, Sorcha bolted up, clutching her throat. "Can't breathe." She clapped her hand over her mouth and froze as Zelia's snoring paused and resumed. *Ivori's ghost stories must be getting to me. Or the sip of absinthe from the bottle Angela snuck into her room? No more of that rubbish.*

Breathe. Sorcha forced her eyes closed. She laid stone still and awake until dawn.

Chapter 7

BON VOYAGE

THE MORNING OF the last full day in New Orleans dawned cloudy and stormy, but at least it wasn't sweltering.

After posting a copy of the group picture to Doris in New York, there was very little to do beyond waiting to board the ship and attending Dr. Banitierre's farewell celebration. Sorcha had worked with him on several occasions since their first awkward meeting. His mesmerizing voice put even the most anxious patients at ease. She had to force herself to pay attention or risk looking like a speechless idiot in front of him.

"Aren't you ready yet?" Zelia asked.

"Almost." Sorcha straightened her skirt, which fit like the day it was made, and spun around. "Ta-da!"

"Healthy and happy is stunning on you, *chère*." Zelia shoved an umbrella in her hand. At the curb, a line of cars waited to carry the well-dressed group to dinner.

"This is a relief." Sorcha touched the comb in her hair. "Spent forever getting it perfect."

Their destination was a restaurant on the corner of *Rues Dauphine and Ste. Anne*.

"So, we need to cross Bourbon?" Sorcha craned her neck to see as much of the forbidden road as possible. *Rain may have been a convenient excuse to keep us from poking around.*

"Nothing here for a proper young woman," Zelia warned.

"Maybe I'm not that proper." Sorcha rolled her eyes. "I understand the birds and the bees. I'm a nurse, after all."

"Welcome to Karen's! Please follow me." A maître d' in a tuxedo escorted them through the elegant dining room to a hidden staircase. At the top of the stairs, waiters drew back velvet curtains to reveal a chandelier-lit hall.

"I love the flowers and this china." Sorcha gravitated to a mural of historic New Orleans, horse-drawn Mardi Gras floats and masked revelers tossing beads. Candles floating in crystal centerpieces reflected emerald walls and silver accents. "Breathtaking."

Dr. Banitierre slipped in while everyone was occupied with the setting. His three-piece suit was midnight blue—almost black, impeccably tailored and accented by a deep crimson cravat. "Good evening, ladies."

Butterflies took flight in Sorcha's stomach. *I feel underdressed. Drink, please?* Like a mind reader, the waiter appeared carrying a tray of sparkling glasses, a slice of strawberry floating in each one.

Dr. Banitierre offered a flute. "Nurse Alden, champagne?"

"Please, call me Sorcha." She forced herself to take a ladylike sip.

"Very well, Sorcha. Enjoy the evening." Each word he spoke floated in the air like a feather. With one hand casually in his pocket, he flashed the signature smirk and turned his attention to a room full of guests.

"There are seating cards with our names on them!" Angela gestured toward the long table. "I adore fancy."

"Pfft." Zelia swept past Sorcha. "We need to find you a man your own age. Proper lady or not, that is never going to work."

"I don't have time for a man." *She assumes I have a crush on Banitierre—totally ridiculous.* "I live in a convent, work non-stop, and we're leaving town in twenty-four hours." Sorcha didn't mention becoming paralyzed whenever the medical director spoke to her.

Dinner started with a choice of crawfish bisque or seafood gumbo.

Whiffs of exotic spices wafted through the room as waiters hand-served guests from plates of trout amandine, blazing red Creole shrimp, Andouille sausage, beef with Béarnaise sauce and a steady flow of pale champagne.

Dr. Banitierre offered a simple toast. "To a fine medical staff. It's my honor to embark on this trip with each and every one of you."

The room raised their collective glasses, and Sorcha shot a quick glance around. *Sometimes these nuns do drink.*

"To the Sisters of the Peace."

A fleeting chill shot up Sorcha's spine. *Must be getting tipsy.* She shook her head clear, reinforced her smile and sipped more champagne.

Dessert was bananas and vanilla ice cream in a sauce of sugar, rum and liqueur. As part of the event, waitstaff prepared the dish in the dining room. Sorcha flinched as the dishes ignited, burning off the alcohol.

"Zel, I'll be right back." Sorcha's uneventful trip to the restroom ended when she rounded the corner and tangled her feet in the fringe of a rug. Twisting backward, she struggled to regain her balance. She expected to feel the hard floor against her face, but instead strong hands caught her and returned her squarely to her feet.

"Careful." Dr. Banitierre stomped down the curled edge of carpet.

Where did he come from? Sorcha gasped for air and leaned on a narrow table for support. *The hallway was empty a second ago.*

"Maybe you've had enough to drink. Did I hurt you?" The doctor reached out to straighten Sorcha's disheveled blouse, brushing the skin under her collar. He snapped his hand back as his eyes shot around the corridor.

"No, sir, I'm fine." *He smells like cinnamon with a touch of vanilla...or maybe it's just leftover dessert?* Sorcha coughed to hide the blush creeping into her cheeks. "No more champagne, promise. I don't want to ruin your lovely party."

"Well, as long as you're all right. Did you eat enough?"

"Plenty." Sorcha rubbed the twinge in her neck. "You barely touched your dinner, though."

"Don't worry about me, *mademoiselle*." Dr. Banitierre swept his hand out to usher Sorcha back into the banquet room. "I rarely go hungry."

Sorcha rejoined her friends for coffee as the party began to break up. As they piled into the waiting cars, the sky opened up with a deafening crack of thunder.

"Holy!" Sorcha hauled Zelia into the backseat by her sleeve.

"It's just the New Orleans rain, *chère*. Relax."

Relax? A last glance out the car's rear window revealed the cathedral, fully illuminated by a lightning bolt cutting the sky like the sword of a god.

After checking that the shutters of their room were securely shut for the third time, Sorcha lay in bed grasping her locket, trying to push the nagging feeling of dread away. *It's already tomorrow and I have the worst headache—ever.* Sorcha closed her eyes and prayed for a sleep without nightmares.

Raimond Banitierre makes my hair stand on end. Dream about that instead.

Chapter 8

INVERNESS

SORCHA'S FEELINGS OF impending doom finally faded when she joined her friends gathered around their luggage in the foyer. Each nurse was allowed a trunk and a small satchel.

As Sorcha left the convent, she took a wistful look back. *This place was a refuge when I desperately needed a home. I miss it already.*

Their ship was ready and waiting. Jointly owned by Sisters of the Peace and The East India Company, the Inverness accommodated passengers and cargo. Compared to the sleek Atlantic liners Sorcha gazed at in Manhattan, this was a secondhand row boat.

Sorcha scanned the dock and ship decks. Dr. Banitierre wasn't visible anywhere in the chaos. The nurses shuffled down steep ladders to cramped quarters to inspect their home for the next few weeks. The cabins were nothing more than storage lockers with dirty portholes.

"It's just temporary, girls—at least we won't be lonely." Zelia patted the mattresses and chose an upper berth.

"What a dump." Angela held her nose. "Let's go back outside."

They arrived on deck in time to see the final member of the expedition emerge from the back seat of the sedan in a long-sleeved shirt, gloves and a wide-brimmed hat. Dr. Banitierre's gait gave him away; it was the stride of a commanding officer.

"He must have known about the small cabins. He wore all his

clothes." Sorcha squinted at dark hair brushing the doctor's shoulders. *Was his hair that long last night?* Three short blasts of the ship's horn, followed by a long one, and they were on their way. *Hope this adventure brings me closer to actually being somebody—to make Mum proud. Time to stop running and start building a legacy.*

The Inverness navigated sharp bends and strong currents down the Mississippi River, while Zelia pointed out landmarks in both St. Bernard and Plaquemines Parish.

Ivori stood alone, staring into the flats. The breeze ruffled her rich, brown hair—just a shade darker than her skin.

Sure she's disappointed I didn't quit. As the twinkling lights of New Orleans faded, Sorcha realized that nobody from New York would believe that she'd taken a chance like this. She gasped as the deck boards curled and twisted under her feet and returned to normal in a blink.

Damn visions haven't stopped.

The team had little to do except dive into their books about tropical diseases and fall asleep to the gentle rocking of the waves.

Sorcha woke to moaning and the violent tossing of the ship. "Angela, turn on the lamp!"

Zelia screamed and covered her eyes. "Turn it off—grab that bucket from the corner!"

Like dominos falling, as soon as one girl started vomiting, so did the next and the next. Sorcha quickly found herself playing nurse to a hallway of green people. Day after miserable day, the ship rolled and pitched so viciously that she needed to brace herself against the walls to avoid falling down.

How did Mum survive a voyage like this at seven months pregnant? If I don't get some fresh air, I'll get sick too.

"Nurse Ald—Sorcha, are you okay?"

"Yes—grand." Sorcha pushed a wild tangle of hair away from her face and fumbled for the sides of the bench. "Must have dozed off."

"Don't get up." Dr. Banitierre placed his hand on her shoulder. "I didn't mean to scare you. All your friends have been so ill, and you look a bit drawn yourself. Have you been eating?"

"A little, usually out here on deck. We just need to get off this ship."

"Soon, a few more days. I've heard how well you've tended to everyone. You're a strong woman Sorcha, and a skilled nurse. We're lucky to have you on this journey."

"Thank you, Dr. Banitierre. I'll try not to disappoint you."

"Not possible, my dear."

The trip had done nothing to change his captivating smile and charm. *Those eyes...so intense.* Aside from being pale, he looked healthier than anyone else on board.

"Make sure you don't miss the beauty on this voyage. Look at the stars. What do you see?"

Sorcha tilted her face up and pointed at the pure black sky. "I only know Orion, the Hunter."

"Look at those five." He steered her toward another constellation. "The Southern Cross."

"How did I not see that? It was just a jumble before, now it jumps out like a beacon."

"You should wear your hair down more."

"Sure, Dr. Banitierre." She pretended to concentrate on playing with her shiny waves while sneaking glances at his profile in the moonlight. His presence put her at ease, as if they'd been friends for years.

Chapter 9
CPR

THE INVERNESS DOCKED the next day at dusk. Older locals hawking their goods on the pier scattered when Dr. Banitierre led his team off the ship to the train station. A few young men offered free fruit. A brave child snuck something yellow in his pocket.

"Holy moly, it's still hot." Sorcha mopped sweat off her forehead and unconsciously tucked the locket under her blouse. "Do they know him?"

"What do you mean?" Zelia asked.

"People are pointing and cowering as if they're afraid of Banitierre."

Both women watched him pull a lemon from his coat pocket, cringe, and fling it into a hedge with enough force to break branches.

"Well, he's been here before. God knows what went on." Zelia pushed her onto the train. "It's a long ride to the foothills of the Himalayan Mountains."

"How long?"

"Six hours," Zelia said.

"Feel like I'm going to faint." Sorcha swayed and cracked her knee on the wooden seat.

"Just lean on my shoulder. Let me take care of you for a change."

The next thing Sorcha knew, she was sitting bolt upright and blinking against the bare light bulbs of the train car. "Did I pass out?"

"Hours ago." Zelia held her at arm's length. "You were flailing in your sleep. Nearly slapped me."

"Sorry, I had a nightmare."

"I'll say." Zelia waved off concerned Sisters and co-workers.

"Ugh." Sorcha pulled a scarf across her face. "Dusty."

"In your dream?"

"No, that was about a stone goblin slobbering all over me."

"Deep breaths." Zelia coaxed Sorcha back against her shoulder. "We're almost at the station. Then, we have to hike."

Sorcha didn't feel any more confident when the team ended their trek in front of dilapidated huts in a barbed wire enclosure. "Don't know if I can handle this."

"That's the hospital?" Ivori clapped her hands over her eyes.

"Where do we even start?" Angela asked.

"I'm positive we can conquer this." Zelia grasped both her friends' hands and Ivori's sleeve. "We're from New Orleans."

The Sisters took charge, ordering supplies placed on the decaying porches and pointing the staff to their accommodations. Each house had two large rooms in the middle with a tiny bedroom on each corner, overloaded generators for electricity but no running water or sewers.

This was not in the magazine advertisement. Sorcha sat on the squeaky bed and rubbed her bruised knee. *All I want is a bath.*

Right away the nurses learned that in Nepal, a bhisti was your best friend when you needed hot water. Alfred, their bhisti, went to work filling small tubs adjacent to the bedrooms.

Sorcha slid into the water and scrubbed travel dust off her body, rinsing her hair twice before the water cooled. Wrapped in a towel, she was busy detangling her waves when she saw something huge slithering from under the tub.

Sorcha froze. The most blood-curdling scream she ever heard came from her own mouth. Like a flash, Alfred appeared, grabbed the snake and twisted off its head.

"I'm going home!" Sorcha knocked over Sister Ann on her way out the door.

"*Chère,* it's dead." Zelia and Angela, still half-dressed from their interrupted baths, both grabbed Sorcha's hands to keep her from running into the yard.

"Ladies, snakes are common here." Sister Ann snapped her fingers. "They crawl through holes in the floor. We'll make sure all the gaps are plugged, and then we need a good night's sleep."

Morning light greeted the staff with a sprawling property in need of serious repair. Split into teams, they filed and organized a path through the clutter. In a few short weeks they learned that most patients were employed by prominent British families on military assignments. Though the building appeared in poor condition, they found the staff well trained, and the medicine up-to-date.

Of all the new therapies and advances from America, heart massage for patients in cardiac arrest was received with the most enthusiasm.

"It's a cutting-edge technique." Sorcha flopped in a chair and gulped water. "But Dr. Banitierre swears he's seen it work many times."

"We need to get this perfect." The local nurses pushed their American counterparts to keep practicing. "We're going to save so many people. By the way, Nurse Alden, our quietest patients have become chatterboxes around you."

"Little old men talk my ear off."

"That's because she listens." Zelia patted Sorcha's hand. "Her compassion for the elderly—it's her gift."

"You're embarrassing me." Sorcha tapped her watch. "Let's go, our shift starts in five minutes."

The hospital housed several long-term patients who needed more assistance to perform daily activities than their families could provide at home. Sai Parrell held the status of a local hero in town, where he once saved several children from a vicious tiger attack and lost use of

44

both legs as a result. He treated his nurses as extended family members and made them feel at home in a strange land. He was also the most stable and healthy patient in the hospital.

Sorcha was at the far end of the hospital when she heard Angela shouting.

"Sai—Sai! Wake up! Somebody get the doctor—we need to start CPR."

By the time Sorcha arrived, Dr. Colby was performing compressions on the man's chest. Another device forced air into his lungs. Every time she checked for a pulse, she found none.

"Come on, Sai. Come back." Zelia took over chest compressions. "We need you."

After an hour of the best care they knew how to give, there was still no response.

"Time of death: 4:42 pm. Sometimes, despite our strongest efforts..." Dr. Banitierre drew a sheet over the body and ran out of comforting words. "I'll inform the family. Everyone, pull yourselves together. We have a hospital full of patients."

Sorcha spotted an unfamiliar face peeking around the curtain. "Sir, may I help you? Are you family of Mr. Parrell?"

The man was about Sorcha's height with dark eyes and shiny black hair. Yesterday she would have found him handsome, but today, it felt inappropriate. *His eyes—they swirl.*

"No, I'm Dr. Ashayle. This is my first day." His words were soft with no discernible accent. "May I assist?"

"Thank you. We're almost finished, but I appreciate your kindness." *He must be new. Doctors don't help nurses with dead bodies.* "Would you check the veranda and assure any family that they can come in soon? This patient is—was—a nobleman. 'Tis a tragedy for everyone. All that CPR practice, but this time it didn't..."

"You did everything possible."

Sorcha swiped a tear with the back of her hand. *Stop blubbering in front of the strange doctor.* "I apologize. We're after having a rough day."

"I'll check the veranda right away, Nurse...Alden," he read from a badge pinned to her crumpled uniform.

Sorcha swallowed as her heart leapt into an unfamiliar flutter and she fought the urge to hug a complete stranger. *What's wrong with me?*

"I'm sorry for your loss. I hope I'll have the pleasure of working with you under better circumstances." He walked away in the direction of the waiting area, and Sorcha returned to their favorite patient—a man who would never tell his tall tales and silly jokes again.

Sorcha cried that night for all that had been lost that day and many days before. *I miss you, Mum, what the hell am I doing here? Days like this feel like nothing I do makes any difference.* Her headache was like a vice around her skull. She resorted to begging Ivori for aspirin. *I must look like a mess—she was decent to me for a change.* Sorcha's thoughts grew jumbled after she swallowed the pills. *Hope it was really aspirin. Oh well, as long as I sleep, it's a blessing.*

In the distance, strains of a melancholy violin wept. *How long has that music been playing?* It blended into the night as if it had been there forever.

Chapter 10

INVITATION

SAI'S MEMORIAL CELEBRATED his life and delivered a stirring tribute to the children he saved.

Zelia opened the hospital door and groaned at the frenzy. "Life moves on."

"Sai's bed won't be empty for long." Sorcha trudged into the hall.

"May I have some help in here?"

"Who's shouting?" Zelia asked.

Sorcha tugged a privacy curtain aside to find Dr. Ashayle struggling to dress an intravenous line. "I've got this."

"Okay." Zelia disappeared to start her rounds.

"You know, you should ask for a nurse to assist you with procedures, Doctor. That's what we're here for." Sorcha mustered her best smile, opened the missing supplies and expertly finished the bandage.

"The hospital is so busy and you nurses work like a force of nature—I wouldn't want to get in the way."

Sorcha absorbed the compliment and jolt of energy that seared the air when their eyes met. *Whoa.* She busied herself cleaning up until Dr. Ashayle disappeared and then turned her attention to the patient, who gave her a thumbs up.

"Hush now, you didn't see anything, right?" She nodded until the man dropped his mischievous grin and mimicked her motion. *Great, now my shaky social skills are entertainment for the patients. Not sure a romantic connection will sit well with the Sisters.*

As much as Sorcha adored the coffee in New Orleans, the tea in Nepal was her favorite discovery. The kitchen staff made it fresh several times a day, stirring in loose mint, ginger spice, cloves, cinnamon, and black pepper until it had just the right amount of kick. The carafe in the lounge was always full, and she was topping off her cup when Dr. Ashayle walked in.

"Pour you some tea?" Sorcha shocked herself with courage.

"If you would be so kind." He grabbed a cup and held it motionless.

Soft, steady hands. Wonder how those fingers would feel on my skin. Sorcha blushed and pushed the thought away.

They sat at opposite ends of the table, sipping and sizing each other up.

"So, has the hospital been what you anticipated?" Sorcha admired the glow of his bronze skin. "Hope we haven't scared you off."

"Not in the slightest. I didn't know what to expect, but I've been pleasantly surprised with your colleagues' skills and care you've given the working people of my country."

"The community has been so gracious and accepting. We're enjoying almost everything, though the weather is a challenge. We're used to heat, but the wind and dust..."

"Rainy season is right around the corner," Dr. Ashayle said. "Have you spent any time outside the hospital or do they work you to death?"

"I've been to the market. Dr. Banitierre insists that we always travel with escorts—guards, really." *New Orleans was dangerous, but this place is brutal.*

"Maybe I can arrange to take you on my next supply trip into town."

He wants me to go?

"You wouldn't have to carry or lift anything. They send a crew for that—you'd just be my assistant. We can make a side trip to show you the sights. I know the perfect spot."

"I would love to, but we'll, em, need approval." *He does want me to go…with him.*

"I'll take care of it," Dr. Ashayle said with a flick of his hand. He didn't appear worried that the permission would have to come from Dr. Banitierre.

I don't remember the last time I saw our boss. Must be back to ruling the night shift.

Noise from the hallway jarred Sorcha back to reality. "I have to get back to work. Let me know if I can help you with that supply run." She scurried out of the room looking for something to do—anything to pass the time. *Wise choice or not, I'm enchanted.*

Two days crawled by before Sorcha heard another word about the trip. So far, no one had noticed her interest in Dr. Ashayle—at least they hadn't commented on it. Just before dinner she received a message to report to the medical director. This might be the consent for her trip into town or a massive disappointment. She crossed the courtyard at dusk, making her way through the miniature jungle to his office.

Dr. Banitierre was seated behind a gnarled wood desk, writing in a ledger by lamplight. The faint scent of incense hung in the background. "Sorcha, sit." He gestured to well-worn chairs.

Sorcha examined the doctor's face. *I haven't really spoken to him since our constellation lesson on the deck in the middle of the ocean. Four months ago.* Dr. Banitierre had grown a moustache and beard, trimmed carefully around his chin. If it was possible, he appeared even more distinguished and totally at ease in this foreign land.

"Dr. Ashayle has requested your assistance for his trip to Karikar. I'm inclined to allow it, but I wanted to talk with you first. Are you comfortable with this young man? If not, I can assign the duty to someone else."

"Yes, sir, I would very much like to go." *Don't sound ridiculous.* "Dr.

Ashayle seems quite polite and professional."

"Very well. Enjoy yourself, stay close to our people. If you ever need to speak with me, you know where I am, correct?" Dr. Banitierre motioned to the study.

"Yes, sir, thank you." Sorcha struggled to hide her excitement. Out in the garden, she quietly clapped her hands and spun in a circle. *Tomorrow!*

Raimond's polite smile vanished once Sorcha stepped off the veranda.

Why the hell did I just agree to that? Ashayle has adequate medical skills, but he's arrogant and full of himself. I need a reason to fire him—anything—or maybe I should just rip his throat out. He swiped a dusty clock off his desk and tipped over both chairs before he stormed out of the office.

Rounds with the senior doctor were mercifully quick that evening. Raimond knew it was a risky dalliance, but every night he followed the same lonely ritual: standing in the shadows and watching Sorcha from the cover of the dark garden. Her violent nightmares were no secret to him. So far, no hypnotic or suggestive powers he possessed had been able to lessen her symptoms. *Her aura is amazing—vibrant and innocent. I can't steal any more energy, tempting as it is. I'm causing the headaches and most likely the dreams too. Didn't I learn my lesson years ago?* Despite his best efforts, innocent blood had been spilled and lives ruined. *My fault.*

Frustrated, he skulked into the dense forest to patrol the village perimeter through the darkest hours of the night.

Chapter 11

KARIKAR

SORCHA FOCUSED ON getting ready for her trip to Karikar without broadcasting frayed nerves to her roommates. Dressed in her nurse's uniform and a light jacket, she snuck on a brush of lipstick from her French Market stash. *For courage.*

By the time Sorcha arrived at the caravan, they were packed and ready to go. She hopped into a dusty sedan and slid across the seat. Dr. Ashayle climbed in next to her.

"Nurse Alden."

"Good morning, Doctor." Sorcha returned his professional smile as the line of cars crept out of the compound. *Deep breaths.* Layered scents of sandalwood and balsam filled her lungs.

In the madhouse of the town market, Sorcha checked the freshness of produce and said yes or no to boxes unveiled from rickety trucks. The whole transaction took under two hours from start to finish.

"We have some free time. What'll it be?" Dr. Ashayle pointed in two directions. "Tea under the tent or shopping?"

"Em…tea." Sorcha slid into a seat in the café and sipped from a cup placed in front of her. "It's good, but not as tasty as the hospital's recipe."

The doctor got comfortable in a chair across the table. "I agree, Nurse Alden."

"Too formal. Call me Sorcha."

"All right. First names it is, as long as you call me Vir."

Sorcha studied his nametag.

"Vir…rhymes with beer."

"Ah, okay." *I'll have to get used to being so informal.*

"It's a family name that means brave."

"Intriguing." She silenced her thoughts to listen to his silky voice. "Tell me more."

"I went to medical school in London, on a scholarship from my community."

"Not even a trace of an accent." Sorcha took another slow sip of tea. "Were you born here?"

"About fifty miles north, in another small village. But my family is from the country they now call Iran."

Sorcha's eyes wandered across his fine bone structure and full lips with fresh perspective. "So, you're Persian."

"I am." Vir winked and tipped his cup.

"Why did your family move?"

"Politics or a better life?" Vir shrugged. "Never seemed to like it here, though. My turn—where are you from? How did you become a nurse?"

"I was born in New York, and nursing is a family tradition."

"Do I hear a hint of an Irish accent?"

Sorcha rested her chin in her hand. "You do."

The drivers honked their car horns to signal the end of free time. As they began preparations for the trip home, Sorcha visited the restroom to tuck her hair into her cap and dab on a little more lipstick. She hurried back to the waiting cars and caught Vir whispering with the driver.

"Have I missed something?"

"I had to beg and plead, but we're making the short detour I promised you." He took Sorcha's hand and gave it a quick squeeze.

She squeezed back without thinking.

Vir's perfect spot was well off the main road. Dark woods gave way to a valley of purple flowers. Above them, snow-covered peaks soared into the clouds.

Sorcha tumbled out of the car before the driver fully opened the door. "Can't believe this is so close to our hospital. It's like another universe."

"Those are the Himalayan Mountains—tallest in the world." Vir tapped her arm to pry her attention away from the view. "What do you think?"

"Spectacular! I know it wasn't easy bringing me here." Their gazes locked and for first time she truly appreciated the intensity of the coppery flecks in his brown eyes.

"But worth it."

"Dr. Ashayle? Nurse Alden?" The driver called across the clearing. "It's getting late."

"Feels like someone is always interrupting us." Sorcha glanced at her wristwatch, and then gaped at the dial. "We've lost track of time somehow."

How long do I have to wait to kiss him?

When the caravan arrived at the hospital, Sorcha dug out her clipboard and supervised the unpacking and organizing of boxes. As the job wound down, the long day began catching up with her. *Home, food and sleep.* Prickling on the back of her neck froze her in place. *I'm being watched.*

"Vir?" Her heart jumped as she spun around, but the piercing eyes she found belonged to Dr. Banitierre, standing in the shadows of the deep veranda around his office. *Vir and I haven't done anything wrong. Why do I feel queasy?* Sorcha put her head down and ran to her house.

"So, how was your trip? Did you have fun?" The nurses showered Sorcha with questions the second she slipped through the door. "Did you buy us anything?"

"Was I supposed to bring gifts?" *Never crossed my mind.*

"No, they're just kidding. Alfred drew you a bath." Zelia grabbed a slice of bread and steered her away from the group. "Eat this. I'll fix you a plate."

While Sorcha soaked, she let the day's events run through her mind. Aside from Dr. Banitierre's disturbing look, it was amazing. Vir was spontaneous and easy to talk with. She recalled the strong grip of his hand and soft touch of his fingers with a pleasurable shudder and instantly hot cheeks. *Even better than I imagined. Has it only been a few short weeks since I met him?*

Zelia knocked gently on the door. "Don't drown in there."

Sorcha pushed away an image of herself climbing into a box while someone shut the lid. "I'm getting out now." *Ugh, enough with the visions.*

"Do I have to check for snakes?"

"No, Alfred has blocked off the gap in the wall."

"Good night. I'll talk to you tomorrow."

"Good night, Zel." *I'll tell her everything—just not yet. I need Vir all to myself for a little longer.*

Ducking behind the drapes, she peeked into the darkness of the veranda, feeling prickly again. She snapped the curtains shut, rubbed her bleary eyes and crawled under the covers.

A sad and lonely violin cried far in the distance.

Who in the world is playing at this hour?

Chapter 12

FIVE SHARP

"*CHÈRE* STOP PICKING and eat."

"This food makes my tongue burn." Sorcha dropped her fork. "Just can't." *I didn't see Vir all day. I'm nervous with him—jittery without him.*

"Let's get some air." Zelia grabbed their tea cups and headed for the veranda. "So, anything new with you? I feel like we never talk anymore."

She knows something's up. "I think I'm falling for someone." Sorcha gave up hiding her goofy grin.

"Just so we're on the same page—you mean Dr. Ashayle, right?"

"Yes, who else would it be?"

"Phew, I worried you were going to say Banitierre. I've seen you talk to him, and the tension between you...it looked like something might happen."

"I told you, it was never like that." *Almost like that.*

"Never mind him, let's talk about Dr. Ashayle. He's very handsome, but..." Zelia leaned forward. "Is he stuck up?"

"I don't think so."

"It's just...his demeanor and voice, we all thought he was snooty at first." Zelia shrugged. "Sorry."

"He isn't, you'll see." It dawned on Sorcha that outside of Vir's birthplace and medical school, she knew very little about him.

"Sorcha, have you ever really had a boyfriend?"

"I, em, why would you ask that?"

"Because." Zelia put her tea down and intercepted Sorcha's drifting gaze. "We're roommates and we've talked about everything, but never that."

"There was one boy." Sorcha frowned at the memory. "Back in high school."

"What happened? How long were you together?"

"Long enough. He was so sweet and kind, I was lucky to have him."

"But?"

"But one night, during a blizzard, we almost, you know...a near disaster."

Zelia straightened her back.

"My mum worked double shifts and his apartment was the only place with heat. But I panicked, ran out into the snowy street and never talked to him again."

"You weren't ready or didn't know what to expect?"

"I thought I knew." *Being naked in front of someone... I was not ready for that.*

"Maybe your subconscious was telling you he wasn't the one?" Zelia tapped her forehead.

Sorcha leaned back and let her mind wander. She flinched in her chair at the vision of a monkey dancing in a smoky fire.

"Have you heard a single word I've said, *chère?*"

Sorcha shook her head. Her biggest fear was that the spark between her and Vir would be snuffed out. Either Dr. Banitierre's disapproval would ruin it, or she would panic again and wreck everything. *His lips look so soft—what if...*

"I said, Dr. Ashayle seems like a suitable choice."

"I'm not sure it ever was a choice." Sorcha blinked hard and forced herself to focus on Zelia's voice.

"What in the world does that mean?"

"I'm sorry, I have no answers for you—plus I don't want to jinx anything."

"You sound like Ivori now." Zelia poked Sorcha with two fingers. "Are you being watched too?"

"Ivori seems to know more than the rest of us combined. Now that you mention it, I have felt watched." Sorcha left out the part about Dr. Banitierre's harsh stare.

"This place is creepy at night. Animals scream in the garden and wake me up at all hours."

"Monkeys, maybe?" Sorcha scanned the dark trees. "Have you heard the violin music?"

"Nope." Zelia took a deep breath. "Just monkeys howling like they're being strangled."

The frantic hospital workload left little time for chance romantic meetings. Sorcha knew when Vir was working; her heart jumped every time she read his signature on a patient's chart. Maybe a ghost signed his name because he seemed to be everywhere, but she rarely saw him in person. Waiting for him to make the next move was excruciating.

One evening Sorcha paced the garden until she saw Vir emerge from the hospital, his white coat slung over one shoulder. Looking around to be sure nobody was watching, she took a few quick steps to catch up to him. "Dr. Ash—Vir. Are you done for the day?"

"Yes, walk with me." He motioned toward a secluded part of the garden. "This being cautious is getting tiresome. I've wanted to talk to you and I really don't care what any nosey people say. As long as we stay professional in the hospital, it shouldn't matter what we do outside, right?"

A weight Sorcha didn't know she carried, lifted off her chest. "I agree. I need to see you more than just to nod in the hallway. The festival in town, em, are you planning to go?" *There, I just asked him out.*

"I wasn't sure, but I'll be your escort. Then everyone will see us together."

"Do we have a date, Doctor?"

"Thursday at five o'clock, I'll be holding the car door for you." Vir erased the distance between them in one stride. "Sorcha, I hope you forgive me."

Before she said a word, he cupped her face in his hands and kissed her, gently at first but growing in intensity and depth as the seconds passed. Sorcha pressed against his body. *This is it—the kiss I dreamt about.* Spooky chanting filled her ears as she closed her eyes and kissed him back.

Sorcha didn't shrink away when the kiss ended. "So, Thursday?"

"Five sharp." Vir stepped back as quickly as he had approached her, tipped his chin down and disappeared.

He glides when he walks.

The door chime on Thursday evening caught the attention of the entire house.

"Sorcha!" Angela called out. "You have a visitor."

Whole hospital heard that. Smoothing out the black skirt and crimson cotton blouse, Sorcha made one last check of her lipstick and hair. She grabbed her small purse, wrapped it around her wrist and hurried to the door. Her appearance in the entry collided with deafening silence. *Did I forget a piece of clothing?*

"Sorcha." Vir held out his hand and guided her down the stairs. "You look ravishing. I've never seen your hair down—it's gorgeous." He twirled one of the soft curls in his fingers and placed it back on her shoulder.

"Thank you. You look dashing as well." Black trousers and a white collared shirt were a perfect contrast to his rich, smooth skin. Sorcha's heart fluttered remembering their first kiss. *I'd very much like another.*

After the village band's first set, Vir coaxed Sorcha away from the punch bowl and paper lanterns.

"But we just got here." Sorcha pretended to drag her feet.

The full moon shed barely enough light to follow a winding trail in the deep forest.

"The clearing is right ahead." Vir clutched her hand.

Sorcha's jaw dropped when she saw thousands of delicate flowers blooming in the deep grooves of ancient tree bark. Some petals were multicolored, while others were solid. They were all vibrant, including blossoms of pure white.

"They're rare orchids—the roots draw the moisture from the air." He reached down for a flower that had fallen to the forest floor. "I don't like to pick these, but this one dropped here especially for you." He held it up so Sorcha could inhale the scent and then tucked it behind her ear. "So beautiful."

As good as their first kiss was, the second kiss was better. In the scattered glow filtered through swaying trees, Vir took Sorcha's hands and lifted them to his lips. He kissed each knuckle, never taking his eyes off hers as a light breeze swirled around them.

"You look like the girl from my dreams, sparkling in the rays of the moon." He grasped one of Sorcha's wrists and gently bent it behind her back, pulling her close. "I've got you."

Sorcha's knees buckled, but Vir held her steady. "You do have me."

"Indeed." Vir's voice was a breathless whisper.

Electricity ricocheted from Sorcha's ears to her fingers, down to her toes and back again as she met his kiss, immediately deeper than their first one. His free hand found her neck, squeezing gently at the base of her throat.

The dirt beneath their feet quivered and startled them out of their trance.

Sorcha's back stiffened. "Did you feel...?"

Vir took a step back. "Yes, but I think I heard something too."

Sorcha put her finger to her lips before tiptoeing to the edge of the clearing and peering into the brush. "I saw a shimmer."

"Don't call me crazy, but I've seen that a million times." Vir crouched over her shoulder. "My parents always said it was my mind playing tricks."

Two figures zipped behind a hulking tree to avoid Sorcha's eyes searching the shadows.

"The King must be getting restless," one man whispered.

"That's only a warning, brother." The second man twisted his mane of black hair and flicked it over his shoulder. "Let's grab our target and end this charade once and for all."

"You can't be serious, Chapal. He isn't alone and I think we're intruding on a private moment."

"Recall Father's exact words, Lock," the long-haired man hissed. "Bring. Me. My. Son. If that's even him."

"You haven't guarded him in over decade. That's our brother."

"Not if I can help it. Why are we hiding like imbeciles? Because of some little—" Chapal charged for the clearing until Lock wrenched him back by his neck. "Get your damn hands off me."

"Just..." Lock saw blue fire flare in his brother's eyes. "Simmer down. We're better hunters than this."

Chapal's fingers stretched into claws for a split second as he raked his hair and drew black blood from his own scalp. "Father called me an incompetent in front of the entire royal court. I can't return without...it's not my fault this human's parents were granted so much extra time, on top of an obscene commission."

"Father's waited centuries for this specific bloodline to mature. Destroying it now would be unforgivable."

"Oh, of course, the bloodline, the power," Chapal snapped. "Yet, Father let this prize specimen leave the continent for medical school? Maybe he's going soft, like you."

"We'll find him alone, mate." Lock gritted his teeth and looked away to hide his own blue fire.

"Your irritating accent returns with your anger."

"If you don't turn into a lunatic," Lock pressed his palms together in front of his face, "our mission will be a success. Take his scent."

Chapal drew a deep breath and punched a tree trunk into splinters. "Our entire army and a pack of tigers are waiting just over the ridge. We could take both humans without a trace, in seconds flat."

Lock ducked behind the huge tree. "Great, they're both looking now."

"Does he hear us talking? How is that possible?"

"He's Dorje, Chapal. Like you and me."

"I'll agree to retreat, one final time. But I'm ravenous and someone has to pay the price."

The violence of the second earthquake cleaved branches from their trees. Lock and Chapal flashed into the clearing in time to see Vir grab Sorcha's hand before she ran down the wrong path. They both disappeared into the woods, toward the party.

"She's a pretty sheila, but…" Lock shook his head. "Where was she going?"

"He could find a more suitable mate." Chapal pointed across the valley to the moonlit mountain peaks. Avalanches of snow exploded from under the clouds, burying everything in their paths. "Want to go home empty-handed?"

Lock shook his head again. "Absolutely not."

Chapter 13

VIOLIN

HOSPITALS WERE WORSE than high school. Everyone knew everyone else's business. Plenty of people saw Vir and Sorcha disappear into the woods at the festival and come running back when the ground shook.

"The earthquake was terrifying." Sorcha hid her face in her hands.

"And common for this region," Zelia said.

"Everyone laughed at us."

"*Chère*, they're jealous."

Sorcha slumped onto the bench in front of her dressing table. "Of what?"

"The power couple. Young, beautiful and in love."

"Love is a stretch."

"Since the festival, he's been here every night for dinner or tea. It's obvious Vir adores you." Zelia picked up a lock of Sorcha's hair. "Split ends."

"What do the Sisters think?"

"He's a gentleman and gives them no excuse to object." Zelia grabbed scissors. "Let me trim an inch."

"Just a wee inch." Sorcha stared at her friend's smile in the mirror. "He adores me?"

"Maybe you caused the earthquake."

As happy as she was, Sorcha's nightmares grew worse. *Blood everywhere, sticky and warm.* She screamed, but her voice was choked into silence. Sharp teeth slashed her neck and ripped into her face.

Help me.

Sorcha woke up drenched, muscles aching from her struggle against an invisible demon. *There must be marks.* She stumbled from bed, her clumsy fingers lighting an oil lamp to inspect her neck in the mirror.

Not even a damn scratch.

"Oh my God, am I crazy?" Sorcha leaned on the bureau, trying to fight off terror lurking around the edges of her mind. *Fresh air.* The power of the dream melted away as she listened to the violin strings weep into the night.

Wait, who's playing that instrument at three in the morning? Sorcha pulled on a robe and wandered into the garden, following music with only a tiny lamp to guide her through the maze of trees. *Should have left a trail of breadcrumbs.* Creeping onto a veranda, she peered into a dimly lit room.

"You play violin?"

Vir dropped the bow and spun to the door.

"It's okay—just me." Sorcha gasped at her white gown and the lamp in her hand. "I must look like a ghost."

"More like an angel." He set the antique violin down and took the lamp from her hand. "What are you doing wandering around?"

"Couldn't sleep…nightmares." Sorcha felt the room spin and Vir's strong grasp around her waist. "You're not wearing a shirt."

"It's the dead of night." Vir cradled her in his arms and sat on the bed.

"I never sleep." A sob caught in Sorcha's throat.

"Shhh, you're safe. They're just dreams." He leaned back and brushed a quick kiss across her forehead.

Sorcha froze in his embrace. *He's half-naked.* She sensed none of the panic that consumed her the last time she was in this situation. *Not yet.* Without thinking, Sorcha traced her fingers down the middle of Vir's chest and onto his stomach, slipping lightly to his thighs. *He smells like the heart of the forest, where orchids bloom in the night.*

"Somebody could catch us." Vir swallowed hard and struggled to keep his composure, as his hand fumbled with the tie of her dressing gown.

"We can keep a secret, right? I want this—I want you," Sorcha whispered, her eyes glued to his skin. *This is nothing like the last time.* The rest of the world drifted away.

"Sorcha, you're shaking—are you sure?"

She met his smoldering eyes. "You take my breath away."

Vir pushed Sorcha onto the soft bed with one finger and lay down next to her, untying her nightgown's ribbon with one hand.

"I've never, I mean…" *I have to tell him I'm a virgin.*

"That means you're mine."

The gas lamp in the corner flickered. The flame battled back to life twice before it burned out.

Sorcha's fingers fumbled into the waist of his pajama pants. The drawstring fell loose, and then it wasn't tied at all. He slipped out of the cloth and in one perfect motion rolled her on top of him. *Breathe.*

"Take this off." He lifted the flowing nightgown and pulled it over Sorcha's head, casting the last piece of clothing to the floor.

Sorcha's arms slipped across her chest, but Vir gently nudged them away.

"Look at you." His hand slipped to the base of her hip, his thumb swirling circles inside her thigh.

I'm ready this time. Sorcha ran her eyes over him, all of him, illuminated by the single candle burning in the room. She tossed her hair aside and leaned to kiss his lips. The moment her mouth touched his, he cupped her breast and rolled over again. He pulled back and let his tongue wander to her chest, lingering and teasing the sensitive skin. Her belly tightened under his feathery touch. Every nerve fired like crazy as his fingers edged closer to the very center of the fire.

Taut muscles rippled under Vir's skin. "I'll be gentle, promise." He pressed against Sorcha and she instinctively arched her back against the sheets, molding to his body.

Vir crushed Sorcha's hands to the bed on either side of her head and groaned in her ear.

She winced into the sheets and bit her lip at a hot, searing pain she didn't expect.

Vir froze. "I'm sorry. I'm so… Do you want me to stop?"

"No, just go slow, please…" *Do not stop.* Her body was pulled and driven to move with his as the pain flared and faded.

Vir slowly shifted inside of her. Sorcha willed herself not to cringe as his pace quickened. A sharp pinch at the base of her neck made her cry out.

He felt her muscles jump and used the energy to pull her hips against his. "Can't help it—I bite."

"I like it." Sorcha wrapped her arms around his back. "More." His movement and the constant caress of his fingers between her legs drove her wild. The sensation was hurtling her toward an abyss, the precipice of a cliff. She was almost there—*almost…*

"Give in Sorcha, let it go." Vir took a handful of her hair and guided her mouth to his, stealing the air with his kiss and pushing her off the invisible edge.

I'm falling. Sorcha's cries were muffled by his flesh, her hands twisting the bedsheets as he dove off the cliff right next to her, a blur of tangled hair and deafening heartbeats. *Still falling.*

And then, sweet peace.

The cotton sheets felt heavenly, like fine silk against Sorcha's naked skin. As much as she wanted to drift off to sleep with Vir, the gravity of what just happened was sinking in. *Can't afford to get caught in a man's bed.* She would be sent home in disgrace. *I have to get out of here, while it's still night.* Sorcha struggled with the tangled sheets.

"No angel, stay." Vir's hands searched the darkness to stop her.

"You know I can't."

"It was your first time." He sat up, perhaps forgetting he was still naked, or maybe he didn't care. "And you have to run away."

"Just for now." Sorcha pressed her lips to Vir's and lingered longer than she planned. She fumbled across the floor for her nightgown and yanked it over her head. Her locket was snarled in her hair, but untangling it could wait. Every fiber in her being wanted to crawl back into that bed.

Move it!

Sorcha's escape back to her room didn't go smoothly. "Ow!" She stumbled hard into a low branch and skinned her knees on tree roots.

"Who's there?"

Sorcha recognized the voice and froze. "Ivori?"

"What the hell are you doing out here?" Ivori's eyes darted around before zeroing in on Sorcha. "Wait, where were—"

"Never mind me, you're hiding something. What's burning?"

The girls stood motionless, so close they felt each other's breath.

"I never liked you." Ivori jabbed her finger at Sorcha's chest. "Or your wicked eyes."

"That's sweet." Sorcha grabbed the finger and bent it back. "I don't like you much either, but if you mention anything to the Sisters, I'll let them know you were cooking a skinned chicken in their garden."

"For your information, it's a monkey."

"The one from outside my window? Thank God someone made that bloody thing shut up."

"You play all innocent, but this is the second time I've caught you sneaking around." Ivori snatched her hand away. "I'd love to slap your face."

"Go ahead. But remember what I did to Dr. Winters."

"Little New York bitch."

"Dry up, Ivori." Sorcha feinted towards her and chuckled when she flinched away. She stalked back to her room amidst birds chirping in the dim light of dawn. *No point going to sleep now.* She spent the next hour unwinding her hair from the chain around her neck and savoring Vir's woodsy scent that clung to her skin like an invisible glove. *This will be one tough secret to keep. Falling for him was truly never a choice.*

Chapter 14

LAST RITES

"HELP!" SCREAMS FROM outside the hospital compound pierced the early morning air. "Please, someone help us!"

Sorcha dropped her breakfast and ran behind Zelia toward the front gate. A wall of sickly sweet air hit them in the face. "I smell blood."

"What happened?" Sister Ann pushed her way to the front of the crowd. "Oh my God in heaven. We need the doctors—all of them."

"Was it that damned tiger again?" Sorcha grabbed a handful of towels to hold pressure on one of the villager's wounds. "The one that attacked Sai?"

"Please, nurse, my son. I think the beast dragged him away." The man clutched at the air, looking for anyone to hold onto in the chaos. The voice sounded familiar, but Sorcha couldn't recognize it. There were more bones than skin.

His face is gone. Sorcha pressed her mouth into her arm to hide a gag, then gently extricated herself from his trembling grip. "We'll find him, sir. Just lie back and let me help you."

"Everyone stop." Dr. Banitierre's commanding voice cut through the bedlam. "Remember your training. We need to be organized and efficient or we can't help anyone. It's all about teamwork now."

"Zelia?" Sorcha met her friend's eyes as they loaded more villagers onto stretchers.

"I know, it's gruesome." Zelia tossed over a bucket of gauze. "All we can do is our jobs."

Furious activity consumed the hospital in the battle to save lives. Tortured cries of families searching for loved ones ripped through the valley. By evening, the wails had been replaced by ominous silence and the unmistakable smell of death.

"Hi, Angela. You're taking over for me?" Sorcha slumped onto a chair next to the only survivor.

Angela nodded, pulled up another seat and flipped the chart open.

"Where do I start?" Sorcha dropped her face into her hands. "Unidentified, middle aged male. Status post…em, animal attack?"

Angela patted Sorcha's hand. "I know, it's awful."

"Could one beast have done all this damage to so many?"

"Unlikely."

"I have nightmares like this." Sorcha stood and took a deep breath. "He has a shattered skull, bilateral rib fractures, and a traumatic, right above-the-knee amputation."

"There's blood dripping from his ears." Angela leaned forward and stared at the green spikes of the heart monitor. "Hemodynamically stable?"

"Surprisingly, yes." Sorcha found a medication list, pointed to each name and recited dosages. "Exploratory abdominal surgery revealed a ruptured spleen and lacerated liver."

"Mental status?" Angela gently touched the patient's swollen eyelids.

"No response to verbal or painful stimuli. Zero. Might be a blessing."

The village plunged into deep mourning—at least a dozen precious children had been lost. Space was cleared in one of the hospital buildings to prepare bodies for funerals that would span the next two full days. Some families had no one left alive to attend their burials, so shifts of staff members organized to accompany each victim.

Sorcha sunk into the refuge of her bathtub and scrubbed off the grime. *Blood and God knows what else.* Less than twenty four hours ago, she was making love to Vir. *Feels like another lifetime.* Sorcha collapsed into bed and for the first time in weeks, no nightmares woke her. No monsters dragged her to death. The demons were all too real and roaming outside the barbed wire fence.

Vir watched somber processions file in and out of the compound for hours. He scanned the yard for a glimpse of Sorcha, the graceful wave of her hand or flutter of her hair in the breeze. *Nothing.*

"Dr. Ashayle?" Zelia knocked on the door to the doctor's lounge. "It's time to go."

"On my way." Vir tossed his white coat aside in favor of a dark jacket. "Any chance you've seen Sorcha?"

"She's attending the last funeral, the one added at the end of today. Anything wrong?"

"Not at all." Vir held the hospital door open for Zelia and the other nurses. A twinge of loneliness ached in his chest. *This is not what I planned.* He came here for the experience, to work hard and earn respect. Getting involved with a young nurse threw a wrench into things. *But I can't get her out of my head.*

The service went without incident until the end when crashing noises in the jungle startled the party. The locals put their heads down and hurried on while the hospital staff cringed, but stopped to look.

"Have they caught the animal responsible for all this carnage?" Angela inched behind her friends.

"Nope, and they've been chasing it for years," Zelia answered.

"Don't let yourselves get separated." The guard urged the group forward. "Not safe."

Vir pushed the women in front of him, speaking to the guard only when they were out of ear shot. "Keep a close watch on the rest of today's events. Use that rifle if you need to. It's getting dark already, and we've seen what these beasts can do. Something just feels…off."

Chapter 15

MONSTERS

SORCHA WRAPPED THE blue cape around her nurse's uniform and shivered in the evening chill. *Damn schedule changes. I'd give anything to feel Vir's arms around me right now. We've barely spoken since our night together.* She tucked a stray hair into her cap, bowed her head and crossed her heart before the mourners headed toward the compound. *Wonder if he misses me?*

Walking at the end of the funeral procession, Sorcha absentmindedly checked for her locket and found it wasn't around her neck.

Panic drove her trembling hand as she searched inside her blouse and uniform to see if it had fallen off.

Sorcha slowed and scanned the path behind her. *Stupid chain must have broken.* If it dropped in the cemetery, it would be gone by morning. Thieves roamed freely at night, stealing anything left at the graves. *How can I get there and back without anyone noticing?*

Pretending to tie her shoe, Sorcha deliberately let the group walk on. Nobody looked back. She retraced her steps to the gravestones and scoured the ground. Nighttime was swallowing the forest, but the warped tree she leaned on during the service was easy to spot. She slowly turned in a circle, her eyes straining to focus.

"Oh, thank God!" Sorcha caught the faint twinkle of gold in the moonlight. Lunging across the ground, she grabbed the locket, folded it into her fingers and touched it to her forehead. *Now, catch up with everybody else.*

With the locket jammed deep into her cape pocket, Sorcha sprinted for home.

The creature struck from the left.

Sorcha's ribs splintered like twigs as the beast clamped huge jaws around her waist and razored her skin to ribbons. She was tossed like a rag doll into a headstone, demolishing the ancient rock and shattering her spine. Sizzling pain exploded and then ceased, replaced by a blast of cold. Sorcha struggled to focus on the burning blue eyes and jagged teeth of a wicked tiger.

Blue fire.

Laughing at her broken body, the savage creature pierced her neck with its fangs and gulped.

Frosty serpents slithered through her veins as they were drained of life. *Sticky dark blood everywhere but inside me—my blood.* Voices Sorcha didn't recognize buzzed next to her ear.

"Did you check to see if she's dead? Wait, who am I kidding? Of course she is—you've killed everyone."

The tiger can talk?

"I executed our plan, followed the scent. She shouldn't have been here."

Two beasts? Another killer.

"Haven't you taken enough life this week? Exceptionally sloppy."

"I know you want our brother alive, but I can't risk the competition. Father already ignores me."

"The depth of your insecurity boggles my mind. If this was our sibling, would you have murdered him and told Father it was an accident?"

"Would you have allowed it?" The first killer snarled. "Perfect brother."

"I can't keep up with you when you're this deranged." The second killer knelt beside Sorcha and gently closed her eyelids. "Such a pretty

72

young thing. What a waste."

Not fair!

"Leave the animals and thieves to clean up this mess. Forget her."

They're gone—I have to catch up with my friends. Why am I not waking up?

Sorcha fought to stay in her body, but the vapor of her spirit hand couldn't hold onto the ice cold human fingers. She hovered over the gruesome death scene. *Where have I seen this before? Me, alone in a cemetery, shredded beyond recognition?*

Even soaked in blood, the blue cape was unmistakable. Her hand was still buried in the pocket clutching her precious locket.

Those pictures. My family tree is dead. I was the last one and I failed them. I never made anything out of myself. Do I float away now? Can I see my Mum in heaven? She'll know I didn't deserve this.

It started gently at first and built in intensity.

Mum?

Sorcha felt her soul being pulled down—wrenched down toward the slaughter and searing pain.

Oh God, I'm being crushed by needles!

All at once she was sucked back into her bloody corpse.

Time screeched to a halt.

Life, as she knew it, ended in midnight blue.

Chapter 16

SEARCH PARTY

THE EXHAUSTED FUNERAL party locked the hospital gates against the jungle, not realizing they were short one nurse. Staff staggered through dinner assuming Sorcha was with Vir, while Vir believed she was with her roommates. The thought didn't cross anyone's mind that she wasn't safe in the compound until Zelia knocked on her bedroom door.

"Sorcha, are you asleep?" Zelia knocked again and peeked in at a perfectly made bed. "She must be with Vir—that girl is pushing it." She scowled at her watch and answered the front door chime. "It's about time you brought her home."

"What do you mean? I thought Sorcha was here." Vir peered down the hall.

"She most certainly is not here. We thought she was with you."

Overhearing the conversation, Angela crept closer. "She must be at the hospital."

"Ivori is on duty." Zelia pushed her way out onto the veranda. "I'm sure she and Sorcha are bickering through the halls like sisters."

With everyone searching, they quickly determined that nobody had seen Sorcha since the final group of mourners left the yard—hours ago.

"Like I said, before you crashed through the wards and scared all my patients." Ivori slammed a chart on the counter. "I am not Sorcha's babysitter."

Zelia looked at the ceiling. "We need to tell Dr. Banitierre."

The group plowed across the garden to the medical director's office and barged through the door without knocking.

Dr. Banitierre thumped his ledger closed. His expression flared from irritation to worry at their grave faces.

"Sir, Sorcha is missing. She's gone!" Angela blurted out.

Everyone else spoke at once, explaining where they thought Sorcha had been and how they discovered that she never came home.

"Just stop—stop talking!" Dr. Banitierre stood. "Angela, wake up Sister Ann. Zelia, gather the guards. Mobilize our resources."

The nurses scampered off, leaving the two men alone in the office.

"I'll be with the search party." Vir spun to the door.

"The hell you will, Ashayle. You've done quite enough." Dr. Banitierre threw the younger doctor aside. "Stay here. That's an order!"

News of Sorcha's disappearance traveled like lightning. Villagers and staff struck out on foot and in any vehicle available. They combed the woods and spread out toward the cemetery, the last place Sorcha was seen alive.

Mother Superior grabbed Dr. Banitierre's arm as he followed the searchers out of the yard. "Find her. She won't survive out there alone." She locked onto his gaze with her own. "Raimond, please."

The locals didn't dare enter the graveyard at night. Legends of devils and demons had been spun around every campfire since they were children.

"I'll cover the burial grounds." *I have nothing to fear from the dead.* Dr. Banitierre shook off his peculiar feeling of dread and stepped over a crumbling wall. Sorcha was his favorite, though he tried hard to hide it. She inspired him, as only a few had ever done before.

Inside the stone perimeter, nothing seemed out of the ordinary until it hit him—a low electric charge humming close to the ground. *Definitely not human.* The vibration was weak but unmistakable. *Monster.* He moved like a blur from headstone to headstone, making sure nothing crept up behind him. *But only one.* A hundred feet from the twisted tree, the stench of death assaulted him.

"Oh no—not again." Raimond shot across the clearing and dropped to his knees in a pool of blood. Sorcha's blood. Brushing matted hair aside, he looked for a spot on the mangled girl to check for a pulse. *Please, please.* He found nothing. The body was stone cold. *How many hours has she been lying here, murdered?* He cradled her head in his lap, while his eyes flashed red. Dark veins blasted across his skin.

"Doctor?"

The single, spoken word jarred him to the core. Wavering blue fire stared up at him.

"Sorcha?" *Weren't her eyes hazel?*

"I can't move. Think something bit me."

"You're okay." *Liar.* He forced a smile. *Think. What is she?* Raimond knew himself. He knew the vampires in Europe and America—he'd turned many of them himself and none had sapphire eyes. *Where have I seen this before? Unless...no.*

"I want to go home, sir, please."

Her body shrunk as he held her. "You need blood." Raimond wrapped her battered body in the cape and looked around for a source of life to complete her transformation. He cornered a searcher and dropped the three-hundred pound man like he was a child. Hoisting the unconscious villager over his shoulder, he returned to what remained of Sorcha's body. Her blue eyes were open, but the color flickered like a dying flame. Raimond positioned the man's arm over her mouth and ripped an artery open with his fangs. The process only required seven drops of blood to complete, but he let her swallow more. He shoved the man away while his heartbeat was still strong.

Blood rolled down Sorcha's throat and her limbs started to tremble. She clawed at tree roots and struggled to sit up.

"Don't fight it, Sorcha." Raimond restrained her hands. "Now, everything changes."

Sorcha's eyes flew open to see Dr. Banitierre hovering. *Why is there blood on his face? I'm so thirsty. Ugh—what tastes like metal?* She swallowed several times and coughed at the giddy flurry in her chest. *Maybe I'm not going to die after all.* Then, her heart faltered. "It's not working. Need more blood—another transfusion."

"That's enough for now, you're in shock."

Her hands clutched at her ribs, sunk past raw flesh and scraped exposed bone. *Something's not right.* Sorcha's final three heartbeats sounded like canon fire in her ears—and then nothing. *How am I still awake?* The tingling flare in her chest shot sparks to every nerve ending in her body. Her veins quivered as if something was waking up inside them. A violent reflex bolted her upright.

My eyes...so fuzzy. Sorcha watched her boss take a long drink from a stranger's arm.

"Thanks buddy, you saved a life here today." Raimond focused on the villager's glassy eyes before he sent him on his way. "You hit your head on a tree limb. Be more careful."

What?

Sorcha sat stone still. Things seemed too bright for nighttime in the forest. She jammed her bloody fingers into her ears. The deafening silence sounded alive. Other than prickling under the surface of her skin, she felt very little, as if her body belonged to someone else.

"Sorcha, we need to move. Not safe here."

Home. She struggled to stand and follow on legs of jelly.

"Let me carry you. It's quicker." Raimond scooped her up under her shoulders and knees, like a child.

Sorcha tried to keep her bearings, but everything was a blur until her feet hit the ground of a hill behind the hospital. Even though they were far away, she clearly saw Zelia pacing the porch and Angela in the window washing her hands, staring off into the night. *I can hear their heartbeats.*

"No!" Raimond's grasp halted her before she took more than a few steps. "You can't go to them."

"What do you mean? Why not?"

He gripped her hand so hard it crushed her fingers.

"Vir can help me, please!"

"Most likely, your attacker thinks you're dead. If they figure out that you aren't, they may come back to finish the job, which will place everyone around you in danger." He nodded toward the compound. "They could slaughter Vir, your friends, every patient in that hospital."

"A tiger would kill innocent people looking for me? Ridiculous." Sorcha fought with all her strength to free herself from his grasp, but it was like smashing her body into a steel wall.

"Very soon your own craving for blood may be more lethal than the predators."

"That's crazy! Let me go—" The screams never made it past her throat. Raimond's hand clamped over her mouth so tightly, the teeth wiggled in her head.

"I can't explain this to you right now." Raimond turned her until their faces were inches apart. "I need to go inside for supplies. You, stay here. Do not move, do not scream and do not follow me. Remember what I said about putting everyone in danger?" He paused to let his instructions sink in. "Am I clear?"

"Yes." Sorcha crumpled to the ground, the urge to run strangely gone. *Dr. Banitierre looks different. His eyes are darker.* "You said we were going home." She felt like crying, but no tears ran down her face.

"We are going home—to New Orleans."

New Orleans? She sat on the hill like a helpless spectator and watched the doctor sneak into his hospital. He cleared the twenty foot high, barbed wire barricade in a single jump and expertly avoided the staff, as if he knew where they were going before they did. Through his office windows she saw him fill a bag with extra clothes, medical items, money, and dusty books. He grabbed a few bottles of wine and slipped silently out of the compound.

"It's almost dawn. We need to get inside." Raimond inspected Sorcha's hands. "Can't see bones anymore. You'll be a hundred percent with rest and a little nourishment. And then, immune to my power."

"Dr. Banitierre, when are you going to tell me what's going on?"

"I'll tell you everything as soon as I'm sure. Trust me a little longer?"

She had no choice but to trust him.

Their hiding place was a well-disguised cave in the brush. She crawled into a back corner and fell unconscious, not sleeping exactly—just not awake. When Sorcha opened her eyes, it was dark again. She found herself staring at Dr. Banitierre, watching him flip pages of an old text. "What are you reading, sir?"

"You need to start calling me Raimond. I'm not your boss anymore." Without moving his head, he lifted his gaze from the book. "Say it."

"Okay…Raimond." *Doctors and their first names again.*

"I'm trying to figure out what happened to you, what you are."

"I don't understand. I just want to get better."

"I know. I promise, you're healing. Here, drink some wine."

"That's all we have—wine?"

"Yes, this is the whole menu."

Sorcha took a sip and gagged at the sour taste. *That wine is spoiled.*

While Raimond left again, Sorcha paced the cave but didn't dare step foot over the threshold. *Wouldn't it be safer to travel in the daylight?* She stared at her hands for a long time. They were connected to her body but they didn't feel like her hands. Her face felt odd, too—smooth but not soft. *My teeth feel broken. I need a mirror.* She tried to drink rivulets of water from the cave walls to quench her thirst, but her stomach immediately and violently rejected it.

"Where have you been?" Sorcha grabbed onto Raimond's arm the second he appeared. "It's been hours."

"Convincing the villagers that I found your remains and that I'm returning to New Orleans immediately, to assist your family with burial."

"They believed that?"

"Blamed it on the damn tiger."

Sorcha's mouth dropped open. "Actually…"

"I couldn't face the Sisters. I had a letter delivered."

"Wait!" Sorcha found her voice. "My friends think I'm dead? Vir thinks?"

"It's crucial that everyone believes it." Raimond nodded. "Especially him."

"I'm so confused."

"Things aren't adding up just yet, but you're safe with me." Raimond steered her into the dark woods. "Your cape—over your head."

I'm sorry, Vir.

Chapter 17

HELL

VIR SENSED SOMETHING wrong as staff filed into the chapel for a meeting. He watched Mother Superior and the Sisters pass around a sheet of paper and whisper, as if they didn't believe what they were reading.

"Dr. Banitierre never came home." Angela tugged on Vir's sleeve. "He must still be out there searching—right?"

"It is with great sorrow that I must…" Sister Ann cleared her throat and choked back sobs. "Nurse Alden's body was found in the woods. Dr. Banitierre has taken her home to notify family and assist with her burial."

Stunned silence followed the announcement until Angela's wail pierced the air.

Vir watched his friends collapse and cling to each other in slow motion. He pried Angela's shaky hand off his arm and staggered to his room.

In the blurry days that followed, co-workers knocked on the door with offers of food and company. At first he refused with a polite smile. As time crept by he slammed the door in their faces or refused to acknowledge them at all.

"She can't be gone." She was just here—in his bed only days ago, so alive and so radiant. *How the hell could this have happened? There were guards—didn't they notice her missing? Why was she ever alone?* "Why!"

When he splintered every piece of furniture in his room, all the nearby houses went silent—nobody knocked on the door again. Vir stood naked in the chilly breeze of the open window, night after night, cultivating hatred for the monsters outside the gate.

I don't care who sees me. I think I love...loved her. There was no grave to visit, no place to leave flowers. *It's like she never existed.* Even his sense of being followed and watched, disappeared. He had hated those specters since childhood. Science discounted their presence, but now he felt oddly alone without them.

I want out of this hell.

Chapter 18

PERKS

RAIMOND BOOKED EMERGENCY passage on an old cargo ship. "Sorcha, climb in." He held a trunk open. "You'll be safe if you stay hidden."

"Tigers attacked me. Talking tigers. Don't you believe me?"

"You've been through a lot. Rest." Raimond shook his head and clicked the lid shut.

Pulling the cape around her, Sorcha lapsed into dreamlessness and let time pass. She woke to the sound of lines being thrown and the ship's engine sputtering away from the dock.

"Time for some air." The trunk creaked open. Raimond offered his hand and led her up to the main deck. The moon spilled a river of silver on the calm water, revealing how poorly the ship had been maintained. Paint peeled off the vessel's flat surfaces in chunks and bolts had rusted several doors shut.

"Is this wreck going to make it?" Sorcha toed warped planks. *I've seen this before.*

"Hope so. I didn't have time to shop around."

Lovely. The moon's glow almost felt like the sun, not warm, but invigorating. "There's the Southern Cross." Sorcha's eyes lit up. "See? I paid attention."

"I know you did." Raimond tucked a strand of hair behind her ear. "We'll talk tonight."

Sorcha ducked below deck and plopped down next to the trunk, resting her head against the raw steel of the ship's hull. *Another cold and miserable cabin—no furniture, not even a cot.* The vibration of the ship's giant screws wobbled through the waves as if engine parts were loose or broken. *I'm hungry—ravenous.* She scanned the bleak room with her enhanced eyesight. A soiled, scabby rat waddled across the floor.

"Ugh." Sorcha pinched her nose closed, while her other hand shot out like a flash of lightning and jammed the rat into her mouth.

"Yuck." Her voice was muffled beneath soggy rat hair. Sorcha swallowed until no blood remained. *What the hell is wrong with me?* She stared at the red stains on her fingers and licked them clean. *Totally disgusting. Took the edge off though.* She hunted for another filthy fur ball.

Before Sorcha could devour a second rat, Raimond walked through the door leading a goat. He threw the bolt at the sight of her face and the creature in her hand. "That's revolting—even for me." He grabbed the squealing body and tossed it over his shoulder.

The rat banged off the wall and Sorcha howled with laughter. *I must be delirious.* "What's with the goat?"

"The goat is dinner." He dragged the animal closer. "I've found they replenish their blood volume quickly; perfect for trips. If the worst does happen—nobody misses a goat. Watch and learn."

Sorcha flinched.

"Relax, the adorable fellow will be fine. Think of it as—milking." He motioned for her to pay attention.

She watched through her fingers as Raimond bit down on the animal's neck, taking a long slow swallow. *Ick.* "How did you do that?" *Who would eat fur? Wait—I ate fur.* She almost understood as he lifted his blazing red eyes, clearly showing her the changes to his face, translucent skin traced with black veins and fangs dripping with blood.

Do I look like that? Deep inside, Sorcha was beginning to understand what Raimond was. *No, no, no—this isn't for me, there has to be a way out.* Her mind wanted to run, but her body begged to stay.

"Your turn."

"Can't." Despite her mind's protest, Sorcha found herself inching closer to the bloody mess, clutching the trunk, trying to stop from sliding across the floor. *But that smell...*

"You can and you will. There's no choice."

The pull of the blood was strong and her thirst scorching. Sorcha found herself kneeling next to the goat. Her fingers brushed her lips and a hint of sharpness on two front teeth.

"Be gentle, or try to be. Trust your instinct."

In a blur, Sorcha's jaws clamped down on the thin neck. The skin ripped under her tiny fangs and blood poured down her throat. *A little watery, fur tickles.* She kept drinking, feeling life and strength course through her body with every swallow.

"Enough." Raimond grunted as he pulled her away. "Don't kill him—we need this little guy for a few more weeks."

Sorcha was definitely not finished, but he had the animal out of the compartment before she ripped it to shreds.

I've turned into a monster.

"It does get easier." Raimond sat down on the floor and took both her hands, holding tight when she cringed away. "Don't be afraid. You aren't alone."

"This will never be okay." She felt as though tears should well in her eyes, but again, none flowed.

"Let me tell you what I know. Remember those books from my office?"

Sorcha nodded silently.

"It took a while for me to figure it out. I've seen your kind before, but not for over a hundred years."

"My kind?" *How old is he anyway?* She recalled Zelia saying that he had been a doctor at Sisters of the Peace since before anyone could remember. *That makes more sense now.*

"Sorcha, you were attacked in the cemetery by a Rakshasa, probably more than one. It's a rare vampire species from eastern Asia. I've only seen two in my life. In France, 1799."

Vampire. I don't want to hear that word.

"Rakshasa are stingy with their blood and rarely reproduce. It's uncommon, but it happens. Your blue eyes gave you away."

"No, they're hazel, or light green."

"Ancient vampire venom is potent. It's almost always fatal, but if a victim survives or the killer is careless, there's a chance the bite can change a human into Rakshasa—with burning sapphire eyes."

"But yours aren't the same?" Sorcha stared hard at his face.

"I'm not your sire."

Sorcha collapsed against the hull. "So, I'm a vampire? I saw Dracula in the movie theater."

"Yes, you are." Raimond brushed her cheek with his knuckles. "So am I—and it's nothing like that movie."

Raimond made a ritual of nightly strolls under the moon. He paced the deck or flopped on his back and stared at the sky, always lost in his own thoughts.

Tonight, Sorcha waited on the stairs, ready with her questions. "So, you were born before 1799?"

"Sort of. I actually died in 1789, at the age of thirty-three."

"Explain." Sorcha leaned in. "Please."

"I was fatally injured during the French Revolution. A stranger offered to save me, but it was a trick. He was building an army of vampire servants to supply him with victims."

"So, you decided to be a doctor because…that was the only job available?"

Raimond tucked his chin and pressed his lips into a tight line, trying not to smile. "I was trapped in a horrific life for years until I escaped to America and enrolled in medical school."

"Can a vampire be killed?"

"Yes, there are ways."

"And how do you create one?"

Raimond shook his head. "That's a discussion for another time. You're fully mended. I want to show you something." Raimond pulled her down the narrow hall to a small cabin with a mirror.

Sorcha hesitated. "Is it bad?"

"Far from it." Raimond propelled her across the floor.

At first glance, nothing had changed. "I thought vampires couldn't see their reflection?" She leaned closer to the mirror and rubbed grime off the glass.

"I told you, this isn't the movies. We still have souls."

Sorcha touched the skin of her face, smooth and pale—not sickly, but deep alabaster. Her cheek bones were more defined, lips plumper but with a pale blue tinge. Her eyelashes were longer and darker. "I didn't believe you." Sorcha batted her new fringe. "But, my eyes are light blue, almost lavender."

"Look at the dark reds in your hair." Raimond stood behind her and fluffed waves out over her shoulders. "And, how long it's grown."

My teeth. Sorcha kept her lips closed, not ready to inspect them yet. *I don't want to believe this.*

"You'll get used to it. There's a lot to learn, but there are some perks too." Raimond massaged Sorcha's shoulders and smoothed her hair. "Talk to me, what is it?"

"Why did this happen?" Sorcha slumped to the floor, cradling her face in her hands. "Am I being punished?"

"Why?" Raimond cringed.

"I'm—not." Sorcha struggled to get the words out. "Em…"

"You can tell me anything."

"A few nights ago—I'm no longer a virgin." *There it is, my big confession from another lifetime.*

Silence cloaked the room as Raimond faced the wall and pinched the bridge of his nose so hard it bled. "No, the attack was a random act of brutality. Wrong place, wrong time."

Sorcha climbed up on deck and lingered for the rest of the night, staring up into the cloudy sky. No stars. *No daylight for me ever again.* Raimond brooded downstairs. *Probably still hungry.* They shared one of the bottles of wine in his bag, and she figured out it wasn't just wine.

I'm catching on.

Raimond appeared without a sound. "Your cape. It's chilly up here."

"I don't feel it."

"Well, you look cold," Raimond answered. "I cleaned it up a little."

"Thank you." Sorcha let him drape the cape over her shoulders, dug into the pockets and pulled out her locket. *I forgot all about this.* "Ow—damn it!" She recoiled and dropped the pendant, sending it skittering to the edge of the deck. "It burned my hand."

"A lady doesn't curse." Instantly Raimond was at the rail, picking up the necklace with a black cloth and dangling it away from his skin. "Must be gold. We can't touch it."

"Gold? I thought..."

"Silver, like the movies?" Raimond raised a brow. "Gold represents the sun. Silver, the moon."

"Oh, I get it. The sun is our enemy. But, that locket was my mum's. I was after losing it in the cemetery. Went back, and that's why I was attacked. I almost threw it overboard."

"I'll keep it for you." He wrapped it safely in the cloth. "How's your hand?"

"Not exactly sure." Sorcha watched a black scar twist and change in front of her eyes. "Now would be a good time to tell me about more perks."

Raimond didn't answer until they were below deck. "Hmm, let's see. How about this?" He turned to face her and then he disappeared.

"Hey!" Sorcha whirled from a tap on her shoulder to see Raimond behind her, then he was gone again, back to where he started. "Whoa."

Raimond motioned for Sorcha to follow him and in a flash he was at the end of the long passage. "Come on, you try it." He crooked his finger in front of his face. "Just run and give a big push."

"Okay, here goes nothing." Sorcha took a few quick steps and pushed off. The doors of the hall were an instant blur. It was exhilarating until she ran squarely into the wall at the end of the corridor. Flat on her back, she blinked her eyes and rubbed her forehead.

"What happened?" *I must look ridiculous.*

"You can't run through walls. Guess I should have mentioned that." Raimond turned away to keep from laughing in her face.

Sorcha brushed herself off and followed him at a safer speed. "Do I just drink blood?"

"Well, yes and no. Fresh blood is the best and you'll need it on a regular basis. Regular food might taste good going down, but not coming up. Wine, scotch or any kind of straight alcohol is safe, but it doesn't provide nutrition."

"I get tipsy from one drink." Sorcha rolled her eyes. "Recall the champagne incident?"

"You'll probably have a little more tolerance now."

"You said vampires could be killed."

"We can, just not easily. Fire is deadly, as is a stake to the heart. Gold will melt your flesh, but wood is the real killer. Your body can't heal that, or push it out. Combined with gold it sets you on fire."

Sorcha absorbed the information for a few minutes. "Animal blood or human?"

"Animals will keep you alive, but human blood is what makes you strong, preferably from a living..." Raimond hesitated. "Donor."

"Have you had any human blood on this voyage?"

"No, and I'm feeling a bit shaky at this point."

Sorcha watched his eyes dart to her and then away again, pretending to focus on a dusty handrail.

"I plan on explaining how all of this works, but it takes some time. You can't go around biting people. It's not, let's say—socially acceptable."

"Can I kill them by accident?"

"Very easily." Raimond's face remained serious. "So, you see why I've kept you away from the ship's crew? The impulse to feed on humans can be impossible to control at first. But I have something else to teach you, just as important as feeding your body with blood. You also need to nourish your soul." He pointed to the center of her chest. "You can just die and continue to exist as a vampire, or live a glorious life and thrive as one."

"How?"

"You absorb energy and vitality from humans without ever touching them. Pick and choose the gift you want and take it. Done right, they don't even have a clue."

"I definitely want to learn that." Sorcha was relieved to hear about something other than blood.

"I will gladly teach you, but use your power carefully. When you're complete, you'll be many times stronger than me. Your species have been the vampire elite for a millennium. They don't reproduce, because they don't want to create any threat to themselves. Rakshasa are also more violent than most."

Sorcha fought her panic. *I didn't choose this situation—what if I can't handle it?*

"You can handle it."

Sorcha glanced around. *Did I say that out loud?*

I can hear your thoughts. That's another skill you possess.

His lips weren't moving but she heard his voice loud and clear. *Vampire mind games.*

Sorcha spent nights learning to put a protective wall up around her thoughts. Listening to Raimond's thoughts was quite easy when he allowed it. *Not much to do at sea besides eat and think. Poor goat is almost dry.*

On the last night of the trip, she found Raimond on deck, leaning on the railing. "Are you smoking?" Sorcha stepped closer, struggling to identify the strong scent. "Oh, I've had one of those. Cloves, right?"

"Have you now?" Raimond arched his eyebrow. "Those nuns are losing control."

"I choked but I liked it."

"Ah, I'd like you to try again." He spun the cigarette in his fingers. "It'll help calm your cravings when we get back. I'm sure you remember the throngs of people in New Orleans."

Sorcha wrapped her lips around the cigarette. The familiar smell wafted around her body like a blanket. "I'm not coughing."

"Are you breathing?"

"Oh, wait." Sorcha popped her hand over her mouth, feeling for air movement. "Nope."

"Stop heaving your shoulders. You realize you don't need oxygen to survive, right?"

"No…yes?" Sorcha stretched her arms out and closed her eyes. "I've got it now."

"Inhale when it's convenient, or if you need your sense of smell." Raimond offered the cigarette again. "Suck in, like you're drinking through a straw."

Sorcha finished the cigarette, assuming Raimond had more.

One more night—I can't wait to be off this ship.

Chapter 19

STONE GOBLIN

THE SHIP DOCKED during the height of day. Sorcha hid in the trunk until dusk and waited for porters to deliver her like a piece of luggage.

"I don't want anyone from the hospital to see you, so don't thrash around in there." Raimond locked the trunk to keep anyone from accidentally opening it. "I'll be right next to you."

Bracing herself in the darkness, Sorcha listened to the voices of the movers as they hoisted her up on deck. Louder than the voices was the alarming sound of heartbeats and rushing blood. Sorcha's stomach clenched, and her throat burned all the way through her chest. *Raimond was right to worry about my cravings.* She listened to his voice direct the porters to a high rise on Canal Street. He had told her about the penthouse with its sweeping views of the river, historic neighborhoods and even the hospital entrance—just high enough to rise above the pounding pulse of the local population.

"All clear." Raimond flung the trunk open.

Blinking at the sudden light, Sorcha climbed out into a spacious parlor. She followed Raimond across the polished hardwood floor of the flat and watched him toss the shattered padlock in the trash.

"Nobody else is home." He motioned to a cozy chamber off of a long, picture-lined hallway. "This can be your bedroom."

"Who else lives here?"

Raimond ignored the question, but handed her a towel and robe. "You could use a long soak in the tub. I have errands to run."

Sorcha peeled off her filthy clothes. *I must smell awful.* Plunging into the fragrant bath, she remembered the marvel of hot water from a faucet. *Heavenly.* Grabbing a bottle of shampoo, she lathered her dirty hair and slipped underneath the bubbles for an extended soak, no breathing necessary.

Wrapping the luxurious towel around her hair, Sorcha swiped steam from the corner mirror. *Those baggy clothes hid something else.* The woman staring back at her was not the scrawny, bony girl she remembered. *How did I miss this?* Running her fingers down her neck, she touched her fuller breasts and curvier hips before she grabbed a robe. She tried to rub away the hollow scalding in her chest. *I know I'll never see Vir again, but he liked me the way I was. I'd trade all this beauty to make love with him again in my skinny, human body.*

The skyline view drew Sorcha through the parlor and onto a balcony that wrapped the entire floor. Twinkling lights in one direction and the blackness of the Gulf in the other. *How does a doctor from a charity hospital afford a place like this?*

Sorcha recognized Raimond's specific, organized energy as he came through the courtyard and up the stairs. He burst through the door with both hands full of bags.

"I went shopping."

Sorcha was amazed at the assortment of clothes. Skirts, blouses, dresses and underwear—fancy, matching sets. *How did he know my measurements? I didn't even see the change until an hour ago.* In the past, she would have blushed over lacey bras and panties. Now too much had happened.

"You can fiddle with all this later—right now you need to put these on." Raimond held up a black long-sleeved shirt and black pants. "Your hair is beautiful." He secured it at the base of her neck with a ribbon. "But tonight it might get in the way."

Across Canal, onto Royal, past the cathedral, left turn toward the party noise. Strangers saw Raimond and instinctively stepped back.

Sorcha had walked this path as a young woman, steering clear of anyone who looked threatening. Now, it was different. Bombarded by the acrid smell of flesh, she gravitated toward bars spilling out loud music and drunk patrons.

The human pulses vibrated the center of Sorcha's chest and clobbered her eardrums. *Heartbeats.*

"This way, we're going to dinner." Raimond's vise grip guided Sorcha down a crooked alley that ended on a garish street.

Rue Bourbon. Finally.

Their destination was a damp courtyard, where two disheveled figures stared blankly at a moss covered wall. Raimond blocked her path. "The idea here is to drink enough to quench your thirst—not kill them. It's a fine line."

Nausea twisted Sorcha's stomach. *How can I hurt these innocent people?* The pounding tempo in each man's neck overrode her hesitation. Blood threatened to burst out of their arteries. *Not a glimmer of fear.* "Why aren't they running?"

"I was here already tonight. They won't give us any trouble." Raimond pointed to the inside of one man's elbow. "Avoid the delicate neck area, for now."

"Why?" *Who cares, I'm famished.* She lunged, clamping her fangs into his arm. The skin was as soft as the goat's, but the blood wasn't watery. *Chocolate syrup meets cherry soda.* Drawing her face back to look into his eyes, Sorcha dragged the man down onto the cold stone of the courtyard, latching back onto the limp arm.

"That eccentric heartbeat is your signal to stop." Raimond needed all his strength to disconnect her jaws from the wilting man. They wound up a tangled heap in a stone fountain, under a dripping gargoyle.

"The drooling goblin—from my dream."

"What?" Shaking his head, Raimond gazed into eyes that had turned from pale blue to burning sapphire. "You'll need some practice. It's not necessary to wear your dinner."

Sorcha looked down at her blood-soaked shirt. Her face was sticky too but she felt so alive and powerful, it didn't matter. Her gaze shifted toward the second man. "Ooooooo…"

"Pace yourself." Losing his grip on Sorcha's arm, Raimond yanked her back by her hair. "Let's clean up this fella first. He can't go out onto the street looking like he got bitten." He sliced his finger on his own fangs, rubbing the blood into the victim's arm. The sloppy wound started to heal immediately. "You try now."

Sorcha followed his lead and the scar faded into unbroken skin. "I'm still hungry."

"Watch carefully." Raimond bared his fangs, pulling the second human's head to the side and exposing the bounding pulse in his neck. "Only bite hard enough to puncture the skin, then let the heartbeat drive blood down your throat."

"Got it—no throat ripping. Why did you put them under such a trance?"

"Would you rather they fight back?"

"Maybe a little."

Sorcha marveled at Raimond's skill. *Looks effortless.* He took two long swallows and disengaged, offering his student an unmarked section of flesh. *Blazing red eyes, flexing muscles—and fangs under his smile. Erotic...devastating. Hope I blocked that thought.*

Sorcha pushed the images away and followed Raimond's instructions to the best of her ability. "How was that?"

"Not bad, for a beginner." Raimond examined the bite, bigger than his and not as tidy. "Practice, practice."

"Won't be a problem." Sorcha's thirst felt endless. She sliced her finger, covered both wounds and watched them heal. "That's amazing, but now what—they tell all their friends that vampires ate them?"

"No, that's the next part of tonight's lesson. Planting your version of events." Raimond maneuvered Sorcha until she stared into the first man's glazed eyes.

"What do I say to make him believe me?"

"I'll show you." Raimond traded places with her.

Sorcha watched as the air turned hazy.

"You went out to a party and someone slipped something in your drink. You and your friend passed out behind the bar."

The man repeated the statement back word for word.

Raimond pointed toward the second man. "You try. Concentrate and make a connection. Look deeper than his eyes. Force your words into his mind."

It took Sorcha a few tries to get any results at all. The man seemed confused. He repeated back a story but not the correct one. *This needs practice too.*

Raimond stepped in, easily planting the correct version and dumping both men on the banquette. He moistened a cloth in the old fountain. "Clean up." He motioned to Sorcha's face and neck. "Wear my jacket, your shirt is drenched with blood."

Stepping over the pile of humans, they emerged from the darkness of the alley. Sorcha reached behind her head, untied the hair ribbon and shook soft waves around her face. She walked down the middle of Bourbon as if she owned it, oblivious to the crowds that parted in front of them.

"Fascinating, right?" Raimond said. "First time I came here I didn't leave for weeks."

Dazzled by the lights and action of the formerly forbidden street, Sorcha gawked into crowded bars full of masks and burlesque dancers, until the clicking of a door stole her attention.

"Where are you going?" Raimond stayed glued to her side.

Sorcha marched up to a baker. He swept the banquette in front of his shop with one hand, while eating with the other.

"Still hungry?" Raimond watched the stranger's broom stop moving. "Sorcha?"

"I want that croissant." Sorcha pointed to his hand.

"This one?" The baker mumbled, struggled to swallow and patted his apron pocket. "I have another."

"She can't—" Raimond tried to stop Sorcha before she seized the wrapped pastry, but she was too fast.

"That one's on me." The man's eyes boldly wandered up Sorcha's arms to her hair, and landed firmly on her lips before he noticed Raimond's glare. "Sorry man, she's a dish."

"Hey!" Sorcha cringed as Raimond pried the croissant from her fingers.

"No harm done." Raimond pulled a bill from his pocket and chased the man's hand until he accepted it. "She'll eat it later."

"Take care of her."

"I plan to." Raimond steered Sorcha down a dark side street.

"Give me back that croissant."

"So you can do what?" Raimond grabbed his throat. "Throw it up?"

"I can't even have one bite?" Sorcha asked. "Can you eat it?"

"Someday, maybe. I'm working on a solution." Raimond rubbed Sorcha's shoulder and nodded to a figure huddled in a doorway. "Would you try and give it to her? She won't accept anything from men."

"This city is such a conundrum. Money and glitter on one block, then poverty and desperation on the next."

"A worldwide issue, and not just a human one."

"Ma'am." Sorcha knelt next to the woman and offered the croissant. "Are you hungry?"

"Only if it's extra."

"Yes, ma'am. I've had more than enough."

"You're an angel."

Sorcha's lip quivered. "Someone else called me that, once."

"Everyone can see your radiance, dear." A lone tear rolled down the woman's wrinkled face. "You shine from the inside out."

Chapter 20⊙

MARIE

CLAIMING EXHAUSTION, SORCHA left Raimond alone with his cloves. She collapsed in bed and pounded her fist into the pillow. *My bloody death in the woods, hiding in the trunk and now the drooling goblin—the damn visions are coming true!*

Sorcha stared at the ceiling until sleep took her eyes by force. She dreamed of soft lips trailing over her neck, across her breasts and down to her hips. *Whose lips?*

Her body was skin and bones. *Thinner than I remember. Sick and weak.*

Long dark hair fell across the stranger's face, hiding his identity. Muscles like steel rope rippled in his back, naked down to the silk sheet wrapped around his narrow waist. *His skin is smooth and cool, like nothing I've ever experienced.* She groaned under the pierce of sharp teeth. *Can't move.* The faceless man grasped her neck. *He's crushing my throat. My ears are ringing. The demon is killing me—the human me.*

Sorcha bolted awake, clawing at her chest. It seemed like an eternity before she remembered her location. *That dream was the ruined memory of my night with Vir.* Her sleepy eyes checked the clock on the nightstand. Half five. *PM?* It was always pitch black behind the shades. Flicking on the small bedside lamps, Sorcha glanced around the room, really seeing it for the first time. The soft light revealed soothing green walls and rich mahogany furniture, including the four-poster bed she slept in. *Not a speck of dust anywhere.* She brushed her hair into submission and willed the remnants of the nightmare away, then pulled a robe over her silk pajamas and peeked out the door.

Raimond sat motionless facing the only light in the parlor, a crackling fireplace. He flicked his gaze over Sorcha's face. "You slept well?"

"Yes, very. My room is beautiful."

He nodded, his expression unchanged. "Go, pick out something to wear. We're entertaining a guest tonight." Raimond turned his attention back to the fire.

In front of her armoire, Sorcha flung the door open and stood perplexed by the array of clothes. Everything was beautiful, finer than anything she had ever owned. She pulled out a knee length, burgundy skirt and black silk blouse before she rifled through a bureau drawer full of stockings. She chose a nude pair and matching dove grey satin bra and panties. The ensemble hugged her new curves. She dabbed on lipstick from a pot in the top drawer, eerily close to the hue she picked during her shopping trip with Zelia.

Zelia would never believe this is actually me. Sorcha spun left and right. Satisfied with her appearance, she left the bedroom to join Raimond in front of the fire.

At sunset, Raimond threw heavy drapes open to the black sky. A light breeze blew through the French doors. After the doorbell rang at eight o'clock, he ushered in a petite woman wearing a tailored suit. Her shoes and bag complemented the outfit perfectly, but her best accessory was a wide, disarming smile.

Heartbeat.

"*Bonjour*, Marie," Raimond said. "Let me introduce my newest associate, Sorcha Alden."

"*Bonjour*, Sorcha. A pleasure to meet you."

Sorcha returned her firm handshake, noting a French accent similar to Raimond's.

"Marie LaCour owns several establishments around the city. She's a quite a successful business woman." Raimond poured a glass of scotch for Marie, one for himself and red wine for Sorcha.

Plain, boring wine. As they sipped, Sorcha listened to Raimond catch up on local news sprinkled with a bit of gossip. The strength and breadth of Marie's position in New Orleans was not lost on her.

So much personality. Back when he was my boss, he was a man of few words. He doesn't wear a wedding band. I wonder... A glare from Raimond warned her that she hadn't protected her thoughts.

"Sorcha, are you ready for your next lesson? Marie has graciously offered to be our subject."

Sorcha's jaw dropped.

"Not that kind of—remember what I told you about absorbing the essence from someone without ever touching them? Marie has volunteered to donate her energy so you can learn how to tap into it."

I'm lost, Raimond.

"Excuse us for one moment, Marie." Raimond pulled Sorcha into the kitchen.

Why do we have a kitchen anyway? It's not like anyone cooks actual food.

"Are you okay?" Raimond tilted Sorcha's chin up until her eyes met his.

"I'm trying to remember everything." *Hungry.*

"We'll take it slow. You've endured so much, but I promise you'll enjoy this."

Raimond searched for something to relax her. He uncorked a bottle of blood wine and poured a glass.

Sorcha finished it in one swallow. *Still hungry.* "Does Marie know about us?"

"Yes, she's a rare human friend, something to remember for the future. Concentrate on the qualities you admire in her. Strength, intelligence and anything else you picked up on." Raimond led her back to the parlor. "Don't close your eyes. Use them to extract the energy from her soul. You can't really hurt her—just lean back and pull."

Sounds simple enough. Sorcha targeted Marie's twist of golden hair. To her surprise she felt a subtle jolt. *Pleasant, like a warm breeze.* She refocused and pulled a little harder. The result was well worth the effort. Marie's energy provided Sorcha a calm strength deep in her being—different from the physical boost of drinking blood.

Raimond is right, I do like this, but I'm still...hungry.

Sorcha barely registered the flush of her skin and the slice of pain in her gums before Raimond flashed between her and Marie.

"No feeding." Raimond pointed his finger in Sorcha's face, moving it from side to side as she struggled to look around him. "No."

"Can't help it."

"Yes, you can." Raimond snapped his fingers close enough to brush her eyelashes. "Put the fangs away."

Sorcha clamped her hands to her cheeks and pushed against her teeth, as if she could shove them back in her skull. *Help me.*

"Think about something else, makeup, music, flowers—girly stuff."

Sorcha pictured orchids, violins and coffee. Three things that made her sad, but didn't make her crave blood. She felt her face shift first, as if ribbons were being pulled under her skin.

Sorcha rubbed her smooth teeth. "Gone?"

"Yes, and your eyes are almost hazel," Raimond answered.

"Oh, so they change back? I look normal."

"You could say that."

"That was close." The phase back to her human form seemed much slower than her change to vampire. The gnawing drive for blood still simmered just below the surface.

Fight it.

"Thank you for everything." Sorcha shook Marie's hand. "Your friendship and kindness."

"I look forward to speaking with you again, dear."

After Marie's departure, Raimond fussed with the fire, adding and rearranging logs to perfection with brass tools. "So, absorbing the energy? That was good?"

"Excellent. Thank you for being patient with me."

"It's my job, Sorcha, and my pleasure."

"And I really didn't hurt her?"

"The human soul replenishes itself easily. Aside from a dull headache, adverse reactions are rare."

"I suffered from unexplained headaches when I arrived in New Orleans."

"Lots of vampires roaming the city." Raimond stoked the blaze that illuminated his muscular frame. "I think you deserve a night of room service. Mind the fire."

He was gone before Sorcha realized that she was holding the poker. Raimond returned with a young couple, thrilled to be invited to a dashing doctor's penthouse. He played the charming host, pouring drinks, chatting about local attractions. In a half-hour they were tipsy from glasses that never ran dry.

Smart choice—tourists. When Sorcha tried her hand at vampire mind control, the dinner guests set down their drinks and stared blankly into the fire.

"Nice job." Raimond motioned for her to sample the woman first. "Remember what I taught you. Be gentle and tidy. You're standing on my antique rug."

Sorcha bit into the woman's neck with all the delicateness she could manage. The sweetness of female blood was another surprise. *I definitely prefer this.*

"Slow down. Do you feel her heart skipping?" Raimond's fingers dug into Sorcha's shoulder. "That's how you know when to stop—so you don't kill people."

Sorcha disengaged from the pumping artery, licked blood from the wound and sucked every trace off her fingers. She let the woman fall back against the chair. Not a drop spilled onto the prized, silk carpet.

Raimond made quick work of the man, satiating his thirst with effortless swallows.

Sorcha sent the couple on their way with a story about an evening out that found them aimlessly wandering the streets. Tonight she found the energy to smoke with Raimond, overlooking the seductive lights of the city. Even so many floors up, disjointed chords and threads of melody wafted in the breeze.

"You have a lot to learn, but I'm impressed. You didn't ruin anything."

"Helps that the rug is red and black."

"Tomorrow night." Raimond patted her hand and stared at the dark horizon. "A new challenge."

Chapter 21

ACCIDENT

THE FRENCH QUARTER provided perfect hunting grounds for training a young vampire. If anything got out of hand, it could be explained away by whisky or absinthe. Tall tales and drunken mishaps wove the nightly fabric.

"How about that one?" Sorcha pointed to a stumbling man.

Raimond shadowed her as they zipped from doorway to doorway. "He's pretty tall. Can you handle it?"

"Hope so." Sorcha broke into a smooth stride, knocking the drunk into an alley with her elbow as she passed. Turning slowly, she scanned the nearby buildings for an audience. Convinced nobody was watching, she yanked her victim out of the garbage by his necktie.

"You're an ugly one. No wonder you were alone."

"Not anymore." The man swayed and caught his balance on the wall. "I've got you, hot schtuff."

"Had one too many, I guess?" Sorcha ripped the man's shirt away, exposing his neck and chest.

"That's more like it. Name your price, kitten."

The stench of bad breath made Sorcha recoil from his slurred words. "This is a freebie." Her sharp fangs pierced skin that disintegrated like brittle paper. More blood oozed from the surrounding tears than the actual puncture site.

What the...? This blood is revolting.

"Let go!" Raimond separated Sorcha's teeth from the drunk but not before his neck snapped like a twig.

"Did I kill him? I'm so—so sorry."

"It happens. More than any of us want to admit." Raimond held her hair back as she wretched over the body.

"I couldn't or didn't stop, even though his blood tasted like vinegar."

"I should have stopped you." Grabbing the man's scalp, he tipped the lifeless face back. "See this?" Raimond popped a set of fake teeth out of the corpse's mouth. "Two lessons for tonight. Bad teeth equal an unhealthy victim, and you need to know how to dispose of a body."

Following instructions, Sorcha helped wrap the corpse in old curtains and followed Raimond as he navigated the labyrinth of back alleys, her dead man flung over his shoulder like a sack of potatoes. Heading away from the river, they crossed a wide street in a blur.

Sorcha pointed to a dangling sign. "*Rue Rampart?*"

"Yes, stay clear of that building." Raimond pointed to a red, brick church. "The priest in residence there is not our friend."

Sorcha stopped at St. Louis Cemetery's gate, the only break in a full city block of concrete wall. "It's locked—what now?"

"You could snap that lock with your pinkie finger, but we'll go over the top."

Sorcha made the leap straight up with ease and admired the view.

"Not a sightseeing trip." Raimond flung the body onto the wall before jumping up himself and kicking it unceremoniously off the edge. "We aren't done yet." He led the way inside the cemetery barrier, coming to a stop in the farthest corner.

Sorcha followed, dragging the carcass by his foot. "Where are we putting...this fella I killed?"

"In here." Raimond yanked off a rusted metal plate to reveal a compartment as deep as the wall was thick. "You have to let the guilt go."

Sorcha drew a deep breath, peered in the hole and then at her teacher.

"This is for anyone who doesn't have a private crypt like—" Raimond gestured to the city of concrete tombs jammed inside the perimeter. "Bodies aren't buried in the ground here; they have a nasty habit of floating up and landing in people's front yards. They stay in the top part of the crypt for a year and a day. The heat turns them to ash, and then they're swept into the bottom to mingle with…whoever."

After sealing the dead stranger in the wall, the pair took a meandering path back to the front gate.

Sorcha stopped short at a vault surrounded by flowers, trinkets and flickering candles. "Unique energy."

"The crypt of a gifted voodoo priestess." Raimond pointed to a worn inscription on the door. "A queen in her own right."

"Oh, yes, I've heard about her from a co-worker. Remember Ivori?"

"Local girl—never smiled—kind of morbid?"

Sorcha giggled at the description. "That's her. She talked about voodoo royalty often. I didn't believe half of what she said."

"She probably spoke more truth than you realize."

Sorcha concentrated on the back of Raimond's head as he led the way back to the Quarter.

Raimond watched Sorcha learn to pick suitable targets and become at home in crowded bars and clubs. At first she was satisfied to follow drunks at the end of the night, snatching them into alleys when they were alone and easy pickings. She had no trouble enticing men with a wink of her eye or a flip of her hair, but with experience she began to embrace the challenge and taste of a woman.

Sorcha's preferences in blood didn't bother Raimond, but her choice of energy patrons was another story. He firmly believed in letting her develop her own personality, but his idea of a strong essence was a business owner, tradesman or philanthropist. Her idea of power was entertainers, musicians and dancers. She found admirable qualities in all of them. *Her human compassion is intact.* He stood guard from a distance, secretly missing the naïve nurse who turned his life upside down. *From pure and dazzling to snapping a drunk's neck in a few short months—she's complicated and addictive.*

Underneath all the flash and excitement, a darker problem lurked. *Never mind the strippers and singers; it's the brutality that disturbs me most.* It was subtle but unmistakable. Raimond knew he had kept his student isolated longer than necessary out of selfishness. She sensed the vibes other vampires in the Quarter gave off. To add to the pressure, his own family was growing restless at the plantation.

"Keep in mind, as glamorous as this all looks, the politics are dirty." Raimond held the penthouse door open. "Don't underestimate anyone."

"Why are you telling me this now?"

"Your family wants to meet you."

"Should I distrust my own family?" Sorcha tossed her jacket on the chair and crossed her arms.

"No, at least not the ones you'll meet tomorrow, anyway."

"How big is this family?"

"Huge—spread around the globe. But one step at a time." *And the roles change, again.*

Chapter 22

FAMILY

SORCHA WOKE ON a Tuesday assuming it would be like any other night—dance, drink and sleep. Life was one big party, ending in a marathon bubble bath. As she brushed out her hair, her feet began to tingle as if a hive of bees had awakened under the floor. *No heartbeats, just static.* Dressed in her new favorite outfit, flowing silk pants and a matching button down shirt, she ventured into the parlor.

Raimond held court in the kitchen, surrounded by three vampires who hung on his every word. As Sorcha entered, the strangers directed their collective attention to her.

"Sorcha? Raimond didn't tell us you were so beautiful." A petite girl stepped up to grasp Sorcha's hands. "I'm sorry. I'm Lily—this is Julia." She pointed to a blonde woman with mint-green eyes. "And, Steven." White freckles dappled the red-haired man's nose and cheeks.

Impeccably dressed in a shirt and tie, Steven seemed like a stuffy southern businessman, until he opened his mouth. "You beautiful creature. We've waited so patiently to meet you."

"You've been an ogre." Julia squawked when he crammed his splashing drink in her hand.

"So have you, blondie." Steven took Sorcha's face in his hands and kissed her lightly on both cheeks. "Welcome to our family!"

In a whirlwind, Sorcha was ushered into the parlor. Lily sat at her side, staring intently at her hair.

Raimond busied himself building a fire.

"Do you all live here, in the penthouse?" Sorcha examined each new face.

Julia stood with her back pressed to the wall. "Raimond is a duke, his royal home is Normandie Hall. Did he mention that?"

"Noooo..." Sorcha arched an eyebrow.

"Figured as much." Julia frowned. "He's the leader of the most powerful vampire coven in the South."

"Coven?"

"Yes." Raimond brushed dirt from the firewood off his hands. "And I'd like you to become a member, if you agree of course."

"I, em, yes," Sorcha said. "Where's Normandie Hall?"

"Way out in the country, up the Mississippi," Lily said. "You'll adore it."

"It's stunning, but the food is boring and we've been stuck there for months." Julia peeked at the dark sky before snapping the drapes back. "Let's go out and eat."

Sorcha couldn't tell if she was annoyed or joking.

"I assume you taught her how to feed, Raimond?"

"Yes, Jules. What do you think I've been doing?"

Jules?

"Get changed, honey—let's see what the duke taught you." Steven's eyes sparkled as he gave Sorcha a gentle push toward her room.

His skin is so white I can almost see my reflection.

Raimond stopped the older vampires before they left the parlor. "You three, I have hospital business, so watch her. I mean it. And Jules, take it easy, she's a newborn."

"Not your blood," Julia said.

"Treat her like she is." Raimond started to point at Julia but wound up pressing his palms together. "Please."

Sorcha's first night out with her family was a complete success. Julia

110

and Lily must have been withering from boredom at the country house, because they hit the bars with a vengeance. Steven was more subtle but equally insatiable. His choices alternated between quirky and stoic, but always perfectly groomed men. They danced, picked victims, drank their fill and went back to repeat the cycle. By midnight three of the four who had been new acquaintances the previous evening strolled arm in arm most of the way to the penthouse.

Julia walked on her own, ignoring Steven's comments even when he dropped back to link elbows with her.

"You can't deny that Raimond taught her well," Steven whispered.

"She's a beast."

"And a damn sexy one." Steven kissed Julia's cheek. "Who will never go hungry."

"I see you've adopted Raimond's favorite, dirty habit." Steven found Sorcha on the balcony and plucked the brown cigarette from her hand. "Good news, it won't kill us."

"Where is Raimond, anyway?"

"At the hospital. You know he's still the medical director, right?" Steven stifled a sneeze. "Ugh, sorry."

Going back to work never even crossed Sorcha's mind. *How does Raimond concentrate around all that blood?*

Julia and Lily joined them, drawn by the magic of the cloves. Sorcha suspected they had questions, but nobody wanted to be the first to ask.

Lily gave in and started the interrogation. "Where are you from? How did you get turned?"

"Do you have a boyfriend?" Julia asked.

The first two answers were simple. Sorcha avoided the boyfriend topic altogether. Her stomach twisted at the thought of Vir.

"What's up with your eyes?" Lily asked.

Sorcha remembered Raimond's eyes turning red when he drank. Sometimes, she even caught a flash of green. "I've seen the blue…if that's what you mean?"

"She means when you feed," Steven said.

"Julia, get some wine. The real stuff." Lily dragged Sorcha in front of a giant mirror at the end of the hall. She waved the wine under her nose, pulling it away at the last second. Alcohol almost masked the smell of blood. Feeling the color rise in her face Sorcha grabbed for the bottle as Lily tossed it to Steven, keeping it just out of her grasp.

"Look!" Lily pointed at the reflection.

"Yikes." Raimond had shown Sorcha her new eye color, but never this intense, sapphire flame.

"Murder—I mean—wow." Steven braced himself on the wall. "Sorcha, what are you?"

Sorcha described what she remembered of her attack and repeated Raimond's explanation of the Rakshasa.

"I thought those ancient vampires were only legend." Steven tilted his head. "But that blue is unique."

"Enough about me," Sorcha said. "I want to know about all of you and how everyone became part of Raimond's coven."

"Do I have to tell this whole starving-to-death story?" Julia looked at Lily and Steven. "Again?"

"Come on, Julia, be nice for a change," Steven huffed.

"Fine." Julia eyed Sorcha up and down. "Paris, 17th century. A band of travelers needed a female companion to run their scams, so they changed me. Bastards were reckless enough to get caught and burned. Not me."

"Sounds awful," Sorcha whispered.

"Try living it." Julia turned to stare at the wall. "I stowed away on a sailing ship and landed in Barbados. Keeping a low profile is nearly impossible when you're ravenous. A local witch took pity on me though, said she knew a doctor who could help. My only chance. That's when I met Raimond. He's a saint. Took him ten years to piece me back together."

"I'm not as old as…her." Lily shot Julia an abrupt glance. "I was born in a New Orleans brothel. My mother was abducted from Japan when she was twelve. They allowed her to keep me, but that life was a trap. One night, a fire swept through a row of houses on the edge of the Quarter. My mother pushed me out the attic window, but she didn't make it. Raimond found my broken body on the street. He scooped me up out of the gutter. Healed me with his blood. Julia's right—the man is a saint. He raised me in this penthouse as his own daughter. When I turned eighteen, grown and educated in the finest schools, he allowed me to make my own choice—human or vampire." Deep emerald flashed through Lily's eyes. "You see which path I chose."

"Okay, my turn." Steven clamped his hand over Lily's mouth. "I was a teenager, running with a gang. Bad neighborhood." He pointed upriver. "I'm sure you've never been there. After a street brawl, I landed in the Sisters of the Peace emergency ward."

"Steven, you had another asthma attack," Julia said.

"I got beat up." Steven brushed off her comment. "The doctors did everything possible, but I was too far gone. Raimond, who diagnosed me with asthma when I was eight, stayed in the room after his colleagues left my corpse for the nurses to wrap. I floated above and watched him change me—saving me. My soul was sucked back into my body, and then he smuggled me out of the hospital and set me up at Normandie Hall."

"Sucked back in…" Sorcha recalled. "That's what happened to me. It hurt."

Steven reached for the whisky. "Hurt like hell."

"So, I know my blood can fix little bite marks, but it can heal big injuries too, like Steven's and Lily's?" Sorcha asked.

"Almost anything, except…hasn't Raimond told you any of this?" Julia snapped. "You sound ignorant."

"Only a little, about the gold and wooden stakes." *What's her problem?*

"Okay, there's no coming back from a golden stake to the heart.

Being decapitated, burned or having your heart ripped out are fatal also." Lily spun an empty wine glass in her fingers.

Sorcha pushed farther. "How is a vampire born? Can anyone make one?"

The room plummeted into silence.

"She is ignorant." Julia stomped into the kitchen.

"It's possible for any of us to make another vampire, but strictly forbidden," Lily whispered. "By Raimond."

"Sorry to break the gloomy mood, but I need sleep. Tomorrow night we go dancing!" Steven looked the girls over, shaking his head. "And this mess will never do. We're going to that new club on Decatur. Dress to kill, ladies." He shooed everyone toward their bedrooms, cackling at his own joke.

Steven's room housed stockpiles of clothes for himself and everyone else. Fashions had been evolving, especially for the young people of underground New Orleans. Skirts and dresses were shorter and blouses tighter. The heels were sky high.

From Raimond's frown, Sorcha assumed he didn't approve.

Sorcha listened to her siblings chat and joke about sex and how they took frequent advantage of humans and vampires alike. Though she had used her looks and charm to lure unsuspecting victims, it was only a tease. She never had any interest other than sinking her fangs into a victim's neck and sucking out as much liquid life as possible.

I slept with Vir. A fleeting, big mistake that ended there. Need to stop yearning for someone I'll never see again.

The new club was located in a converted warehouse with a rear courtyard entrance. Sorcha glanced up at the grimy glass surrounding them and did a double take. *Is that a skeleton peeking out of an upstairs window? Creepy is the culture in this town.*

Painted wood doors swung apart and Sorcha's eyes shot open at the charged atmosphere. In front of her, a sea of gyrating bodies danced under the vivid colors of flashing lights. *This is no smoky little jazz club.*

"Forget the dreary dives and filthy streets." Steven took a bow in front of the chaos. "Welcome to the future of New Orleans nightlife."

A high stage faced the cavernous room. Bars lined the walls and a balcony circled the entire space.

The music was a change too. *I love it—piano and drums.* The crowd throbbed with luscious heartbeats. *Plenty to choose from later.* Sorcha was introduced to more members of her future clan. "Doesn't our family live at Normandie Hall?"

"Thousands are members of the Banitierre coven. Not all of them reside with us." Steven dropped his voice. "Thank the Lord."

"Who's the bald man?" Sorcha nodded to the balcony. "His eyes have been daggering a hole in my back since we arrived."

"That nasty piece of work?" Steven turned back to the stage. "Cole—head of the Victoire coven. Our families have no relationship. Stay far away."

"No problem." Sorcha flicked invisible bugs off her arms.

The night ended with the usual feast, same blood only better-dressed vessels. The Banitierre family set out for home, giggling and recounting their favorite moments. As they rounded a dark corner, Julia narrowly avoided tumbling over a crumpled figure.

Blood.

They all smelled it at once.

The scent is familiar. Sorcha crept closer. "Wait, Alexa?"

"Who?" Lily asked.

"I met her on the train to New Orleans." Sorcha looked from face to face and back to Alexa's splintered bones and ragged, bleeding neck. "We have to help her."

"Vampires did this." Julia scanned the dark streets and run-down townhouses. "I still feel static."

"I think she's dead." Steven knelt close enough to feel a faint pulse. "Correction, almost dead."

"I'm getting Raimond." Julia vanished in a blur, toward Sisters of the Peace.

"Can't we save her with our blood?" Sorcha smoothed Alexa's soggy curls away from her eyes. "I'll do it, just tell me how, please. Lily?"

"No, move over." Lily took her place on the blood soaked pavement with the limp form in her lap. Sorcha watched Lily's fangs slice a tiny wound into her own wrist. She held it over Alexa's mouth, and let black blood trickle down her throat.

"Lily." Raimond appeared out of the fog. "You do realize you're in the middle of the street? Have you learned nothing from me at all?"

"We found her here. She's—"

"Sorcha, I don't mean you." Raimond flung Alexa over his shoulder and turned his anger on the others. "I'm taking her to the hospital. The human one. The rest of you—to the penthouse. Immediately."

They ran home at full speed, skipping the stairs and climbing up the side of the building onto the balcony.

"What now?" Sorcha turned away from the hospital lights and faced the dark streets of the Quarter.

"We wait for Raimond." Steven followed her gaze. "What are you staring at?"

"The block where the attack happened. Those buildings are not empty."

From the cover of an overgrown balcony, Cole Victoire had watched the street scene unfold. "I hate those arrogant, entitled Banitierres."

"Why the hell did you call us off?" A blond vampire tossed his hair back and leaned on the iron railing. "That was a rare crack in their armor. A gift."

"Not the right time, Nicholas. I do hope the victim doesn't remember any faces." Cole pointed to the blood puddle in the gutter.

"Your coven sisters were sloppy, again."

"The meddling outsider was damn near dead, until that new girl showed up."

"Blue-eyes seem like Duke Raimond's weakness. Might just be the answer to our problems." Cole crossed his arms. "Wouldn't mind a taste of that little vixen's blood myself."

"But we could have taken them all out—they were totally unprotected." Nicholas clenched his fists. "Don't you want New Orleans for yourself?"

"Patience, young one." A sneer flickered across the bald man's face. "Our time will come."

Chapter 23

BANISHED

BANITIERRE FAMILY MEMBERS changed out of their bloody clothes, and returned to the parlor, one by one, to wait in silence. Raimond entered the penthouse as the first rays of dawn pierced the horizon.

Sorcha saw the anger in his eyes, but his voice had softened.

"Alexa made a miraculous recovery. I have no problem with saving Sorcha's friend, but not in the middle of a public street. I've taught you the mistakes of our ancestors—please don't repeat them." Raimond traced his moustache with his fingers. "There's been enough carousing. Tomorrow night, all four of you will go to the plantation. Sorcha, a word, please."

Sorcha remained in the parlor with a lump in her throat while the others shuffled out. "Sorry, I panicked."

"I'm not angry with you." He steered her toward the sofa. "You're still young. I don't expect you to know everything." He guided Sorcha's chin with his fingers until she had to meet his gaze. "Normandie Hall is stunning in the spring. I'll join you there in a few weeks."

A weight lifted off Sorcha's shoulders and she collapsed into the silk pillows.

"Your friend will recover, but she's been snooping around the Sisters of the Peace and the Quarter, looking for you—told everyone the story of your death was a lie."

"I'm not surprised. She thinks the whole city is haunted. She's kind of right."

"Apparently, she runs with a bad crowd and visits the Emergency Ward often."

"Should I talk to her?"

"No, I took care of it. You're not to go anywhere near that hospital. Alexa is on her way back to Nashville, undamaged." Raimond patted her knee. "Go to the plantation—you'll be safe there."

Sorcha retreated to her room. *Alexa, your curiosity almost got you killed.*

Chapter 24

NORMANDIE HALL

THE NEXT NIGHT at dusk, Raimond carried his bottle of scotch to the street and supervised his somber family piling into the car. "Cheer up, kids. You'll be at Normandie Hall by ten o'clock and it's only four weeks until spring. You know what that means."

Tension hung in the air like invisible fog for the two-hour drive.

"Sorcha, it's not like we are being sent to the pit of hell." Julia rested her chin in her hand and stared out the window. "Our home is one of the grandest mansions in the South. Oh, and by the way, don't curse around Raimond."

"Wait." Sorcha leaned forward. "After all this blood and death, Raimond is hung up on cursing? You just said hell."

"He's old-fashioned that way." Julia waved her off. "And hell isn't a curse word. It's a place."

"The party is in a few weeks. We'll need to get the tailor in as soon as possible," Steven said.

"What party?" Sorcha let her eyelids drift closed.

"Only the biggest bash of the season—the place to be and be seen in the vampire world." Steven shook her shoulder. "Magnolias blooming, candles everywhere, music and dancing 'til dawn. We kick off spring in style."

"We're here!" Lily pointed through the trees.

Sorcha strained to see through the tunnel of ancient boughs. Like a curtain being drawn back, the canopy ended and the car emerged into a clearing. Her eyes were drawn up the slope to a magnificent white building with lights twinkling in every draped window. Lush, tropical vegetation threw shadows that swayed in the gentle night breeze. Sorcha tumbled out of the sedan before it stopped, staring at double staircases curving up to a veranda lined with rocking chairs. Porches and galleries wrapped the entire mansion.

"This is Raimond's house?"

"The fortress of the Duke of Normandie," Julia answered.

They piled up the stairs, ladies on the left, gentleman on the right. Lily explained to Sorcha that it was an old custom.

A man in traditional uniform threw open massive double doors. "Welcome home, Lady Julia, Lady Lily, Lord Steven."

Heartbeat.

"You must be Miss Sorcha. I'm DeLynch. Welcome to Normandie Hall." He gave a slight bow, nodding toward the rest of the staff. "If there is anything you need, we're here to serve."

"As per Raimond, Sorcha will be taking the Myrtle Room." Julia fired off orders on her way down the hall. "The trunk is jammed with luggage, and more is on its way. Get it all to the correct rooms."

"Very well." A snap of the butler's fingers sent staff flying to retrieve suitcases and ready the rooms.

What's that bitter smell?

"Time for the grand tour!" Steven pointed out details as they walked. Every room featured high ceilings, sparkling chandeliers and antique furnishings.

"This clock must be twelve feet tall." Sorcha traced her fingertips over dark swirls in the polished wood.

"Some loud-as-hell relic Raimond rescued from France. Salvaged wood from the hull of a Dutch sailing ship. Blah-blah." Steven pulled her away. "The house is wired for electricity, but every room still has a working fireplace. I saved the best for last."

Behind meticulously carved doors, the soaring ballroom occupied a full wing of the mansion. Iron-railed balconies ringed the upper gallery. Built in a graceful curve, the French doors of the west wall spilled onto a sweeping patio and garden.

Floor to ceiling snow. Sorcha recalled a blinding vision: columns, ornate moldings and curtains of pure white. Mirrors framed in polished metals shone like jewels. *I've seen this.*

"For the parties." Steven flipped on the chandeliers. Soft color from the crystals reflected on the gleaming dance floor and turned the ceiling into a dome of colored glass.

"Whoa." Sorcha gaped at the grandeur.

"This is Penny, your maid." Steven shooed Sorcha toward the stairs. "Follow her."

The second floor of the manor held twenty-two bedrooms. The Myrtle Room was at the end of the east wing, with a view of the back gardens. A canopied bed was anchored against one wall opposite a seating area, a small fireplace and another chandelier. Polished rosewood furniture complemented rich hardwood floors.

Can't believe I live here.

Penny arranged clothes in the substantial armoire.

Heartbeat.

"What would you like to wear for dinner, Miss?" Penny asked.

The scent of these humans is sour.

"Dinner?"

"The family meets in the drawing room at midnight. You can freshen up in here." Penny opened the door to a well-appointed bath. "I'll lay out the black skirt and purple blouse. Ring me when you're ready."

Sorcha took a quick bath and pulled the bell. Penny helped her slip into the conservative outfit and expertly brushed her long hair into full luster.

"Will dinner be crowded, Penny?"

"Sixty-three live here in the estate's wings and cottages. I'm sure they're all anxious to meet you."

Dabbing on a bit of lipstick, Sorcha turned side to side.

"Ready?" Lily poked her head around the door.

"Hope so."

"Come on, you're the guest of honor."

Sorcha shuffled behind Lily's braided black hair to sweeping stairs that spiraled the foyer. She gripped the curved railing with shaky fingers, pausing to admire the intricate, inlaid tile of the grand entrance. *Getting used to this extravagance may take some time.*

Laughter and voices from the front parlor fell silent as she passed through the arched doorway.

"Everyone—" Lily stepped forward. "Miss Sorcha Alden."

Sorcha shook hands and greeted so many people, she was sure she wouldn't remember their names.

"Come, Sorcha." A friendly man wearing spectacles ushered her into the dining room. A long table was centered in a warm yellow hall lined with artwork. Three sparkling chandeliers lit perfect place settings. The older man reintroduced himself as Benjamin and offered Sorcha a seat between himself and his wife, Vera. "Meeting so many strangers can be overwhelming, but you'll feel better after you've eaten."

Staff entered the room in a single file parade. They stood back after arranging platters and chalices on the table.

"I haven't had anything but blood and alcohol since my transformation." *I thought normal food was off limits.* Trays uncovered in unison revealed cakes, chocolates and pudding. *Apparently, I'm wrong.* The goblets were filled with blood.

Benjamin whispered gleefully in her ear. "Straight from the vein."

Sorcha took tiny bites at first. *If this is a customary dinner, what's the spring gala like?*

"Would you like a bit more, dear?" Benjamin held a full platter of pastry. "It's safe for you."

"It's heavenly." Sorcha helped herself. *Haven't eaten this much since…the convent.*

A place set at the head of the lavish table remained conspicuously empty.

I miss Raimond.

Chapter 25

PACIFIC OCEAN, FEBRUARY 1936

THE TRIP BACK to New Orleans was not a smooth one for the Sisters of the Peace. Seasickness hit with a vengeance again, even before a vicious storm nearly sunk the old ship. Nurses and doctors huddled below deck and prayed to live through the night. The morning following the tempest left a battered and beaten Inverness adrift on a dead calm sea.

Vir staggered to the deck, picking his way around debris to a bench at the bow. "What the hell ever possessed me to go on this voyage?" He popped open the buttons of his shirt and leaned back, welcoming the sun to beat on his bare chest.

"At least we're still alive."

"Geez, Ivori." Vir's eyes flew open. "Why are you creeping around?"

Ivori kicked splintered wreckage aside and made room for herself on the bench. "The question is, what are you doing here, Dr. Ashayle?"

"Meaning what?" Vir fumbled to fasten his shirt. "In this seat?"

"Truth is, this bench was Sorcha's favorite spot. She wasted hours up here studying stars." Ivori pulled a loaf of bread out of a bag and tore it, offering half to Vir. "Eat something, before you go and starve."

"Thank you." Vir inhaled the food. "How long will it take to get to

New Orleans, now?"

"Weeks, probably." Ivori squinted through the sun. "Anyone from your family know you're on this ship?"

"Nope. If this thing sinks, I disappear without a trace. Just like Sorcha."

"This trip's been cursed since the beginning, but I'm pretty certain we'll get home at some point." Ivori stood and brushed the crumbs off her shirt. "Last night, I wasn't so sure."

"Cursed?"

"One way or the other. Don't you agree?" Ivori walked a few steps before she backed up. "Please, don't take this the wrong way…"

"Does it matter?" Vir shaded his eyes against the sun glare. "You'll speak your mind anyway."

"If you're looking for closure, New Orleans is the perfect place to talk to the dead."

Chapter 26

NORMAN ISLAND

IN SEARCH OF legal advice, Raimond set sail for the Caribbean hideaway of Crown Prince Draven Norman. His history with Norman ran deep—he owed his life to the prince's mercy, but their relationship was adversarial as often as it was friendly. His rented boat bobbed in uncharted waters for hours before he saw a glimmer of light. Steps carved into a cliff led to a terrace on the island's highest peak. Stone fire pits lit the midnight sky like it was high noon.

Draven's blond hair whipped in the wind. Raimond dropped to one knee in front of the prince.

"How many times have I told you to stop doing that?"

"I'm never sure whether to believe you." Raimond rose and joined Draven to stare at the moon's reflection on the black sea. "Any wild stories for me?"

"Not this season," Draven said. "An exotic bore, if you must know."

"You might need to actually look for a bride, instead of standing here surveying your kingdom." Raimond looked down at the rocky beach. "Unless you expect her to wash up on your shore?"

Draven's mouth twisted into a smirk. "I have miserable luck when I invite females to visit."

"That was one time, and you scared the lass to death."

"My family would never have accepted her. Enough idle chatter.

You must be famished."

After a night of gorging themselves on royal, private stock, Draven and Raimond didn't stir again until the next sunset. Deep inside subterranean catacombs, limp drained bodies littered the floor. The humans would live, but they would be useless as blood donors for at least a week.

Untangling himself from a pile of naked women, Draven rose and dressed before nudging a fully clothed Raimond. "Come, allow the staff to tidy up this mess." The prince unlocked his office door and settled behind a desk. "Let's hear your story. Surely, it's long and complicated."

Raimond recounted the Nepal trip, including the night of Sorcha's attack and the aftermath. "I always assumed my emergency bag would be for me—not one of my nurses." He closed the office door before explaining his research of the Rakshasa and why he thought they were behind the recent tragedies in that region.

"I know of that ancient species, but haven't seen one in nearly a century. They keep themselves hidden in the mountains." Draven wrinkled his brow. "Your nurse has those eyes?"

"My first clue. She was also unusually strong, even for a newborn. I've spent months training her in the right way to do things, using all the knowledge from my own mistakes."

"Yet?"

"I've taught her to be precise, not to spill a drop of blood. She's a quick learner, but she has an edge of violence, not driven by hunger— just a current of evil I catch from time to time." Raimond paused. "I also don't think anyone restarted her heart after she died."

"Hmm, certainly sounds like Rakshasa. Those bastards murder for sport. The more brutal, the better. An accidental transfer of their blood or venom could change her without any intervention."

"She claimed she was attacked by talking tigers. I didn't take her seriously."

"Legend tells of Himalayan vampires who take tiger form. I'll speak to Father about it." Draven reached for an old ledger. "You drank your fill last night, but you aren't yourself. Either none of those women appealed to you, or you've something else to confess."

Raimond rested his face in his hands. "It's that obvious?"

"It is to me."

"Do I have a conflict of interest, integrating Sorcha into the family?"

"Not if you first explain our laws and the advantages of being part of your coven. She sounds like a strong woman with a fiery streak. Let her make her own decision. Of course, leaving her unprotected would be foolish and dangerous."

"Even for a minute."

"I would very much like to perform the initiation ceremony at the Equinox Gala." Draven ruffled the ledger's pages and tossed it away. "I propose that I come to Normandie Hall, get acquainted with Sorcha and ascertain whether she's competent to make the decision. Then, you can proceed with a clear conscience."

Raimond flopped back in his chair. "I'll take you up on that offer."

"And if the sire arrives to claim her?"

"I'll fight." Raimond bared his fangs. "I'll win."

"Relax, old fool. The next time you see that girl, she'll be sitting under the columns of your palace, sipping wine in the moonlight."

Chapter 27
PRICELESS

SORCHA'S TOUR OF Normandie Hall continued after dinner. She trailed Lily and Steven through the ballroom, into the formal gardens.

"Nobody told me about the food." Sorcha settled onto a bench with a view of the main house.

"Well, the recipes are secret, plus your body has to be ready. Newborns need to stick with liquid nutrition." Steven examined Sorcha's face. "How do you feel?"

"Grand and strong. The blood was fresh?"

"We have donors here at the estate, collected from every corner of the globe," Lily said. "They're downstairs, hidden from prying eyes and living in complete luxury. I'll show you tomorrow."

"You can drink directly from any of them if you get hungry. They rather enjoy it," Steven explained. "A trip to their quarters is like perusing the menu at a five-star vampire restaurant. Every evening, veins are tapped and donations poured into chalices minutes before we sit down to dinner. It's painless all around, although it does lack the excitement of the hunt."

"And the servants?"

"Most of Raimond's security is vampire, but the house staff are human. Generations of the same families work here. They're trustworthy and well compensated for it."

Sorcha crinkled her nose.

"The smell is Artemisia. Silver sage, originally from a castle in Wales. An effective vampire repellant to safeguard our humans. It's poisonous if you ingest it." Steven pointed to the far corner of the plantation. "Don't even touch the leaves."

"You look exhausted. It's been quite a night." Lily took Sorcha's hand. "Let's get you to bed."

Sorcha tossed and turned all day. Behind her eyelids, she was thrown violently from side to side and hurled out of her berth. *The Inverness?* She heard voices crying, praying and begging for their lives. The steel hull groaned in agony under crashing waves. A freight train of wind roared overhead. Long tentacles spun from the deep, dragging the ship down into silence.

Sweet silence and light.

Ivori handed her a glass of champagne.

Oh Lord, we must be dead.

"Miss, wake up."

"Don't touch me, Ivori." Sorcha swatted fingers off her shoulders.

"Miss Sorcha, please."

Struggling to focus on a figure floating in front of her, Sorcha bolted up. "Penny?"

"Yes, Miss." The maid touched Sorcha's forehead. "Are you unwell? You screamed in your sleep."

"Just a nightmare, but I'm never going back on that horrid ship." Sorcha glanced around the room, recalling the previous night and her new home in bits and pieces. "Do I smell coffee?"

"Freshly brewed." Penny arranged a tray over Sorcha's lap and filled the fine china cup.

"Can I drink this? I mean—do the others?" The aroma brought memories crashing back.

"Indeed they do, every evening. Black, maybe a dash of sugar. Our duke's custom blend."

Sorcha sipped the steaming coffee. Mellow buttery flavor exploded on her tongue. "Oh, that's divine!"

Wearing a light linen dress, Sorcha made her way to the front parlor, where Steven and Lily paced the floor. They both looked closely at her eyes.

"Hungover?" Lily asked. "You ate and drank a lot last night."

"Well, I did feel a bit queasy when I woke, but I had some coffee and the symptoms are gone." *Nobody will understand how much I missed coffee.*

"You're strong for a young one." Steven grabbed Sorcha's hands. "We have a full evening planned. You'll need to pick a dress for the Gala. It's only three weeks away."

The tailor arrived at nine o'clock with trunks of fabrics and patterns. His crowd of apprentices set to taking Sorcha's measurements. She looked at Steven helplessly as she was pushed, pulled and turned in every direction.

"Get that bust measurement right. We can't have the top drooping like the last dress you made for Julia. Frankly, I don't know how you girls walk around with..." Steven gestured at Sorcha's breasts.

Sorcha glared at him as apprentices pushed her arms up, wrapping the measuring tape around every curve of her figure. "Being flat-chested is no fun, either."

"I didn't know you before, but that is no longer an issue."

Choosing fabric was far more enjoyable. The samples were rich, saturated colors, perfect for a formal evening in a white ballroom. The men would wear black tails with classic white shirts. Custom-made cravats provided splashes of color.

Digging through the trunks, Steven emerged with a vibrant blue fabric—silky without being shiny. He held the color up to Sorcha's face along with a coordinating swatch of tone-on-tone design. "Perfect with your eyes. Now, to pick a pattern."

Sorcha smiled as she went along with Steven's suggestions. *What a charade. I'm just a pawn in these party plans.* The crew of tailors exited the house with strict instructions and a mountain of work to accomplish. Most of the women had ordered new dresses—some of them more than one. The men had standing orders for formal wear to be delivered the week of the party.

The midnight meal was a scrumptious encore of the night before. The specialty of the night featured Pacific Island blood. Sorcha pretended she tasted the difference.

After dinner, the family dispersed into small groups, some going for walks, others heading into the wine cellar. Several married couples in residence retired to the privacy of their own cottages, while the younger vampires gathered in the drawing room.

Steven herded the group into the dark ballroom. "Time for dance lessons. Sorcha, what's your pleasure?"

"My what?"

"Ballroom dancing. Can you?"

"I can waltz a wee bit." Sorcha recalled standing on her mother's feet in their tiny living room in New York.

"The waltz it is then." Steven dragged a Victrola out of the parlor and sorted through a stack of old records until he found the right one. "Sorcha, I'll be your partner. Lily, lights, please!"

The week at Normandie Hall passed in a blur of dance lessons and dress fittings. Sorcha had no doubt that her gown would be beautiful, though she still had very little idea what it would look like. The tailors returned to drape, pin and fuss while Steven circled like a shark, snapping out orders.

Sorcha thought she knew how to waltz. *Wrong.*

Most of the vampires in residence were forced to practice dance after dance, while Steven pointed out their every flaw. "Elbows up, hands back. Maintain eye contact!"

"Is this a party or a Broadway show?" Sorcha complained. "My feet are killing me."

"More than six hundred guests are invited to this Gala. You are the host family." Steven gestured to the entire group. "Everything you do will be scrutinized, especially you, Missy." He pointed his finger dramatically at Sorcha. "You'll be the center of everyone's attention. Most will be gracious, but others—not as much."

"What's that supposed to mean?"

Shouts in the hallway were punctuated by slamming doors and the crash of china.

"What the devil is going on out there?" Steven disappeared to investigate the commotion without answering Sorcha's question.

The dancers took full advantage of the break in the action to collapse on the ballroom floor. *We must be some sight. Twenty vampires lying in a circle, staring at the moon through a fancy skylight.*

"Damn, that thing is magnificent," Lily said. "Wonder how they got it up there."

"Lily, language!" Julia shook her head. "That priceless skylight was lifted with pulleys, chains and horses."

"Attention everyone!" Steven burst back in the room. "Raimond will be home in two nights." He paused and dropped his voice to a whisper. "With Prince Norman."

"Who?" Sorcha sat up, looking from face to face for a reaction. Some gasped while others rolled their eyes.

"Crown Prince Draven Norman rules the North American continent," Steven said. "He's handsome, arrogant and very, very formidable."

"More powerful than Raimond?"

"Show me the flowers!" Steven spun in circles. "Send that wine list to Ben and Vera."

Julia waved a dismissive hand in his direction, turning her serious face to Sorcha. "Yes, more powerful. Raimond has no living sire, but the prince is his direct superior."

"What happened to his sire?" Sorcha assumed that meant the vampire who made him, not his human father.

Julia slouched to the floor. "Faison sired countless vampires in the dark days after the French Revolution to serve as his slaves and bring him humans to feed on. He brutalized his victims, who were mostly helpless women and children. By all accounts, his taste for infants was ghastly, as was the horrific treatment of his own family. He kept them chained, beaten and burned. Many didn't survive."

"Raimond?" Sorcha rolled over to face Julia.

"He knew he had to stop that villain, even if it cost him his own life," Julia said. "He and his inner circle ambushed and killed Faison in a bloodbath covering miles of French countryside and a vacant castle. A few cowards ran off and informed the vampire court of the massacre. They traced Raimond to America and brought him up on murder charges. Killing another vampire is illegal, unless it's in self-defense or extreme circumstances."

"Prince Norman was chosen by the king to preside over Raimond's trial," Lily said. "Creatures came out of the woodwork to defend him. Vampires, witches, wolves...even humans and it worked. Not only did the prince spare Raimond's life—he appointed him duke and granted him stewardship of New Orleans."

"All this history." Sorcha massaged her temples. "So much I don't know."

Julia stood. "Oh, and just so you don't look like an idiot, address the prince as 'Your Highness' and don't look into his eyes until he grants you permission. I know Raimond is laid back, but during formal functions such as this party, you should address him as Duke."

"I'll remember that." Sorcha watched Julia stop Steven as they passed in the ballroom doors.

"How about you quit the dance marathon and teach Sorcha something useful," Julia said. "If she looks foolish, it's your fault."

"Yes, ma'am." Steven saluted Julia and stuck his tongue out at the back of her head.

Sorcha followed Lily downstairs and let her introduce the blood donors. *She wasn't kidding when she said they lived in luxury. I expected some*

kind of dungeon. The space mimicked the mansion's footprint: furnished from floor to ceiling in silky fabrics, lush carpet and oversized furniture. Food and drink flowed freely as a collection of beautiful people lounged, minimally clothed and tangled in each other's limbs.

Heartbeats.

"Do you want to feed? Pick anyone you like," Lily said. "They would love a little of your blood too, if you're willing."

"They drink blood? I thought they were human?"

"They are. Vampire blood keeps them strong and beautiful. Many of these people are much older than they look."

"But won't that turn them?"

"It's more complicated than that—you would have to kill them. Please don't."

"Of course not. Anyone?" Sorcha's eyes landed on a brunette, swaying to the faint music and savoring cherries out of a carved bowl. *Why do I feel naked?*

"Go ahead." Lily nodded. "That's Rayna—I think she's your type. Take some energy too. You haven't had much since the night at the club."

Sorcha felt fingers tug at the hem of her skirt as she slipped through the crowd. "Hello, Rayna." She offered her hand in greeting.

Rayna smiled, not taking Sorcha's hand but instead lightly kissing her on both cheeks. "Welcome, Sorcha. We've been waiting for you." The girl led the way to a low chaise in a private corner of the room. "Drink?" She tipped her head to the side, exposing the perfect, unmarked flesh of her neck. Blood pulsed in vivid arteries under nearly transparent skin.

"Oh yes, please." In a mirror Sorcha watched her own eyes ignite into blue fire.

"It's better skin to skin. Don't be shy."

Sorcha offered no resistance as Rayna unbuttoned her blouse, gently pushing it off her shoulders. Without thinking she unzipped her skirt, letting it fall to the floor, leaving her in only an ice blue slip.

Rayna turned her back and relaxed her slender body, waiting for the next move. Sorcha knelt, lightly caressing the back of her neck, feeling the warmth rise from her skin. Lowering her fangs to Rayna's neck, she inhaled her scent—faintly familiar spices and smoldering jasmine. *My weakness.*

Rayna reached up and released clips that held the hair piled on top of her head. Waves of silk tumbled around their faces like a veil, as Sorcha's fangs pierced skin. Rayna gasped with pleasure, her spine crushing into Sorcha's breasts while blood filled the vampire's throat. Rayna's life rushed in, charging Sorcha with power and strength. She drank enough to quench her thirst and then focused her eyes down, onto the rise and fall of the girl's chest.

"Rayna, may I?"

"Take all that you need."

Sorcha absorbed glorious waves of energy. Rayna's small body hid a treasure chest of unexpected optimism and unscathed love for life, nature and dance. *She was a dancer.*

Sorcha sat back, hoping she hadn't taken too much.

Rayna gazed up through her tousled hair. "Yes?"

"That was divine." Sorcha took Rayna's face in her hands. "Do you want to drink from me? I don't know how to do it."

Rayna pulled a small dagger out of a drawer. "Give me your hand. You'll barely feel it, promise."

Sorcha offered her open palm. A rivulet of dark blood sprung to the surface from a tiny slice. Rayna lowered her lips, cautiously licking and coaxing blood from Sorcha's veins.

Sorcha flinched. *Tickles a little.* Rayna looked up with questioning eyes.

"All good."

Rayna gulped blood until she was full.

Chapter 28

ROYALTY

ALL THAT WAS left to do was wait. With preparations complete, the entire household squirmed in a state of poorly disguised panic, anticipating the arrival of vampire royalty.

"I found dust." Steven held up his finger, showing off invisible dirt. "It's awful!" Maids scurried to polish and tweak parlor knickknacks.

Sorcha was fairly certain of how to greet the prince. She ran the instructions through her head. *Eyes down, hands at your side—wait, what do I call him again?*

"Steven, sit down." Julia hissed. "You're making everyone nervous."

"The cars are here. Places, everyone." DeLynch herded the family into the foyer. Sorcha hurried to her appointed spot inside the curve of the grand staircase. Penny had brushed Sorcha's hair into soft waves and secured it with a silk hairband, leaving a few pieces loose to frame her face. She nervously smoothed her crimson skirt and strained to hear footsteps.

A man in formal military attire entered, followed by security and royal valets. Sorcha shivered from a blast of energy, stronger than all the vampires she had ever met put together.

"His Royal Highness, Prince Draven Norman." The guard's voice echoed and all heads bowed as DeLynch ushered the visitor across the threshold.

Sorcha peeked through her hair as the prince proceeded down the receiving line. His back remained poker straight while he acknowledged each member of the family by name.

"Miss Sorcha Alden." The prince lifted her hand to his lips.

English accent? Sorcha wasn't sure what she expected a prince to look like. *He's flashy. Young.* His pale skin was flawless. She squirmed under his intense gaze. A calculated smirk hooked the corner of his mouth. *Arrogant.*

"Your Royal Highness, it is a great honor to meet you." Sorcha spoke her lines. *Thank God I paid attention to Steven's lessons.*

"The pleasure is all mine." Locks of blond hair drifted across his face as his steel eyes locked on hers, leveraging the full effect of his royal charm. "I look forward to getting to know you better."

Sorcha remained frozen as he moved on to the next person in line. She glanced toward the door and returned the smile of another man. *Raimond. I've missed you.* He nodded his approval and she took a deep breath, and then another, even though she didn't need to.

Family gathered in the front parlor while the royal party settled into their quarters. The prince traditionally occupied a large guest suite in the main mansion, with sweeping views of the front lawn and driveway. Dinner would commence when the prince was ready. Raimond appeared in time to position Sorcha behind her chair, next to his customary seat at the head of the table.

"Good evening." The prince sat at the opposite end of the table, and the rest of the dinner company followed his lead. He briefly stared at Sorcha and Raimond before putting the room at ease with colorful stories of recent escapades in the Caribbean and South America. He made a point of connecting with each person, asking their opinion on topics that seemed to suit them.

Sorcha's chest quivered when his attention landed on her.

"Miss Alden, I've heard of your penchant for fine coffee."

"Yes, Your Highness." She cleared her throat. "The coffee in New Orleans is the best I've ever tasted."

"Have you tried Galleyson beans from New Zealand? A very distinctive, complicated taste."

She shook her head.

"I'll send for some and look forward to your review."

Dinner ended abruptly when Prince Norman excused himself for the evening, anxious to walk the grounds and inspect the upkeep of formal flower beds. Raimond spent time with Julia, Steven and the staff reviewing plans for the party.

Sorcha's attention drifted to the group of vampires that strolled the moonlit garden. *A charming prince on the surface, but underneath all the trappings, something less glamorous is lurking.*

"Sorcha, may I have a word?" Raimond dismissed the others, leaving them alone in the parlor. "I apologize for taking so long to join the family. I was waiting for the Sisters of the Peace to return, but their ship's been delayed again. I'll send flowers when they arrive." Raimond kissed her lightly on each cheek. "I trust you've enjoyed yourself?"

"Absolutely. This house is amazing." She told him stories of obsessive dance lessons and dress fittings.

"Be kind to Steven. He struggles with his identity."

"He seems supremely confident."

Raimond nodded. "That's an act."

"But..."

"Are you going to ask me if he's homosexual?"

"I wasn't. But I know what that means, Raimond. I learned."

"If they talked about it in nursing school, there's much more to understand."

"They gave us a pamphlet." Sorcha stared at her feet. "But never said the word."

"Our family is a sanctuary, free and safe for everyone to be who they truly are. Always remember to cherish love, whenever and wherever it finds you." Raimond brushed his hand across her cheek. "Not to change the topic, but the prince wants to have a private meeting with you tomorrow, to discuss the ceremony."

"Ceremony?"

"The ritual at the Gala to make you a formal family member. The prince presides over major events, and he's agreed to explain the legal portions to you. It's his area of expertise." Raimond produced a black velvet pouch from his breast pocket. "Almost forgot, I brought a gift."

Sorcha untied a delicate ribbon and a disc slid into her palm. Her fingers traced the *fleur-de-lis* carved into each side. "Past, present and future."

"Who taught you that?"

"Zelia, my roommate." Dangling the polished wood object by its black cord, she gave Raimond a questioning look. "You said their ship was delayed. Is everyone safe?"

"Perfectly." He clicked a tiny latch and sprung the disc open.

"My locket." Sorcha's bottom lip trembled. "My pictures."

"I commissioned a jeweler to carve this case out of a fallen redwood branch. Those trees are thousands of years old—their wood is sacred." Raimond stepped behind Sorcha, brushed her hair aside and fastened the clasp behind her neck. "The gold is still underneath, but now you can actually wear it."

Sorcha twirled the locket in her fingers. "How can I ever thank you?"

"I'm just glad to see you so happy."

"This plantation...was it named for the prince?"

Raimond softly rearranged the hair over her shoulders, while she examined the carvings in the redwood. "Yes, it reminds him of a favorite estate in France."

Convinced everyone was upstairs in bed, Raimond stood in the unlit window with his cigarette, replaying the events of the night in his mind. *The country air agrees with Sorcha. Draven kissed her hand with more than the customary royal formality. Should have expected that though, he was a world-famous playboy in his glory days.*

Having Sorcha's locket reworked so she could wear it was a stroke of genius. The only thing missing from the evening was the long, searching kiss he wanted to coax from her lips. He had been so close to giving in to the temptation. *Soon—after the ceremony. Family first.*

"Raimond."

He spun around at the voice.

"I assume that you're waiting to sign her before you bed her?"

"Jules, keep your voice down." Peeking down the hall, he clicked the doors shut behind her.

"You may be pulling the wool over these fools' eyes," Julia gave a dismissive wave toward the sleeping house, "but don't forget I'm older than you—I always know what you're up to."

"Yes, and you never let me forget it." Raimond leaned against the window frame. "I'm trying to do what's best for her and our family. Think it's easy?"

"No, I'm sure it's not. Don't get hurt." Julia poked him in the chest. "Again."

Chapter 29

GARDEN DISTRICT

IVY-COVERED WALLS disguised a flurry of activity in a forgotten house on Terpsichore Street. Members of the Victoire coven were bound together by blood, but they were not one big happy family.

"Cole, why are we going to this ridiculous party? Don't we hate the Banitierres?" Kettly wrestled with two evening gowns, not satisfied with the fit of either.

"Can't we at least get a tailor?" Danielle whined. "This is a pitiful joke."

Cole Victoire sat in his study surrounded by dusty books, trying to massage away pounding in his head. Building a family quickly had forced him to choose quantity over quality. Kettly and Danielle were nightly, painful reminders of his strategy.

Kettly stomped into the office struggling with the zipper on her aqua dress. "Can't you at least get this place fixed up? I feel like Cinderella getting dressed in a garbage dump."

The house looked like a wreck, but Cole had no interest in renovations. The façade kept nosey neighbors from knocking on the door in the middle of the day to deliver a pecan pie.

"Really, Cole? Have you heard anything we've said? Do we have to go to this damn thing?"

"It's a night of free blood and booze. Seriously, Kettly, that frock is ugly. Find something else."

Both girls shrugged him off and walked away.

"Anyone else here?" Cole stood and slammed his knuckles into the wall.

A bookcase swung open and Nicholas appeared. "Yes, boss. Those tramps would be funny if they weren't so irritating."

"I would have ripped their throats out long ago, if it weren't for the convenient sex, which we both regularly enjoy."

"I'll get them under control, sir."

"You'd better." Cole hurled Nicholas through his study door, turned around and kicked the splinters. "Fix this mess."

"Where the hell is all this rage coming from?" Nicholas pulled wood fragments out of his skin.

Cole rubbed his temples. "Can't get that blue-eyed jezebel out of my head."

Chapter 30

REVEL IN IT

PANIC OVER HER private meeting with Prince Norman made Sorcha jittery. Instead of gnawing her nails off or twirling her hair to shreds, she opted for a visit to the basement.

Rayna met her at the door with a glass of wine. "Sorcha, the prince just wants to meet you to explain logistics and answer your questions."

"Can you tell me something about him? Where he's from? Anything?"

"Ummm, he's from Switzerland, or that may be just a rumor. I know he grew up in London and Paris."

"Wish you could come with me." Sorcha had grown fond of Rayna as far more than a food source. *I don't like the idea of sharing her with anyone else, either.*

"I'll be at the Gala and ceremony. It's one of the few nights of the year that we mingle with family upstairs."

"That makes me feel better."

"Then, go." Rayna pointed to the stairs.

Sorcha took a few deep breaths and climbed to the parlor.

"Come in, please." Prince Norman set aside his cigar and ushered her to a seat on the plush sofa.

"Thank you, Your Highness."

"For the purpose of our meetings, which may be lengthy, I would prefer to be on a first-name basis." Sitting on the low table across from the sofa, the prince offered his hand and re-introduced himself. "Draven Norman, charmed."

Again, Sorcha was staggered by the jolt that arced from his skin to hers before they even touched. *Guess I won't be out of here in an hour.*

"So, what do you know of the ceremony to be performed at the Gala?" He poured two glasses of wine and focused his penetrating gaze on her.

Sorcha sipped and stalled. "Well, I know it concerns vampire law. That's pretty much it."

"My goodness, we've plenty to discuss. Make yourself comfortable and we'll get it sorted." Draven snapped his fingers, ordering more wine before he relit his cigar. "Some of the vampires in this house, sired by Raimond himself, are automatically members of his coven. They share his blood. Others have sworn allegiance to him over the years. During the Ceremony of the Equinox, at the moment of spring's solstice, you will become a free entity. That is, as long as none of your ancestors come forward with a claim."

"Has anyone come looking?"

"Not as of yet." Draven assessed Sorcha's reaction. "Being free can be splendid, but it leaves you a target for unscrupulous vampires— and there are many. I'm sure Raimond would defend you to the best of his ability, but as a Banitierre, you'd be protected by legions of sworn members from all corners of the earth. Attacking you would be a declaration of war. It remains, of course, your free choice."

"I don't want to be alone, and I can't imagine being anywhere except with Raimond."

"Understand that by swearing your allegiance, you're bound to obey orders. I don't mean how to dress and such trivial things. In matters concerning the operations and security of the Banitierre coven, complete loyalty is expected. Anything less will be considered treason. Also, you may not break your bond unless Raimond gives permission, or in the event of his death." The prince stopped again— this time for emphasis. "Bad things do happen, Sorcha. Immortal does not mean invincible."

Sorcha winced as she sat back. Knots twisted in her neck. She was just grasping the idea of living forever, now she had to consider that she could die, or worse. *Raimond could die.*

"Young lady, you're positively pale." With another snap of his fingers Draven summoned a butler serving chalices of fresh blood. "Drink." He lifted a cup to his lips, watching intently as she did the same. "Ah—there it is."

Oh terrific, am I dribbling? Sorcha dabbed her mouth and chin with a napkin.

"Your eyes, Sorcha. I see the legendary flicker of blue. We'll feed together soon—the original way."

Sorcha grabbed the arm of the sofa against a spiraling flash. *Green—wet grass, thunder and birds.*

"Are you troubled?"

"Em, I see things." Sorcha bit her lip.

"That's unsettling." Draven urged her into the cool breeze of the veranda. "What manner of things?"

"Not sure, really." Sorcha settled into the rocking chair. "Bits and pieces, but some of it comes true."

Draven changed the subject. "Do you know how tomorrow's ceremony is performed?"

"No clue."

"It's not difficult. First, you'll confirm your identity by signing your name in the book. Then you'll swear your allegiance to Raimond and his clan by drinking his blood."

"I can do that?"

"Of course. You've not had any?" Draven acknowledged the shake of her head as an answer. "His blood seals the bond and he's forever part of you."

"And the book?" Sorcha put the chalice down and rubbed her palms in the fabric of her skirt. *I don't know anything.*

"It's the sacred record of Banitierre lineage. After you drink, I'll slice your hand with an ancient dagger. Your new blood will flow into your signature—on your very own page. After you're presented to the family, the party will commence."

"So much to understand, but I should be used to that. Most days are revelations to me."

"It gets easier. Have you been instructed in self-defense?"

Sorcha's face crimped into a scowl. "I need that too?"

"You do, although after the Gala will be fine. I'll insist on it." The prince's gaze drifted. "I think that will be sufficient for tonight. But Sorcha…"

"Yes?" She admired the prince gently rocking his chair. *Such dark eyelashes for his fair complexion.*

"I hear commotion in the ballroom at night. Are they teaching you to tango?"

"No, Steven has spent weeks trying to teach me to waltz. I may be hopeless."

"Steven?" Draven cringed. "That boy irks me. Ask Rayna to instruct you. She's an amazing dancer."

"I will." *Does that mean the prince wants to dance with me? The Gala is five days away. It'll be a miracle if I make it through this whole thing without falling on my butt.*

Sorcha feigned exhaustion and retired to her room after dinner. She dismissed Penny, made sure the hallway was clear and crept down the back stairs to find Rayna.

"You have to teach me the tango." Sorcha recounted her conversation with the prince, word for word, in between swallows of Rayna's blood. "Isn't that crazy?"

"Not really. He's quite the dancer. Maybe he's sick of having only me to partner with every year." Rayna made quick use of the dagger and took a long drink of Sorcha's blood. "I'll make it fun. Let's go to the ballroom."

Hours flew by to the steps of the Latin dance. Rayna taught Sorcha how to move using fingertip caress to guide the swing of her hips. She spun around to execute the man's steps, never breaking skin contact.

"This is a bit…"

"Intimate?" Rayna asked. "We drink blood."

"The dance seems deeper, if that's possible."

"Draven and I were involved a long ago, if that's what you mean. It didn't work out. He feeds like any other vampire, but powerful ones prefer sex with their own kind. They can't truly let themselves go with a human. Fatal damage kind of ruins the moment."

What is he looking for from me?

"Enough talking." Rayna rubbed her hands together. "Just picture a full crowd—lights, clinking glasses, laughter." She twirled in a circle for the benefit of an imaginary audience as music filled the room. Taking Sorcha's hand, she walked to the center of the dark floor, stepping into the beginning stance and fusing her eyes on Sorcha's. "Relax your neck—concentrate and let everything fade away. All that exists is you, me and the melody."

Rayna's method worked like magic. Sorcha unwound and they danced, gliding effortlessly, two shadowy figures in a majestic theater, lit by faint slivers of moonlight.

Draven masked his power and stayed hidden behind one of Normandie's columns. He watched the two beautiful women move together as one, like lovers in perfect sync, even when they collapsed on the floor giggling like little girls.

"Ladies." Both dancers shot up at his voice.

Sorcha stumbled to her feet. "How long have you been standing there?"

"Long enough." The prince smiled politely as Rayna backed away.

Sorcha's neck prickled as his piercing eyes looked her up, down and through.

"Shall we walk?"

Sorcha glanced at her loose black pants and crimson shirt.

"That outfit will do." Already across the veranda and patio with his entourage, Draven turned and beckoned with his finger. "Let's go,

Princess."

I can't refuse a royal invitation, but Princess?

"Have you ever hunted? Not in jazz clubs or corner bars, I mean— truly hunted?"

"Sometimes Raimond brings people to the penthouse. You know, for dinner?" Sorcha followed his confident strut across the sweeping lawn, glancing back at the sizeable royal guard that shadowed them.

"Yes, I'm quite sure he does. This is all lovely and gentrified," Draven gestured to the glowing mansion, "but it's not the way most vampires live. I assume Raimond hasn't told you much of his personal history, but he was deeply scarred by his past. His sire was—well, he was a prick."

"Julia told me some details, not quite in those words."

"That's why I found Raimond not guilty of murder. In any case, he's been trying to make up for the sins of our entire race since then, toiling in miserable places, saving hopeless people."

Sorcha winced as Draven unclipped her long hair. "That answers a lot of my questions about why he chose to be a doctor."

"He was a career soldier, a rebel commander and a born leader."

Sorcha tugged at the wild locks of hair around her face. *Why are we way out in this field?*

"Just to clarify, I respect Raimond for the man he was, and what he's achieved since I gave him control of New Orleans. The principles and standards he holds for family are admirable. However, it's my responsibility to make sure you know what you are and how to survive on your own."

"Thank you for helping me with all this. It's overwhelming, to say the least." *I can't see the house anymore.*

"So, our lesson for tonight is about hunting, but more importantly it's about chasing and catching. This man, here," Draven selected one of his guards, "will run across the field, and you're going to capture him and drink. He's a human, but a resilient one. His job is to escape. Your job is to bring him down."

"What if I hurt or kill him? I was taught to be gentle and precise."

"He's employed by me for this sole purpose. If I haven't killed him yet, I doubt you will. We'll give him a head start—half the distance to the trees. Ready?"

"Guess so." Sorcha was unclear about what was going to happen, but there was no time to plan. The soldier bolted across the field.

As the man reached the middle of the clearing, Draven shrugged out of his dinner jacket and cracked his knuckles. "Let it fly, Princess. I'm right behind you."

Sorcha sprung forward, locking onto the heat signature and scent left by the runner. She wasn't fooled by his zigzag pattern and covered the distance between them in the blink of an eye. Her final steps were perfect and accurate as she tackled a man three times her weight, ripped into his neck and hit the ground with the impact of a thunderclap. They twisted and rolled on the ground as one. Sorcha finished drinking before their momentum came to a halt. She disengaged and landed on her toes in a circle of fire, shoving wild hair out of her streaked face. She dabbed a spot of blood off her lip, as if she had just sipped tea from a fine china cup.

What is the prince gawking at?

Draven had been alive for centuries and known countless vampires, but nothing rivaled the beauty of Sorcha's evil smile. Her brilliant blue eyes were a peek into her staggering power and the door had only been cracked open.

"That's my girl. Revel in it!" Draven pumped a fist in celebration. He let Sorcha walk ahead of him on the way back to the mansion, admiring the new confidence in her stride. What he really wanted was to rip her clothes off and ravish her in the middle of the soggy hayfield. However, taking a female claimed by another would create a scandal, unless he convinced her to choose him over the duke.

Raimond waited on the veranda with his arms crossed.

"Where were you two?" His mood didn't improve when he saw the grass stains on Sorcha's clothes and the unruly state of her hair.

"On a picnic, old chap. Such a pleasant evening." Taking hold of her arm, Draven steered Sorcha around Raimond. "Upstairs, directly. You look perished."

Dangerous energy arced across the foyer.

Sorcha shot Raimond a guilty look and scampered up the curved staircase as the grandfather clock chimed five times. She hid on the landing and watched Draven admire the clock.

"The first time I saw this timepiece was in 1560 at Chenonceau. Glorious party, splendid fireworks, but the French had snakes in their garden." Draven traced the scrollwork with his fingertip. "The secrets this face must hold."

Raimond hurled a wine glass across the room. "Enough reminiscing! I know what happened out there tonight. How could you? You know how brutal her ancestors are."

"Calm down, bloody hell. She showed amazing control. You've taught her well, but it is possible to shelter someone too much. She needs knowledge of her primal force to be able to control it. Otherwise, she's a ticking bomb."

"I'm trying to do everything right." Raimond raked his hands through his hair. "Smothering her."

"I'll give her my blessing to join your family, but you must teach her to defend herself. You, more than anyone, know the significance of those skills. I can send one of my specialists if you like."

"No, thank you, I'll train her myself. She doesn't need to be manhandled by your goons. But you make a valid point, she needs to learn the ways of the world."

Draven poured a scotch and pushed it across the table.

Raimond drank it in one gulp. "And tonight, how was she?"

"Magnificent. Truly magnificent."

Chapter 31

DEMANDS

THE EVENING OF the party kicked off before sunset, the equivalent of early morning for a house full of vampires. Sorcha's eyes fluttered open and settled on bustling around the armoire.

"Whoa, is that my dress?" She threw the blankets off and flipped on the chandelier. The blue fabric leapt to life in the soft glow. Her fingers caressed the subtle tone-on-tone pattern. *Steven outdid himself.* A silver slip lay on the nearby chair; its boning and fluffy layers would give the skirt perfect fullness.

"Breakfast is served!" Steven and Lily barged in, carrying coffee and chalices of blood. "You have to eat early today—you'll need your strength for tonight. Hurry up. Hair and makeup take time."

Sorcha fiddled with her food, spun her glass and left everything but her coffee on the tray before retreating to a tub full of bubbles.

"Quit stalling in there!" Steven pounded on the bathroom door while Rayna, Julia, and Penny paced the floor. When Sorcha emerged in her slip, she was pushed into a chair in front of her dressing mirror. More maids scampered through the door and went to work painting her nails and setting her hair in curlers.

Lily babbled as she applied false eyelashes, strand by strand. "I recommend the dark lip stain—less smudging."

Penny spritzed sample perfume on linen strips.

Steven grabbed his nose and sneezed three times. "You know not to spray that near me."

"The spicy jasmine, please." Sorcha patted Steven's back. "It's just allergies. That slip is beautiful enough to be the dress itself."

"Your allergies are in your tiny mind." Julia snorted.

"Oh, shut up." Steven held a handkerchief over his face and collapsed in a coughing fit.

"Stop." Sorcha held her hands up. "I want a short break and Steven could use some air. You all need to get dressed, too."

Julia stormed out.

The rest of Sorcha's attendants hesitated until she gave each a sincere hug. "You've made me feel like a movie star. Steven, how in the world do you have allergies?"

"Never mind." He dabbed the corners of his eyes with a sleeve. "I'll see you downstairs."

"Can someone send for Raimond? I need to have a word with him." Digging in her nightstand, she found a smashed pack of cloves. *Glad I don't have allergies.* Sorcha straightened the least damaged cigarette and lit it in the doorway of the balcony.

"I've been summoned?" The duke appeared out of the shadows, dressed in tuxedo pants and unbuttoned shirt, missing his tie and shoes.

"That's a dashing look—you should attend the party as you are," Sorcha said. "I especially like the slicked-back hair." *Sultry and dangerous.*

"Touché." Raimond scanned her outfit. "Is that underwear or your gown?"

"Ha-ha. There's an important question I need answered. I want to know the procedure to change a human into a vampire."

He shook his head and his finger in unison. "Way too soon."

"I'm serious—I need to know."

"Do you require my assistance?" The prince appeared on the balcony, like a phantom in a silk robe.

"I don't want to turn anyone. Just to understand, like everyone else." Sorcha looked from the duke's deep frown to the prince, and back.

Raimond's bare feet paced the painted floor.

"Duke, this is bullshit. She has a right to know. With your permission, I'll show her, once and for all, then our night can move forward."

"This is not appropriate." Raimond threw his hands in the air. "And Draven, you know not to curse in front of my ladies."

"Will they be wearing gloves as well?" Draven asked. "Nobody wants a scandal."

"It's Louisiana. It's hot."

"You don't sweat." Draven pinched the air with his fingers.

Sorcha crossed her arms. "I'll leave, Raimond."

"And I'll escort her," Draven said. "With immense pleasure."

"Fine, demonstrate the basics only. None of your artistic license."

Draven snapped his fingers, summoning a tall, well-built valet.

"Ronald here would like to be turned. He's been begging me for years. Tonight is his lucky night."

Ronald's face lit up. "I'm ready, Your Highness."

"Nobody's ever ready," Raimond mumbled.

Without warning, Draven slashed into the man's neck. He swallowed blood with every pump of his victim's heart and sucked harder when the rhythm became eccentric, ignoring all signals to stop.

Sorcha ran her tongue across fangs that now throbbed in her gums.

As the human's heartbeat slowed and ceased, the prince bit his own wrist, tore open an artery and forced royal blood down the victim's throat. Draven drove his other hand through the man's sternum, past ribs and vessels until he grasped hold of the man's lifeless heart.

Sorcha winced and clutched her chest.

The prince began squeezing gently, mimicking a heartbeat,

spreading venom to every cell in Ronald's body.

"Now he needs time to transform. It's agonizing—most of them hallucinate." Draven withdrew his hand and let the body crash to the floor. "To complete the process he'll need to drink at least seven drops of fresh, human blood."

"And what if he doesn't drink?" Sorcha gaped at the writhing man.

"He'll die. Raimond supplied you human blood when you were in transformation. It's my understanding that you were almost too far gone to save."

Sorcha swept her gaze to Raimond. "You did that to me? Reached into my chest and did that—gory, disgusting thing?"

"No, I didn't." Raimond shot a glance at Draven. "It was unnecessary, though I'm not entirely sure why. I assume it was the potency of the Rakshasa who bit you."

"Well then, thank you for saving me."

"So Sorcha, now you're enlightened. Can we please dress for this party? Guests will be arriving any minute." Draven stalked away. He wiped blood from his hands with an embroidered handkerchief and tossed it over the railing.

"What about him?" Sorcha pointed to Ronald. His eyes rolled back as he made futile attempts to stand.

"He'll have his seven drops, but I can't deal with any more of this rubbish now. The equinox is in two hours." Raimond grabbed the newborn by his neck and threw him at the security team. "Lock him in the basement. And another thing—make sure you watch every guest tonight as if your lives depend on it."

Chapter 32

THE WALTZ

AS THE LAST rays of sun relinquished the sky to the sultry power of New Orleans dusk, members of the Victoire coven piled out of their derelict house and into a waiting limousine. The fading light was a blessing for the worn car that had seen better days.

"Is this the best you could do, Cole?" Danielle yanked stuffing from a tear in the car's upholstery. Running her hand over her ass, she checked the crimson silk for tears. "If I rip my gown this night is o...ver."

"Shhh, please behave yourself tonight, for a change." Nicholas attempted to do his job, policing the girls.

The group bantered and complained during the drive from the Garden District, up the river to Normandie Hall. Cole peered down driveways to catch a glimpse of the famous plantations. "Someday it'll be me hosting the Gala of the Equinox, at my private estate."

"Are they going to have food at this thing? I'm starving," Danielle moaned.

"I can't wait to sample some of their private stock. Rumor has it this house has an exotic, living collection." Nicholas shut up after a sharp stare from his boss.

The first glimpse of the gleaming Banitierre mansion brought blessed silence throughout the car. The house sparkled like a jewel on the hill.

Danielle pinched Kettly and let out a low whistle. "Will you look at this place? The dump we live in should be condemned."

"Let me remind you of the rules for tonight's festivities." Cole snapped his fingers. "You may eat and drink as much as you desire. Food, wine, blood; knock yourselves out. If you choose to sample any of their 'collection,' just remember—they're an appetizer, not a full meal." The next statement he directed to Nicholas. "They are for feeding only—this is not a brothel. In short, act like you've been here before."

The leader of the Victoire coven met his escorts at the top of the split staircase. With one girl on each arm, Cole crossed the veranda and waited to be formally invited over the threshold.

Elegantly attired beings mingled throughout the polished home. He peeked at the two girls next to him, noting their nervous glances in the mirror and how they traced their necklines, jewelry and hair without thinking. *Good—they need to be knocked down a few pegs.*

Cole couldn't resist taking a dig at Kettly. "Good thing you went with the black velvet gown. That green thing made you look like a hideous sea monster."

Kettly wriggled her arm out of his elbow and looked for Nicholas.

"You can thank me later." Cole ordered wine and checked his watch. "Bring on the main event."

The stark contrasts of Sorcha's bizarre world had played out in fleeting moments on the balcony. *Repulsive and vile, displayed at my request.* Her species could brutally destroy human life, wiping blood from one hand with family linen while sipping wine from priceless crystal with the other. *Exhilarating too.* Sorcha wanted to rub her face and slash fingers through her hair. *Stop—Steven will lose his mind.*

Inside, Rayna and Penny were dressed and waiting with Sorcha's gown. She stepped into it as instructed. They zipped, fussed and primped before she turned to see her reflection and the finished ensemble for the first time.

"The color and cut are perfect." Penny fluffed the hem.

The dress featured a modest neckline in the front, while the back plunged to Sorcha's waistline. To show off the full effect, her hair was swept up and fastened with diamond pins. If the slip showed when she danced, it would be a glittering peek of silver lace over matching dancing shoes.

"I love it. I love everything—except my locket doesn't go with formal wear." A knock on the door startled Sorcha from reflection.

"Delivery for Miss Sorcha Alden."

Sorcha accepted a black velvet box.

Rayna read the card out loud. "It's a gift from House Banitierre, welcoming you to the family."

Sorcha flipped open the box to reveal a spiral of flawless diamonds.

"That is absolutely formal enough." Rayna adjusted the necklace to sit snugly around Sorcha's throat, following the curve of the dress. Three strands of jewels hung down her back like liquid ice.

"It's exquisite!"

"They're calling for you downstairs," Steven hissed through the cracked door. "We need to go—now."

"Wait, your earrings." Rayna caught Sorcha on the top step of the landing. "Walk slowly, take it all in. This is a big night for you."

Sorcha gulped a breath and peered through the chandelier at the half-moon of painted glass over the stairs. *That window reminds me of a portal to another world.* Eyes of friends and strangers seared her skin as she descended the graceful staircase. Her fingers trembled on the railing until she spotted Raimond's beaming face. Waiting on the bottom step, he extended his hand to escort her, his guest of honor.

The dais was set against a backdrop of open windows over the candle-lit garden. Prince Norman stood motionless as a warm breeze ruffled the sacred family ledger. He handed Sorcha a pen, and she signed her given name in thick ink, on a brand-new page.

That's the black blood from the vision at Mum's funeral. Sorcha willed her expression to remain frozen.

"We will now conduct the ceremony of the spring equinox. When the clock strikes twenty minutes past nine, Sorcha Alden will be free to declare her allegiance to the coven of her choice."

Sorcha peeked around the room. *The vibe isn't entirely friendly.*

Checking his pocket watch against the grandfather clock, the prince nodded. "If anyone has an objection, speak now or forever hold your peace."

The silence was thunderous.

"Very well. The sacrament of the blood."

Without hesitation Raimond bit his wrist and offered it to Sorcha.

She faltered for a moment, before lifting her lips to his skin. *Powerful—sweet—the blood of a master.* Sorcha swallowed and her eyes melted into Raimond's riveting gaze.

Prince Norman sighed and produced a jeweled dagger. He blessed it and effortlessly sliced Sorcha's palm, squeezing her hand and letting blood drip freely onto the signature. The seal of The Crown Prince of North America finalized her allegiance to the Banitierres. Applause erupted in the packed room.

Raimond clasped both her hands in his. "Congratulations, Lady Sorcha. You have arrived." He punctuated the declaration with a subtle bow.

The stranger's hands. Sorcha dabbed her eye where a tear should have fallen. *More visions coming true.*

"A pleasure to meet you. Thank you." Introductions, handshakes and kisses blurred Sorcha's next hour. "So lovely that you could attend." *Just a few more.* She gasped and snatched her hand back, freezing as she came face to face with a bald man. *The creep from the club.*

"Miss Alden, or shall I call you Ms. Banitierre?" Cole brushed

Sorcha's arm with his palm.

Raimond jumped in, snapping his fingers for security. "Victoire, I suggest you step away."

"No harm done, Duke. I was just being polite." Cole dragged his dates forward. "I'd like to introduce Danielle and Kettly, along with my right hand man, Nicholas Victoire."

The women grunted and curled their lips into sneers. Nicholas bowed.

"Well, terrific." Steven steered Sorcha away. "Someone brought whores to a black tie affair."

"I feel their contempt." Sorcha's hand rattled as she accepted a glass of wine.

"The entire guest list was approved and identities confirmed at the door. They don't pose any threat. Drink." Steven directed the glass to her lips. "More."

Butterflies fluttered in Sorcha's stomach when she heard the band start.

"Chin up, dear, shoulders back—you're the envy of every woman in this house." Marie nudged Steven away and steadied Sorcha as she wobbled. "Remember the energy I gave you back at the penthouse? Take a little more now—go ahead."

"Thank you." *Close your eyes, focus and pull back.* Steady strength coursed through Sorcha's veins by the time Marie walked away. She waited her turn as family members were formally introduced in pairs, disappearing to distant applause.

The bandleader's voice boomed from the stage. "For the very first time—the newest member of the Royal House Banitierre, escorted by Duke Raimond Banitierre of Normandie. Ladies and gentleman, Monsters and Angels, please welcome Lady Sorcha Alden!"

When the doors swung open, hundreds of candles adorned the walls like burning gemstones. Raimond grasped her hand and raised it to eye level. Stretching out at full arm's length he presented her in the center of the dazzling ballroom. They turned in a circle, acknowledging the guests around the dance floor and many more ringing the upstairs gallery.

"May I have the honor of your first dance, Lady Sorcha?"

"Yes Duke, but the honor is all mine."

"And the music?"

"The waltz, please."

"The waltz it is." Raimond turned toward the orchestra director. "*S'il vous plaît.*" The band struck up a familiar tune, and Sorcha danced with her patron in front of the dizzying crowd.

Sorcha touched her cheek to Raimond's and whispered in his ear. "Feels like a fairytale."

Raimond slipped his hand further around her waist and breathed in the scent of her hair. "Then I've done my job."

Sorcha let her eyelids flicker and close, her lungs melting with his almond scent.

Family couples joined in slowly, until the entire inner circle was present on the dance floor by the end of the number.

Sorcha kept track of Rayna as she danced and disappeared behind curtains with menacing strangers. *I know we have security, but if one of those freaks hurts her...*

With the party winding down and dawn approaching, the maestro announced the final song. By special request, it was to be a tango.

Oh no.

Draven stalked across the floor, each footstep echoing like a gunshot through the silent crowd. "Ready, Princess?"

With the first notes, Draven led Sorcha to the center of the gleaming floor. She positioned herself as Rayna instructed, leaning into his body and laying her hand sensually on his shoulder. As a pair, they walked backwards and paused to begin the complicated steps.

Sorcha dissolved in Draven's leaden stare. His lips brushed dangerously close to hers more than once before the music ended and the crowd drifted to the edges of the chamber.

A deafening crash of shattered glass broke the trance and a knife of energy sliced between the dancers. Sorcha snapped her eyes around at the empty ballroom. Her feet seemed to have a mind of their own, propelling her toward the main house. Any candles still burning blew out when she passed, as if the air were being sucked out of the room. The second she crossed the threshold, hands reached out, ripping her out of the doorway like a rag doll.

Raimond leapt from the gallery, landing effortlessly with wineglasses still in his hand. "I had a few more to break—just in case."

"Always so dramatic, Duke Raimond. It was merely a dance." Draven's tone revealed no emotion.

"Bullshit—only a dance, like the innocent picnic you went on two nights ago. You know I've claimed Sorcha. I specifically did so, to you." Raimond pointed his finger at the prince. "Your Royal Highness, are you planning to steal her from me?"

"Not tonight. But I'm serving fair notice. If you screw this up in any way, and I mean any way, I'll be there to pick up the pieces. And I promise you, I will not fail."

The prince spat blinding anger like a spray of daggers. He raised his voice so anyone interested could hear. "Spectacular party as usual, Duke." He exited the ballroom and swept the veranda clean of any lingering guests with the force of his rage.

Chapter 33

SUGAR RUSH

SORCHA STIRRED AROUND midday, lying on top of the bedspread, still in her silver slip. Embers from the night before smoldered in the fireplace. Her dress draped across a chair, but she had no recollection of taking it off or getting back to her room. *Being the center of attention is exhausting.* Shadowy memories danced on the fringe of her consciousness. *Something strange happened at the end of last night.* She concentrated on whispers coming from the hall.

"Does that pompous ass think he can take whatever he wants?" Steven asked. "This is our house."

"Keep your voice down," Julia said. "You're speaking of a crown prince."

"That was incredibly..." Rayna started to sob. "She could have been caught in between those two. I'm surprised the house is still standing."

"Does she not see it? She must know about Raimond at least?" Lily asked.

"She doesn't see anything. I think she's in another world, or at least her heart is somewhere else." Julia's voice faded into the distance. "I told you this would happen."

See what? Sorcha's eyes struggled to focus on the figure covering her with a quilt. "Rayna?"

"Yes, honey, shhh—go back to sleep."

"Please stay, my head is splitting." Sorcha clutched at the darkness, finding Rayna's hand and pulling her toward the bed.

"Only if you promise to rest." Rayna climbed in, tucking the blanket around them.

"Will you tell me what happened?"

"Later. You need to sleep now—all that can wait."

Later.

Sorcha didn't open her eyes again until well after dark. Dinner had been delivered to her room and Rayna was gone. She drank and ate every drop and morsel on the tray. Still weak and queasy, she grabbed whatever clothes she found and wobbled into the hall.

Raimond's bedroom—I think it's this one. She prepared to knock and lost her balance. The unlatched door creaked open as she stumbled, revealing an enormous white bed in the center of the chamber. *That carved headboard must weigh a million pounds.*

"Sorcha?" Raimond guided her to a leather sofa. "You look ill. Did you eat?"

"Is Marie still here? Think I need her."

"How did I not see this?" Raimond rang his room service bell relentlessly until valets converged at the door. "Is Miss Marie still on the estate?

"Yes, sir."

"Fetch her—tell her it's urgent."

Marie bustled in a few long minutes later, brushed her hand over Sorcha's cheek and shot an alarmed glance at Raimond. "I worried there would be trouble. Isn't it forbidden for one vampire to steal energy from another?"

"Not for a prince, apparently. He left her almost empty." Raimond paced the room. "Can you help her?"

"Of course." She held Sorcha's chin in her hands. "Try to wake up and focus, dear."

It required all the strength Sorcha had left to pull on Marie's essence.

"I may not be enough, Raimond." Marie slumped back in her chair. "Who else do you have here?"

"A house full of hung over vampires and an entourage who are completely tapped out."

"I have a human chauffeur. He's an exemplary person."

Raimond didn't bother with the bell this time, choosing to yell down the hall for his servants instead.

The chauffeur was a complex man, a war hero, unassuming at a glance but tough as nails on the inside. Sorcha took what she could from him. She found it difficult to absorb energy from a donor with such a different background from her own. "I need to lie down or..."

Raimond dismissed Marie and her employee, lifted Sorcha effortlessly and laid her down on the edge of his bed. "Now you need to drink from me." He nicked his wrist and waved it in front of Sorcha's lips.

Sorcha's eyes fused to a well-placed mirror and admired the transformation of her own face.

"Your blood is almost black." She licked his wrist, savoring the first drops.

"That's because there's no oxygen in it."

Sorcha lunged at Raimond's flesh. *Tastes like candy.*

Raimond caressed Sorcha's neck and shoulders, burying his face in her hair and fighting unbearable temptation. She was in his bed, drinking his blood like an animal, entranced by her own reflection. Her withered soul bloomed with every swallow. She seemed to enjoy his touch—at least she didn't pull away from him. A good first step, but the matter of teaching her to fight threw a wrench into things. He wouldn't be effective as an instructor if they were romantically involved. He lay back in a cloud of blankets and pillows and cradled the Banitierre family's newest Lady as they stared at the ceiling, basking in her just-fed glow.

We'll find out soon enough if your heart is ready to find true love.

Chapter 34

BAR CRAWL

VIR RECOVERED FROM the harrowing voyage and immersed himself in his new job. The hospital wards were crowded and busy, but his favorite shifts were spent in the chaos of the Emergency Ward.

"Dr. Ashayle, always a pleasure to work with you." Dr. Colton and his residents took turns shaking Vir's hand after a hectic night.

"Full moon strikes again." Vir rubbed his lower back before collapsing into the break room sofa.

"And you handled it brilliantly." Sister Ann collected dirty lab coats for the laundry. "The patients are very fond of you."

"A lot of bad things happen in this city. The violence still catches me off guard."

"New Orleans may look like a playground, Dr. Ashayle, but don't let the pretty lights fool you. It's a war zone out there."

"Come on now, Sister. You'll scare the man." Dr. Colton poured the nun a cup of tea and shooed her out the door. "Vir, don't change your mind about our bar crawl. It's a shame you haven't experienced a minute of nightlife yet."

"Don't worry, I'm ready." The only times he'd ventured out of the hospital compound were to visit a nearby diner or stare at the river from atop the levee.

After the first outing with fellow doctors, that all changed. Vir spent every night he wasn't working lost in the French Quarter, drinking in sketchy bars and clubs that vanished in the light of day. He always found his way to the safety of a private, upstairs lounge owned by one of his first patients. Early morning wandering in the streets could be dicey, but the after-hours club had security along with great views of the river and railways. He often envisioned Sorcha strolling and browsing the shops, falling under the spell of the city. Thursday night wasn't particularly memorable until a small group of partygoers swept by him as if he were invisible. They crowded around a corner table, ordered drinks and chatted among themselves.

Vir tuned in to the jumble of voices.

"That mansion was incredible!"

"The new girl, though—total snob. I wanted to slap her face."

"Did you see her dress? To die for!"

"Banitierre was arrogant, as usual."

Banitierre? Vir concentrated on his drink while he eavesdropped.

"Did you see that tango—serious tension."

"The prince looked tasty. I wouldn't throw him out of bed."

Vir fumbled in his jacket pocket, sneaking a glance behind him. Most of the conversation took place between two women wearing extra makeup. *Don't stare.*

"You'll never have to worry about a prince in your bed, either of you," a male voice said. "Didn't you see what happened to the fools lurking in the bushes? Norman can erase you with a sideways glance. Royals have a separate playing field and their own set of rules."

Regular bar patrons kept their heads down as the party rose and paid, obsessed with how many minutes it would take to get home.

They mentioned Banitierre. It isn't a common name—is it? The senior doctor hadn't been seen since he left to search for Sorcha on that terrible night in Nepal, though he still held the title of medical director. His name was printed on every official hospital document. Vir's attention was snapped back by a female voice.

"Did you see that little morsel at the bar? Too bad it's so late. I could use another drink."

"For the love of…" the man growled. "Can we go now before we all burn to death?"

169

Chapter 35

ALLIGATOR HUNT

SORCHA'S SELF-DEFENSE lessons began the night after Prince Norman and his entourage left the estate. The atmosphere at Normandie Hall had been icy since the Gala. She still didn't have a clear picture of what happened at the end of that night.

"You're slacking!"

What Sorcha lacked in training she disguised with sheer strength. Raimond taught her the tactics, but one of his bodyguards acted as her sparring partner. He believed Sorcha wouldn't be able to use her full power against him, thus it needed to be a stranger. She wasn't even allowed to know the man's name.

"Faster!" He snapped his fingers. "Anticipate every move."

"Raimond, I'm way stronger than this fella."

"Trust me, you won't always have that advantage, and choking vampires just wastes time. Fighting has one goal—death."

As much as Sorcha enjoyed driving a blade through the poor vampire's heart, the steel only produced a fleeting wound. Though it was equally useless, she would have preferred every sequence ended with her holding the opponent in the air and squeezing his neck until he fell unconscious.

Raimond's favorite skill to teach involved catching bolts fired from a crossbow in mid-flight.

Seems showy and useless. How many people keep a crossbow and gold-plated weapons in their home arsenal?

Since the conclusion of the festivities, the estate's residents came and went on personal trips. Steven and Lily made excursions into New Orleans, returning every few days to keep Raimond up-to-date on the sloppy, high-profile killings in the Quarter. Sorcha spent evenings in the parlor listening to opera and jazz recordings. Closer to dawn she would sneak downstairs for an hour or two with Rayna. Her human friend supplied her with food, energy, wisdom and the occasional dance break to their favorite steel drum melodies.

Sorcha's self-defense education ended when she passed a surprise exam with flying colors, sensing danger seconds before a cloaked attacker struck. Crouching down, she let the stranger leap, grabbing an arm as he lunged for her throat. Her sapphire eyes blazed as she twisted a shoulder in its socket, shredding muscle and ligaments in one effortless move.

The attacker hit the ground, shrieking in pain. "You win."

"Raimond?" Sorcha stopped her hand short of ripping into his chest. *Cinnamon and vanilla.* "I'm so—"

"Don't even think of apologizing. You did what was necessary; exactly as I taught you." Raimond rotated his shoulder and collapsed into a writhing heap.

"For heaven's sake." Sorcha knelt on the ground and supported Raimond's arm. "Hold still, I hear bones cracking. It's awful."

Rugged physical training triggered Sorcha's craving for violence. *What I wouldn't give for one of the prince's hunt, chase and tackle games right now.* She kept her thoughts as well insulated as possible. Raimond wouldn't appreciate her dreaming of nighttime activities with Draven. Several times during their evenings alone, she tried to broach the topic of the mysterious events that occurred after the tango ended. Even though Raimond was a gifted deflector, rearranging books, stoking the fire, or straightening framed art on the wall, the men's friendship had definitely hit a rough patch.

As Sorcha dressed for another humdrum dinner, she was surprised by a knock on the door. Expecting Penny or Rayna, she almost didn't recognize Raimond wearing work clothes and a sly smile.

"Want to hunt?"

Sorcha looked down at her dress.

"These should fit." He handed over brown cotton pants and shirt. "It may be a muddy business, but I think you'll have fun. Take that locket off too—it'll get lost for sure."

Sorcha changed, pulled her hair back and followed Raimond down the stairs. She thought the cellar ended with the floor where Rayna and the other blood donors lived, but a hidden door led down many more flights.

I can hear the Mississippi. Feel it too. Sorcha touched rivulets of water that ran down the walls of the crude tunnels. "How is this mud not caving in?"

"You'll see. The original passages are in the back, but this is our secret entrance. I need to show you how to get in and out in an emergency." Raimond waved Sorcha along behind him. "There's a password—we change it every few months, especially after a big party when so many have crossed the threshold. Can't have every vampire in the South traipsing in and out of the house."

"What is it?" Sorcha approached an ancient iron gate. Half submerged in river water, its ornate bars twisted like tree roots where they anchored to the walls. *Can't believe that thing has moved in years.*

"The gate doesn't move. You pass through it."

Careful, he reads me like an open book.

"You need the password to get in or out. Don't speak it—ever. Write it on this chalkboard. Either the witch behind the walls accepts it and allows you to pass, or she doesn't."

"There's a witch behind the walls?" *Something else I don't know about.*

"Who do you think holds the walls up?"

173

"If the password is never spoken, how do I—"

Gypsy. Raimond planted the word into Sorcha's mind. "Actually she's more of a dragon than a lady. Go ahead, write it." He handed over a piece of chalk.

Each letter disappeared as Sorcha wrote the next.

"You may pass."

Pleasant voice for a dragon. Sorcha stumbled ahead, knee deep in water as the gate dissolved around her. Behind her the metal returned to its solid form, with her companion still on the other side.

"One at a time. Security measures." Raimond wrote on the chalkboard and nodded to the invisible gatekeeper. "Thank you, ma'am."

"So, what are we hunting?" Sorcha shuffled into the night. The entrance to the tunnel was well hidden, closer to the river than the house.

"Alligators. Their blood is a delicacy. Fresh is the only way to enjoy it."

"Really?"

"Yes, really. They're always here, lurking in the mud, waiting for some foolish animal or human to play on the riverbank. Do you see him?" Raimond pointed to two glowing orbs hovering above the murky water. "Splash around, but let me handle his first assault. Wait until I get him upside down and then go for his heart." He spun Sorcha around and looked in her eyes. "Are you up for this?"

"I am." Sorcha pulled her shoulders back and returned his gaze with confidence.

"Remember—you need to bite hard. Their skin is much tougher than a human's and even thicker than a vampire's."

Sorcha followed Raimond's instructions at the swamp's edge, toying with danger she couldn't see. The speed and strength of the predator caught her off-guard. She jumped back just in time to avoid snapping jaws.

Raimond leapt from behind, standing the alligator straight up before twisting and wrestling him into the black water. Sorcha watched two monsters roll as one, an imperceptible mass of mud, limbs and teeth. Heat rose behind her skin as killer instinct flooded her heart. She crouched close to the edge of the swamp, looking for a chance to join the fight. *Come on, give me a split second.* Sorcha glimpsed the lighter coloring of the beast's underbelly and lunged with all the power caged behind her burning blue eyes.

Alligator scales were like steel skin. Sorcha locked her jaws into the softest flesh and gulped. *Smoky and spicy.* Blood loss weakened the beast enough for her to flip him onto his back in the river mud. Raimond swooped in, draining the alligator's remaining life and ending the fight. Both vampires fell back, exhausted, exhilarated and satiated, staring up into the moonless night.

When Sorcha realized that she was plastered head to toe in foul swamp mud, she searched for Raimond, finding him only by the glow of his eyes. *He's covered in the same muck.*

Meeting her gaze, he started to laugh.

This is a first. Free and reckless Raimond. His version of "revel in it" was just as spectacular as Draven's and all without spilling a drop of human blood. *More spectacular.* Sorcha and Raimond rolled in the mud alongside the carcass of a prehistoric beast, both laughing until their sides were splitting.

"You know we can't go back to the house like this, right?" Sorcha held her mud-covered shirt away from her chest, letting it snap back with a sloppy splash.

"I thought ahead. There are dry clothes in that bag, but we need to rinse off first." He grabbed her hand and flashed toward the river. Without looking back, Raimond stripped off his shirt and pants, throwing them in a crumpled heap. Two steps later he dove into the bend of the river. "I won't look, promise."

Raimond faced the opposite bank and Sorcha peeled off everything except her underwear and followed his lead. *Never thought I would swim in this water.* When she surfaced, he was waiting, eyes gleaming.

"Let me get the mud out of your hair." He gently worked the dirt out of her long locks with his fingers while she tried to rinse her face clean. "Having fun yet?"

"That was an incredible rush! Do you hunt them often?"

"It's more fun, not to mention safer, with company. That beast was over twenty feet long." He finished with Sorcha's hair, and she swam around to start on his.

Sorcha never realized how sensual it was to run fingers through someone else's hair. *This mud is more like glue.* Lost in concentration, she didn't notice her neck sagging.

"Tired?"

"My legs just got heavy—don't let me float away."

"Never." Raimond slipped his arm around Sorcha's waist and swam to shore with powerful strokes. As the water got shallower he walked out of the river, cradling her with one arm.

Sorcha dropped her feet to the ground, never letting go of his neck or breaking eye contact as Raimond touched his lips to hers. *So soft compared to the force of the fangs I just witnessed. Extraordinary.*

Their lips lingered for a few seconds, and like a whisper, it was over.

"Get dressed, it's late." Raimond tossed dry clothes from his bag.

What just happened? Sorcha pulled the shirt over her head first, letting the extra fabric cover her hips until she slipped on pants. *We were almost naked. Did he stop?* She let tangled hair conceal her eyes. *Or did I? And why?*

They returned to the house in silence, shutting the front door as the first rays of sunshine broke the horizon.

"Sleep now." He steered the spent girl up the stairs before he clicked the parlor doors closed behind him.

Not ready for the night to end, Raimond shut the curtains to seal out the morning light. Over a strong drink, he examined his reflection in the mirror. Peering back at him were the eyes of a slightly muddy, but happier man. *That went fairly well—she wasn't revolted at least.*

Chapter 36

HIGHLIGHTS

THE ACTIVITIES OF the previous night left Sorcha pleasantly exhausted and unconscious until after sunset. *So surreal—possessing the skill and power to match an ancient animal.* Her fingers wandered across her lips, recalling Raimond's sensual kiss. *A different side of his soul. Hidden and seductive.* Shuffling outside the bedroom door roused her from daydreaming. *Must be Raimond.* Sorcha jumped up and grabbed a robe, checking her hair in the mirror. She flung the door open to find Steven and Lily giggling.

"Wake up, it's late!" The pair burst in the room, tossing bags everywhere.

Sorcha peeked both directions down the empty hall. *This place—whenever you expect one thing, you get another.*

"What's the matter, aren't you glad to see us?"

"Of course I am." Sorcha gave Steven a hug while Lily rang for the maid.

"Honey, you need some coffee." Lily pecked her friend on the cheek. "What's going on at this stuffy old mansion to make you so tired?"

If she only knew.

"She's probably dying of boredom." Steven unzipped the garment bag and whipped out a shimmery black dress.

"For me?" Sorcha asked. "Awfully slinky."

"Specifically for you. Wait until you see the shoes and stockings that go with it." He rubbed his thumb over his chin. "There's a special plan for your hair."

Sorcha reached back and gripped a handful. "Not cutting it."

"Don't worry." Lily reassured her. "It always grows back to the length it was when you were turned. Faster when you wash it."

"Or get caught in the rain." Steven frowned. "Dreadfully inconvenient."

"How about this?" Lily shook out her own hair, revealing deep red streaks mixed in with her natural jet black.

"Ooo, pretty!"

"Lasts about a week."

"Why all this fuss? Is there another party?"

"Only the preeminent, sold-out show of the season. Remember that new band I told you about?" Steven produced a stuffed envelope from his jacket pocket. "Tickets!"

"We should invite Rayna," Lily suggested.

"I have plenty for everyone, but we need to leave tomorrow night."

"Has anyone told Raimond?" Sorcha looked back and forth between her friends.

"He'll be fine with it." Steven's response hinted that he hadn't considered that wrinkle. "Get dressed. Dinner will be on the table soon."

Sorcha locked herself in the bathroom, using running water as a cover for her racing thoughts. *Raimond is not going to be thrilled about the timing of this trip—and wait until he hears about them messing with my hair.*

Dinner was quiet. Raimond was happy to see Steven and Lily, but his quizzical look told Sorcha that he knew something was up. The sound of clinking glasses and silverware echoed in the room.

"Okay, enough suspense. What aren't you telling me?" He tossed his napkin down and leaned forward, staring briefly at each family member before settling on Steven. "Spill it."

"I have tickets to a concert in New Orleans on Thursday night. If you'll allow it."

"Where?"

"Warehouse Club." Steven exhaled.

Raimond reclined in his chair. "Only if you stay at the penthouse and take my guards. Too much ugliness in the city this summer for you to go alone."

"Come with us, Raimond. I think you'd like this show."

"I'll ride in with you, but I have business to attend to at the hospital."

"We're also dyeing Sorcha's hair blue."

"Blue?" Sorcha nearly coughed wine out her nose. *I thought it would be red, like Lily's.* She shot Raimond a helpless stare.

"It'll be fabulous. The hairdresser is here." Steven yanked Sorcha to her feet. "Don't worry, silly girl, just highlights. Totally subtle."

"Take it downstairs," Raimond shouted down the hall. "No blue dye on my furniture."

The following evening two limousines arrived in New Orleans, their trunks so stuffed with luggage they almost didn't close. The penthouse descended into silence as the merciless summer sun rose above the horizon.

Sorcha's eyes blinked open and she snapped her gaze to a brass clock. *Half two.* Past the dial, she saw someone fussing around the windows. "Fire?"

"What?" Raimond whirled around. "No."

"I saw it." Sorcha sat up. "But it's not real."

"You went to bed early. Another headache?"

"Not tonight. Don't get them as often." Sorcha flopped on her back and smirked. "Since you stopped tapping my energy."

"You knew?"

Sorcha's lips twitched up. "I guessed."

"My apologies. I was in such a bad place, weak and mired in a rut, until you knocked a resident on the floor and changed everything." Raimond drove his hands in his pockets and stared at the ceiling. "Tried to stop the dreams back then...still can't."

"My visions and nightmares aren't your fault." Sorcha rolled onto her side and let waves of hair cascade over her face. "Why are you really here?"

"Just double-checking the drapes." He glanced back at the windows and slumped his shoulders. "Did that sound absurd?"

Sorcha smothered her face in the pillow to keep from laughing out loud.

Raimond flashed across the room. "Shhh!" He pressed a finger to his lips. "May I?" He pointed to the bed.

Sorcha slid over and he wasted no time gathering her in his arms. His kiss was deeper than the first at the river.

"We can't do too much of this here." He leaned back on his elbow. "Thin walls."

"The way you brushed my arm and nudged me during the car ride almost gave us away."

"If I'm pushing too fast, you'll tell me?"

"I will, and you are not." Sorcha shifted closer and inhaled. "You smell like...Christmas."

"That's an odd compliment." Raimond kissed her on the forehead.

"Reminds me of home and happiness."

"After this concert, you and I are going back to the plantation. We need time alone." Raimond ran his hand through her hair, twirling the blue strands in his fingers. "Very tasteful."

"Much as blue hair can be."

Raimond seized the tangles behind her head and coaxed her lips to his. "My wild Lady."

Sorcha drifted asleep in Raimond's arms. When she woke, the only sign that he had been there was a dent in the pillow next to her. Making sure the sun had set, she threw open the heavy drapes, lifted the window and welcomed the river breeze thick with the scent of New Orleans' summer. *I wish it were tomorrow night already.*

Her human life was dead and gone. Moving on with Raimond felt right.

Not just right. Thrilling.

Chapter 37

THE WAREHOUSE CLUB

EVER SINCE THE night of the Gala, Sorcha left the fashion decisions to Steven. For this occasion, her outfit was far more risqué. Beaded embroidery accented the short, jet black dress. It was the backdrop for sky-high heels and stockings with seams running up the back of her legs. The center of attention was her freshly highlighted hair. The best hairdresser in the city spent an hour twisting, pinning and teasing until a lion's mane of vivid blue and rich brown cascaded down her back.

The Banitierre coven strutted past a line of ticketholders that snaked around the block. Steven knocked on the middle of an old wooden wall until a door swung open and they were waved into pulsating darkness.

So many heartbeats.

Flashing his platinum card at two men guarding a velvet rope, Steven led his family past screaming fans and through a set of double doors opened by unseen hands. Inside, their personal bartender stood with his arms folded amidst pyramids of bottles. He had their favorite cocktails already mixed, poured and lined up on the bar. Each Banitierre grabbed their specialty as they walked by, nodding and waving in appreciation.

Sorcha found herself last in line. Before lifting her Garnet Martini, she leaned over the bar and kissed the bartender on both cheeks.

"Good to see you, Jeffrey."

"Hello, beautiful! That was some entrance."

"I want you to meet my best friend, Rayna."

"Pleased to meet you, Rayna." Jeffrey's eyes ran over her black skirt and red vest before he raised her hand to his lips.

Sorcha's heart twinged with jealousy.

The crowd parted as the Banitierres danced their way to a prime spot in front of the stage.

Sorcha breathed in the chaotic scene, a heady mix of incense and expensive fragrance. The big room was as beautiful as she remembered. Bars along every wall glowed with backlit, exotic liquors. The spooky, twisted swamp trees that supported the balcony were strung with twinkling red lights. Carved gargoyles held back velvet stage drapes.

The opening band whipped the crowd into a frenzy while Sorcha danced and mingled, reconnecting with guests she had met at the Gala. *Rayna is beaming.* She rarely got out of the basement, never mind out of the mansion. Tonight, she was part of the family. *Her smile is brilliant. Happy and alive.* Unless someone knew that her luminescence was courtesy of vampire blood, she could pass as an exceptionally beautiful human.

The drums of the headline act rang loud and sharp as spotlights swirled around the stage, finally landing on the lead singer. His long hair flowed over a black, leather coat that hung to his knees. The piano was a flashy centerpiece—dramatic and just the right level of loud, invading every corner like fog.

Sorcha had never heard this music, but it captivated her from the first song. *A blend of blues and opera. Equal parts love and anger.* One particular lyric jumped out and grabbed her. The crowd drifted slowly away as the singer zeroed in, leaving her alone and the center of attention. His words painted a picture of sea and sky whipped into a frenzy, plucking something deep inside Sorcha—as if they poured from the soul of a tortured, lonely vampire. *There is no way this human penned these words alone, odd as he is.* Without thinking, she started to dance in the middle of the room. The man on the stage drew her forward with his eyes, imploring her hips to sway to the crescendo.

Dark eyes, burning eyes,

Glowing beacons in the sky,

Roll the dice,

Take a chance with your life…

Vir. Sorcha hadn't thought of him in weeks. Missing him used to tear her heart apart. *But he's my past.*

Trapped like a girl in a cage,

Dead silent, you yearn to rage,

Hiding in your sleep,

Trapped in dreams, buried so deep…

The music penetrated every inch of Sorcha's body. *I must be a spectacle, but right now I just don't care.*

Your destiny, your forever,

Plans ripped, connections severed,

Pray for release with all your might,

But eternity is a long, bitter fight…

Sorcha glided to the stage, reaching her fingers out to touch the messenger. She drank in the hypnotic power of confidence with her eyes, making it her own. A prickling sensation on her back pulled her attention to the private balcony.

Raimond.

He put his palms together, bowed and planted words in her wide-open mind. *Stellar performance. Be careful. I'll see you later.* In a flash, he was gone.

The music played late into the night—a continuous blur of drinking and dancing.

"Are you all right, honey?" Rayna maneuvered Sorcha's drink out of her hand.

"Grand, why?"

"I'm afraid someone spiked these martinis. You're so…uninhibited."

Steven jostled through the rowdy crowd. "Uninhibited? You mean she's dancing like this is a burlesque club."

"Folks, pardon the interruption." A security guard pointed at Sorcha. "Mr. Barwick is requesting your presence backstage."

"I'd love to meet him, but my friend needs to come with me." She grabbed Rayna's hand and pulled her close.

Steven shook his head.

"What if we took one of the guards?" Rayna asked. "It'll only be a little while, and then we'll meet at that upstairs club—the one with the green door."

"Fine." Steven threw his hands in the air. "But shake a leg."

Sorcha and Rayna waved and disappeared into wispy stage smoke.

We probably shouldn't tell Raimond we did this.

Raimond composed himself on the short walk from Decatur Street to the Sisters of the Peace. His sole intention tonight had been to spy on the crowd, scouting for anyone who might recognize Sorcha. Instead, he was treated to a show that eclipsed the paid entertainment. *I'll never admit this to Steven, but the blue highlights in Sorcha's hair are dazzling.* He couldn't wait to whisk her back to Normandie Hall.

Arriving at the door of the hospital, he switched on the distinguished charm of Dr. Banitierre, just in time. The Sisters and nurses on duty greeted him with energetic smiles.

"I understand there are cases waiting for my consult?" Raimond worked his way down the halls. He visited each room, speaking with patients, scrawling on charts and sending nurses scurrying to follow his orders. At even the slimmest break in the action, his mind wandered. Tomorrow, Sorcha would be his alone. He imagined her silky skin against his body, the taste of red wine on her lips, the groans of pleasure he would coax from her throat.

"Wait." Raimond froze and held a finger to his ear.

"Doctor." A shaky voice barely broke through the commotion. "I need assistance."

The odor burned in Raimond's throat before he turned to find a woman standing in the hall. Her uniform was splattered with red. Blood dripped from her gloves.

"That Alexa girl," the nurse said, "ripped all the sutures out of her leg again."

"Clean yourself up, dear." Raimond strode past the trembling nurse and grabbed an orderly. He followed a blood trail to find a patient trying to break the window in her room. "Where are you going, young lady?"

"Getting the hell out of here." Alexa kicked the orderly and made a dash for the door.

Raimond stopped her with one hand and dumped her back in bed. He barked orders over his shoulder. "Get me a sedative, silk sutures and a surgical mask."

The nurses scattered to find medication and sterile supplies. The orderly stepped behind Raimond and tied a mask around his head before circling the bed to help hold the patient still.

Even though Raimond's face was partially hidden, the orderly flinched back when he saw the doctor's glowing eyes and darkened skin.

Got to get my head on straight. Raimond took a syringe from a nurse's hand and injected the combative girl. *I haven't had a slip-up this serious since medical school.*

Raimond sutured Alexa's jagged wound and planted a suitable story in the orderly's mind. "We're finished here. Keep her restrained until further notice."

The hospital staff answered in unison. "Yes, sir."

"Doctor, thank God you were here." The head nurse pointed in the direction of his office. "Some paperwork on your desk desperately needs your signature."

"I'll check on it tonight or tomorrow, Sister, I promise." He spent the next few hours finishing rounds in the crowded wards.

Surely the paperwork can wait. He paused at the mountain of files on his desk. *Should I look at this mess?* His body overrode his brain again. He slipped out the back door into the city for a quick bite before sunrise.

Chapter 38

MARTIN BARWICK

SECURITY ESCORTED THE guests of honor past a vast entourage and deep into private rooms under the Warehouse Club. All eyes, along with many dropped jaws, followed both girls on their way to visit Mr. Barwick.

Rayna's fingers dug into her friend's arm. "Do you feel like a piece of meat?"

"Stay close, there are some real crumbs down here." Sorcha avoided eye contact and although she took note of everyone, one man in particular made her cringe. Dark olive skin, braided hair longer than hers and eyes so black they looked like craters in his skull. The energy was mostly human, mixed with the spiritual presence found everywhere in New Orleans. *Except that guy is vampire all the way.*

Sable curtains were pulled back to reveal a dressing room brimming with flowers and candles. Soft denim pants and an unbuttoned, linen shirt made the singer appear smaller but no less compelling.

Heartbeat.

Rising to greet his guests, he shook Rayna's hand first and then turned his undisguised adoration to Sorcha. "Good evening, ladies, I'm Martin Barwick."

"I'm Sorcha and my friend is Rayna. We're honored to meet you, Mr. Barwick, and we very much enjoyed your show."

"Call me Martin, and please, make yourselves comfortable." He splashed champagne in elegant flutes and raised a toast. "To the city that never disappoints." His eyes took a quick tour of Sorcha's ensemble, starting at the stilettos, traveling up her legs to the shimmery dress and landing on the crowning glory of her hair. "Sorcha, please don't take offense. Whether you're an angel or a witch, you cast an exquisite spell over the club tonight."

"A witch is close enough to the truth, for now." Sorcha signaled Rayna to close the curtains for privacy. *Let all the gawkers fantasize.* Running her hands over her curves to grab his undivided attention, Sorcha locked onto the singer's eyes, invading his consciousness and replacing his thoughts with her own. *You aren't afraid Martin—this is what you want—what you crave. There is no pain, only pleasure. Sit back, close your eyes and release your mind.*

Sorcha waited for Martin to sink into the abyss of an alternate world before she brushed his hair away and pushed his head to the side. She made eye contact with Rayna for final approval and released her inner monster. She knew the dark bloodlines would bloom first in her eyelids, tracing an intricate map down her neck and then explode across the full expanse of her skin. Rayna's smile told her when her eyes snapped from their natural hazel to a vicious, burning blue.

Savor every drop.

Martin's body gradually went limp and sank lower in the sofa.

Sorcha made quick work of covering her tracks before she offered Rayna her sliced wrist. Her friend's eyes lit up as she tasted Martin's blood, safely buffered by vampire chemistry.

"Are we ready to go, Rayna?" Sorcha froze when she saw tears trickling down her cheeks. "Oh no, what's wrong?"

"The entire club was fixated on you tonight. You're intoxicating when you dance and when you feed. I can't look away." Rayna dried her eyes with her sleeve. "You choose to spend so much time with me; I feel like I won the lottery."

"Whisht, don't cry." Sorcha gathered Rayna in her arms. "I'm the lucky one. You save me every day. Your humanity, love and kindness are keeping me sane."

Rayna's laughter replaced her sobs.

Sorcha pulled back to look in her friend's eyes and followed an urge she had denied before, gently kissing her on the lips.

"He's watching us?" Rayna nodded to Martin.

"I'll fix it." Sorcha delved into the singer's mind, planting a juicy story of a menage-a-trois and erasing any memory of bloody activities. "Let's go."

"If there are photographers or groupies in the alley, keep your head down." Rayna grabbed her hand. "Do not stop."

Two men bickered outside the stage door.

"I can handle heat—I didn't expect swamp air."

"You'll get used to it, mate. Give it a few more days."

Chapal and Lock ducked behind a dumpster as two women burst through the door and scampered off into summer darkness.

"Let's finish her now."

"How stupid are you, Chapal? Father said to capture her and Ashayle. I only saw the Alden girl. You know, your flesh and blood?"

"Go ahead, say it. My latest blundering mistake. How did he even find out this harlot existed?"

"Spies," Lock said. "That ship captain sung like a canary about a hidden passenger with blazing blue eyes.

"You're the favorite son and everything's my fault. So, I plan to erase it—her." Chapal unraveled the braid from his hair. "Father said capture, but kill if necessary."

"If we follow her, chances are we'll find our brother."

"He is not—stop saying that!" Chapal hissed. "Are we even sure he's here?"

"I've just arrived, same as you, and we've been together every bloody minute."

"Ashayle is not our brother." Chapal smashed a dumpster into the crumbling brick wall. "He's a weak, pitiful excuse for a human and a damn foreigner. I'd like to end the whole business once and for all."

"I'm a foreigner," Lock said.

"Do not remind me."

Chapter 39

BROKEN BONES

THE BANITIERRE WOMEN headed straight for the green door club.

Sorcha deflected a jolt of vampire electricity at the door and pulled her friend behind her.

"I'm not that fragile," Rayna whispered.

"But you're mortal. There's Steven, on the balcony."

"Thank the Lord you're okay." Steven stalked across the bar and dragged them back to his table. "Now, I demand details."

Sorcha described the backstage escapade, exchanging a wink with Rayna as she left out their kiss. She wasn't sure what to think about that herself.

Julia nodded to a table in the corner. "Look at those Victoire bitches. Danielle is the one in red and the other one's name starts with K. I don't recall, or care."

Ooo, Julia's claws. Sorcha only had a partial view. "I remember them from the Gala. Nice to my face, but I saw right through their garbage. What did I ever do to them?"

"Nothing. You're royalty." Steven sneered. "They're street trash."

"How about one more drink before we call it a night?" Lily glanced at her watch and craned her neck around. "Where's that waiter?"

"I'll find him." Sorcha rummaged through her purse on the way to the bar. *All heartbeats over here and a familiar voice or a scent—can't place it.*

Probably someone I've eaten. She ignored the feeling until stabbing pain in her stomach stopped her in her tracks.

Not possible. Her eyes fixed on the back of one head and her ears heard only one heartbeat. *Can't be.* Sorcha's legs turned to jelly. An ache crept up her spine while her mind played lightning tag with her senses. *The scent is so strong, I can taste him.*

Just one look. Sorcha approached the man as he stared straight ahead, nursing his whisky like a professional drunk. *What are you doing? Run!* Her hands ignored the searing agony inside her stomach and tapped the stranger's shoulder.

He turned and collapsed when he saw her, striking his head on the bar.

"Vir!" Sorcha propelled herself between him and the floor. A small rivulet of blood trickled from the gash on his head.

Sorcha heard muffled screams and sensed a hostile presence hurtling toward her. *Vampire.* Rakshasa rage rumbled in her chest. She found herself, fangs bared, face to face with Danielle Victoire. "Don't even think about it."

Julia and Lily pushed nosey patrons out of the way while Steven forced himself in between Sorcha and her rival. "Back off, floozy."

Even with Nicholas and the Victoire guards holding her back, Danielle reached for Vir's neck.

Bad move. The skills Raimond taught Sorcha kicked in like second nature. She twisted her new enemy's wrist back until bones splintered.

Banitierre security broke up the fight, while Sorcha held onto Vir with an unwavering grip. Seconds in real time felt like hours.

"Vir, you're okay. I promise." Sorcha rocked his unconscious body.

"Your arm will heal in ten minutes." Steven knocked Danielle backward. "Your makeup, on the other hand, that's a tragedy. Get lost."

"Damn Banitierres." Nicholas swept Danielle against his chest and cradled her arm. "All bullies."

"We need to get out of here." Lily shielded Rayna with her body.

"Not leaving without him." Sorcha didn't budge. *What if he doesn't wake up?*

"Fine." Julia hooked her arm under Vir's shoulder. "Sorcha, take the other side."

A few blocks upriver, they stopped at a crumbling concrete bench. Sorcha laid Vir's still body down and caressed his cheeks. "Please, open your eyes."

"Who is this?" Steven walked in circles. "Do we know him?"

Sorcha looked around, unsure if telling the truth was the smartest move. Her eyes finally landed on Rayna, whose face told it all. *She knows. Every intimate detail.*

"Sorcha?" Vir lifted his shaky fingers to her face. "What happened? Are you a ghost?"

"Don't be scared. You had too much to drink. Where are you staying?"

"Sisters of the Peace, across some streets. I have a place."

"Okay, let's go. It's late." Sorcha rubbed her forehead. *How long has he been here and how the hell did I not know?*

"We can't stroll this tourist home," Steven said. "Not enough time before dawn."

"We'll make it." Sorcha hauled Vir to his feet.

"I'll go with her." Rayna slid her arm under Vir's shoulder. "Can you spare one guard, Steven?"

Steven frowned. "This officially makes my skin crawl."

Sorcha concentrated her full attention on finding Vir's apartment and surviving the last, deadly hour before dawn.

"We'll make sure no Victoires follow you." Julia shoved Steven and Lily away from the river.

In a run-down, Garden District house, dust flew in every direction as the front door slammed open.

Danielle screamed up the stairs. "She broke my arm, Cole!"

"Who?" Cole spun his chair around as family members piled

through his office door.

"That Banitierre bitch—she snapped it in half!" Danielle offered her right arm as evidence. A current of bedlam simmered in the crowd tailing her.

"Everybody, calm down." Cole rose behind his desk. "Which bitch are you referring to?"

"That blue-eyed one. I haven't fully healed, in case you're interested."

"I see." Cole had heard very little from the Banitierres since the Gala. But last night, the energy around Sorcha was volatile. "Why, Danielle? What did you do?"

"Nothing."

"She just randomly attacked you?"

"Some guy fell off his bar stool and hit his head. I smelled blood." Danielle shrugged. "Dinner fell on my plate."

"Was he one of theirs?"

"Never seen him before. He was drinking alone. Anyone here know him?" She scanned the crowded room but every stare was an empty one. "I'll get that little snob."

"Sounds like she claimed him." Cole voice was low and even. "Don't break the code or start a war we can't win."

"Is this another speech about patience?" Danielle heaved a crystal lamp at him. "Why do we always run from them? I want to fight back!"

"Enough!" Cole caught the lamp and shattered it against his desk. "Don't touch any Banitierres or their humans. That's a direct order. We can't match forces with them in an open battle—not yet. Danielle, take your friends and get the hell out of my office before I break your other arm." He pivoted to the dark fireplace as the room cleared. "I need to think."

"I don't get it, boss." Nicholas flicked shards of glass off the sofa. "You've been waiting months for another crack in Banitierre's armor."

"Find out who the human is. It's unlikely all this fuss took place over a nobody." Cole strutted to the staircase and leaned over the railing. "Danielle? We haven't destroyed any bedroom furniture recently."

"Must you be so crass?" Nicholas balled his fingers into fists. "She just got beat up."

"I'll make her forget her stupid arm and give the house something else to gossip about."

Danielle stomped back up the stairs. "I'll pay that girl back if it's the last thing I ever do."

"Kettly is all yours." Cole left Nicholas standing in the office. "After you clean up this wreck—again."

Chapter 40

LAFAYETTE SQUARE

SORCHA AND RAYNA half walked and half dragged Vir across Canal Street.

Sorcha waited for a moment when Vir's eyes blinked. "Where's your apartment, honey?"

"Ummm, St. Charles, I think…by that square? Second floor of a red brick thing. Can't miss it."

"Sounds like Lafayette Square." Rayna batted his fumbling hand away from her face.

Vir was right. The ugly red house stood out on the street like a sore thumb. The trio tumbled into the apartment moments before dawn. Smoke wafted off Sorcha's skin with the scent of burned meat.

"Get in here!" Rayna covered the bedroom window with a blanket. "You'll be safe until sunset."

Sorcha held her nose and flew into the darkness. "That was too close."

"No kidding. What are we going to do about him?" Rayna pointed at Vir, passed out face down. "You better not tell him anything."

"He thinks I'm a ghost." Sorcha sunk onto the bed, shifting Vir into a more comfortable position. The cut on his head had finally stopped bleeding, but the smell still made her gums throb.

Sorcha watched Vir sleep, fighting a tidal wave of emotions. "I've missed him, but I had no idea how much."

"After all you've been through, burying your human feelings was a necessary defense mechanism." Rayna wiped the blood from Vir's face.

"My soul almost exploded when I saw him. Isn't he handsome?"

Rayna sank onto the floor.

"Your hair..." Vir's eyes fluttered open. His hand reached for Sorcha's face and stopped short.

"Welcome back. The blue hair was for a party."

"Angel party?"

"Something like that." Sorcha tumbled into his endless brown eyes. "How long have you been in New Orleans?"

"Two months, maybe. I came back with the Sisters of the Peace. The voyage was a nightmare. Does Zelia know about you?"

"No, and you can't tell her anything either, not a word. If anyone finds out I'm here..."

Rayna shook her head violently and pressed her finger to her lips.

"Vir, you have to promise not to tell anyone, okay?"

"Promise."

Sorcha recalled their first kiss in the hospital courtyard. She brushed her lips across Vir's mouth.

"You shouldn't." Rayna wrung her hands.

Vir gripped Sorcha's neck to steady himself and they spun out of the dingy New Orleans apartment, across time and thousands of miles to the moonlit room in Nepal where they became one—to their last precious kiss.

"After I left your room that night, everything irreversibly changed."

"Don't ever leave me again," Vir said.

"Never."

"Sorcha." Rayna staggered to her feet. "We should find Raimond."

"You find him."

"What do you mean she didn't come home?" Raimond slammed the bedroom door open. His voice echoed like thunder through the apartment while Julia, Lily and Steven cowered in the hallway. "Where the hell is she?"

"Someone she knew passed out and cracked his head on the bar. Sorcha caught him before he hit the floor." Steven and Lily talked over each other. "She insisted on taking him home. She's much stronger than any of us."

"Raimond, she broke one of the Victoire girl's arms." Julia made sure he heard her, loud and clear.

"Why? Why would she ever do that?"

"Sorcha's friend was bleeding, and that Danielle girl went after him. Sorcha snapped her arm in half," Julia said. "I assume you taught her to do that?"

"What did this guy look like?" Raimond grabbed a shirt and directed the group to the kitchen, far away from the windows and the blinding morning sun.

Steven offered the best description. "Tall, striking, black hair, bronze skin. He could have been from the Far East, maybe?"

"His name started with a V," Lily said.

Raimond froze and the kitchen sank into silence.

"What is it?" Julia struggled to get his attention. "Do you know him?"

Finally Raimond moved, rubbing his fingers on the stubble around the corners of his mouth. "Goddamn it, how did I miss that?" He stared past everyone in the room, shaking his head and pacing faster by the second. "I need to go to the hospital. I think I can find her, if I can get to my office."

"Now? You can't..." Julia reached for his arm but changed her mind. "The sun, Raimond, there's no way."

"I'll take the tunnels. Jules, grab my travel bag."

"He cursed in front of us," Lily whispered in Steven's ear. "That's not good."

Three wrong turns later, Raimond tumbled out of a hatch and onto the basement floor of the hospital. After a few buckets of water and a change of clothes, he snuck up the back stairs and into his office undetected. On his desk the pile of files loomed. Reluctantly he flicked papers aside, knowing in his heart what he was going to find. *And there it is—the name I thought I left halfway around the world.*

Vir Ashayle, M.D.

If I cleaned this up like I should have, all this trouble might have been avoided. Idiot. I failed Sorcha as a woman and as her family, just like Draven predicted.

Raimond sat in the dark office, mentally beating himself to pieces. The address on the file read St. Charles Avenue. No tunnels could maneuver him close enough to that building in the middle of the day. *Stay put, Sorcha, until I get there.*

Faint rattling broke the stillness.

Thunder? If the storm was severe enough to block the sun, he might be able to make a run for Lafayette Square. Grabbing a pair of black gloves from his desk, Raimond gingerly nudged the blinds covering the window. *Oh yes!* Storm clouds blackened the sky in every direction. He stopped at his desk and triggered a hidden compartment. *Do I really need a weapon for two girls and a twit? Can't hurt.* After grabbing a long coat and a hat, with antique diamond-tipped dagger in hand, he climbed out the window and onto the hospital roof.

Lightning zinged around him as raindrops fell like bombs—just a warning of the deluge to come. Raimond made most of the trip jumping from roof to roof among the tall buildings. No human eye moved fast enough to register his form, especially in the pouring rain. After a few blocks he dropped to street level, running at full speed toward the address from Ashayle's file. He leapt over the iron fence, ripped off the front door and dove into the relative safety of the grimy hallway. Despite the clouds and rain, tendrils of smoke wafted off his skin.

I'm alive. Where's my family?

Chapter 41

EMILY

THE APARTMENT STAYED dark and still for most of the day while Sorcha lay next to Vir. Her eyes were closed, but she remained fully awake, lost in her thoughts and the sound of rain drumming on the roof and windows.

A zing of energy made her scramble up. "That's not lightning. Rayna, wake up—someone just came in the front door."

Rayna jumped to her feet, wielding the butcher knife she'd been clutching for hours. "The downstairs neighbor?"

"No way." Sorcha's skin darkened into the face of a demon. "It's a vampire. A strong one."

Both girls listened to slow footsteps echo on the stairs.

"Wait behind the door and plunge that knife deep. It's not gold, but it'll slow this prowler down long enough for me to end him."

The stranger ripped the door off its hinges and took two steps into the kitchen before Rayna charged. Using her movement as a cue, Sorcha leapt at the figure.

"Raimond!" Rayna screamed as the weapon was ripped from her hands.

Sorcha changed course in mid-air, smashing against the kitchen wall and sending plaster dust spraying everywhere. "We almost killed you."

"Unlikely." Raimond crumbled the steel knife into dust. "Nice to see you both safe."

Rayna slid to the floor, sobbing. "I didn't know what to do."

"You did everything right. Take this." Raimond unsheathed the dagger and held it out for Rayna.

"I don't want to touch that thing." Rayna tumbled over a chair. She saw the glare in Raimond's eyes and slid her sleeve over her hand before accepting the old blade.

"Go straight home." Raimond shoved Rayna out the ruined door and turned to Sorcha. "Where is he?"

Sorcha nudged the bedroom door open and pointed at Vir, still soundly asleep despite the commotion in his kitchen. "You know?"

"Pieced it together. Have you told him anything?"

"No, he thinks I'm some angel or spirit. I let him believe it for now."

"For now?" Raimond stepped in front of Sorcha. "Try forever. He can't know that you're anything but dead."

"There must be another way. I can't leave him again." Sorcha's gaze drifted. "I promised."

"You need to erase this entire night from his memory." Raimond watched Sorcha's face go blank. "Or I can do it. Come home with me now, please." He reached out to take her hand.

"No."

It wasn't her answer, but the way she flinched away from his touch that hit Raimond like a gunshot to the stomach. "I know what you're thinking, and it won't work. I never talked to you about this because I didn't think it would be necessary."

Because I thought she would be with me. Get yourself together. Be a Duke, not some lovesick fool.

"So that's an absolute—that it won't work?" Sorcha said. "We have a house full of humans and they seem fine with us."

"Because they're property. Food. They signed a contract in blood promising loyalty to my coven. I know you're close with Rayna, but is that the existence you want for Vir?"

"Aren't there any other options?"

"Aside from the obvious one?"

"You mean…" Sorcha nodded. "Yes, aside from that curse."

She feels cursed? "This is dangerous, very possibly fatal—and not just for us, for him too. I don't expect you to understand. You're very young."

"I'm a grown woman of twenty-two."

"I'm well over a hundred. Draven is seven hundred, and there are others far older. Don't forget that our time frame is eternity."

Sorcha stared at her feet.

"Our lifestyle is not typical for vampires. We live in a permissive community, and I love this city, but secrecy is still the key to our survival. There are humans, religious zealots, who would hunt us with torches and gold if they knew what we were." Raimond sagged against the wall. "You kids go to dance clubs and drink from fine crystal. I crawled through filthy streets like a cockroach for the first years of my life, just trying to feed enough to survive. Humans can promise to keep our secret, but even if they give it their best effort, it's next to impossible."

Vir sat up and searched the room for the source of voices.

Sorcha pushed him down in his bed. "Sleep." She covered him with a light blanket and slumped on the floor.

"It's almost sunset, we won't be cramped in here much longer." Raimond settled next to her on the worn hardwood. "Many years ago, when I was young and arrogant, I fell in love with a human woman. Thought I could keep her safe. We played at being careful, but it wasn't enough. Someone must have seen something, or thought they did. Proof isn't necessary when crusaders perceive evil. Funny thing about holy people is, their hate is stronger than their love. One night when I was out, they came to our home and burned it, with my fiancée inside. By the time I returned there was nothing left but ash."

"Raimond, I had no idea."

"They were chasing me, but they murdered a beautiful, gentle young woman. I held myself ultimately responsible and I still do. The guilt of living without her for eternity—I wouldn't wish it on anyone. I had nobody to teach me anything when I was young, but it's my responsibility to prevent you from repeating my mistakes. Think about it." Raimond pointed to Vir. "He works in a convent with nuns and priests who think you're dead. What if he gets killed by people hunting for you? Can you live with that forever?"

Sorcha dropped her face into her hands.

"Plant the idea that you were just a dream and take some time to think things through. This is where eternity works in your favor."

"For now." Sorcha agreed. "Vir, can you wake up for me? You need to listen closely and follow my instructions down to the last detail."

His mind presented a blank slate, easy to control. Sorcha erased any memories aside from a drunken night in the Quarter. She fought back sobs as he repeated the story back to her, word for word.

Satisfied that the situation was neutralized, Raimond led the way back to the penthouse in silence.

Sorcha stumbled along next to him. "What was her name?"

Raimond rarely allowed himself to think of his fiancée; he hadn't spoken of her for decades. Today he reopened that grisly wound in his heart in an attempt save another woman, one he almost made love with twenty-four hours ago. After tonight's events, that was very unlikely to ever happen. *You waited so long—obsessed with being careful, yet you made a mountain of mistakes.*

"Emily. The clock in Normandie's foyer was to be her wedding gift."

"Was she the first nurse?" Sorcha asked.

"*Non, mais…*" Raimond's shoulders sagged. "The first was Aveline, who gave her life for that clock. Said it held a blessing for the future. I'm still waiting."

"I'm so sorry."

"For?"

"Putting all of us in danger and letting Vir see me. For hurting you."

Raimond glanced at Sorcha, still dressed in her party clothes from the night before, blue hair tumbling in unruly waves around her face.

"I know it wasn't intentional."

The real problem was not that Vir had seen her—it was that she had seen him.

The Duke summoned his bodyguards and put orders in place to protect Vir. The human guard was to shadow him during the day and crumble a pinch of silver sage into his tea each morning and evening. His vampire counterpart would cover the night shift and make sure he drank it.

"Both of you," Raimond pointed to his men, "be extra vigilant."

As proud as he was that Sorcha had taken her defense training seriously, he knew that her public attack on a Victoire family member wouldn't go unnoticed. Emotion equaled weakness in the vampire community. At least the sage ensured that Vir wouldn't be eaten.

Raimond dismissed the soldiers with a wave of his hand. "I'll make sure that fool changes the location of his late-night drinking escapades."

Chapter 42

SPY

SORCHA SHIVERED AND swung her legs out of bed. In the fog before her mind cleared, she was still carefree and immortal, on the verge of a romance with a handsome duke. Her heart plummeted as the previous day's events flooded back. Throwing open the drapes, she stared across the river. *It's dark, but you can't run back to Vir. Raimond forbid it.*

"Are you awake?" Rayna crept into the room, looking every bit as petite as her voice sounded. "We're all so worried. Don't you want to go out with the others?"

"Not hungry." Even Sorcha's best smile didn't fool her closest friend.

"Then we'll stay here and talk. At least it'll be quiet."

Sorcha directed her eyes back to the dark horizon. "Where's Raimond?"

"He went to the hospital hours ago. Sit down, let me fix this." Rayna began untangling Sorcha's hair. "I know you're hurt."

"I feel hollow."

"I don't have a solution, but I'm here." Rayna buried her face deep in Sorcha's hair.

"None of what happened changes anything between us, I mean it. Nothing."

Rayna's arms gripped Sorcha tighter as her lips brushed the skin at the back of her neck. "Drink please. Do it for me. Being weak makes everything that much worse."

Sorcha was hungrier than she realized. As cautious as she was, Rayna fell sound asleep soon after she finished drinking. *A hidden blessing. She wants to help, but what is there to say?* Her attention floated through the open window, in the direction of Vir's apartment. If the view weren't obstructed by buildings, she could have seen the peeling paint of his red house.

Wait a minute. Raimond was adamant that Vir didn't see me, but he never said I couldn't see him. She slid out from under Rayna's sleeping body and tiptoed out the French doors, assessing how many roofs she would have to navigate to get in position. *I'll figure it out on the way.*

Sorcha had never tried rooftop hopping but she knew it was possible. *Don't be a klutz.* She gave herself extra room for a running start and jumped as far as she could, tumbling head over heels on the flat surface and sliding to a stop against an old chimney. *Easy jump but the landing needs work.*

Sorcha paused to stare at the main hospital's glowing windows. Marion's rose-colored, glass lamp shone out like a beacon. *My favorite patient. I can't help her anymore.*

Now that she knew the distance was attainable, finding the right vantage point to spy on Vir was easy. Sorcha wasn't worried about anyone seeing her. The moon was hidden behind clouds, and most of the buildings were lower than the one she was sitting on. She didn't have to wait long for him to turn on a light and slump onto his narrow bed.

Hello, lover.

Sorcha watched Vir pick up a textbook and fling it aside after a few minutes. She almost looked away as he peeled off his shirt and stood motionless in front of the crooked bureau mirror. *What's wrong with me? It's nothing I haven't already seen. Besides, why waste that jaw-dropping view?*

Sorcha dove behind a chimney as his attention flickered to the open window. He switched off the light and stared into the black night. She guessed he couldn't see very far, but just in case, she stayed crouched behind the bricks.

Hope no one is spying on me.

On his way home, Raimond detoured to the apartment on St. Charles Avenue. His approach to the gate was stopped short. Slinking back into the shadows, he climbed one of the taller buildings. *The bodyguard is in position.* He shifted his focus to the upstairs window. *Well, there's Ashayle staring blankly into the distance.* A familiar sizzle of electricity hummed from another rooftop. *Damn it, Sorcha couldn't stay away, not even for one night.* Raimond kept a respectful distance. Right now, that lousy excuse for an apartment was one of the safest places in the city. *What did you expect anyway? You've been in love once or twice—you would do the same.* If only it ended so innocently, but the odds of avoiding this train wreck were as impossible as holding the blazing sun beneath the horizon.

The elaborate dance continued for a week. Sorcha watched Vir, Raimond watched Sorcha, and Rayna waited at the penthouse to pick up the pieces. The universe was stuck in a cycle of damage, healing and never-ending heartbreak until Raimond made a decision.

"Where is she?" Sorcha flew into the parlor, minutes after dawn.

"I sent Rayna back to the plantation," Raimond answered. "Wasn't safe for her here. You should go back too."

Sorcha slammed the bedroom door, screamed and pounded her fists into the walls. "How could you!"

Raimond bolted to her room. "Shhh—stop, before the police show up." She thrashed and howled like she was fighting for her life. Raimond wrestled her to the floor, smothering the sound of her voice

208

with his hand as she attacked every exposed inch of his skin with her fangs. He never really believed Sorcha would leave without a fight, but this was more than he had bargained for. *I can't even be angry. She's too young to handle all this heartache.*

"I'm sorry, but you're going to kill me or yourself." Raimond bit his lip and slammed her head into the floor. Inspecting his bloody clothes, he had a hard time determining which of his wounds was worst. Chunks of flesh were missing all over his chest and arms.

After laying Sorcha's unconscious body on the bed, he rooted through his medicine cabinet for a sedative: a distant relative of wormwood, minus the poison. Hopefully it would be effective long enough for her mind and body to reset.

Time for the back-up plan. Unless I'm willing to do the unthinkable, and I'm not, a safe alternative is better than…whatever just happened.

"Oh, my head." Sorcha squeezed her eyes shut to lessen the throbbing pain.

"Sorry." Raimond appeared at her side. "I hoped the sedation would last longer."

"What happened—how are you still—" Sorcha touched an open gash in Raimond's flesh and watched blood pour through her fingers.

"You almost ripped all my skin off, but I'll live. Your headache is courtesy of me, again."

"No, I couldn't have. Why?" *Did I actually do that to him?* The memory of her attack on him returned with a wave of visceral shame.

"Wait, before you get upset again, listen to what I have to say. I know this has been a nightmare for you. I've had guards on Vir day and night, after your little incident with the Victoire girl."

"You know I broke her arm?"

"Off the record, I'm impressed." Raimond slumped against the bedpost. "I've also been dosing Vir with silver sage, so nobody has him for dinner."

"I never thought of that. I know you don't really like him."

"But you do." Raimond attempted a smile. "So that means his safety is important. The precautions have worked well so far, but I can't keep him home or at the hospital forever. He'll need a secure destination for his party habit and the green door club is not that place anymore."

"Is anywhere safe?"

"Remember the dinner I had on the night before our voyage?"

"The upstairs room with the Mardi Gras mural." *Good memories from a different lifetime.*

"That restaurant, Karen's, is owned by Marie's family. There's a bar hidden in the back of the building. It has tight security and an exclusive guest list. Vir will be protected there, as will you—if you choose to spend time with him."

A few moments passed before Sorcha understood the full meaning of his statement. "So, I can meet Vir? Let him see me?"

"Keep up with the angel story. You've convinced him so far."

"I would hug you, but you're still bleeding. How is that even possible?"

"I tell you that you're strong and you don't take me seriously." Raimond winced. "You should."

Sorcha picked up his limp hand and held it to her cheek. "What can I do?"

"I need to drink, maybe."

"From me?"

"No, I'm sure there's still sage in your veins." Raimond struggled to rise. "Might do more harm than good."

"Rest." Sorcha caught him as his legs tangled. "I'll take care of you, for a change."

"Sorcha?" The voice was raspy and barely recognizable.

"Yes, Raimond?"

"Be careful—please."

By the time Sorcha returned, Raimond had slipped deep enough into a coma that she sliced the first human's wrist herself and held it over his mouth. "Come on, drink."

When the older vampire stirred, his hunger returned with a vengeance. Sorcha barely had enough time to pull him off the first victim before it was too late, quickly replacing him with a second course. Halfway through the blood volume of the third man, Raimond began to regain some semblance of control. When he closed his eyes again, he fell into an easy sleep. The hovering specter of death vanished.

"You scared me." Sorcha brushed the hair from his eyes. *I need to stop taking him for granted. Not only did I break his heart, but tonight I almost killed him. And why? Because he tried to save me. He's been saving me since the moment I died.*

And I'm still in love with another man.

Chapter 43

KAREN'S

VIR'S WORK KEPT him busy enough that he hadn't considered a night out, until now. Sauntering down cobblestone streets, an unfamiliar building drew him in like a magnet.

Karen's. It doesn't ring any bells, but the last lucid memory I have is ordering a whisky in the green door club. Ceiling fans hummed, turning the candle-lit restaurant into a pleasant reprieve from the oppressive summer humidity. Delicious smells from the kitchen met him as he passed through a room of crowded tables.

"Dr. Ashayle, welcome. They're expecting you in the back." The waiter nodded in the direction of an arched doorway concealed by shadows and ushered him into a lavishly furnished lounge. The air inside buzzed with the low murmur of conversation. The lights were bright enough to see that the club was well attended yet dim enough to hide the members' faces unless one was part of their inner circle. Instead of being intimidated, he felt oddly at ease, even as a party of one.

The bartender greeted Vir as he approached the bar. "What will it be tonight, Dr. Ashayle? Blockers delivered two crates of absinthe today. It's perfection. First drink is on the house, made the old fashioned way."

"I'd love one." *This place might be part of my blackout tour, and I'm starting the night with absinthe. I remember promising someone I'd go easy on the booze, but just one couldn't hurt.*

Sorcha obsessed over her outfit and hair for the special occasion. She pulled her waves into a loose knot and decided on the darkest purple dress. Butterflies fluttered in her stomach when the maître d' waved her past tourists and locals crowded around the entrance to Karen's. The atmosphere of the private lounge was quiet, but the aura of power was unmistakable. Her eyes adjusted to the dim lights, zeroing in on the handsome man sitting alone at the bar.

Vir. Sorcha arrived at his side just as he looked down into his drink. One second he was a solitary reflection in a large mirror over the liquor bottles and the next time he looked up, she was there.

"My angel." His perfect face exploded in a grin. He grabbed her neck and guided her lips to his.

Does he remember? Every moment Sorcha kissed him, their time spent apart faded more into the distance. "I've been keeping an eye on you." Traces of absinthe on his lips made her feel lightheaded.

"I need more than your eyes, Sorcha."

"You have my eyes, my body and all of my heart."

Vir crushed Sorcha against the bar as his lips urgently parted hers, his tongue swirling and caressing until she allowed him to kiss her as passionately as he wished—as deeply as physically possible.

To hell with the audience. This man is mine.

"For an angel, you're so real and alive in my arms."

"And your kisses sweep me away like I'm in the movies. I think we're making a scene." Sorcha slipped back onto her own bar stool.

"I don't care."

Sorcha held up her right hand at eye level, palm facing him. "Go ahead, like a mirror."

Vir lightly placed his palm against hers, gasping at the contact. "You zapped me." He concentrated on Sorcha's tiny hand next to his.

"Kind of tickled."

I must be crazy. Sorcha marveled at the gentle pressure of each soft fingertip on hers. *This is as intimate as the kiss.*

"Tell me what you've been doing since you came to town." Sorcha listened to him talk about the voyage and the storm, all the hours he had been working and his favorite local restaurants. *He's taken to the city, just like me.*

"They don't make tea here like they do back home. Tastes funny."

Sorcha covered a giggle with the back of her hand. "Switch to coffee."

Never breaking contact with Sorcha's skin, Vir ordered another drink. "Now, what have you been up to all week?"

"Just this week?"

"Well, since the last time I saw you."

"You remember?"

"Yes, it's funny. That night is a complete blank, except now I vividly remember you tapping my shoulder at the club, catching me as I fell, walking me home and staying with me until I fell asleep. There was a lot of other jumble—people talking or fighting, but your face is crystal clear. You were wearing a black dress and high heels." Vir reached around and gently freed her hair, letting it fall in long waves. "No more blue?"

"It was temporary." Sorcha rested her face in the smooth skin of his palm. "You liked it?"

"It was wild." Vir nodded. "So, while I was working, what did you do with all that free time?"

"I was taking care of people."

"Of course, you're a nurse. Were you watching my window?"

"How did you know?" Sorcha watched his lips move with the words.

"Not sure. I just sensed that I was secure."

"You're safe here." She didn't mention the bodyguards. "But not the place by the river. Don't go there anymore."

"This is much nicer anyway. Absinthe is better too." He drained his glass and signaled to the bartender for another.

"I've tried it a few times. Ick." *Wormwood.* Sorcha stuck out her tongue. "Be careful with that stuff—it makes people do crazy things like fall off bar stools."

"It's one of my favorites, but I enjoy a good port just as much. Would you like another glass of wine or maybe that martini with the raspberry?"

"Yes, I'll have the Garnet Martini special!"

The hours slipped away in simple conversation. The bartender made a fuss over polishing crystal, approaching when Vir excused himself to the restroom. "Miss Alden, I have instructions to remind you of the time."

"Are you closing?" Some of the patrons had left, but the club was far from empty.

"The sun will be up in less than two hours."

"Oh!" *Sunrise. I lost track.* Sorcha sighed as Vir's arms wound around her.

"That's a stunning couple in the mirror."

They definitely were quite a pair—his dark features and jet black hair next to her pale complexion. She watched as he trailed kisses down her neck. Thankfully he wasn't paying attention to her eyes and the beginnings of blue fire under her natural hazel. *Keep it under control.* Sorcha made a point of feeding well earlier in the evening. *That flash of blue was a different hunger.*

"It's getting late. I need to get home."

"No." Vir kept his hand firmly entwined in her hair.

"It's almost five in the morning."

"Come home with me."

"I can't—not tonight. What's your schedule?" *I'd leave with him, but Raimond would have a breakdown.*

"Don't care." Vir lightly kissed her cheek.

"You do care. Don't be wacky." Sorcha pulled away gently.

Vir sighed, considering the upcoming week. "I'm actually off today, so I can see you again tonight." A genuine grin regained control of his face.

A pure smile—untouched by darkness.

"So how about ten o'clock—right here?" Sorcha forced herself to stand and break his embrace.

"Perfect."

"Vir, you still can't tell anyone that you've seen me, or we'll never be able to meet again. It's a matter of life and death." Sorcha locked onto his eyes and drove the words deep into his brain. "Do you understand?"

"Yes, nobody can know that I saw you. But I don't have to forget?"

"Better not." Taking a last sip of the martini, Sorcha kissed his mouth and headed for the door. She emerged onto the dark street and nodded to the guards. "Follow him back to his apartment—stay close." Even in the rush to get home, she detoured for a few minutes to stare at Sisters of the Peace. *I could make it in that fifth floor window, just to prove I'm still a nurse.*

Raimond was waiting in the silent, dark parlor when Sorcha got home. "Everything go well?"

His faint smile was meant to be effortless, but he didn't move a muscle or bother to blink his eyes. A full-blown fit of jealousy would have been more subtle.

"Yes, grand. Nice place."

"There was a delivery for you. I left it in your room."

"Thanks. Good night." Sorcha couldn't get down the hall fast enough. She leaned on her door and clicked it shut behind her. *You seriously hurt him. There's no real way to fix it, either.* She flipped open the pink card on her special delivery.

From your garden.
Miss you.
Love, Rayna

The bouquet combined all her favorite flowers from Normandie Hall. *So sweet. I wish she were here so I could tell somebody about tonight.* In truth, if she came home giddy from a date with Vir, Rayna would listen to all of it and be happy, but it would hurt her.

She doesn't deserve it any more than Raimond does.

Chapter 44

NEXT IN LINE

THE FOLLOWING EVENING, Raimond didn't leave the privacy of his room until he was positive the apartment was empty. He had no desire to ruin Sorcha's date, and he would have to fake any pleasant interaction with her.

I'm hunting Uptown, nowhere near the stuffy old Quarter. He whisked a razor over his stubble and stopped short, the full bottle of after-shave still in his hand. He placed it on the marble counter, held his nose, and knocked it in the trash. *Enough smelling like someone's damn Christmas tree.*

Raimond was tackled the second he opened the front door. Caught completely off guard, he struggled to defend himself. *I'm so sick of everything and everyone—why bother fighting anymore?*

"Did you think I wouldn't find out, Duke?"

"Norman? Get off me, you pompous ass." Raimond's survival instinct kicked back in with a vengeance and just enough strength to throw his assailant into a china cabinet. "What the hell is wrong with you?"

"Where is Sorcha, you moron? My spies tell me that she's been seen in public—kissing a human? I thought you had things under control. You screwed up, did you not?"

"You have no idea what you're talking about, as usual. She met the human in Nepal before she was turned."

"How did he wind up here?" The prince picked himself up,

brushing slivers of glass off his clothing.

"He arrived with my medical team a few months ago. I knew nothing about it."

"Aren't you the director at that pathetic excuse for a hospital? I respected your claim to her, but I made it very clear that I was the next in line."

"I was distracted and didn't read my files. That part is my fault, but even if I'd taken her, or you'd taken her…" Raimond smoothed his hair back with both hands. "She would've dumped us. They were already lovers."

"Lov—are you serious?" Prince Norman threw everything in arm's reach. "You knew about this?"

"She told me during our voyage across the Pacific that she thought the attack was punishment for giving her virginity to that man. I should have ripped his throat out when I had the chance."

"So, why the hell didn't you?"

"He never did anything wrong. I was waiting for an excuse and looking for one, believe me."

"There." Draven crossed his arms. "That is your weakness. You needed some honorable reason; you couldn't just end him. Now he's here, putting us all in danger and taking what's ours."

"Don't you think I know that?" Raimond kicked fragments of wood across the floor. "Just so we're clear, you're paying for all this damage."

"I don't give a rat's ass about your furniture. Why not just kill him now?"

"Why do you think? She'd never forgive either of us."

"She'll get over it."

"You haven't seen her with Vir. Killing him would be an eternal mistake."

"I'll be the judge of that. Your chance may have passed, but I'm not giving her up to some human loser." Prince Norman straightened his tie and flashed to the door. "I'm taking what's mine. Scandal be damned."

Hidden in the shadows of a club where he'd been a member for decades, Draven spied on Sorcha and Vir for hours. Between the chitchat and kissing, they spent most of the evening with hands touching, palm to palm. The simple contact was publicly acceptable, yet deeply sexual at the same time. Whether he liked it or not, too many had seen Sorcha and her human, lost in each other's eyes, mingling souls through their skin. They were clearly an exclusive pair. None of his family or staff could pass off the human's demise as a random accident. His enemies definitely wouldn't.

Danielle Victoire dragged her friends across a dark rooftop.

"Another exhilarating night of stalking." Kettly crossed her arms and pouted.

"Lay off. This is important." Danielle peeked over the roof's edge at the front door of Karen's. "Nicholas, did you take care of that dancer and her big mouth?"

"She made things difficult, but it's permanently shut. No more investigating Sorcha's death or talking to the police," Nicholas answered. "Left her corpse in a dumpster."

"Did anyone check the bar by the river?"

"I've been there every night," Kettly said. "Not one exciting thing has happened since your fight."

"That's because everyone is here." Danielle counted security guards and rolled her eyes. "Banitierre soldiers and Royal Guard."

"This place is seriously private, Dani." Nicholas pulled her out of sight. "We can't buy or lie our way into that back lounge."

"I'm terrible at being patient, but when I get my chance, I'll make the most of it," Danielle said. "They'll all be sorry."

Chapter 45

NO GUILT

SORCHA SPENT THE next evenings at Karen's, consumed with Vir, sharing the same space, breathing the same air. They made the move from bar stools to a secluded corner of the room, but she never shook the feeling that the walls had eyes. Being human would have made things simpler.

I need some advice and a plan. I'm going to have to make a quick visit to Normandie Hall.

"As much as I don't want to leave the city right now—"

"No, not again." Vir grabbed her arms and locked his eyes on hers.

"Only for a few days. To sort some things out."

"I'm afraid you won't come back."

"I will." Sorcha worked her hands through his hair. "I promise."

"Come home with me. I want to be with you." Vir glanced around and dropped his voice. "You know what I mean."

"I want that too, but it's complicated."

"When are you leaving?"

"Tomorrow." Sorcha rested her hand on his chest and felt his muscles twitch under the cotton dress shirt.

"I can't stand to be here alone."

"Don't worry, time will fly."

Through the guards, Sorcha arranged for a car to take her back to the plantation. The Dragon Lady let her pass through the river tunnel with no hesitation.

Sorcha had to tell Rayna the truth. She didn't come all the way out here to lie. Hopefully she'd know what was safe to do next. If only she could find Steven and Lily. Julia was always on Raimond's side, she'd steer clear of her.

Sorcha tiptoed to Rayna's suite and listened for noise from inside. Hearing none, she let herself in.

A figure jumped from the shadows, wielding a gold knife. "Get out or I'll scream."

"Don't stab me." Sorcha tossed up her hands protectively.

"Oh Lord, I'm glad to see you." The knife clattered to the floor as Rayna flew into her friend's arms. "Shut that door before we wake the whole house up."

Sorcha threw the bolt. "Why are you crying? Did something happen?"

"I've heard rumors about you and Vir. I know it's selfish because I think you love him, but I feel like my soul is being ripped in half."

No words were going to comfort Rayna. Leaning close enough to feel the moisture from her tears Sorcha kissed her friend on the lips. Her hand wandered over the soft curve of her hips and rested on her thigh. All the passion for Vir she'd had to hold back ignited genuine desire for Rayna.

"Don't stop."

Sorcha claimed Rayna's mouth for her own, falling back into a deep sea of pillows.

"Let me undress you," Rayna said.

Sorcha's clothing was simple. As the fabric fell from her quivering skin, Rayna christened the newly exposed areas of flesh with gentle kisses and flicks of her tongue.

Rayna's outfit was just as easy to dispose of—Sorcha surprised herself as she ripped the one-piece dressing gown free, tossed it to the side, and exposed every glorious inch of her perfect dancer's body.

This was uncharted territory, but Sorcha took Rayna's soft gasp as a sign of success. She went to work kissing every sensitive zone she knew of, from her earlobes, down her neck and past her perfect breasts. Inching farther down Rayna's stomach, she licked gently around her navel, working down her belly and dragging long hair across her skin like a spray of feathers, landing on a spot inside of her thighs. Sorcha focused her touch on the center of Rayna's being, making small circles and building momentum until her friend arched her back, shrieked into a pillow and collapsed into an exhausted heap.

"Sorcha, I have to say, I'm shocked—in a good way. Where did you learn?"

"Honestly, I'm as surprised as you." Sorcha tightly spooned Rayna's spent body. "This could have happened after the night at the Warehouse Club if we hadn't been...you know, derailed by circumstances. I've been in awe of you since the night we met."

"Must have been the tango." Rayna giggled as she nuzzled Sorcha's neck.

"So, if anyone claims that they're just friends with their dance instructor, we know it's a lie?"

"Absolutely." Rayna slid a silk belt from her nightgown and secured Sorcha's wrists to the headboard. "Play along."

Sorcha looked at her bound wrists, down at her naked body and back with wide eyes.

Rayna's expert tongue and fingers stroked Sorcha's body, starting with her neck and ears, moving down between her breasts, tracing a line to the middle of her stomach. Her lips and tongue teased, moving in circles closer to the ultimate destination. Well-practiced strokes caressed her belly while her tongue teased mercilessly. The pace was maddeningly slow, but when Sorcha was ready, there was no stopping her—like a runaway freight train.

Sorcha found it hard to rest, alternating her attention between Rayna's breathing and the ceiling fan over her bed. She swiped a hand across her forehead and then her chest. *No guilt. Not yet.*

Locking the bedroom door was a stroke of luck—a fact neither of them knew until they were startled from sleep by shouting in the hallway. Whoever banged on the door would have barged in if the door hadn't been secure.

Rayna sprung from the bed, silencing Sorcha with a finger to her lips. Grabbing a robe, she fluffed her hair and cracked the door open. "What's the commotion?"

"Have you seen Lady Sorcha?" The man in the hallway sounded annoyed. "The guards say they dropped her off at the door last night, but her room is empty. The staff is in a complete panic."

"Yes, she's sleeping. Or she was." Rayna blocked the entrance with her body. "She arrived exhausted and I let her stay down here. Please stop screaming and tell upstairs that everything is fine."

"You could have at least notified us—they're on the verge of calling Raimond and launching a search party."

Sorcha clapped her hands to her head. *Oh no, I forgot to tell Raimond.*

"Well, there's no need for that. I'll make sure she arrives in her bedroom safely." Rayna slammed the door in the man's face, spinning around as Sorcha peeked out from under the blankets. Both women collapsed in a fit of laughter. Rayna shook a finger at Sorcha. "Apologize to DeLynch and the staff. You probably scared them all half to death. I'll come upstairs later, so we can talk."

The Normandie Hall servants were sure Sorcha had been lost or abducted—an unforgivable sin in the eyes of their master. Sorcha apologized profusely to each and every person she saw. Penny brought a chalice of blood and didn't look away until it was empty. After she arranged Sorcha's hair in a loose braid and put her to bed, she planted herself in a chair, blocking the door.

"Penny, will you be watching me sleep?"

"Yes, my lady. Mr. DeLynch's orders. Guards are outside your balcony door."

"Well, I do feel quite safe." *I hope Vir isn't watching the clock and obsessing over my return. Might be a few nights.*

Rayna was clever enough to bring a tray of steaming coffee and use it as a bargaining chip to talk her way into the room.

"Why are you all treating her like a prisoner? It's a little overboard."

Penny reluctantly left the room after she had poured the coffee personally and rearranged the tray to her satisfaction.

"I know you came here to talk about Vir and vampire problems." Rayna flopped down on the bed.

"And I think I've made things more complicated than ever." Sorcha covered her face with her hands.

"Do you regret what happened between us?"

"Absolutely not. Don't ever think that, Rayna."

"I have no expectations."

Sorcha's jaw dropped open.

"You're royalty. I know my place. You and me, more specifically, what we did, would cause trouble if anyone learned of it. Not because I'm a girl or a human, but because I'm part of the staff. Not that it doesn't happen, it does—and plenty. The key is to keep what happens downstairs, well, downstairs."

"That doesn't fly with me at all. You're equal to everyone else."

Rayna laced her fingers with Sorcha's. "But I'm not, that's reality. I signed my life away a long time ago."

"How exactly did that happen? Why aren't you vampire? You must have had opportunities."

"Raimond found me in New Zealand decades ago, searching for exotic blood to stock the reserves of this empire. He drank from me a few times and decided I was special."

"You are." Sorcha kissed her knuckles. "Were you two lovers?"

"No, but he was quite the player back then and he loved to dance.

I learned a lot about the lifestyle. Raimond believes in full disclosure. The possibilities fascinated me, but I chose to hold onto my humanity—the best of both worlds. I can go out in the sun, eat regular food and drink enough blood to look twenty-five."

"How old are you?"

"Eighty-seven, maybe?"

Sorcha wrote a question mark in the air with her finger.

"Never mind. I know you're considering taking the next step with Vir, but is that why you came home? Did Raimond say something?"

"Raimond hasn't talked to me in a week. He arranged a safe place for me to meet with Vir, but it's a bar and privacy is nonexistent. Can't go home with him or bring him to the penthouse. It's a dead end."

Rayna leaned against the bedpost. "I'm sure Raimond is devastated. You know he fell hard for you, right?"

"We almost made love the day before the concert. So much almost happened that night, and so much changed in a split second."

"Wait until Draven hears about this, if he hasn't already."

"What does the prince have to do with anything?" Sorcha asked. "We haven't seen him in months."

"They almost dueled in the ballroom, on the night of the Gala. Over you. Could easily have knocked the whole house down."

Sorcha collapsed into the pillows. "Nobody ever told me exactly what happened."

"Draven respected Raimond's claim to you, but just barely. He declared himself next in line. Why do you think we whisked you out of there? Too many times vampires have fought over a woman, only to have her injured or killed in the crossfire."

"How dare they treat me like a piece of meat!"

"The culture is progressive in some ways," Rayna sighed. "Still painfully archaic in others."

"The prince is devious and not my type at all."

"Men like that don't take no for an answer. I'm sure he won't tolerate your love affair with a human well. You haven't seen the last of him." Rayna pointed to Sorcha's fangs. "So, what does Vir think of the new you?"

"He doesn't know, really. Thinks I'm an angel."

"Guess that's fine..."

"Like a ridiculous, flying around the ceiling angel," Sorcha said.

"There's a big difference between thinking something and believing it." Rayna rested her hand over her heart. "When are you going to tell him the truth?"

"Raimond says I can't, that it would be too dangerous."

"Yes, Raimond says, but you're going to have to tell Vir something, especially if you take him to bed. He'll notice the difference and could easily get hurt."

"This feels hopeless and it can't be okay with you."

Rayna slowly released a deep breath. "I promise to support you, no matter what. Steven can help you to find a more private location."

"Julia's jealous, isn't she?" Sorcha asked. "Even though I was never with Raimond?"

"You stole his heart anyway. She's fiercely loyal."

"Steven and Lily completely abandoned me."

"No, they didn't."

"Raimond sent all of you away so I'd leave the city and Vir?"

Rayna nodded.

"We're not anyone's possessions or playthings." Sorcha kissed Rayna's hand again. "Not sure how, but someday, I'll make it different."

Chapter 46

MARIGNY

WHILE EVENING COCKTAILS were served in Normandie's parlor, Steven and his entourage made a noisy entrance. "Sorcha, darlin', how is every little thing?" He began the formal greeting of kissing both cheeks and changed his mind, opting for a full hug. "We've been worried."

"Sorry to interrupt, Mr. Steven," DeLynch said. "Lady Sorcha has a phone call."

Sorcha looked back and forth between the two men. "We have a phone, now do we?"

"Raimond had lines run last week." Steven shrugged. "Keeping up with the times."

"The Duke, for you." The butler handed her the shiny receiver, turned his nose up and stalked away.

Sorcha stared at DeLynch's back and then at the phone. "Raimond?"

"I'm glad you're safe. You caused a bit of a stir."

"I know. I fell asleep downstairs." The once comforting voice raised a shiver of anxiety inside her. "I've apologized to everyone. Twice. Is everything okay there?"

"No worries. Dr. Ashayle is offering to cover everyone's shifts. Guess he doesn't want to go home. Other than that, nothing out of the ordinary."

"I just needed to clear my head," Sorcha said. "It's been difficult."

"Understandable. Take your time; you have plenty of it. May I ask a favor?"

"You may."

"You can come and go as you please—both residences are your homes. Just leave a note or a message when you disappear. Some…" Raimond paused. "Suspicious characters have been snooping around."

"Characters?" Sorcha glanced at DeLynch and turned away.

"That Victoire girl—you know the trampy one?"

"You'll have to be more specific."

Raimond chuckled. "The one whose arm you broke."

"Danielle, she's dreadful."

"The guards have run her off several times, along with some other strangers. Too many amateurish killings here lately."

"Vir?" Sorcha asked.

"He's safely working in the hospital. Please, don't take unnecessary risks."

"I will not."

"Good night, Sorcha."

"Wait—" The dial tone buzzed in her ear. "Bye."

Barricaded in the drawing room after dinner, Sorcha filled her friends in on Vir, leaving out any mention of Rayna. Steven listened to her story without interruption.

He's so rarely quiet. Must be serious.

"Let me be crystal clear." Steven rose, checked the locks, snugged the drapes and sat on the coffee table across from Sorcha. "For the record, I don't recommend any vampire taking a human to bed, but I'll give you any advice I can. What have you disclosed about—your status?"

"Not much, but the angel story is wearing thin."

"Honestly Sorcha, if you're taking this step, you need to tell him the truth. If he can't handle or believe it now, it won't get any better after you become intimate."

"I don't even know how to start explaining."

"Then maybe you're moving too fast. What's the rush?"

"Em, this is more complicated than I thought, isn't it?"

"You don't realize your own strength. Do you get..." Steven glanced at Lily and smoothed the pleats of his slacks, one at a time, "carried away?"

"Steven, I've done it once." *With a man.* "I was petrified most of the time." *Not with Rayna.*

"Well, I rent a house in the Marigny for myself and a few others. You're welcome to stay in the guest apartment. We'll go back to the city on Friday."

"Thank you so much for helping me." Sorcha rubbed her forehead. "I've got nobody else to talk to."

"Anytime, darlin'. We're here for you."

"Both of us." Lily gave Sorcha a long hug.

"Please don't do anything until you're absolutely positive you're ready. I don't want to regret this." Steven tossed his drink in the fire. The flames exploded, ignited by pure alcohol. He paused in the parlor doorway. "I'm in the mood for a wingding. Where's the music?"

Sorcha spent the next day with Rayna, trying to get her to open up about her feelings. She hit a wall at every turn.

"Come on—" Sorcha chased her friend as she scurried around the room. "Just talk to me."

"I've told you, I'm fine. What else is there to say?"

Sorcha slammed the suitcase shut and grabbed at the clothes in Rayna's hand. Silk and linen ripped in their struggle.

Rayna tossed the rags away and collapsed on the sofa. "What do you want from me?"

"The truth." Sorcha kneeled in front of Rayna, grabbing for her hands until she caught them. "Simple as that."

Rayna let her head tip back. "I've told you, I'm at peace with all of this. Do you want me to be devastated?"

"Of course not."

"Just because I'm coping doesn't mean I don't care." Rayna extricated her hands from Sorcha's and finished the packing in silence.

Sorcha left Normandie Hall with Steven and Lily at sunset on Friday, promising Rayna she'd be back, giddy with excitement about returning to Vir.

Now I feel guilty.

Steven's hideaway didn't look like much from the street, but tucked behind the security of high walls, it was a gem. Candles softly illuminated every lush corner of the courtyard garden where a gentle waterfall gurgled in the center of the flagstones. Food and wine was served on polished trays, poured in fine crystal and garnished with fragrant flowers—every bit as elegant as Normandie Hall.

"All this," Steven gestured to the local blood brought in for his welcoming party, "is from our little neighborhood. No need to set foot across Esplanade."

Still new to the city, Sorcha had never ventured outside the invisible barriers that framed the French Quarter. She made up for it tonight and fed until she couldn't swallow another drop. "Raimond requested I leave him a message when I arrive. I gave everyone a scare a few nights ago."

Steven lifted his fangs from the flawless skin of a man's neck. "Already done."

"I need to tell Vir also, so he knows I'm back in town."

Steven snapped his fingers to summon his assistant. "Tell him to meet us at Karen's. Tomorrow night, ten o'clock."

"Us?"

"If this man is so important to you, I want to meet him. He needs to know that your family has your back. I'll bring extra security."

"Last time I was there," Sorcha slumped into her chair, "the place was crawling with them. Raimond's and Draven's."

Draven paced his hotel suite, whipped the curtains back and cursed at the New Orleans skyline. "Ronald!" When the soldier didn't appear immediately, he pounded on the wall and hollered again.

"Right here, Your Highness." Ronald snapped to attention in the doorway.

"Have you been drinking?"

"No, sir. You want to kill all the drunken idiots."

"I'm wasting one more night in this eternal party city—that's it. If I don't find Sorcha, the chore falls on you and your men. Have you located this boyfriend of hers?"

"He's a doctor at Sisters of the Peace. Rarely leaves."

"And what have I told you about doctors?" Draven pointed to Ronald.

"Vampires have no use for human heroes."

"Are you sure you're spying on the correct fool?"

Ronald shifted nervously. "Brown skin, dark features, bit moody."

"That's him. Complete opposite of me." Draven flipped blond hair off his forehead. "Another brooding specimen like Raimond, protector of the human race. I didn't have a chance."

"Permission to speak freely, sir?"

"Granted."

"Since when do you wait your turn?"

"Excellent point." A spark flared behind Draven's steel eyes. "Tonight, things will change."

Chapter 47

RUN

LILY AND SORCHA ducked into the back room of Karen's, while Steven and his date stopped to chat at every table in the crowded restaurant.

Sorcha scanned the room for Vir. He wasn't at the bar, so she turned her attention to the luxurious furniture tucked around the edge of the room. "I see him." She tapped Lily's arm and deserted her, sliding onto Vir's lap and into his arms before he knew she was there.

"You came back." Vir ran his hand across her face. "My beautiful angel."

"Promised, didn't I?" Sorcha imagined the pain he must have felt when she disappeared in Nepal. "I'll never leave you alone."

"Excuse me, Sorcha—and stranger?" Steven crossed his arms and glanced between them. "Sorry to interrupt. Is an introduction too much to ask?"

He's far from sorry. I can almost see him laughing. Sorcha untangled herself from Vir's embrace. "I'd like you to meet Dr. Vir Ashayle. Vir, these are the friends I told you about, Steven and Lily." *I didn't say much of anything about them. Hope he plays along.*

Vir stood and offered his hand. "Very nice to meet you both. Please sit down, have drinks with us."

Crisis averted—talented lying disguised as manners and charm.

The group's conversation turned into a competitive exchange of tall tales. Vir's recollection of his brush with death on the Pacific crossing was horrific enough to earn her friends' respect.

"I'd like to hear more about Zelia," Sorcha said. "She was my best friend."

"Later." Vir nuzzled her ear. "These friends are still eyeing me up like I'm an unwelcome alien. I know they aren't angels. You aren't one either, are you?"

Sorcha pressed her finger to Vir's lips. "Steven, where's your date, whatever his name is?"

"Pfft, who knows? Probably schmoozing at the bar like he's the mayor." Steven excused himself, dragging Lily behind him.

Sorcha listened to their conversation until the crowded room swallowed their words.

"Well, the doctor is acceptable." Steven tucked Lily's arm into his. "Better looking when he's not bleeding on the floor, but there's some...shadiness there and I don't mean his flawless, black hair."

"He seems exceptional. Don't be so overprotective." Lily glanced back at Sorcha and winked. "Besides, he never lets go of her hand. Isn't it romantic?"

"Only if you like creepy and possessive."

"Shhh! She can still hear you." Lily pushed Steven into the throng around the bar.

"I have good news." Sorcha waited to tell Vir about the cozy room in the Marigny until her family called it a night.

"You're never leaving me again?" He twisted Sorcha's hair in his fingers.

A supernatural jolt of electricity followed by a vicious cold breeze wiped the smile from Sorcha's face. She spun around and scanned the bar. *I know that energy.* Rayna said Draven wouldn't take no for an answer, that he would be back and target Vir. *We need to get out of here—now.*

Sorcha grabbed Vir's wrist and headed for the back door. "Hurry up," she whispered, though she screamed on the inside.

"What's wrong?" Vir struggled to stay upright as she whisked him around furniture.

"Need air." Sorcha tried not to crush the bones in his hand as they skittered through the maze of dark alleys.

"Slow down, you're going to break an ankle."

Hide behind the clubs. With a firm hold of Vir's hand she propelled both of them across Bourbon. She didn't let go until a heavy door clicked shut, leaving them standing in another filthy walkway.

"That was not about you needing air." Vir slumped against the wall and flexed his hand. "Let me guess—angel bullshit?"

Sorcha was on the verge of an elaborate lie when she heard a groan and the unmistakable scent of blood hit her nose. "Hear something?"

"Besides my heart pounding in my ears?"

"A person's hurt back here." Sorcha tossed debris until she found a broken body. "Help me!"

Vir climbed over soggy boxes and searched the girl's neck for a pulse. "Incredibly weak."

Sorcha looked harder at the bloody face. "Alexa?"

"You know her?" Vir asked.

"She's the first person who was kind to me when I left New York." Sorcha hauled Alexa's body into her lap. "You are not dying in an alley."

"We should get to Emergency. I can't do much for her back here."

"She'll never make it to the hospital." *There's only one way.* Sorcha recalled the last time and how angry Raimond had been. This wasn't a public place, but there was one witness.

"Vir, bang on the doors. Pray someone hears you." Sorcha nicked her wrist and pressed it into the dying girl's mouth. She whipped her arm away when Vir turned back, hoping the darkness had hidden her actions.

"Any change?"

Sorcha picked up a faint stirring under Alexa's skin. "Maybe."

"It hurts." The girl's eyes fluttered.

"Hi there." Vir picked up the battered wrist and found a strong pulse. "You're going to be fine, we're getting help."

"Stay with her." Sorcha waited for Vir to look away, located a knob that was easily removed and tore a door off its hinges. "Let's get her inside."

Sorcha could have carried Alexa by herself but chose to keep up human appearances, letting Vir support most of her weight. *Hope he doesn't see the crushed skull and deep lacerations healing in front of his eyes.* Inside, she fumbled for the lights. Even with the electricity on, the place stayed dim and miserable.

"Who did this to you?" Vir dabbed blood from ugly bruises around her ears.

"One of our regulars. He's gotten a little rough with the other dancers, but he tips well so I took the chance." Alexa pointed at Sorcha's blank face. Vampire elixir fortified her voice with each word. "I knew they were lying."

"Nobody lied, what are you doing in this dump?"

"I lost the railroad job and I can't seem to pull myself together. Something always happens. I get sick or behind on the rent. This city has turned on me." Her voice trailed off. "Even the doctor said you were dead."

"Maybe you misunderstood?" Sorcha shrugged to Vir.

"No, Dr. Bandee-something swore you were killed on that damn trip." The girl sat up straighter. "But I saw you after that, dancing with your friends. I got attacked, and all of a sudden I was sitting on my parents' front steps with no idea how I got there. But I remember who did it. Gave the police a description."

"Whisht." Sorcha faked a smile and erased what she could from the girl's mind, running into walls where Raimond had already manipulated details. *Just not enough of them.* "Don't you want a ticket home?"

"I'd prefer the truth and a Sazerac."

"Me too," Vir said.

Sorcha forced her way behind Alexa's eyes again, and turned the question into a statement. "Dr. Ashayle will accompany you to the train station." She shoved a stack of cash into Vir's hand. "Make sure she gets on that train." *In less than an hour I won't be able to step outside this building.*

"Funny thing." Vir wrenched Sorcha to face him—staring into the dark bar before he spoke. "She thought you were dead too."

Sorcha called on every ounce of control not to give away her true strength. "She's fuzzy, almost died."

"Do you think I'm blind or stupid?"

"Em, neither." She wriggled her arm free.

"Tonight, we meet at our usual place. To talk." A fog of tension swirled between them. "Sorcha, I'm serious, I need some damn answers."

"Until tonight, then." Sorcha kissed Vir's cheek. Whether it was fear of the unknown or anger, intensity deepened Vir's features and changed a handsome man into an intimidating force. She wrestled with the temptation to make him forget everything he'd witnessed in the last few hours. *Wish it were that easy. I'm going to have to tell him something. The lies are complicated and exhausting, but the truth might be devastating.*

Even at full speed, Sorcha's arms were blazing red from the rising sun by the time she reached home.

Raimond must have some advice.

Chapter 48

PROOF

RAIMOND ROSE AT sunset, anticipating another full night of drinking and debauchery. He had finally given in and called one of his dearest friends, who also happened to be the most influential madam in New Orleans. Happy to have his business back, she responded by sending a parade of exotic beauties for him to sample. Between the medical mission, saving Sorcha, helping her assimilate into vampire life and then waiting for her to return his affections, he had neglected himself for a year. Vampires often endured long periods of celibacy for various purposes, but there was no reason for this torture to continue.

Nightlife in the city was barely underway when Raimond took his first break. *I'm thirsty, again.* He extricated himself from the tangled limbs and hair of naked women, heading straight for his favorite scotch. He wasn't alarmed by sounds of shuffling in the hallway; the next wave of ladies was expected to arrive at any minute. He paused to find a pair of pants and changed his mind. *Why bother? Might as well show off the assets I've been blessed with.*

The bottle exploded when it hit the floor.

"Sorcha!" The last person Raimond expected to see was staring through his bedroom door, first at his body and then behind him at the explicit scene in his bed. "This—this is not what it looks like."

Sorcha crouched to check for a pulse on a woman in the doorway. Feeling none, she checked a few more bodies and found corpses. She clapped a hand over her mouth and flashed back to the parlor. "Oh yes, Raimond, it's exactly what it looks like—and after all your snobby preaching."

Frantically wrapping a sheet around his waist, Raimond chased her down the hallway. "I'm sorry, I didn't think you were coming home. You're supposed to be at Steven's."

"No need to apologize. This is your apartment. You can do whatever or whomever you want here. My mistake was showing up without calling first." She turned herself into a blur, shooting out the door and down the stairs.

"Damn it girl, come back!" Raimond watched from the balcony as she disappeared into the crowded streets.

Sorcha kept running until she crossed Canal Street and disappeared into the heart of the Quarter. *I'm such a hypocrite. I dumped him for another man and threw it in his face, but those women were stone-cold dead.* Stopping at the front bar of Karen's, Sorcha ordered a shot of tequila. *I'm on my own now.* Glancing around to make sure Draven wasn't lurking, she had two more for good measure.

Vir was waiting in their favorite corner, holding a glass of wine he hadn't touched. "Wasn't sure you'd show up." His face remained frozen in a frown.

"Why wouldn't I?"

"Because you know I'm going to ask for the truth. I saw too many crazy things last night."

"Keep your voice down. This isn't a conversation we can have in public."

"We're in luck." Vir dropped a heavy key and a note on the table.

Lady Sorcha and Escort,
I reserved this fabulous room for tonight, but my plans fell

through.
Don't let it go to waste!
Fondly,
Steven

"Let's find this address." Sorcha walked out the door, assuming Vir would keep up. Halfway across Jackson Square she realized he still lagged two blocks behind. She made a weak effort to slow down as she examined the door numbers.

"Here." She handed him the skeleton key. The lock looked like an artifact from the previous century. "I hope whatever's inside lives up to the drama of this entrance."

The substantial door swung open with a moan. Muted chanting greeted them in the shadowy stairwell. A square table sat empty, set with fine china and two untouched glasses of wine. They followed the staircase around the room's perimeter, emerging into a stunning crimson and purple lounge. Chanting gave way to the faint ringing of bells and the overpowering aroma of incense.

"Damn." Vir's jaw dropped.

"Damn is right. Check out the bar. Top shelf everything."

They spent the next half hour exploring the deep corners of the suite. Walls were decorated in ornate mirrors, Egyptian artifacts, carved animals and portraits of exotic women.

At last, Vir touched Sorcha's sleeve. "Hate to risk breaking this mood, but I felt your strength last night. I saw the mangled door and watched a girl recover from fatal injuries. You're not a ghost or a garden-variety angel. Are you a witch?"

"Absolutely not." Sorcha snatched her arm away. *Why am I offended? I use that cover story all the time.*

"Okay, then what? I won't judge you, promise. Don't you trust me?"

"Of course, or I wouldn't be here, but I've been warned not to—it can be dangerous. For both of us."

"I believe you, but I need to know what I'm up against." Vir led Sorcha through the labyrinth of purple to a velvet sofa, gathering her onto his lap and into his arms.

"I'm afraid you'll run from the real me."

Vir traced her face with his fingertips, pressing softly on her bottom lip before he kissed it. "My perfect girl. I'll never run. I love you—no matter what."

"Please don't call me a witch. I can't stand it." *He loves me?*

"I take it back then. I want you—just you."

"Vir…"

"Just say it, I'm begging." Vir pressed both Sorcha's hands in his own and struggled to make eye contact while she stared at the wall behind him.

"Do you remember, em…stories you heard of the Rakshasa when you were a kid?"

"Silly legends told to frighten children."

"Not entirely silly. I was attacked by one of them, after the funeral. I lost my locket and went back, looking for it."

"You were attacked by Rakshasa? I can't believe it." Vir touched the amulet around her neck. "You're sure? What do you remember?"

"The violence of the impact, teeth shredding my flesh—then the cold. I was almost dead, but some of their blood must have mingled with mine. And then someone saved me."

"Who?"

"That's not important now. You wanted my story." Telling the truth carried risks and Sorcha was trying hard to limit the danger to herself.

"Okay, I'm listening. What are you, Sorcha?"

"I'm Rakshasa—like my ancestors. A vampire." Sorcha slid out of his limp arms and across the sofa to watch his reaction. "Surely that's not what you wanted to hear."

Vir's wide-eyed stare turned into a scowl as he shook his head.

"Should I just leave now?"

"I knew something wasn't right, but this is unthinkable. You look and feel—Rakshasa are hideous monsters. How can you be related to them?"

"I'm not just related, I am one of them. It was an accident, an unforgivable mistake. The result is the same. Still sure you don't want to run?"

Vir sighed, closed his eyes tightly and let them drift back open, his expression frozen and unreadable.

I don't blame him if he rejects me. It was a long shot.

"I promised I wouldn't run. Show yourself to me—the real you." Vir shrugged out of his white shirt, stepping in front of a gilded mirror. "Prove to me that you truly are a vampire."

He may regret losing his innocence.

Their eyes united in the reflection of the wavy glass.

Tell him as little as you can get away with and show him even less. No human can absorb this reality—no matter how much they desire it.

Sorcha let her true nature loose with a sliver of blue eyes and the slightest hint of dark veins shadowing the periphery of her face.

"I want to see your teeth."

Sorcha's nose tickled with the odor of a burned out fire. When Vir pushed his fear back with squared shoulders, she curled her lips and revealed the smallest amount of fang she could manage. Blood slammed against the vessels closest to his skin.

"Shit." Vir cringed at the sight of her teeth.

"Have I proven myself now?" Sorcha crushed her face into the back of his neck. She inhaled his scent with deep gasps and fought her desire with sheer willpower.

"Do you want to drink from me?"

"I do not. You're my lover, not my dinner. Will you still be one with me—now that you know the truth?" Sorcha unzipped her black dress and let it drop to the floor. She wrapped both arms around his chest, caressing his bronzed skin, gently kissing his shoulders and working her way up the back of his neck. *Sandalwood and smoke. Irresistible.*

Vir whirled around, clamping his hand around Sorcha's throat and forcing his lips as close to hers as possible without actually touching. "Still mine?"

"Hell yes, I am." Sorcha drew an involuntary breath as he lifted her off the ground and wrapped her legs around his waist. *Where did this brutality come from?*

Striding to the innermost room, where the human universe grazed the supernatural realm, Vir crushed Sorcha into a cloud of velvet cushions and tassels. He fixated on a garment of lace, the last barrier between her naked skin and his flesh.

I hear his blood rushing. Down.

Starting at her neck he worked methodically, ripping the slip down the middle of Sorcha's thighs and setting her body free.

"I'm totally and completely yours."

"Death and demons won't steal you from me a second time." Vir plunged into Sorcha with the desperation of a man trying to reclaim the last, precious shards of a lost love.

In vivid contrast to her first experience, Sorcha felt no pain—only sheer ecstasy. *Be gentle. Remember all the warnings. Don't let the monster completely out of her cage.* Surprising both of them, Sorcha rolled over, positioning herself on top of Vir, and took control of the crescendo. She drove him toward the climax he desired, stopping only when they were both satisfied.

He loves me. Bells were still chiming in Sorcha's ears when she looked at the watch on Vir's wrist and the ugly bruise under it. "Wake up!"

He squinted at the dial. "Can't we sleep a little more?"

"Oh good, you're alive." Sorcha stretched the full length of her naked body next to him. "Do you remember everything I told you last night—'bout me?"

"Yes, and a few other things too. You were different...in a good way. So free, so powerful." Vir pinned her underneath him in one motion. "A little wicked."

"Much as I'd love to do this again, I need to get home before sunrise." Sorcha winced as her fingers traced welts on his back. "The stories you've heard about vampires burning up in the sun are true."

"I'm coming home with you. I won't take no for an answer."

"That was my plan before we lucked into this room." Sorcha wiggled free and tossed his shredded clothes on the bed. "You need a new wardrobe." With a wink, she led the way out onto a balcony overlooking the dark street, still wet from the customary morning cleaning.

"The stairs are that way."

"Who needs stairs?" She climbed onto the iron rail that ringed the building.

"What are you doing? You'll fall." Vir grabbed frantically as she danced, just out of his reach.

"You really think vampires fall? Climb up here with me, we're taking the easy way down." Sorcha held out her hand, gesturing with her fingers.

"You're nuts, know that?" Stepping on a chair he took a long look down to the street before he stepped onto the iron rail. "I must be nuts too."

"Open your eyes. I won't let go." Sorcha's rock-steady grasp convinced him to take a peek around. "Promise."

"How are we getting down?"

"Trust me." She wrapped her arms around his waist and jumped. Vir's fingers dug into Sorcha's back until he realized they were floating in a slow spiral. She let him take in the view of the square and cathedral in the eerie predawn light, before landing gently on the flagstones. His expression registered complete shock.

"Little taste of the perks." Grasping his hand, Sorcha took every shortcut she knew to make it to Steven's safe house before the rays of dawn broke the horizon. She had turned cutting it close into a high art form.

He loves me.

Vir slept soundly for most of the day, leaving Sorcha plenty of time to rehash the last twenty-four hours. Last night, again, alarmingly random events sent her hurtling toward another life-changing decision. She thought she handled it fairly well.

Questions and answers, death and demons, that's all. The sex was way better than I expected. Didn't kill him, either.

Proof of her core transformation was as clear in that performance as the first time Sorcha glimpsed her own fangs. The woman who flaunted her body and drove her lover to a mind-blowing orgasm was universes away from the naïve orphan girl who ran from New York. *I need to confide in someone.*

"Dear Lord, yes, I got stood up." Steven rubbed his eyes and tried to wrestle the blankets back from Sorcha's grasp. "No, I don't want to talk about it."

"Never mind that. You need to hear my story—it's juicy."

"Wait, this is about you?" He bolted up and fumbled on his nightstand for a bottle of wine. "What the hell happened last night? You're glowy."

After a hesitant beginning, Sorcha guzzled the wine and started talking. She babbled until she spilled everything, from Raimond's murderous orgy to Draven's stalking, and on through the highlights of her escapade with Vir. "That room was magical."

"And an impossible reservation. I booked it five months ago."

"There is one other secret, and it complicates things further. You're the only person I can tell." Sorcha confessed her relationship with Rayna.

Steven drained the remaining wine, nearly choking on the last swallow. "Don't tell anyone else about that for now. And not for the reason you're thinking, either. There's a lot of illicit history—we'll talk about it some other time."

"That's cryptic."

"Sorcha honey, you've done an exemplary job handling this situation. Mature vampires have wilted under less pressure."

"I didn't say a word about you, or Raimond. I very deliberately told him only about myself." Sorcha twirled her hair with shaky fingers. "Didn't even let on this was your house."

"Well, if he's going to be spending any time here, we can't avoid bumping into each other. When he wakes up, bring him to the parlor."

"You're sure?"

"The most important thing is that he doesn't see you or any of us feed. Other 'oddities' can still be explained away by magic, but not blood activities. Any further questions trouble boy wants to ask, he can ask me."

Chapter 49

INTERROGATION

STEVEN LEFT SORCHA in Lily's capable hands. His mission was to find Raimond and fill him in on current events. Despite the unfortunate naked caper, an uncharacteristic blunder for a man of his standing, the duke needed to be made aware of any threat to his family.

A search of the customary haunts turned up empty; tonight Raimond was being his usual, elusive self. Steven finally let himself into the abandoned penthouse. He sunk into a comfortable spot on the softest chair. "Why can't I ever walk in on anything scandalous?"

Raimond slipped in moments before sunrise. His eyes narrowed at the sight of a visitor camped in his parlor. "Steven."

"Raimond. Bring home any sleazy little trinkets?"

"Are you scolding me? You aren't interested in the equipment my guests are born with."

"Fine, no debate there. I'm here to discuss what happened after you damaged Sorcha's eyes with your little display." Steven peered under a sofa cushion. "Also, to look for bodies."

Raimond stopped slamming cabinet doors and sat down as he listened to Steven recount what he had learned. "All this in the few hours after she left the penthouse? We need to talk to Ashayle and find out what he believes."

"Let's not forget that our girl is in love with this character." Steven frowned. "I can't just read a human mind, either. How do we handle that?"

"Interrogation."

"Do we have time to grab him?" Steven nudged the drapes aside and looked skeptically toward the brightening horizon.

"We don't have to go anywhere." Raimond grabbed the telephone off the table and spun the dial. He turned his attention to the Sister who answered, requesting that Dr. Ashayle do him a favor after his shift.

"Murder." Steven crossed his arms. "You took my advice and installed phones everywhere."

"That jargon is wildly inappropriate."

"But it's hip."

"Can we focus?" Raimond banged his forehead on the wall. "Ashayle will be here any minute."

Both vampires were ready for the doorbell chime in the first hazy minutes of New Orleans morning.

"Steven." Vir flinched away from the door. "Dr. Banitierre asked me to make a call to this address. Must have gotten it wrong."

"No, you're in the right place." Steven ushered the doctor across the threshold, relieved him of his black bag, and threw the bolt.

Vir's eyes flashed with recognition as he looked for escape. "Demons—"

Raimond slipped from the shadows and clamped his hand over Vir's mouth. "Sorry pal, we need to find out how big a liability you are."

Steven forged a note and Vir signed it under duress.

Please forgive me Sorcha.

In order to make up the work I've missed, I'll be on house calls all day. Until tonight.

Love always,

Vir

"Is this thing sappy enough to do the trick?" Steven asked.

"Makes perfect sense," Raimond said. "He's missed enough shifts to be fired outright."

After hours of questioning, neither vampire had anything left to ask. Raimond jammed a pillow under Vir's head. "All he cares about is his night of passion with Sorcha, and how to get more of the same."

"Typical man." Steven tossed a blanket in Vir's direction.

"He's devoted to her, and in spite of everything he's learned, his commitment hasn't changed. He's more in love than ever."

"I think he sensed you were his competition for Sorcha back in Nepal. You must not have been very subtle."

"And neither are you," Raimond said. "He met you a week ago and knows all about your preferences."

"Another judgmental one."

"He'll come around. You're one of the strongest souls I know, Steven."

"Still a lonely soul."

"Love visits everyone in its own time. Be patient."

"I have a hard time believing anyone would choose..." Steven mumbled, "me."

"Stop selling yourself short. Of my entire family, you're the one I'd choose to stand beside me in battle." Raimond nodded at Steven's dropped jaw. "You're ferocious, and I trust you with my life."

Raimond positioned himself to be the first thing Vir saw when his blurry vision cleared. "Welcome back, Dr. Ashayle. You've been unconscious for hours. Be more careful where you walk."

"This was no accident." Vir rubbed his head. "You, sir, are a disgrace to our profession."

"So, report me. But first convince us you understand what's expected where Sorcha is concerned."

"Behavior that hurts her will not be tolerated." Steven waggled his finger from across the room.

"My family, my rules," Raimond said. "If you want to end your relationship with her, we'll help you leave town immediately."

"I'm not going anywhere. Where's Sorcha?"

"She's safe at home. Listen Ashayle, you're a decent doctor in spite of your lousy attendance record, so I've resisted the urge to dispose of you. That being said, I have little use for you other than protecting one young woman's heart." Raimond paused to assess the reaction. "We're going to reinforce the concept of secrecy as it pertains to life and death. If you truly love Sorcha, you'll guard our secret with your life. Understand?"

"I do love her and I keep my promises. Cut the bullshit. Sorcha showed me what she is—I assume you two are the same."

"In every way that matters." Raimond snapped his fingers. "Little help here?"

"I miss being a thug." Steven uncloaked a face he rarely used, pure black eyes framed by skin with veins so dense that he was barely recognizable. "Would have been more fun if I could breathe."

"Let's finish this." Raimond grabbed his terrified employee by the throat and snarled through gruesome fangs. "Break your word and I'll throw your body in the swamp and feed your heart to the fire. Accept the terms?"

"Yes, sir." Vir gasped for air as he crashed to the floor. "May I please see Sorcha now?"

Vir followed Raimond and Steven to the club, amazed by the army of guards that blended in and out of the crowd. "How long has all this security been tailing me?"

"For weeks, idiot. Pay more attention to your surroundings." Steven shooed him away.

One glance at her boyfriend's bruised neck, company, and disheveled state made Sorcha realize something had gone wrong. "What did you cretins do to him?"

"Look at his pretty face." Raimond waved his hands in front of Vir like a magician. "If we really wanted to hurt him, he'd be dead. Rules of conduct needed to be established. None of it was recreational."

"You forged that note." Sorcha whipped Vir behind her.

"No, Steven did," Raimond said. "I'm sorry about the other night at the penthouse. It was sloppy and wrong. Not my finest hour. Can you forgive me?"

"Maybe, if Vir isn't hurt."

"I'm perfectly healthy." Vir patted Sorcha's hand. "Those two are scary, but I stood up to them. I'm never leaving you."

"Did they tell you to leave me?" Sorcha willed blue fire to ignite her eyes.

"They offered me an escape from all this cloak and dagger business, which I flatly refused. You're stuck with me."

"In a dangerous mess that you don't deserve."

"Exactly where I want to be. Touch me, beautiful girl." Any lingering pain and anger faded as they pressed their palms together.

"Shhh, let your hazel eyes come back." Vir smirked at Raimond over Sorcha's shoulder.

"That hand thing is too freaky." Steven shook his head. "Their skin is almost liquid. Could you imagine if he became a—"

"Don't even go there," Raimond snapped.

Every being in the vicinity, human or otherwise, responded to the waves of energy that radiated from the couple. Sorcha and Vir were too entwined with each other to notice how others retreated, but nobody missed the malicious flash of power when it ripped through the cracks in the building. Banitierre guards reacted with precision, separating the family from the impending confrontation.

Raimond remained in place with his arms crossed. "Prince Norman, what an unpleasant surprise."

"Tread carefully, Duke, you still serve at my pleasure." Draven clasped his hands behind his back. "I'll whip this town into shape myself. My subjects here could use a healthy dose of fear."

"You can have the city, which you've never wanted, but I'll fight to the death for my family."

"Then you can stand down. I mean your family no harm. Merely here to claim my princess, as promised."

Is he talking about me? Sorcha's mind spun. *I'm not his princess!*

"That's not going to happen. She's made her choice and though it pains me terribly to say—it isn't you." Raimond turned his face into a mock frown. "I'll defend her human as a member of this family as well."

"You're protecting that filthy runt, now? I'll rip his spine out before he touches her again."

Vir listened silently until he heard the comment about his spine. "What the—"

Sorcha clamped her hand over Vir's mouth as Steven simultaneously clamped his hand over hers. Julia turned around to glare at all three, warning them with a slicing motion across her throat.

"I'm sure you recall their intimate connection? As we've discussed before, are you willing to make that eternal mistake?" Raimond held his ground, making an effort not to ignite the prince's wrath any further or block his exit.

"I'm not inclined to fight tonight. Far too fond of this dinner jacket." The prince tilted his head to the heavily guarded corner. "I know you've heard every word of this exchange, Sorcha. I'm willing to wait for you to tire of your feeble partner and embrace the power of my royal bloodline, but my patience won't last forever. Yes, Princess—I'm speaking specifically to you." He shot her a withering glance before exiting the room, immediately enveloped by royal secret service.

"Who the hell was that guy?" Vir started firing questions the minute the atmosphere cleared.

"A vampire monarch," Raimond answered. "Not your biggest fan."

Steven brushed himself off with disdain. "Let's get out of here.

The Warehouse Club is every bit as safe as this joint, probably more so considering what we just witnessed. At least the music will be better."

The Banitierres spilled into the street, their security fanned around them like a blanket.

Sorcha let go of Vir's hand long enough to match strides with Steven. "So, I assume you revealed all my secrets?"

"Only the ones that saved your life. What if Raimond hadn't been here tonight, when your royal suitor showed up to claim you? A lavish prison cell in the Alps has your name written all over it."

"Now, you're scaring me."

"You should do the Irish accent more often," Steven said.

"What?" Sorcha froze for a second. "No."

"So...minxy."

"Steven." Sorcha slapped his arm.

"Suit yourself." Steven stuck his nose in the air. "I am shocked that Raimond defended Vir the way he did, considering."

"Hello, I can hear you." Vir jogged to keep up with the vampire's comfortable walk. "I always suspected that Banitierre didn't like me. Now I'm starting to understand why."

"Don't expect any of that to change, either. He only defended you because Sorcha is his...family." Steven bit his tongue, and swept his entourage through an eerily lit portal where they made their customary dramatic entrance.

"Jeffrey?" Raimond's eyes darted around sprawling room. "Jeffrey!"

A bartender dashed out from behind stage curtains, waving his co-workers away. "Right here, sir!"

"Please attend to my family personally," Raimond said. "It's been a rough evening."

"Certainly. Sazerac for you tonight?"

"Sounds refreshing." Raimond shook his head when Jeffrey pointed to the lemon wedges. "Don't ruin it."

"Gentlemen and ladies, to what do I owe the pleasure?" Jeffrey straightened his bow-tie and bowed. "Didn't expect to see you until the Masquerade."

With the Banitierres distracted by their bartender, party girls skulked around the edges of the room, paying specific attention to Vir.

"Damn, he's a hot piece."

"Danielle, you need to move on—plenty of tasty blood to drink in this town." Nicholas whispered in her ear as Kettly steered her away. "None of us wants to be slaughtered because you're stuck on that specific blend."

"What a bunch of losers. No imagination. You may be content to slither through filth for the next hundred years, but I'm aiming bigger and better. What I want is that man, and I don't mean for a quick bite. I'll drain him, change him and keep him as my personal sex toy. And I'll enjoy the hell out of rubbing it in that little bitch's face."

Chapter 50

BUBBLE BATH

"MASQUERADE?" SORCHA DRAGGED Steven upstairs to the balcony so they could speak without yelling over the band. Vir trudged behind them. "Fill us in."

"The Masquerade Ball is the jewel of the fall events, the sister party to our Equinox Gala. It's being held here on October 29, so we can be safely home by the first minute of Halloween," Steven said. "Summer can go, and take this dreadful humidity with it."

"Isn't Halloween a celebratory night in the Quarter?"

"Yes, but it's notoriously violent, so Raimond insists the entire family spend it locked behind Normandie's walls. I'm already designing everyone's outfits. Lily works magic with the masks. I guess we'll need to dream up something for—" Steven looked Vir up and down and pulled Sorcha to the side. "I apologize for breaking your confidence but I'm not sorry. Vir has good intentions, but this unconventional affair makes us all vulnerable. Your personal business with Rayna is still a secret. Keep it that way."

Sorcha was finally free to give Vir her full attention. "I know you didn't hit it off with Steven, but he's family."

"I respect his loyalty."

"This Masquerade is news to me," Sorcha said, "but you're invited. A soiree with masks and ball gowns sounds exciting."

"It's been an eye-opening few days." Vir touched his neck and winced. "That prince guy is keen on you?"

"Something like that, but there's nothing charming or romantic about it. He's used to getting what he wants. I'm sure he'll be back at some point."

"And Banitierre? Tell me the truth—did you sleep with him? He's extremely possessive and protective of you, much more than I would expect from a friend."

"I did not. Remember what I told you that night in the upstairs lounge?" Sorcha asked. "I'm completely yours. Raimond's saved my life many times. I've paid him back by hurting him and putting him in the impossible situation of having to defend both of us. He needs time to recover. Grief, sadness and anger are all amplified for a vampire. Any one of them can be paralyzing."

"When can I be with you again?" Vir asked.

"Come home with me. Now."

The couple arrived at Steven's Marigny compound surrounded by more security than the leaders of most nations.

Sorcha locked the door behind her, hoping it sealed all the ugliness out of their private oasis. She filled the old claw-foot tub with steaming water and suds in her favorite fragrance. "How do you feel about a bubble bath, doctor?" Dropping her robe, she shot a seductive glance over her bare shoulder and disappeared into the bathroom.

Vir glided under the water, pulling Sorcha back into his muscled chest and tucking his chin around her neck.

She rested her head back against him and allowed tension to flow out of her neck under his skilled fingers. "Is the water too hot?"

"Perfect for me, but what about you? Your skin still feels cold." His hand dipped under the layer of bubbles, skimming the curve from Sorcha's breasts to her hip. There was an audible catch in his breath as she arched her back and shifted her legs for his wandering fingers.

"Show me where."

Without thinking she placed her hand over his, directing their interlaced fingers lower, until she gasped in pleasure. "Gently, please."

"That's it, good girl." Vir buried his face in the damp tangle of

Sorcha's hair as he gingerly stroked the exact spot she led him to, pushing her closer and closer toward the edge of bliss. "Don't hold back." Anticipating the precise moment she would go over the brink, Vir squeezed his arms around her body, absorbing her waves of pleasure in his steel grip.

Instinctively Sorcha wrapped her legs around Vir as he lifted her from the tub, ignoring how much bathwater spilled as their embrace progressed to the bedroom. Bubbles sprayed in every direction as Vir flung Sorcha into the sheets, pinning her under his dripping body. He lavished her with kisses, pressing her into the silk, hovering just above her. Sorcha ran her hands down his spine, from his shoulders to his hips, tugging, urging him to continue.

"I think I was too rough last time. Don't want to hurt you."

"You won't—can't. Let me help." Sorcha reached between their wet bodies, needing both hands to guide him inside.

"I want you."

"Then take me." As Sorcha arched her back, Vir lost any thread of control he was clinging to, burying himself to the hilt. Drawing a ragged breath, he began the journey. Momentum and rhythm built until neither could hold back any longer. The unmistakable pinch of teeth on her neck sent Sorcha hurtling back to her first experience with his raw, physical power.

He bites—how's that for glorious irony?

They lay still for minutes or hours; all that mattered was sunset and sunrise—at least for one of them. Pulling a crumpled pack of clove cigarettes out of the bedside stand, Sorcha offered one to Vir. From the hesitant way he leaned in as she flipped open the lighter, she assumed that he had never tried one before.

"Are these things legal? I feel a little buzzed." Vir whisked away a puff of smoke. "So, tell me about Normandie Hall."

"It's a few hours up the Mississippi. The perfect Southern mansion, complete with a ballroom. I know you'll love it."

"I've never been inside a house like that in this country, though

I've visited some castles in England that you would adore. Do you actually live there or in the city?"

"Both, but we gather at the plantation for holidays, just like a normal family. There was a fancy party a few months ago. Next year you'll attend as my date." *If Raimond allows it.*

"Can I ask you a serious question?"

"Shoot."

"If you bite me, will I turn into a vampire?"

"You will not. 'Tis way more complicated than that. Don't worry." Sorcha patted Vir's hand.

"And if I bite you? What happens then?"

"Nothing really. I mean some humans drink vampire blood to extend their lives—it's an acquired taste. The effects are the same as a drug, a strong performance-enhancing one. It's also highly addictive."

"All my instincts are warning me to run from this—except I'm so curious. I don't want to turn into a vampire ever, but I need to know more." Vir flipped around to face Sorcha. "I want to drink from you."

"Nope. Maybe you shouldn't smoke any more of this." Sorcha pried the cigarette from his fingers.

"Why? I just want us to be inseparable."

"I'm right here. I'm real and I'm never leaving you."

"I'm not letting this go, Sorcha. I want it for myself, for both of us."

Chapter 51

WARNING

OVER THE NEXT weeks, Vir worked the graveyard shift and spent most days in the Marigny, unless Sorcha decided that he should sleep in his own bed. Forgetting that he was a human who needed food and rest was easy. The dark hours were free for her to gallivant with friends, but after her hunger subsided she quickly tired of the bar scene. She preferred to watch the windows of the hospital, specifically Marion's. *Don't see many nurses in that room.*

When Sorcha quizzed Lily and Julia about Halloween season, she learned that the coven held a meeting on the night of the autumnal equinox. An ancient family of witches conducted the vampires-only blessing of protection for the upcoming month of danger.

"You don't need to plan much for the Masquerade Ball," Lily said. "We'll make you and your fella look smashing."

Sorcha clapped her hands. "Can't wait to see the masks."

Julia snickered at her excitement.

"Vir is invited, Julia. I know you don't approve," Sorcha said, "but I don't need your permission."

"It's the most secure location in the city that night," Julia said, "and that is the only reason he's included."

The night of the autumnal equinox fell in the midst of a tropical storm that battered the delta with wind and rain. Palpable hurricane anxiety plagued the region for several months out of every year. All creatures, supernatural and human, were vulnerable to the power, wrath and destruction that Mother Nature unleashed. Whether it was luck, or spells and prayers offered up by the odd mix who called this their home, once again the Crescent City dodged the worst of it.

Dressed in somber colors, vampires from covens across the country spilled into the wet streets, streaming in silence toward the fringe of the Treme. As the ruling family, the Banitierres walked directly behind Raimond, leading a march of the undead to a well-guarded site.

A devil parade. I laughed it off when I first heard the term—not so much of a joke tonight.

The guests entered a walled cemetery by the back gate, proceeding down a set of hidden stairs into a long tunnel. River water dripped down the walls and disappeared into the stone floor.

How is this passage not flooded?

The group emerged into a subterranean chapel. Shining tiles decorated with *fleur-de-lis* lined every inch of the curved walls.

Sorcha tried to understand the language of the ceremony, but it was hopeless gibberish spoken by a decrepit old woman. The officiant was a legendary witch and distant relative of the guardian under Normandie Hall. Her spine was so twisted, her face was permanently sideways.

Roussel. That name sounds familiar, but I just can't place it.

A dragon was the central element of this spell. Sorcha watched as the witch chanted over the brimming goblet of blood, drained from veins of the secret creature. *Who knows where they have a dragon stashed.*

Following the crowd, Sorcha found her place in a line leading to the altar. Once there she kneeled, ready to accept the final act of protection.

The witch began to swirl incense around Sorcha's head as she had done for the others and stopped mid-chant. "Rakshasa. You're the Pacific demon who's taken a human lover."

Sorcha was frozen by the eerie smile. *She doesn't have one straight tooth in her head.* "How do you know that?"

"Relax, child. I have a special cloak of protection, just for you." At her low whistle, younger witches appeared out of thin air, carrying wine and dark fabric. They draped silk over Sorcha's head and hair, with enough length to graze the floor. Placing her hand on Sorcha's forehead, the old witch chanted for what seemed like forever before she offered the wine goblet.

Sorcha took a sip.

"My magic will protect you for one full year, until the next autumnal equinox." The witch summoned Sorcha to her feet. "But my senses tell me that your human is in grave danger. Keep your wits about you and your eyes on him, always."

"How can I protect him?" Sorcha grabbed the woman's crooked hand.

"If you want him to be truly safe, change him. Share your power—your hellion blood is the greatest gift he could ever receive. His eyes will blaze with blue fire as deep and fierce as your own."

"No, it's against everything that makes him who he is. He would rather die than be a killer." *Like me.*

"You may not have the luxury of choice. This life is no romantic fantasy. It's a brutal hell on earth. Examine your own heart and be prepared to make that ultimate decision when the time comes."

Long after the witch uttered her devastating words and shook her off, Sorcha stayed riveted at the altar wringing her hands. *There's no way Vir will agree to become a vampire—none. What horrific circumstances could convince me to rob him of his human life?*

"Ceremony's over. We need to leave before the tunnel floods." Raimond gently took Sorcha's arm. "Did the witch say something to upset you?"

"I don't know." Sorcha did her best to avoid his eyes and failed. "Yes, she did—about Vir. She implied he was in danger, and I'd have to change him against his wishes."

Raimond guided her down the tunnel, keeping his hand on Sorcha's back to push her along. As they cleared the top step she glanced back in time to see the tunnel fill with black water, and the steps vanished into the flagstone.

"I know telling you not to worry about Vir's safety won't make you stop, but I've kept extra security on him day and night. What she said about changing him, it's a valid point. But it's a crushing responsibility, and you don't need to make a decision right now. What's wrong with your fingers?"

"Covered in dirt or ashes." Sorcha brushed her hands together. "Don't you see it?"

"Not a speck." Raimond grasped her chin and directed her eyes. "Putting all our personal issues aside, I'm here to help you, whatever you need, whenever you need it."

"I know you are."

"Alright then, let's go find something to eat. Every vampire in the South is roaming these streets. Some poor fool always goes home hungry."

Chapal and Locke lurked behind the crypts, waiting for Sorcha to emerge alone.

"Stay out of sight." Lock yanked his brother back into the shadows. "Attending this ritual was risky enough."

"Why? That Norman Prince isn't here. It's an easy kill."

"Only if you want us dead too."

"Shit." Chapal cursed under his breath. "She's with Banitierre. Now what?"

"I'm not fighting a duke in his home city. I'll try to get close at the Masquerade next week."

"What, no invitation for me?" Chapal asked.

"Masks or not, you don't exactly blend into the crowd, mate. All you're missing is the Samurai sword."

Chapter 52

THE CROSS

AN UNEVENTFUL WEEK had passed since the protection ceremony, but Sorcha couldn't shake the ill feelings. The few hours she spent with Vir felt distant and tedious. Knowing she was keeping something from him, possibilities with devastating implications, was enough to kill the romance for her.

Just life or death, human or monster. No big deal.

The young vampire had also lost her appetite, which did nothing but make her weaker and more depressed.

"Another tequila." Sorcha sat at the bar alone, rejecting any human offerings sent by her friends. She found something distasteful with every one of them.

I need fresh air. Throwing a stack of bills onto the bar, Sorcha led her nervous bodyguards into the chilly autumn night. She stopped to admire the cathedral and St. Anthony's Garden, which was as enchanting as ever.

Nothing has changed—except me. I dreamed of attending mass in that church, but I can't even step inside. Bet I can climb up on that roof, though.

Making sure she didn't have an audience, Sorcha chose the darker of the two alleys, a sketchy walkway that ran down the side of the cathedral. Taking a few steps as a running start, she used the scrolled iron fence to vault onto the church.

"Here I am, case anyone wants to strike me down." She scampered to the highest point, navigating the spine of the building as if it were a balance beam. *Higher is better.* Sorcha scaled the steeple, boosting herself to the top in one strong leap. Still expecting death by lightning at any second, she wrapped her hands around the crowning jewel of the cathedral, a giant cross.

"Ow, hot!" Sorcha pulled her palms away and gripped the cross where her blouse protected the inside of her elbow. "Must be gold in this thing."

The view was striking and crystal clear in every direction. From the bright glare of the city to the gas lamps of the residential streets, the light always surrendered to the blackness of the sea, the lake or the bayou. Sorcha's spire felt like the brilliant center of the universe but one look straight down reminded her how much tequila she drank.

Whoa…that is some long drop. If I fall, will anybody care? Who am I really? The daughter of a dead nurse, the royal subject of a prince and a duke, both of whose advances I've recently refused.

"Who am I?" Sorcha took a few test steps around the small sill that supported the cross. *The secret lover of a girl chained to a life of blood slavery and the vampire girlfriend of a human who still struggles with my existence. I've always been obsessed with becoming someone special. All I add up to is a sad collection of negatives.*

Sorcha forced her eyes up, and twirled around the ornament. Little by little, the fear of falling drifted into the background.

"Come down right now." Raimond's voice blasted up from the black roof.

"What are you doing here?" Sorcha slipped, hugging the thick metal and fighting dizziness. "Can't look down."

"Next time, consider that before you start pole dancing on a rooftop cross." Raimond held out his arms. "Jump. I'll catch you."

"If I fall, I won't die, right?"

"No, but when you shatter every bone in your body it's still horrific. Trust me." He kept his arms wide open. "How drunk are you, anyway?"

"Pretty drunk." *His arms look like a better option than the flagstone steps.*

"Figured as much. Please, I'm not mad but you're scaring me. Close your eyes and let go."

"Promise you won't drop me?"

"I'm a duke—I don't drop women."

Sorcha didn't really jump; it was more of a free fall. Raimond kept his word and caught her, even though the distance and force of the drop drove them both into the slate shingles. As soon as his strong arms wrapped around her, tears broke free. She hadn't cried since before the attack in Nepal, but she made up for it now.

"I thought I couldn't—" Sorcha wiped her cheeks and gaped at both her hands covered in blood.

"You can cry, but it's messy." Raimond handed her a handkerchief and held her until the wracking sobs faded. "Times have been hard, but you were handling it all so well. What changed?"

"That witch called me a hellion. I just wanted to be a good nurse. How did I end up a blood-sucking killer?" Sorcha's tears welled up again.

"That old bat? I'll have a word with her. Witches are always so dramatic. They can't even open a door without hocus pocus and abracadabra. Ooo!" Raimond wiggled his fingers around, coaxing a giggle out of Sorcha. "I know that's not the whole story."

"I was one of the top nursing school graduates in New York."

"*The* top graduate. I made some inquires after you knocked Dr. Winters on his keister."

"I'm sorry. That was about Miss Marion."

"What else is bothering you?"

"Here I am with all this magical ability and I'm too late to save my mother. Now, I feel powerless to save Vir."

"I know this is not the path you planned, but in the grand scheme of the universe, you're exceptional. Your mother would be proud."

"I feel God doesn't exist anymore, not for me anyway."

"Maybe not the one you knew as a human. But I believe there's a Lord somebody, somewhere, watching over all of us."

Sorcha tipped her head back until she was face to face with

Raimond.

"You know I respect your choices, right?" He nodded until Sorcha mimicked the movement. "Your friends and very extensive family love you. Plus, your gentleman suitor worships the ground you walk on. You were a heroine of the community in Nepal and you're equally popular here in New Orleans—perfectly capable of dancing on rooftops, but not this drunk and weak. I insist that you sleep at the penthouse today. After this little display I'd like to keep my eye on you."

Sorcha followed him down the slope of the cathedral roof and into the narrow streets. *I would definitely have fallen.* A quick stop in the corner bar provided enough blood to take the edge off her hunger. *Teetering on the edge of a church spire feels like it happened to someone else, in a different lifetime.*

Sorcha was happy to be safely in the penthouse, pulling the sheets back on her bed when a soft knock pulled her attention away. She opened the door to find Raimond drumming his fingers on the wall.

"Sorry to intrude. Just wanted to let you know I sent a message to Steven assuring him you were safe and that you would be spending the day here. I'm sure he's heard about your escapade. Word travels fast in this town."

"Course it does."

Silence swirled in the hall.

"There's a question I've been—" Raimond leaned on the doorframe.

Sorcha's fingers fidgeted with the chain around her neck. "I'm still so sorry for…"

"No, not that. Let me explain." Raimond pointed to the locket. "You try so hard to disguise your heritage. Why?"

"Mum was convinced that it would give me a better life." Sorcha's face fell. "She endured a lot of prejudice against the Irish."

"And the accent?"

"All the time Mum spent coaching it out of me, I was secretly memorizing every syllable. I loved who she was…who I was."

"You can stop hiding who you are," Raimond said. "Things are different now."

"Dr. Raimond Banitierre, I will take your advice. It's a sparklin' new world." Sorcha's lips twitched up playfully. "That was a bit cliché on purpose."

"I also called Normandie Hall, and Rayna will be here by the time you wake up. Things are about to get hectic leading up to the Masquerade Ball. I know you two are close friends, and she seems to calm and comfort you better than anyone else."

"Perfect." Sorcha forced her smile wider, said good night, and gently shut the door. She slammed her mind closed for the short walk to the bathroom and blasted running water as soon as she reached the faucet.

Jayz, how am I explaining this mess to Rayna?

"Good morning, sweetie." Rayna snuggled under the quilt and slipped her arm over Sorcha's shoulder. "Raimond sent for me. Something happen?"

"Where do I even start?" Sorcha had been awake all day, tossing and turning, debating how to handle the conversation. She rolled over and gathered both Rayna's hands in hers. *I miss her. So much.*

"I'm going to come right out and—I'm sleeping with Vir. If you run away I won't blame you one bit." *Please, please don't.*

Rayna rose to get off the bed and fell back with a sigh. "That's why Raimond called."

"More likely because I got depressed, drunk and almost fell off the roof of the cathedral."

"Why—how? Where the hell was everyone?"

"Wasn't their fault, I ditched them. Raimond swooped in and saved me, again." Sitting up in bed, Sorcha studied her best friend's face closely. "Why exactly didn't you run away just now?"

"I'm willing to share—not thrilled, but you did meet Vir first. That is, if you still want me."

"Rayna, of course I still…you accept me for who I really am. I'm afraid he sees me as some unholy freak of nature."

"And what if he finds out about us?"

"I'll figure that out when the time comes. Vir acts like everything's fine, but he still grieves for a girl who gave him her virginity on the other side of the world. I'm not her anymore." Sorcha pretended to study the drapes.

"No, you aren't. You're Lady Sorcha of House Banitierre. Be proud of who you are and don't ever forget it." Rayna swept Sorcha's unruly hair aside, kneeling behind her and enveloping her in an embrace. "I promise I'll treat him as one of our own family. If you love him, he must be special. For you, I can and will do anything."

"Doesn't seem fair." Familiar tears were close to breaking through again.

"Life is seldom fair, but this is my choice. Please don't cry anymore. Think about something else. What makes you smile?"

"Right now?" *Nothing.*

"Come on, how about the Masquerade?"

"I hear we're going to Steven's place tonight for fittings. Does he dictate everything, like the Gala?"

Rayna rolled Sorcha back into bed, pinning both her hands against the sheets and kissing her lips with the softness of butterfly wings. "Almost. He rules the wardrobe detail with an iron fist. The gowns are a beautiful canvas, but Lily's masks are the masterpieces."

Thank you Lord, or whoever answered my prayers. She didn't run away.

By midnight, Vir was neglecting the cup of coffee in his hand, completely distracted by the chaos around him. The parlor of the Marigny house had turned into masquerade fashion central. He watched as all the women were measured, re-measured, poked and prodded by a gang of tailors. "Didn't realize this party was such a production. Is all this fuss normal?"

"Steven treats every decision as a personal challenge." Sorcha tucked her legs under her on the overstuffed sofa. "He lives for all the drama and gossip surrounding the first family of New Orleans."

"Admirable." Vir's voice dropped to a whisper. "A little overboard, maybe."

"You think this is nuts? You should see him giving dance lessons."

Steven huffed loudly. "Okay, you two. Do you think I'm deaf? Vir, get up. I need measurements. Kindly put the cold coffee down before you slop it all over my fabric." Steven turned his attention to choosing an appropriate outfit for a human at a vampire party.

Traditionally, the men wore classic tuxedos and basic black masks, with the exception of the elders, who often hid their faces behind family heirlooms. Masquerade style had changed over the centuries, but jewel tones and glitter were still reserved for the ladies.

Sorcha didn't know what she expected, but the masks were beyond anything she imagined. There were so many variations to pick from, all of them uniquely beautiful. A black velvet work of art drew her in. The lace patterned edges were adorned with deep blue sapphires. Delicate filigree on the right side extended up and down, covering part of her cheek and forehead. "I want this one."

"Are we geniuses or what?" Lily flipped her hair back. "That was actually Steven's design."

"Because?" Steven tapped his ear.

Lily couldn't hide her smirk. "He knows you best."

"And howl!" Steven pumped his fist in the air.

Raimond surprised everyone as he swept into the room, peeking over shoulders and murmuring his approval. "I assume my tuxedo will be pressed and hanging in my closet by Thursday?"

"Yes. I know how to delegate." Steven snorted and plucked his champagne off the table. "Honestly."

"Excellent. Everyone will dress at the penthouse and return there afterward. I've secured the lower floors so we'll have plenty of space. Promptly at sunset the following night, we'll leave for Normandie Hall. This is my favorite party of the year, but unfortunately I can't stay to help with makeup and jewelry." Raimond turned his attention to the only human in the room. "Ashayle, let's take a walk."

Vir rose and followed the master vampire across the Marigny. Raimond stopped on the French Quarter side of Esplanade and pointed to a vacant block. "See that?"

"Dead grass?" Vir asked.

"Avoid it like the plague. I know for a fact bodies are buried there and they've never floated up."

"Real bodies?" Vir ran to catch up.

"I've made a decision, doctor. The danger of leaving you here alone is far greater than bringing you along. After the festivities, you'll accompany us to the plantation."

"I appreciate the invitation." Vir staggered on the banquette, hands on his knees, out of breath. "But what do I tell Sisters of the Peace?"

"I'm in charge. Don't tell them anything. You're missing so often, most likely nobody will notice. Make no mistake, this is less of an invitation and more of an obligation." Raimond stopped abruptly in front of Vir's apartment building. "Pack your crap. You don't live here anymore."

"Don't I have any say—"

"No." Raimond aimed his finger at Vir's face. "And at this party, don't engage with anyone who isn't...us."

Draven cranked down the limousine window and inhaled. "There's just something about this city. She wraps her arms around you like an old flame." Tired of waiting, he kicked the door open and jumped over the gutter. "Ronald!"

"I thought you were sick of New Orleans, Your Highness?"

"I was more than a bit annoyed after my soldiers lost Sorcha and Vir in the alleys, but we've moved past that ugliness. And I got to fire people."

"As your new chief of security, I assure you that past mistakes have been corrected." Ronald picked up the luggage. "You're still planning to attend the Masquerade Ball?"

"I replaced the board of directors and arranged the whole thing myself. I'm hosting the damn party."

"I thought you said it was boring and predictable?"

"That's why I've changed the location to a trendy club." Draven stopped in the lobby and stared at Ronald. "Do you memorize every word I say?"

"It's my job, sir. What about the orchestra?"

"We'll have the traditional pageantry at the beginning of the evening, but I booked that Barwick fellow to entertain after midnight."

Ronald hit the elevator button. "The old ones won't like it."

"Ancient stiffs. They need to understand that youth and change is as important to the survival of the vampire species as are history and ritual."

"I heard gossip that Barwick got Sorcha to perform quite a solo number this past summer."

Draven punched his soldier's arm. "I'm hoping for an encore."

Chapter 53

MASQUERADE

SUNSET GRACED MASQUERADE night with bold streaks of red and purple across the sky. At the Banitierre's Canal Street apartment, staff members worked furiously. Freshly pressed gowns and tuxedos were delivered, and last-minute alterations completed.

Sorcha blinked her eyes open. *Coffee.* She caressed the empty pillow and sheets next to her. Vir finished moving out of his Lafayette Square apartment the day before and was tucked away on the floor below. As excited as she was about tonight's affair, Sorcha couldn't wait to spend time with him at romantic Normandie Hall.

"Ladies, hair and makeup—pronto!" Steven barked orders and pushed everyone in the proper directions. "Gentlemen, get dressed and get out of the way."

"Need coffee." Sorcha shuffled into the kitchen.

Julia peered past the drapes and up at the sky.

"Not a drop of rain in sight." Steven fluffed her long blonde hair.

"Says you." Julia held her palm out the window.

"Might pour tomorrow." He snapped his fingers at the hairdresser. "But a chin length bob would be smashing for tonight."

Sorcha lifted the china cup to her lips. "Where's my dress?"

"In Raimond's room, oversleeper." Steven shooed her down the hall.

"Raimond?" Sorcha knocked on the open door. "You in here?"

She found her black dress hanging in the cherry armoire. She traced her fingers over the fitted waist and slightly flared skirt, embroidered with platinum beads and crystals. "If you think this is too short, it's Steven's design. Where in the world are you?"

Sorcha hooked the dress hanger over her finger and peeked into the empty bathroom. She inhaled warm spicy fragrance. *Where is that scent coming from?* She followed her nose to a bottle in the trash. *This is full—*

"Sorcha!" Steven barged in. "Your shoes."

"Stilettos?" Sorcha jammed the cologne bottle into her bathrobe pocket.

"Long legs. Daring hemlines." Steven pointed from her feet to her head. "Signature blue highlights. Move!"

Sorcha scampered back to her room and hid Raimond's cologne in the back of her linen closet. *Now, I'm worried. Why would he throw that whole bottle away?* Her mind wandered while the hairdresser twisted, teased and secured her locks with invisible pins. The dress was deliberately understated so all the focus would be on the sapphires and sparkle of the black lace mask.

"My God, you're magnificent!" Vir stood frozen in the bedroom doorway.

"You're pretty handsome yourself," Sorcha said. "Did Steven choose the silver dress shirt?"

"Of course he did, to show off his skin and striking eyes." Rayna arrived in the chamber, holding a scarlet mask trimmed with black ribbon.

Sorcha touched Vir's elbow. "This is my best friend Rayna. Rayna, Dr. Vir Ashayle."

Vir lifted her hand to his lips like a perfect gentleman. "I think I remember you from the green door club, and then my apartment?"

"That would be me. You're looking well. Ready for this party?"

Sorcha's gaze darted between Vir and Rayna.

"Hope so," Vir said. "Not sure what to expect."

"I heard a rumor that Martin is performing tonight." Sorcha drifted back to fuss in front of the mirror.

274

"By the prince's formal invitation, I'm told." Rayna gave Sorcha a subtle wink and a handful of jeweled bangles. "Wear them all, the more the better."

Steven rapped on the door. "Masks on—time to go!"

Elegantly attired party guests spilled out of every building. The crowd grew louder and tighter as they funneled through the narrow streets. Security created a visible barrier between the first family and less trusted covens while additional soldiers guarded them from stealthy tactical positions.

Sorcha sensed Vir shrinking from the vibe that hung like electric haze in the air. She hooked her arm through his elbow. "Stick close. You have me and an army of bodyguards. Plus, this is supposed to be fun."

"Even after years of medical school in London, I've never attended something this fancy. These people are pretty intimidating. I feel like a bug about to get squashed by a tank."

"That's a normal reaction. I'm still getting used to it myself."

"Some of these masks are spooky. A few are downright ugly. What if I lose you?"

"You won't. Concentrate on your sense of smell." Sorcha stepped close enough to Vir to feel his muscles twitch. The masks played tricks on the eyes, but their bodies had memories of their own.

"You're wearing my favorite perfume."

She offered the pale skin of her throat to his lips. "Take a deep breath and hold onto it all night." *He's too shy to kiss me in this chaos.*

"Come on, lovebirds. Steven is waving us through the invisible door in the wall again." Rayna grabbed the couple's hands and dragged them through the private entrance.

The big room gleamed with decadence, decorated with hurricane lamps and twinkling lights in all the vibrant colors of autumn. The orchestra occupied every square inch of the elevated stage. Later tonight the place would transform into a seductive party, but for now it was an elegant ballroom, complete with strains of civilized music and small talk.

Sorcha tugged on Rayna's blouse. "When do I have to dance?"

"The first number is ceremonial, executed by the leaders of prominent families," Rayna said. "As a Banitierre, you'll join the couples on the floor after the formal segment is complete."

"That's an incredible relief." Sorcha spun back to face Vir. "I forgot to ask you one important thing."

"What's that, beautiful girl?"

"Do you know how to waltz?"

Decked out in their best disguises, the Victoires joined the throng entering the Warehouse Club through a narrow alley. Security guards used the opportunity to inspect each guest.

"Those goons better not lay one filthy finger on me, Cole. They treat us like common criminals and get away with it. Doesn't it infuriate you?" Danielle ran her hands over her red dress and readjusted the silver ribbons on her mask.

"You're lucky to be invited, and I'm quite sure no one will think you're hiding anything beneath that outfit," Cole said. "The seamstress must have been short on fabric because it's borderline obscene."

"So you keep reminding me. Yet you enjoy what's under it on a regular basis." She shook free of her escort as soon as they entered the club. "I'm getting a drink. You're on your own."

"I assume you'll make yourself available for the first dance? Or shall I find another partner?"

"Oh don't worry, I'll be ready. It's an honor to be on the dance floor with these snobs, right?"

"It's a party, Danielle. Try to have some fun."

The Victoires staked their claim in a prime spot for the opening festivities. With her friends watching, Danielle threw back several shots of vodka before picking up her martini glass and turning to face the room.

Kettly sipped her first drink slowly, struggling to see past the fringe of her mask. "You need to take it easy with the booze. Nervous about dancing with Cole?" She glanced at Nicholas who gritted his teeth and spun away.

"I'm getting loosened up. What are you two, my damn babysitters?" Half of Danielle's martini sloshed from the glass when a stranger collided with her arm. "What the hell is your problem?"

"My apologies, miss—I'll buy you another."

"You'd better." Danielle blotted her dress with a napkin. "Sap."

"Hold on there." The stranger motioned for a fresh drink. "We've gotten off poorly. Let's start over. I'm Lock. Your name is?"

"Danielle. If this is your pickup technique—lousy."

"I overheard you chatting with your date on the way in."

"So, you're an eavesdropper too? Enchanting."

"Now, don't give me the glassy eye. You weren't exactly whispering. Fight with him often?"

"We disagree on a few things. I hate people." Danielle faked interest in her martini as she snuck a better look at Lock's chestnut hair and pale eyes. "Your accent, is it English?"

"Australian." Lock tilted his head and flaunted a bright white smile. "Now, who do you hate?"

"See those two over there?" Danielle pointed at Sorcha and Vir.

"They look positively…well dressed and…awful." Lock's head shake turned into a nod. "I'm sure they're just hideous once you get to know them." His eyes lingered on a man behind the couple. "Who's that bloke?"

"The one ordering everyone around? Steven Banitierre. Nobody cares about him. But that bitch and her boyfriend—I'd love nothing more than to kill her and suck him dry."

"Such violence from a beautiful creature."

"I'm not known for my friendly disposition."

"Well, I'm famous for making dodgy choices, and following rules bores me to tears." Lock looked into the crowd and back to Danielle. "Maybe I can help make your wishes come true."

All voices in the room hushed in anticipation. Only the faint clinking of crystal and rustling of gowns could be heard as Prince Norman emerged from draped velvet curtains. Striding to the center of the stage, he swept his royal gaze across the masked crowd.

"Ladies and gentleman, I can see you've pulled out all the stops for our lavish Masquerade. Is everyone ready to dance the night away?" The prince raised his arms to acknowledge cheers and applause. "Excellent. Maestro, whenever you're ready." He descended the stairs to join the revelers. The orchestra began to crescendo as honored couples made their way to the dance floor, each man and woman taking their places in a long line.

Steven nudged Sorcha. "Watch carefully. Someday, you'll be expected to participate."

Although they were works of art, the masks were also highly effective disguises. Only Sorcha's closest friends were recognizable, but she easily picked Raimond out of the troupe by the seductive way his body responded to the music. *There's no substitute for first-hand experience.*

Raimond chose Marie to be his partner and share in the honor of the formal dance. From their comfort and precision, Sorcha assumed this was not their first time together in the spotlight. Placing their palms together without touching, the couples executed steps around an invisible axis, eyes locked in concentration. They seamlessly switched hands and directions, finishing the sequence face to face, both hands up and only the slimmest margin between them.

Damn, sexy dance.

As the couples joined their right hands, Sorcha focused on Draven's blond hair and the heartbeat at the end of his outstretched arm. "Steven, who is the prince's date? Don't recognize her."

"Gwynevere, she's new. One of the priestesses from his private island, maybe?"

"Sounds so medieval. Is King Arthur here too?"

"Who knows, but the lady can dance. They must practice—dancing, I mean." Steven forced his face straight. "Are you and Vir ready?"

"Hope so." Sorcha fidgeted with her bracelets. "You'll tell us when?" *They're all so perfect. Were Raimond and I that glamorous when we swept through the white ballroom?*

The couples on the floor began a formal waltz.

"There's your cue. Vir, give me that damn drink. Couldn't wait until later?" Steven held out his palm. "Nervous?"

"What's the matter, Steven?" Vir asked. "Jealous?"

"Don't worry, I'll be there to pick up the pieces when you fall on your ass."

Sorcha looked back and forth between the men in disbelief as she tugged on Vir's sleeve.

Steven's worries were unwarranted. After draining his drink and handing over the empty glass, Vir assumed charge.

"May I have this waltz, Lady Sorcha?" He held his partner's hand high and locked his brown eyes onto hers.

"You may, Dr. Ashayle." Sorcha didn't even have to think about the steps as he led, whirling her in the classic pattern while expertly navigating the crowded floor. *Apparently he learned something other than medicine in England.* At the end of each box step Sorcha felt her hips swing. Nothing registered to her senses but the intoxicating scent of Vir's skin, his smoldering eyes and perfectly trained movements. The music ended to a deafening ovation. *Could've stayed lost in that waltz forever.*

Raimond patiently waited his turn to speak to Sorcha, finally kissing her on both cheeks. "To answer your question—yes, it was that glamorous when we danced at Normandie Hall, but your current partner seems more than capable." He nodded toward Vir, leaning on the bar, chatting with Jeffrey.

I left my mind wide open for Raimond to read, again.

Raimond excused himself as Sorcha received her favorite drink from a waiter's hand.

Cocktails flowed freely as the hours flew by. More and more, Vir looked at home in the company of the Banitierre family and friends. He even danced with Rayna. Both Steven and Raimond warned Sorcha to be cautious and vigilant, as the formal portion of the affair was almost over and many of the elders and their security teams were departing for private dinner parties. Avoiding Draven had been a daunting, all-night mission, and Sorcha almost lost the battle when the band struck up a familiar tango.

Not again.

The prince's steel eyes pierced through the room until Rayna stepped up. Everyone present took a subconscious step back as the professional dancer and the dashing monarch commanded the empty floor.

Chapter 54

AFTER MIDNIGHT

SORCHA MET RAYNA at the bar when the music ended. "You saved my night. The tango didn't end well last time."

"Anything for you. He actually asked me to apologize for his bad manners."

"Is he serious about that new lady?"

"I don't know. She's odd and he's unpredictable. Enough of him, Martin's up next." Rayna rubbed her hands together. "Time for the fun part."

"Come on, let's get a good spot!" Sorcha dragged Vir and Rayna to the center of the packed dance floor.

Barwick and his band burst out amid white smoke and a drumroll as the clock struck midnight. He looked every bit the eccentric entertainer in his carved leather coat and flowing, black hair.

"Happy Halloween, ladies and gentleman! What a fine, fine crowd. I know it's gettin' hot in here, but let me see you all with your masks on for just one number. All right, all right, let's blow the roof off this joint!"

The music was as dynamic as Sorcha remembered, and tonight it had an extra kick: Since the band had become so popular, the entire orchestra of classical musicians requested to play the remainder of the evening in accompaniment.

Bold and dominating, the piano rattled crystals on every chandelier.

Sorcha's new favorite lyrics were saved for the final encore. The closing song recounted a love so strong that it was blind, unconditional and eternally forgiving. One heart was kind and innocent, the other evil and black, both joined as a united force against the cruel world. Vir and Sorcha swayed to the seductive music, fully occupying each other's personal space.

The words hit home with him too.

Sorcha used her prime position on the dance floor to draw Martin's energy. He acknowledged her and nodded his approval of Vir, who danced most of the night with his arms wrapped around her waist and his face buried in her hair.

Martin is a believer and the macabre significance of this night is not lost on him. Sorcha absorbed the pleasure he took in commanding the spotlight of the masked vampire ball, on the eve of the most haunted night of the year, in the heart of the spookiest square mile in the world.

After the final notes faded, the humans needed sleep and their vampire companions craved blood. A handsome stranger approached Sorcha, tripped over his own feet and dumped a glass of red wine onto her dress. He apologized with a distinctive accent. In the bottleneck of the club's exit, her friends and bodyguards were distracted long enough for the world to unravel.

Vir dropped his drink as a vampire flashed in front of him. Her lips curled inches away from his ear.

"Hello handsome, I've wanted to tap those exotic veins since the first time I laid eyes on you."

"Danielle." Sorcha lunged toward the confrontation, restrained by security. "Let me go—she'll kill him!"

Screams echoed throughout the club as celebration ceased, fangs were bared and battle lines drawn.

The attacker's red dress split up the seam as she grabbed Vir by the hair. Danielle licked her lips as her eyes left his pulsing artery and wandered down his body. "This was much too easy." Her break in concentration gave Rayna a few seconds to wrench Vir out of the way. She flung him to the side and planted herself in front of angry fangs that tore full force into her neck, driving her to her knees.

"Rayna!" Sorcha recognized another face mired in the frenzied crowd. "Nicholas? And you called my family bullies."

"I swear I didn't know she was planning this, Sorcha," Nicholas answered.

"The whole Victoire family is trash." Sorcha fought against impenetrable blockade of killers in expensive clothes. "Won't anyone stop her?"

The few humans still in attendance dropped to the floor to avoid bolts of electricity bouncing between the walls. Members of the royal security force reacted, but too little, too late.

"Foolish little twit." Danielle's eyes turned a lethal red. "You ruined my perfect moment." Even with all the Banitierre resources hell bent on rescuing her, Rayna would have been dead if Draven hadn't stepped in.

The prince whisked Rayna away from her attacker, tossed her to Raimond and inserted himself in the line of fire. "Go ahead, bitch. Try and bite me."

Danielle's rage shattered like a pane of glass, replaced by terror.

"That's what I thought." With one hand, Draven lifted Danielle up by her neck. "Get this straight, little coward. Attacks on my clan— humans included—are not tolerated." One flick of his wrist sent her hurtling across the room before he turned his attention to the head of the Victoire coven. "Cole, this troublemaker will not show her face at any of my functions for several years—make it forty. If she does, I'll make a gruesome example out of her, and you."

Royal secret service pushed the family to a fleet of black sedans behind the club. Sorcha managed to make eye contact with Steven, Julia and Lily as they were stuffed into the first limousine. Crushed between Vir and Rayna, she struggled to inspect her friend's wound. "Your neck is destroyed, and still bleeding."

"I'm so cold," Rayna sighed. "Can you turn the lights on in here?"

"Those aren't good signs." Vir shed his jacket, tearing off what was left of the sleeve to hold pressure on Rayna's neck. "I know Raimond gave her a good dose of blood during that commotion. Why isn't this healed by now?"

Without considering her audience, Sorcha sliced an artery and let Rakshasa blood run directly into Rayna's ragged wounds. Like magic, the edges of her skin started to knit together. "That's more like it. You saved Vir—I don't even know how to thank you."

"Told you I'd treat him like family." Rayna's smile flickered.

"I thought you meant passing him a casserole at the dinner table."

"Since the three of us are alone, I need to ask. Sorcha, have you..." Rayna cleared her throat and rubbed the fading scar on her neck. "Did you drink from Vir yet?"

"No, never. I thought I wasn't supposed to—Steven said."

"Forget what Steven said. Being the first to drink his blood is as fierce a connection as taking someone's virginity. If you don't do it, somebody else will. Unless you're opposed, Vir?"

"I've been begging for weeks. I want to be a part of her, to share everything." Vir ripped open the collar of his dress shirt, exposing bare skin.

Sorcha cringed against the window, wishing she could climb out and run.

"Maybe we should start with something a bit less extreme. Vir, give me your hand." After ensuring that the car's privacy curtain was tightly closed, Rayna pulled a pin from her hair, sending her tresses tumbling around her shoulders in waves. Expertly, she pierced his palm, allowing bubbles of blood to seep to the surface. "Sorcha, get in here."

Transfixed by the rivulet that ran across her lover's hand, Sorcha inhaled the fresh scent of life. Vir's heartbeat slammed in her ears like a bass drum. When she looked up, the fire from her eyes tinged everything blue. "Are you sure?"

Vir's fingers trembled. "Sure as I've ever been."

Dropping her lips to his palm, Sorcha licked the droplets already outside his skin. Becoming braver, she closed her lips around the small puncture and drew elixir from his body. Vir groaned with pleasure.

This blood, his blood—delicious. Sorcha scared herself as delicate sipping turned into a cruel gulp. *Damn.* Using the car seat for support she dragged herself away and buried her face in her hair.

"I want to go one step farther." Vir dabbed at his wound. "I want to drink from you too, like Rayna does."

"How do you even—"

"That we are not doing in the car." Rayna expertly tucked the pin back into her hair as the black sedan screeched to a stop. "There'll be plenty of time at Normandie Hall to work everything out. Vir, this stays between us."

He nodded his head.

Only one drop of Sorcha's blood was necessary to seal the hole in Vir's palm, as if nothing ever happened.

Sorcha gritted her teeth. "I really loathe Danielle."

Outside the Warehouse Club, Cole dragged Danielle relentlessly through an early morning thunderstorm. "I warned you, time and time again, to stop antagonizing the Banitierres. What the hell were you thinking?"

"I just hate that bitch so much—I lost my mind." Danielle sobbed and staggered toward their sorry limousine.

"Well, now you can hate them from another continent. We can't risk pissing off Prince Norman again. I'm sending you to Europe for a few years, until things cool down here."

"Are you kidding? What are we going to do in Europe?"

"Not we—you. I have associates in Paris. You can stay with them, but if you don't behave, you'll be sleeping in the street. My home is New Orleans and I can't overthrow Duke Raimond from France."

Chapter 55

Happy Halloween

BEFORE THE FIRST rays of sun peeked above the horizon, the penthouse doors and windows were locked and shrouded against the outside world.

After Steven convinced Rayna to eat breakfast and take a long bath, Vir carried her to bed for some precious sleep. "Her wounds are completely healed. Still amazing to watch that happen."

"She should have healed much faster." Steven shuffled out the door and popped back in. "Watch her, Ashayle."

Vir checked and rechecked the site where the enemy tore Rayna's flesh open. The only evidence of trauma was a faint, pink splotch.

"I recall you lost some blood too." Sorcha curled up on Vir's lap with a soft blanket. The overstuffed chair at the foot of the bed was a perfect spot for them to watch Rayna while she slept.

"I feel fine and closer to you than ever. In spite of the ending, I had a fantastic evening. The music, the dancing and then what transpired in the car was purely intoxicating."

"In a few short hours we'll be at Normandie Hall. I can't wait to dance with you in that ballroom." Sorcha rested her head on Vir's shoulder.

"When will you allow me to drink from you? I'm not giving up, you know."

"When Rayna is strong enough to help us and I'm sure we have complete privacy. Our blood is strong and addictive. I've heard it compared to heroin—tried that?"

"Ah, no. I rarely even take an aspirin."

"For that reason alone, we need to be careful."

Vir lowered his lips to Sorcha's forehead, leaving a soft trail of kisses down her cheek until he reached her mouth. "Sleep now, sweet girl. Sunset will be here before you know it."

Confident that security around the Canal Street compound was impenetrable, the duke and the prince conducted a royal summit at the Warehouse Club. Still dressed in their tuxedos, the men approached each other across the deserted dance floor, neither anxious to speak first.

Raimond broke the standoff, offering mismatched glasses with one hand and a full bottle of a rare, blood whisky with the other. "There's been ugliness between us recently, but I need to thank you for stepping in and saving Rayna. She would have been dead long before I broke through that crowd. I'm not sure any of us could have changed her. That girl's so accustomed to vampire blood, she may have developed some resistance."

"There's no way I'd allow that miserable little troll to kill Rayna. My history with her is far too precious." Draven accepted the liquor. "That Victoire female caused serious damage. If there wasn't such a judgmental audience, I would have simply ended her and erased the whole problem."

"Sorcha and Danielle have had run-ins before."

"I recall something about a fight and a broken arm. She's no match for Sorcha and she knows it, so she went after Vir. In any case, I've made sure she won't be a bother for a good while. It would be best to keep your family in this hemisphere for the next few years."

"She's been banished to Europe?"

"Paris, specifically," Draven said.

"My hell on earth." Raimond downed the entire contents of his glass in one swallow. "Don't worry, I won't be tempted to visit."

"So, you're locking your entire clan down at Normandie Hall in honor of Halloween? Again."

"Still the safest option." Raimond grimaced as he slammed another glass of whisky.

"And Ashayle, how long are you planning to let that fool remain human?"

Raimond turned to face the empty hall. "I don't want to take away anyone's choice. Reputable sources have told me he doesn't want to be changed."

"That's very noble of you, but I believe you're thinking with your heart, not your head. Often a fatal mistake." Draven loosened his tie as he drained his glass. "This is unique and tasty. My compliments."

"I admit, I've disliked Ashayle since I met him. Still blame him for everything that's gone wrong, though clearly it's not all his fault."

"He's a nuisance, yet here he is, living large and painting the town red with a lady that you and I both adore. Remind me again Raimond, why is he still breathing?"

"Because Sorcha loves him. If I've learned anything in the last century, it's that trying to manipulate true love backfires every time."

"His humanity is a dangerous liability to all of us, specifically your coven." Draven placed his empty tumbler on the edge of the dark stage and drifted toward the door. "He'll have to be dealt with sooner rather than later. You know it and I know it."

Raimond watched Draven leave and slumped to the floor, suddenly alone in the deafening silence of the abandoned warehouse. Tossing the glass aside, he swigged whisky directly from the bottle. Strewn around him were discarded remnants of last night's festivities. Glitter, streamers, stray beer bottles and a large bloodstain offered a glimpse into how quickly celebration could turn into tragedy. The path ahead was crooked at best, treacherous and deadly at worst. Blood would be spilled, and hearts were bound to break.

Your heart is already broken, soldier. Happy Halloween.

Chapter 56

NEW YEAR

BOTH DOCTORS IN the penthouse examined Rayna and proclaimed her healthy enough to travel.

Steven fussed from the time she opened her eyes, continuing relentlessly as the caravan exited New Orleans city limits, bound for the safety of the country fortress. As per his instructions, the family dressed in subdued colors more appropriate for a funeral than a holiday.

Sorcha had described Normandie Hall to Vir in great detail, but words would never do the estate justice. She kept a close watch on his face, anxious to catch the reaction to his first glimpse through the tree canopy.

"This the place?" Vir asked.

Instead of the budding flowers and twinkling lights of spring, the house had taken on a sinister aura. The windows and galleries were dark except for the glow from countless jack-o-lanterns, staring into the night like miniature sentries. A line of fire encircled the entire compound. Unseen forces dropped the flames down just long enough for the parade of cars to snake past.

Witches.

At Raimond's command, the shield of fire rose, flames soaring into the sky, sealing them off from the outside world.

"Very impressive, but not the sparkling castle you described.

Imposing would be more accurate." Vir joined hands with Sorcha as they crossed the threshold into the soaring foyer.

"Dr. Ashayle, welcome to Normandie Hall. I'm DeLynch, I'm in charge of the staff here. If there is anything we can do to make your stay more enjoyable, please let me know."

"Thank you, Mr. DeLynch."

"Penny, Lady Sorcha's personal maid, will be your attendant. I've been informed you'll be dining with the family this evening. It's essential that you only eat and drink what Penny serves you, sir." DeLynch nodded and disappeared.

Sorcha responded to Vir's raised eyebrow. "Humans don't usually join us for dinner. You can't eat or drink most of what's on the menu. Here's Penny now—you'll like her. Very sweet."

"Dr. Ashayle, your wine, sir." Penny delivered a crystal glass on a polished silver tray.

"Thank you, Penny. Please call me Vir."

"Yes, sir, Dr. Vir." With a quick smile she returned to the kitchen.

"What can I say, it's formal here." Sorcha led Vir into the low-lit front parlor. She greeted family members and made the necessary introductions, but only part of her attention remained on them. The wall of flames reflected in the jeweled mirrors was visible from every corner of every room.

"Don't look so afraid, Sorcha. The fire is there to protect you."

"But em, Steven, don't you see the people?"

"What?"

Sorcha pointed to the fire's edge. "I just saw hundreds, all carrying gold weapons."

"You're imagining things." Steven took Sorcha's drink and waved it under his nose. "No more of this...or that." He stuck his tongue out at a piece of floating fruit.

"What, exactly, is the aversion to lemons?" Sorcha asked.

Steven nodded his head toward the back parlor. "He hates them."

"Dr. Ashayle, a moment please?" Raimond beckoned from the open doors. "Sorcha, I'd like to speak with you also." The latch clicked shut behind them. "Vir, I just want to make it absolutely clear that you will not be sharing a room with Sorcha under my roof. Appropriate accommodations will be provided in one of our guest cottages. I'm not a fool—you're both consenting adults. What you do at night is your own business, but during the hours between sunrise and sunset, you are not permitted on the second floor of this house. Am I understood?"

"Yes, sir."

"I assume you've been instructed on what to eat and drink in a mansion full of vampires?"

"Only what Penny serves me," Vir said. "Sir."

"That's correct. Vomiting on my antique furniture is not acceptable." Without looking back, Raimond threw the doors open and strode out in the direction of the dining room, tossing back his whisky on the way.

"He has a thing about his antiques," Sorcha whispered. "No throwing up tonight."

Vir swallowed a mouthful of wine. "Always a sound plan."

After the meal was cleared, guests gathered and milled in the foyer.

"Did you enjoy dinner?" Sorcha was happy to see that the staff had taken her suggestions and prepared one of Vir's favorites, seafood gumbo with shrimp and crab accompanied by a hunk of fresh French bread.

"It was delicious. I wasn't revolted by your dinner either. I know I was being watched." Vir's eyes crinkled with a smile as he accepted the next glass of wine from Penny.

Another waiter appeared with goblets for the undead guests. "For the toast, Lady Sorcha."

"This clock." Vir stepped closer and peered under black fabric that draped the face. "So intricate. It shows the phases of the moon."

Steven swept past with Lily firmly in his grasp. "Come on, it's almost midnight. Ballroom's open."

"Lady Sorcha." Vir offered his arm.

"Dr. Ashayle." Sorcha tucked her right hand comfortably into his elbow as they blended into the wave of guests.

In spite of the dark and creepy atmosphere, the ballroom couldn't help but shimmer. The chandeliers remained dark, leaving the task of illuminating the room to strategically placed candles and the flickering glow thrown from the fire. At precisely midnight, silence fell over the crowd that had grown to include servants, security guards and blood donors who called Normandie Hall their home.

Twelve chimes rang from the grand clock in the foyer.

Raimond lifted the ceremonial goblet high above his head, turning his eyes to the muted colors of the skylight. "In memory and tribute to all that have gone before us, all that have contributed to the success and strength of our coven, your sacrifices in life and death will never be forgotten. To the Banitierres!"

"To the Banitierres!" Every soul in the packed room responded as one.

With his official duties complete, Raimond watched the gathering from a far corner of the empty gallery. Instead of the constant interruption of servants, he opted to bring bottles of liquor upstairs and pour for himself.

Listening closely, he heard Sorcha questioning Julia. *It's her first Halloween as a member of this family, and Banitierre traditions differ greatly from other covens.* The mournful strains of the string quartet were a stark contrast to the wild excess taking place in the French Quarter tonight. The underworld treated this holiday as a free-for-all, but Raimond preferred to use it as a time of reflection. Most considered vampires to be the top of a vicious food chain, administrators of unspeakable bloodshed and damage. *Nobody considers how much tragedy we endure—the death of our own kind and the slaughter of innocent friends and family.*

As an original member of his coven and second in command, Julia was entrusted with the job of conveying to young associates the importance of their ancestors' sacrifices, along with the wisdom not to repeat mistakes of the past. Whether they believed it or not, Sorcha and Vir's romance drew uncomfortable parallels to prior catastrophes.

Emily, my darling, this tribute is my best effort to honor your memory, but it doesn't bring you back. Raimond set the tumbler on the floor and rubbed his eyes. *Every time that damn clock chimes, my heart shatters a little more. I need to stop drinking before I'm sobbing like a lonely fool in my own ballroom.*

Tomorrow at midnight, the day of remembrance would end. The shield of flames would disappear, and the mansion would shed the cloak of gloom and be resurrected to her sparkling glory.

New Year's Day at Normandie Hall was the first day of November.

Chapter 57

BEDLAM

FAMILY TRADITION OR not, Draven wasn't about to waste another Halloween marooned in the countryside, pining for lost loves or reopening ancient wounds. Supernatural energy soared from the streets in waves, visible, palpable and intoxicating. His party on the rooftop terrace offered a stunning view of the French Quarter and beyond while eliminating the risk of being down there, in the bedlam.

The guest list included a representative from every officially recognized vampire and witch's coven in the South. The Caribbean contingent had shown up in full force, carrying musical instruments, bearing gifts of spice and rum and lending their accents to the buzz of conversation. Hundreds of floating candles made the swimming pool glisten in front of Draven's favorite steel drum band.

"Love the island flair, Your Highness." Ronald let the way as Draven navigated a line of guests.

Tonight, rules against feeding in public were ignored citywide. The only thing that flowed more freely than blood was sex. On the elegantly lit deck, vampires drank openly from their own dates and a variety of escorts provided by the royal house.

"Just get me past this insufferable crowd," Draven hissed through his formal smile. "Gwyn is waiting for me. I'm parched."

He had spent the hours before sunset surrounded by naked women, exquisite specimens whose sole occupation was to please him in every way. Knowing his legendary, carnal drives, the staff procured a supply of human flesh to satisfy him. Unlike other celebrations, this year the harem was mainly window dressing, since one woman had become the monarch's favorite lover.

"You've been a different man since that freak storm washed Miss Gwynevere up on your beach," Ronald said.

"Swimming the channels of Norman Island." Draven chuckled. "A bizarre notion of fun." He had been so preoccupied by Sorcha that he hadn't paid much attention to who was right under his nose. Gwyn did everything he asked of her, including allowing him unrestricted sexual freedom to enjoy whatever and whomever he pleased, without the slightest hint of jealousy.

"Have you decided what to tell your family?" Ronald asked. "About her lack of traceable lineage, I mean?"

"I'll worry about that when the time comes." Draven shook the last guest's hand and nodded to the massive men guarding a hidden staircase. "Take your pick of the humans. I'll have no further use for them."

Lush tropical plants and lavish furniture decorated the oasis under a crisp autumn moon and stars. "My Gwynevere." Draven took her delicate hand, fully intending to kiss it like a gentleman, sweeping her off her feet and into the fierce grip of his arms instead. One lightning motion propelled them both across the deck and into a mountain of pillows. Pressing his body against hers, he made sure she felt every rippling and hardening muscle. He tangled his hands in the dark waves of her waist-length hair, pulling her mouth to his. "You have me all to yourself—no more orgies. I sent the females away. I desire you and only you."

"Not females." A sly smile curved Gwyn's full lips. "We're women."

"Very well woman, I can't promise I'll always be gentle, but I guarantee you'll be satisfied."

Gwyn groaned under his demanding kiss as he pinned her hands behind her back.

Draven's lips drifted from her mouth to the bounding pulse of her neck, lingering to inhale her scent and driving himself wild before his fangs even broke the skin. He was tender until the first drops of blood filled his mouth and then he threw caution to the wind, locking his jaws into her flesh like a predator, draining her to the point that she almost lost consciousness. "Drink from me now, my love. You'll be better than new."

Gwyn's eyes glowed with the strength of a thousand humans as she licked her lips for every trace of royal elixir. The prince never broke contact with his lover's skin, caressing her face and holding her hand obsessively. Suspecting nothing amiss, he dipped his head to receive a message from Ronald. His face froze and the atmosphere transformed in an instant.

"Danielle is still bloody here?"

"She's killed six tourists on the Canal Street pier."

Draven pointed to soldiers standing guard at the wall. "Find that bitch and deliver her to the house on the corner—alive! Cole Victoire, too."

"Right away, Your Highness."

"Gwyn, sweetheart, I hate to leave, but one particular coven is a never-ending source of irritation for me. I'll be back by sunrise and I expect you naked and waiting in my bed."

"Of course, my prince, but stay close to your bodyguards. The streets are treacherous."

Ronald let out a low whistle when he saw Royal Street packed with vampires, zombies, witches and creatures that only crawled out of the swamp for wicked occasions. All watched the procession intently, leering from every rooftop and doorway. "Any tourist foolish enough to be out at this hour deserves whatever misfortune befalls them."

Danielle covered her face as she was thrown across the floor, skidding to a stop in front of the prince.

"Ms. Victoire, I ordered you out of this city."

"I leave tomorrow, Your Highness. Surely I'm allowed to feed before I'm trapped on that ship for two weeks?"

"I couldn't care less if you starve to death. Your suffering is well deserved. Oh look—your boyfriend." Draven grabbed Cole by the throat the second he was dragged into the garden. "I blame you for your own actions, Danielle, but I blame him more."

The head of the Victoire coven flailed helplessly as the prince spun him toward the center of the room, then brutally snapped his neck.

"Cole!" Danielle clawed her way across the stone floor.

"If I see your face again I'll kill him for real. Now get the hell out!"

"Cole!"

"Throw them in the river. If we get lucky, the scum will wash out into the Gulf." Draven stormed out the door and down the street. He crossed the hotel lobby loosening his tie, fully intending to relieve his frustration in the bedroom.

"Prince Norman."

The voice sent shivers up Draven's spine. He halted the guards with a flick of his wrist.

A wrinkled woman appeared from behind a column, leaning on a cane for support and squinting to focus her cloudy eyes.

"You're the Roussel witch who conducts the blessing ritual."

"Yes, Your Highness, I am. You should have killed that Victoire girl when you had the chance. This is the second time you've let her go. She will be gravely dangerous in the future."

"I wish you told me that sooner, madam." Draven fished in his pocket and handed the witch a wad of bills. "But I appreciate the warning."

Lock struggled to haul his brother away from the balcony railing. "Keep your head down, Chapal. What if the prince sees you?"

"That one is as unattractive as his brothers."

"How many Normans do you know?"

"Four, including him. All dolts. He gave your little girlfriend a rough time back there."

"Business associate—please."

"Strong choice." Chapal applauded slowly and returned his attention to the festival in the street. "Did she give you any useful information before she was strangled?"

Lock waved to the revelers and their colorful cocktails. "Apparently, the Banitierre coven abandons the city every Halloween."

"Who in their right mind would choose to miss all this?"

"So you won't complain that we have to wait around for their return?" Lock asked.

"I can survive a few more nights." Chapal held his palm out. "Got any more of those glass beads, brother?"

Chapter 58

BLOOD BANK

SORCHA LAY AWAKE for hours, stroking Rayna's hair as she slept. Vir wasn't permitted upstairs during the day, but donors had free rein and the help was far too busy maintaining the mansion to police the downstairs crowd. Aside from a brief house tour, the sheer number of vampires behind the shield of fire made privacy scarce. Vir was whisked away to his quarters a few minutes before sunrise without time for much more than a goodnight kiss. *Hope tonight is more fun.*

"Wake up, Rayna. I hear Penny in the hallway. She can't catch you in my bed." *Lovely girl, what am I going to do with you?* Since Vir and Rayna had become better acquainted, they appeared to have hit it off. *Good news, except she isn't happy.* It was evident in her eyes and undeniable in her tortured sleep. Uninterested in sex or blood, she preferred to bury her face in Sorcha's hair and hide from whatever haunted her dreams. The sleepy girl shuffled out the balcony door just as the maid entered from the hall, her silver tray piled high with pastries.

"Good evening, my lady. I've brought coffee for you and breakfast for Dr. Vir. Everything on this tray is safe for him to eat. I've pulled out dresses for tonight. After midnight there'll be a jazz band and dancing, so festive colors are appropriate. Let me know which you prefer."

Rayna offered Penny an innocent smile as they crossed paths in the bedroom doorway.

"What did you do—run around the outside of the house?" Sorcha whispered.

"Something like that. Vir will be here any second."

Vir was still admiring the upstairs décor when Sorcha opened the door. "Angel, you look beautiful this evening."

"You're too sweet. I just got up and I'm sure I'm a mess. Was your room acceptable?"

"More than that. The carriage house is like a luxury hotel."

Rayna poured coffee. "I spoke with Julia earlier. She mentioned that it might be better if Vir ate dinner downstairs with us, at least for tonight. Please, don't be offended. She's concerned that Raimond is dealing with so much adversity and drinking too much. An uncomplicated, vampires-only dinner might help."

"No offense taken. This is Raimond's home, and I don't want to cause any trouble," Vir said.

"Everything on our table is edible, always delicious and I'll have you back in the ballroom before midnight." Rayna shut the door quietly behind her.

Sorcha wandered to the balcony door, her heart twisted with guilt. "I think I have to get ready now." *What I really want is a few moments alone to think, and scream at myself.*

"Of course, I'll meet you in the parlor for drinks." Vir squeezed her hand. "Sure you're alright?"

"Yes, grand—a bit scattered." Sorcha forced a smile as Vir grabbed two croissants on his way out the door. She plucked a croissant from the tray and fought the urge to lick the crust. "Damn it!" She hurled it into fireplace and kept her thoughts hidden until she was safely under the cover of running bathwater. *Selfish and unfeeling and careless—who knows how many stupid things I've said. I'm hurting Rayna, Vir and Raimond at the same time and I've no clue how to stop.*

Somehow, Sorcha avoided smashing the bathroom mirror with a soap dish. The angry vampire reflected in the steamy glass was not a pretty sight. Her eyes were more black than blue, and very little white skin peeked out beneath dark veins. *Pull yourself together—freaking out won't help anyone.*

Right on cue, Rayna appeared in the parlor to collect Vir.

"I'll be back before you know it." Vir brushed a kiss on Sorcha's cheek.

Now I really feel incomplete.

DeLynch steered Sorcha to an empty seat, far from the place she had occupied with her date the previous evening. She was already settled, napkin across her lap and chatting with Ben and Vera when the chair to the left moved. Raimond gracefully slid in and filled the vacant space.

"Good evening." Raimond countered her blank stare with his signature smirk.

"I didn't expect to be seated next to you with all these honored ancestors in attendance. Surely someone will be insulted."

"Who cares, unless you want me to sit somewhere else?"

"No, this is perfect. May I please have some of that wine?"

Tilting his head to hide a wider grin, Raimond grabbed the full bottle.

Before they indulged, every member of the family joined hands high above the table in a solemn blessing. The surge of vampire power completed an electrical circuit that no human could have survived.

Although he was being sneaky about it, Sorcha caught Raimond peeking at her several times while he held her tiny hand in his larger one. *He looks happy and comfortable. Sending Vir downstairs with Rayna was the right decision.*

Vir fought to ignore the growling in his stomach while Rayna guided him around the dining room table, and through a litany of introductions. Once the aroma of cooking reached his nose, the names became a blur. In between bites of fried chicken and gulps of wine, he caught snippets of an argument between Rayna and her colleagues. *Fresh meat and idiots? Makes no sense.*

Rayna dropped her silverware and tossed her napkin down.

"Planning to finish that gumbo?" Vir pointed to the bowl.

"It's all yours." Rayna forced a sweet smile. Once he was mesmerized by gumbo, she snapped around to scowl at the long table. "Have a little respect for Lady Sorcha's gentleman friend. He'll never be one of you."

"What's that about Sorcha?" Vir dabbed his chin with white linen.

"Never mind, honey." Rayna pushed another plate in front of him. "Crème brulee."

After two helpings of dessert, Vir wandered to Rayna's sitting room, shed his dinner jacket and flopped on the sofa. "It's pleasant down here and incredibly quiet. I don't feel constant static frying my brain."

"That's because we're humans, unlike the volatile company upstairs." Rayna clicked the door shut.

"So, everyone at the table was part of the staff?" Vir asked.

"I'm not sure you understand, this is the blood bank..."

"Oh." Vir's face started out blank and transformed as his mind worked. "I had no idea. All of them?"

"What do you think the vampires drink?"

"Please, excuse my wacky questions. I never really considered how all of this worked. They drink from you?" Vir pointed to her neck.

"Sometimes, when it's personal. But on an everyday basis, I tap a vein." Rayna indicated the inside of her arm. "Let it flow into a pitcher, sterile and anonymous."

"You're happy?"

"For the most part. We're treated extremely well, but that vapid conversation." Rayna waved her hand in the direction of the dining room. "Sometimes, my life feels like an eternal dead end."

"How long has it been?"

"Sixty years, maybe? I stopped counting."

Vir choked on a mouthful of wine and motioned to her face. "Just from drinking their blood?"

"Potent blood. It pays to work for royalty. Remember when I tackled you at the Masquerade Ball?"

"You hit me like a tank. Your youth is astonishing, but my whole life I've been the smallest man in the room. I'd do anything to wield a force like that."

"Well, I won't even consider it 'til all this family leaves. Every year, more and more show up—it's a house full of strangers." Rayna shook out Vir's dinner jacket. "I promised Sorcha she'd be holding your hand when the clock chimed midnight."

"You look like a ravishing twenty-year-old." Vir straightened his tie and offered his arm to Rayna.

"You're quite the perfect gentleman. I can see why Sorcha is so enamored."

Vir's legs buckled halfway up the stairs. "Feels as if my hair is standing on end. Not pleasant."

"It should ease up a little when the house is less crowded," Rayna said. "Vampire energy never really goes away though, so get used to it."

The ballroom was already open and swarming with guests. Sorcha stood at the far end of the theater, engaged in an animated conversation with Raimond and a circle of family.

Vir stopped short. "Can you explain to me what their relationship is—my girlfriend and Banitierre? I'm not blind. I can see the way he looks at her. Is it because he's her sire or…?"

"He didn't create her, but he did save her back in that cemetery. He's her protector and the head of her family. She joined this coven by choice, and his blood will always be a part of her." Rayna waited for more questions.

"So I don't have anything to worry about?" Vir shot a glance back in Sorcha's direction. "They're both glowing."

"My advice is don't waste time worrying about what you can't control. If Raimond didn't want you here, you'd be dead already. Just take care of Sorcha and make her happy."

Sorcha excused herself and bounced across the crowded floor to her friends. "How was dinner?"

"I'm stuffed." Vir tipped Sorcha's chin up and kissed her mouth. "Missed you though. Let's get drinks."

"I'll catch up with you later, Vir." Rayna drew Sorcha aside. "Make sure he eats real food. The man gobbled dinner."

"I'll insist on it." Sorcha glanced at Vir's slim figure, leaning on the bar.

Rayna stood on her toes and whispered in Sorcha's ear. "Being hungry might not be his only problem. He's determined to drink blood, and his craving for strength... Sorcha, most humans who'd sell their soul for vampire power become vampires, whether they want to or not."

Before the echo of the twelfth chime faded, Normandie Hall came to life like the sun breaking out from behind typhoon clouds. The wall of fire dropped and disappeared without leaving even a scorched blade of grass behind. Chandeliers flickered on one lamp at a time.

Vir surveyed the ballroom with wide eyes. "Now this is the palace you described."

"Look up." Sorcha pointed to the skylight.

Drums rolled and music burst into the room. Following Raimond and Julia's lead, Vir extended his hand, palm up, tilting his head in the direction of the dance floor. Sorcha enthusiastically accepted and found herself twirling around in his expert embrace for hours. After the last romantic dance of the night concluded, she snuck Vir out to the candlelit patio. "Whatever happened to your violin?"

"I have it, or what's left, packed in one of the boxes."

"That doesn't sound good."

"I kind of smashed it after your accident."

Sorcha winced. "Can it be fixed?"

"Don't know. I'll show it to you tomorrow."

"Let's walk in the garden." The following hours strolling the estate were magical. Sorcha stored away the sight of Vir smiling, tie hanging loosely around his neck, carrying a bottle of wine with his arm casually slung around her shoulder.

Memories to last forever.

They made their way across the shimmering grass of sloping fields, kissing as they walked, never breaking their embrace. In front of them was the setting moon, the mansion a sparkling backdrop like a mirage.

So spontaneous, pure and gloriously human. The happiest I've ever seen him.

As they lounged in the tall grass she thought back to the first time she had laid eyes on him. A dark day in a faraway hospital, when he offered kind words to help her through the tragedy of a patient's death.

From that moment, I loved him with all my heart. I still do—with whatever heart I have left.

Chapter 59

DRINKING AGE

THE NEXT NIGHTS saw the population of Normandie Hall dwindle back to normal numbers.

Vir ate his meals downstairs with Rayna or joined Sorcha in the main dining room when Raimond wasn't in attendance. Whenever possible, he reminded the girls of his desire for vampire blood. They stalled, but the excuses were wearing thin.

After considering the options, Rayna decided the safest place for the event would be the privacy of her own suite. "Sorcha, I still have reservations."

Wrapped in silk bed sheets, Sorcha crammed both hands over her eyes. "I'm not pushing for this, but he certainly is and I don't want him to resort to someone else. There are plenty of vampires with questionable scruples. Maybe he won't like it."

"We can only hope. Bring him downstairs after dinner." Rayna slipped out the balcony door.

Vir followed the usual routine of sleeping until noon and then making his rounds of the compound. He chatted with security, got a second cup of coffee from the kitchen staff, chose clothes for the evening and joined the family in the parlor for cocktails. His final destination was the dining room with place settings for the few remaining guests. "Sorcha, why so quiet?"

"Just lost in my thoughts." During their customary after-dinner walk,

Sorcha revealed the plan.

"Oh yes!" Vir pounded his fist into his hand. "Right now?"

"Raimond is staying in the city. No time like the present, I guess."

Rayna double-checked the lock on her door, walked away and returned to check it again. "Vir, you can change your mind at any time, you know that, right?"

"Yes, I'm aware. That's not going to happen."

"Okay then. Sorcha, give me your hand." Rayna sliced the vampire's palm and directed a stream of blood into a crystal goblet. She chuckled at Vir's vacant expression. "Were you going to suck blood out of her neck like Dracula? Can we hang onto a little civility, please?"

"I never know what to imagine around here," Vir said.

"Be careful, and expect to be revolted the first time. It's warm and thick." Rayna stuck out her tongue. "Tastes like metal mixed with swamp water."

The cut on Sorcha's hand stopped bleeding and healed without a trace, rendering about as much blood as two fingers of booze.

Vir waved it under his nose. "Yuck, smells like—blood." He took the smallest sip possible, contorted his face and gingerly placed the glass down on the table.

If there is a Lord, please make him hate it.

Both girls jumped back as he grabbed the glass a second time, slammed the blood down like a shot and staggered away.

"What part of be careful didn't you understand?" Sorcha scrambled across the room. "Here, drink some water."

"No, I need something stronger to get rid of this taste." Before Rayna could pour whisky in a tumbler, Vir grabbed the bottle and took a long gulp. "Holy shit, I don't know which one burns worse." He crashed against the wall and slid down until he was sitting on the floor, head cradled weakly in his hands.

"You look a little green." Sorcha had no idea how to help him.

"Give me a minute."

"Is this normal?" Sorcha asked.

"Sort of." Rayna nodded. "Most people don't drink it that fast. In hindsight, a little less blood in the glass would have been safer."

Vir tore his shirt open and wiped sweat from his forehead. "Don't know how or why I just did that. Almost like my hand was controlled by someone else."

Rayna looked at Sorcha and back at Vir. "He'll feel better in the fresh air."

With one girl under each of his shoulders, they made their way up the stairs and dropped him in the wet grass.

"Now what?" Sorcha asked.

"I would say he needs to walk it off, if he could actually walk."

"All right, let's go." Sorcha was easily strong enough to haul Vir to his feet and drag him until he started to move on his own. She threw her most confident smile over her shoulder while Rayna shook her head in dismay.

A few steps from the forest Vir wheeled around and kissed Sorcha's neck. "I want to make love to you."

"Now? You were unconscious five minutes ago."

"Well, I'm back and I'm wide awake."

"Right out here in the open?" Sorcha asked. "Like exhibitionists?"

"No, right there in the woods like animals."

"Take it easy. My family can look out a window at any time."

"I'm sure they know what we do in the bedroom." His embrace swept Sorcha off her feet, crushing her against the trunk of a twisted tree.

Grabbing Vir's shirt, she steadied herself and ripped the fabric cleanly from his chest.

"Let's go, lady." Vir forced Sorcha against the rough bark as he fumbled to undress her.

Using the tree for leverage she boosted herself up and wrapped her legs around his waist.

With an unmistakable tearing sound, Vir flipped Sorcha's ruined panties over his shoulder and started to unzip his trousers before he stopped short.

"What are you waiting for?"

"Sorcha, do you hear something?"

"I do not."

"Birds. I hear—can't do this with all that noise."

Sorcha's back slammed into the gnarled tree roots as Vir whirled away, clamping his hands over his ears. *Did I just fall? Holy…he dropped me.*

"I'm sorry. I didn't mean—it's just—don't you hear wings flapping around us? It's driving me insane and it's so damn bright out here, my head is going to explode."

"Vir, I think you're hallucinating. Let's get you back to your room." *Something is very wrong.*

Tossing aside what was left of his shirt, Sorcha carried Vir back to the guesthouse at vampire speed. *Nobody needs to see him half-naked, cringing away from invisible feathered creatures.* As gently as she could, she laid him in his bed and looked around for a blanket. What she saw next froze her in her tracks.

Who is that? She stared into a familiar face that wasn't entirely familiar. The man in bed resembled Vir, but he definitely was not her boyfriend.

"I saw you."

Stifling a scream, Sorcha jumped back, clutching her chest. "What?"

"I saw you zooming." Vir flicked his eyes open.

"Zooming?"

"That ridiculous running you and your friends do when you think I'm not watching. I can see you."

"Jayz, go to sleep. You scared the hell out of me tonight."

"Good night." A content smile transformed his face as he drifted off.

Definitely his face this time. "Good night, lover." She climbed down from the second story and gasped when a pair of birds shot up from the damp lawn like glowing bullets. "What the—"

Vir's voice chimed in the fringe of Sorcha's hearing. *Free me, angel.*

Sorcha spun around in time to see a shadow dart across the window of Vir's room.

Free me. Please.

Chapter 60

THE CALM

VIR'S MOODS SWUNG between ecstasy and depression, with no apparent trigger for the changes. Some nights he asked for Sorcha's blood, other times he had no interest. His subsequent reactions hadn't been nearly as violent or disturbing as his first experience and she never confided the details of that night to anyone, especially not the way his face changed into someone else. The key to keeping him healthy turned out to be strictly limiting his consumption to a few drops. Almost daily he apologized for dropping her.

"Will you please forget that," Sorcha begged. "I wasn't hurt and I should've been able to catch myself. Raimond will be home any minute and he says he has important news."

The small group of family remaining at the mansion gathered in the parlor. After drinks were poured and everyone had the opportunity to shake Raimond's hand or kiss his cheek, he summoned Sorcha and Vir to the upstairs library.

"Dr. Ashayle, you have a few weeks free and I have a career opportunity for you."

Early the next morning, Vir began his new job as a traveling physician in rural Louisiana. By the end of the first day, Sorcha could tell his outlook on life had improved. *He simply missed being a doctor*. He worked all his life for the privilege to be a healer, to share in the joy of life and ensure the dignity of death. Even though she knew he loved being close to her, it was unhealthy for him to lie around the mansion day after day, doing nothing and waiting for the next demented thing to happen.

At the end of his first week, Sorcha had a special gift waiting.

"This is a surprise! I didn't think there was any chance my violin could be fixed."

"Will you play for me?"

Vir picked up the instrument and the bow, expertly adjusting the strings as he walked out onto the moonlit balcony. After tucking the polished wood under his chin, he started to play. The violin sounded as pure and fluid as ever, singing the same wistful notes that mesmerized her in Nepal. Vir lost himself in the melody, coaxing harmony out of the strings with the movement of his body. The outline of his figure blurred as if a puff of smoke had blown through.

Spooky.

Sorcha was fully aware that her blood altered him, but more and more she was convinced that none of the changes were improvements. After making love, Vir would gasp for air as if something or someone was smothering him.

"Drink from me." Vir stood naked in front of the mirror. "I enjoy watching."

"You're so weak…"

"It doesn't hurt, Sorcha, just the opposite, like another orgasm. What flavor am I?"

"Complex, citrusy with swirls of sugar."

"You don't have to heal those marks. I like the way they look."

"You might, but your patients may disagree. Now close your eyes and rest before you need to get up."

The middle weeks of December brought torrential rain to the Mississippi River Delta. Every day the skies would open up and soak the landscape until the earth couldn't hold any more. Flooding triggered an early start to the year's influenza outbreak. Many nights, Vir came home exhausted from losing patient after patient to complications from the virus.

"Drink, Vir, come on. You need it just to survive."

Sorcha and Vir let their minds wander together during the trip back to New Orleans. Christmas at the plantation had been a smashing success. For a full week they toasted celebrations piled high with gifts, and packed with family and close friends. The feasting and drinking continued until sunrise forced the party to end.

"Sorry to cut our holiday celebration short." Raimond cranked the limousine window open to a gust of humid air. "Sisters of the Peace is already swamped with patients."

"Am I back on the schedule?" Vir asked.

"As of January first. Keep that in mind on New Year's Eve."

Sorcha's fingers drifted to stroke Vir's hand. "Draven's party, right?"

"Last official event of the calendar year." Raimond's eyes wandered across Sorcha's vacant face. "Should be a subdued, black-tie affair, but who knows. Draven's been carrying on all over town with Gwynevere, like a teenager in heat."

"She seemed a little odd." Vir stared out the window.

"Well spoken, though," Sorcha said.

"I know he's wanted a bride." Raimond peered up at the dark clouds. "Not sure if she's the one or he's just tired of looking."

"Has Draven changed her?" Sorcha's tilted her head. "He made such a big fuss over a human in the vampire fold creating vulnerability with deadly consequences."

Raimond leaned forward and tapped Sorcha's knee. "Is everything all right with you two? You're distant."

"Oh yes, perfectly fine." Sorcha nudged Vir with her foot. "Aren't we?"

"Looking forward to getting back to work, sir."

"I've heard you play that instrument." Raimond pointed to the violin case in Vir's lap. "Maybe you could learn some more cheerful melodies?"

New Year's Day marked the proverbial calm before the storm. By the first week of January, Sorcha knew this was no normal outbreak. The patients were incredibly sick and the hospital staff stretched so thin, only half the people that needed care got treated and even fewer survived. Sorcha paced the parlor, waiting for Vir and Raimond to come home every morning. They discussed their worst cases, slept for a few hours and dragged themselves back to work. As essentially different as they were, neither man was eating well or resting enough and they both looked like hell. She spent evenings in the Quarter visiting her old haunts, but the public was scared and the streets were deserted. One morning, Vir arrived so tired and weak that Sorcha carried him to bed. Her blood was the only thing keeping him going, and she gave him more each time he drank.

Weary of sitting by and watching her colleagues struggle, Sorcha took to staring at the hospital windows and debating whether to take a dangerous chance or not.

What the hell, I'm going in. I'm a nurse and a damn good one.

In the darkest corner of the building she scaled the wall, bouncing from one ledge to another and landing on a fifth-floor windowsill. The latch snapped off the window like a brittle twig.

"Marion." Sorcha flashed across the room and squeezed the lady's hand as she blinked furiously. "It's okay, I'm here. When is the last time anyone brushed your hair?"

Sorcha busied herself cleaning the room, and fussing over her patient. "Marion, can I tell you a secret?"

Marion blinked once for yes.

"You may disapprove." Sorcha read Marion's two blinks for no and launched into her story about Vir and Rayna. "I need to clarify my situation with her, don't I?"

Marion blinked once.

"Who am I kidding? I have to break things off. The secrets and worrying plus all this sneaking around is exhausting. If Vir found out, he might say he understood and that he doesn't mind the relationship, but on the other hand, he might feel betrayed." Sorcha brushed a pink tear off her cheek. "Such a beautiful girl with a dirty little secret."

I have to go home.

Zelia juggled patients' charts and bumped the glass door open with her hip. "Why is it so dark out here?

"Because it's three in the morning." Ivori's voice squawked across the deserted patio. "And don't you turn that damn light on."

"I'm trying to get some work done."

"It's called a break for a reason."

Zelia sighed and flopped into a wrought iron chair. "How did I get stuck working the night shift with you?"

"Because people are dropping dead." Ivori struck a match and lit a candle. "I love this time of night, though. This is the closest to peaceful New Orleans ever gets. What do you hear?"

"You're right. Nothing."

"I didn't say that."

"It's completely still. All the late-night drunks have passed out and the crack of dawn risers are catching a last wink."

"Listen." Ivori pulled on her earlobe. "The spirits are all around, whispering their secrets."

"You're nuts." Zelia patted her pockets. "I have charting to do."

"And you're in denial. Did you see our gloomy priest hanging around in Emergency?" Ivori handed Zelia a pen.

"Unfortunately, I did. He heard that Alexa girl spouting her craziness about Sorcha before Dr. Banitierre sent her home. Again."

"Kind of makes you think…"

"I don't have time to think."

"I caught that holy fool sneaking around our barracks yesterday, close to your room."

Zelia stopped writing and dropped her pen. "He interrogated me about the Nepal trip last week. Gave me chills."

"I think we need to move out of the barracks. Something's not sitting right with me."

"We need to get back to work." Zelia grabbed her papers. "Thank you for taking care of Miss Marion tonight."

"I thought *you* got her ready for bed. The orderly heard a ruckus in there earlier."

"I wasn't in that room," Zelia said.

Ivori sauntered to the patio door. "Neither was I."

Chapter 61

ALWAYS

"I PROMISE, VIR." Sorcha pressed her lips to his forehead. "I'll only be gone a day, two at the most. I can't do much to help around here anyway. I left you half a glass of 'you know what' in the medicine cabinet—don't forget to drink it. When I get back, hopefully you'll have some time off and I'll take you out, anywhere you want to go."

"Hurry home. I know I'm barely here, but it helps to have you waiting for me. As terrible as things are right now, I know my soul is always safe here with you."

"I love you." Sorcha kissed his mouth then turned away before she changed her mind. She tossed a note to Raimond on the hall table. She would have told the duke where she was going in person, but he was traveling again, tending to New Orleans vampire business that the prince had dropped in his lap when he disappeared during his own party.

"Love you too, Sorcha. Always."

Damn, I don't want to abandon him, but he deserves the best of me, the best of everything. I'll do whatever's in my power to give it to him.

The last time Sorcha glanced back, she saved the image of Vir smiling down the stairs as he waved goodbye.

Love that smile.

The trip to Normandie passed quickly and Sorcha arrived before midnight. She barely flinched at Rayna's scream when she barged in her bedroom. "Jayz, don't go waking the whole house, now."

"You look like you need to feed." Rayna offered her neck and Sorcha gulped her friend's blood so forcefully the girl cringed with pain.

"Sorry, I think I'm losing my mind." Sorcha wiped blood from her chin with a silk pillowcase. "Came here to talk."

"Your voice, Sorcha—" Rayna stumbled back and crashed onto the edge of the footboard. "Your accent only comes out when something's wrong."

"You can't even imagine how bad things are in the city—everyone's sick and hiding in their houses. But there's more." Sorcha dove in and drank more than she planned. Overcome by the lethargy that followed a big meal, she flopped down next to Rayna and passed out.

"Rayna! Sorcha!"

Both girls were jarred awake by panic in the underground chambers.

"Raimond?" Rayna whipped her bedroom door open just as he arrived.

"Where's Sorcha?"

"Right here—what is wrong with you?"

"We have to leave immediately. Vir is sick." Raimond grabbed both girls and dragged them up the back stairway at full speed.

"What do you mean sick? He was fine a few hours ago."

"I mean sick, Sorcha. On death's door. He collapsed at work. Rayna, get in the car."

"No." Sorcha slumped against the trunk, fighting a wave of dizziness and freezing pain in her chest. "Raimond, where—"

"I had him brought to the penthouse. The hospital can't do anything." Raimond wrenched Sorcha into the car and stepped on the gas, breaking every speed limit between Normandie Hall and New Orleans. "If Vir caught the flu everyone else has, he may need your blood to help him get well. I don't know what's different this year, but none of our normal treatments have any effect."

"He's already had my blood."

Without slowing down Raimond looked at Sorcha, glanced in the mirror at Rayna and then back at the road. "How much and since when?"

"A lot—for the last few months."

Clenching his jaw, he maneuvered the car down the winding road. "How often?"

"Almost every day. Lately he's been so tired. Is this my fault?"

"No, but it's probably what kept him from succumbing to the virus for this long. However, if he was already dependent on your blood it won't be enough to heal him. You may need to…"

"What?" Sorcha lunged across the car, forcing herself in front of the driver's face. "You can't possibly mean—"

"Stop! You'll make me crash." Raimond swerved and kept the car on the road. "Let's just see how bad it is before we panic. We're almost there."

All of Sorcha's restraint vanished when she saw Vir. His skin was grey and his eyes sunken. Blood dripped from his tear ducts. Breaking free from Rayna's grasp, she grabbed his limp hand.

"He looks like he's already dead!" Sorcha searched his neck frantically for a pulse, finally finding the weakest heartbeat imaginable. "How the hell did this happen in twenty-four hours?"

"A decision needs to be made quickly," Raimond said.

"Honey, I know you can you hear me. Please wake up." Sorcha cradled Vir's head in her lap and stroked his face as he drew a few ragged breaths. "I don't want to…he never wanted this."

"Either you do it or I'll do it, but right now you're wasting precious time he may not have." Raimond grabbed Sorcha's chin and forced her to look into his eyes. "The only choice left is our life or his death.

Think hard—do you want to slide him into the wall at the cemetery? Because we're at that point right now."

"No." Sorcha's mind turned inside out as she wept. "I can't." Life flashed in front of her closed eyelids. *Orchids, violins, midnight kisses, candles, ballroom dancing…is this it?*

"It doesn't have to be."

"Vir, can you smile for me?"

Raimond rested a hand on each of Sorcha's shoulders. "He'll never smile again—unless you make it happen."

"I can't lose him." Sorcha bit her lip and squeezed her eyes shut. "Help me, I've only seen it done once."

"Rayna, you need to step out. Vampire eyes only." Raimond held the door open, waving the reluctant girl through.

Sorcha followed Raimond's instructions precisely. Piercing Vir's neck, she started to drink. His blood, once the sweetest thing she had ever tasted, had already started to die. It was so foul she gagged and struggled to swallow it.

"That's enough. Rip your wrist open and let blood pour in his mouth. That's it. Now find his heart and squeeze—slowly.

Sorcha plunged her hand through Vir's flesh and bone. She hesitated when his eyes flew open and rolled back in his head.

Vir choked. Green bile erupted from his mouth and nose. Sorcha's arm drooped.

"No, no!" Raimond snapped his fingers in front of her face. "Keep going!"

Forgive me lover. Fishing around her dead boyfriend's chest, Sorcha found his shriveled heart and began to massage it with her palm, careful not to tear the tissue with her nails. She coaxed the magic of vampire blood through Vir's body until Raimond instructed her to stop.

"Now we watch and wait. You did well. It's not as easy as it looks."

"How long until we know for sure?" Minutes ticked by as Sorcha watched the progress, or the lack of it. "Raimond—how damn long?"

"Go clean up, and please don't curse."

"Draven changed a human without spilling a drop. Why am I a

319

colossal mess?"

Raimond sunk deep into a chair, dropped his elbows to his knees and rubbed his forehead.

Sorcha saw the tremor first. "He moved!"

"I don't see anything."

"Just look, Raimond. His right hand—his fingers! I'm here Vir." Sorcha rushed to the bed, grabbing his wrist and recoiling immediately.

"Were you expecting a pulse?" Raimond lifted Vir's eyelids, one at a time.

"I felt slithering under his skin."

"Well, congratulations, it worked. Now, we need to get him into the basement."

"It's filthy down there. Why can't he stay in this bed?"

"Transformation is an ugly business—it's much safer downstairs. In fact, after you help me get him settled, you and Rayna are to stay in the penthouse until I call for you." Raimond flung Vir effortlessly over his shoulder, treading down flight after flight until they were well below sea level.

"I think I need some air. Don't feel well at all." It was too late. Sorcha vomited waves of black blood, drenching the floor and her clothing.

"What the?" Raimond froze. "Wait a minute, I've seen this before. It's not influenza—Rayna! Call the hospital. Tell Sister Ann to evaluate everyone for plague. Go!"

Shuffling and crashing on the stairs sent Raimond flying to the door "What now?" He whipped the door open to see Draven clutching a crumpled body in his arms.

"I need you, Banitierre. Gwyn was fine when she went to sleep and then a few hours later, I found her like this. I'll beg for your help if I have to." The prince stared at Vir's body. "What happened to him?"

"Like you care?" Sorcha hissed. "I hope you're happy now."

"Sorcha, enough, nobody's happy here." Raimond bent over to examine Gwyn. "Her symptoms are identical to Vir's. Draven, it's plague. You need to change her."

"No, I promised her it would be her choice. She isn't ready." Draven shoved Raimond to the side, grabbing Gwyn's limp wrist. "The goddamn plague again?"

"She may not be ready, but it's her time." Raimond placed the woman's cold hand on her chest. "Don't bother swallowing her blood. It'll come right back up."

Sorcha turned her head away as Draven kissed his girlfriend good-bye. *How ironic. We endure the same heartbreak a few hours apart.* She watched him engage in the brutality she had just finished, rocking Gwyn's lifeless body in his arms on the miserable floor as he waited for her to wake up a different creature.

The duke and the prince sat stone-still in the basement, waiting for the newborns to open their eyes.

"How did you diagnose plague, Raimond?"

"Sorcha vomited Vir's blood almost immediately. You and I have seen that before."

"Something I hoped we'd left in the past." Draven pounded the back of his head on the limestone wall.

"Officially, America has it under control, but a port city is always vulnerable. Vir and Gwyn were too far gone, even for modern medicine."

"Did Rayna give us enough blood?"

Raimond held up a full pint. "Hope so, unless they spill it all."

Gwyn slept unrestrained while Vir was shackled to the wall.

"Get ready, Raimond. He's waking up."

"You're killing me." Vir twisted and rattled the chains, yanking against the cuffs. "Get these off."

"Son, you need to drink."

"No, that's revolting. Get away from me!

"Now you're revolted?" Raimond tried to talk Vir into drinking from a cup but gave up and poured blood down his throat as he choked.

In stark contrast, when Gwyn woke she remained lucid and sipped obediently before returning to sleep.

"Any idea where Vir was born?" Draven sat on a crate and rolled his sleeves down. "His bizarre aura has bothered me since the first time I watched him and Sorcha together."

"Some hut in the Himalayas, I assume. Why?"

"Not sure if you know, but I wasn't born a royal. Back in Europe the Normans breed humans, looking for that one in a million, like racehorses are perfected through extensive bloodline research and a little bit of trial and error. Only one can conquer the winner's circle."

"That's disturbing to say the least. Is arrogance an inherited trait?"

"Don't be naïve. It's been done for thousands of years by ruling families. I might have been horrified by it too, but by the time I understood how everything worked, I was seventeen and about to become an immortal prince." Draven chuckled. "I really didn't give two shits, and yes, I was born a prick."

"What does any of that have to do with him? He's hardly a fair-haired, steely-eyed masterpiece."

"My point is, there have been hundreds of my siblings and half-siblings running around the Alps, living normal, human lives—just not perfect enough to make the final cut. I'll bet the Rakshasa have a similar arrangement in their kingdom."

"If he has Sorcha's blood, he's one of them already."

"Indirectly." Draven tapped his chin and pointed to the vampire in chains. "I also don't think he's native to Nepal, or wherever your little outpost was. I think he's from the desert."

"Desert, as in Africa?" Raimond squinted at Vir. "Him?"

"More like the Middle East. It's a strong resource that no vampire family has tapped for centuries." Draven flexed his neck. "At least as far as I know."

"The only royal family on the Asian continent is Dorje. That's frightening and worse than we originally thought."

"If I'm right and he's one of Ammon Dorje's genetically

engineered candidates, he won't be any normal vampire. When I was turned I became another version of myself. My cheekbones got higher, my hair grew."

"You, with long hair?"

"White-blond, down to my shoulders, and an enormous bother. I need a haircut every two days, sooner in this soggy climate. My body was the biggest difference. I was a bony kid, but I filled out tremendously." Draven stared at Vir's form, sagging from the handcuffs. "That man there—Sorcha may not recognize him anymore."

"Dorjes don't leave loose ends. They'll come looking for him, and Sorcha too."

"They may be here already." Draven clapped Raimond's shoulder. "No worries. My forces will handle it."

Chapter 62

THE NATURAL

SORCHA SPENT THE entire day in bed, too tired to sleep and too devastated to cry. "I didn't take good care of his soul."

Rayna rose from the chair where she had been watching over her friend.

"He said it was safe with me but I let him down. I let him die."

"Nonsense, his soul is still with him, thanks to you. He was human and he got sick, like the rest of this city."

"He'll hate me." Sorcha couldn't control the low wail coming from deep in her chest.

"Baloney. It's an adjustment for sure, but you both have forever to figure it out. You had no choice—really, you didn't."

Rayna nagged her relentlessly to drink but Sorcha didn't want to see blood, much less smell it or drink it.

"Do you feel the building shaking?" Sorcha stared at a glass vibrating on the end table.

"I thought it was thunder."

"I hear screaming, from downstairs. Oh shit, that's Vir. I'm going—"

"Sorcha, you shouldn't." Rayna reached out to stop her, catching nothing but air. "Raimond said—"

"I don't care. His howling is tearing me apart." Sorcha bounded down the stairs. She flung open the basement door and ran into

Draven's chest. The force of hitting an immovable being knocked her to the ground.

"Sorcha, help me." Vir's form was a violent blur of growling and snapping fangs. "They're killing me." The anchors that held his chains creaked where they attached to the stone foundation.

"Didn't I tell you to stay upstairs?" Raimond wrapped his arms around Sorcha. "There's nothing you can do for him right now. This part takes as long as it takes. Your presence only makes it worse."

She braced herself against the doorframe, and fought back. "Why is he acting so crazy?"

"So did you—you just don't remember. Good news, neither will he."

Draven knocked Sorcha's legs free and Raimond dumped her in the stairwell.

"I know you hate us right now, but we're doing you a tremendous favor. This isn't some random, transitioning vampire. He's the love of your life, and some things you can't unsee." The prince slammed the door squarely in her face.

Sorcha hammered the steel with her fists before sliding to the ground. She pressed her cheek against the rough metal. "I'll not be leaving this spot."

"I'm right on the other side. Talk to me," Raimond answered. "The beginning is ugly, but everyone goes through it. Remember the rat incident?"

"Ugh." Sorcha recalled sucking dirty fur. "I didn't know what I was doing."

"My point exactly."

"When he screams, it's like I'm being turned inside out."

"Because he's your blood. His name is already in the book, right under yours. That's the curse of the sire and the deepest bond imaginable. Add in your feelings for each other—I know why you couldn't stay upstairs."

"When can I see him?"

"Soon, a day or two. You have eternity."

"That's what Rayna said."

325

"She's a smart girl. I'm glad you two are so close."

"I can't imagine my life without her." *That's the truth, even if there's more to it—much more.*

Sorcha spent days listening to her soulmate grind through his transition. Draven and Raimond assured her that the horror was normal, but Gwynevere had already been released to a luxurious bed in the penthouse while Vir writhed in the hell and chains of a dank basement.

"You're bringing him out tomorrow, right?" Sorcha glared at Raimond. "No more stalling."

"Maybe at night, if he stops hallucinating. He's angry and it takes me and Draven together to control him." Raimond pointed to a chair, silently ordering Sorcha to stay put.

Angry? He must be furious now that he knows what he is. How the hell am I going to explain it to him?

Vir was obsessed with escaping the basement. "Raimond, let me out of these damn shackles. Don't you think I've been violated enough?"

"You need to back off a little and stop blaming others for—" Raimond rubbed the back of his neck. "Do you even realize what happened?"

"No. Why don't you enlighten me, you monster."

"I'll try not to take that personally. Plague is an ugly way to die, and your case was as nasty as they come. How do you think Sorcha would have survived eternity without you?"

"Plague?" Vir leaned his head back on the stone wall. "New Orleans had a minor outbreak in 1918, but…"

"The death toll was far higher than we reported to the newspapers."

"You covered up the truth?" Vir asked. "I'm shocked."

"I protect the public. Humans panic. Panic kills. Do you recall any details of the patients who crashed in front of our eyes?" Raimond paced the room. "Vitals, skin color, sour smell?" He held a finger up for each symptom.

"You're teaching me about plague now?"

"Never pass up an educational opportunity, doctor." Raimond stepped directly in front of Vir. "Apparently you were drinking Sorcha's blood regularly?"

"So?"

"So, a little swig wasn't going to cure anything. You were as good as gone. Decisions needed to be made."

"And you took it upon yourself to decide for me?" Vir yanked on the handcuffs. "Like when you chose to throw me out of my own apartment."

"Try to make the best of your second chance at life." Raimond played along with Vir's misconception and accepted the blame for changing him. "Are you serious about that shithole of an apartment? I didn't hear any complaints when you were living in high style at Normandie."

"Unlock me."

"Behave yourself." Raimond tapped the key against his palm. "There's a beautiful woman upstairs, waiting for you to return to her."

A flurry of footsteps on the stairs made Sorcha jump to the door, bracing for a confrontation. Vir zoomed across the room, enveloping her in his crushing embrace before she realized she wasn't quite ready for his new abilities. *Zooming—his word, not mine, but amazingly accurate.* Sorcha gave herself up to his desperate kiss. *What's different?*

A rude whistle from the kitchen interrupted the moment. "Bloody hell, was I right Raimond or was I right?" Draven leaned casually on the marble counter.

Doesn't that man ever, ever stop bragging? Before Sorcha could roll her eyes, she actually looked at Vir. Half the furniture in the parlor was overturned by the time she stopped staggering backward.

"What did I do? Sorcha—do I smell? I've been chained up for days."

"It's your face. Your everything." *That's him—the stranger I saw the first night he drank my blood.* Blinking furiously didn't change the view this time. The man standing in the middle of the parlor was definitely Vir, but his voice was the only thing unchanged. *No wonder kissing him felt odd, I had to stand on my tiptoes to reach his lips.* His shredded, bloody shirt barely covered his chest. *He's put on at least fifty pounds of pure muscle.*

"Am I that ugly?"

"Noooo, that's not...see for yourself." She weakly pointed to the hallway mirror and watched him flash across the room.

"No way." Running his hand through his hair and across his face, Vir traced the new contour of his nose and cheekbones. His eyes were still brown but with a hint of the blue inferno that burned deep within. His eyelashes and hair were darker and longer. Pulling at the ribbons of fabric that used to be his dress shirt, he flexed muscles that had appeared overnight. "Is all this permanent?"

"That and more—hope you like it," Draven said. "Guess I can't call you a runt anymore."

The veins under Vir's skin sprung like roots and his eyes burned blue. "My mouth hurts!" Vir recoiled from the demon in the mirror and scanned the room for anything to quench his thirst.

Raimond stepped in front of Rayna.

"I would never hurt her." Vir leaned on the wall.

"No, you'd kill her by accident. Here, have some not-just-wine." Draven tossed the bottle to Vir, who drained it in one swallow.

"Put the fangs away. Take a bath—please. I'll catch dinner." Raimond wrenched Vir around and shoved him in the direction of Sorcha's bedroom. "Draven, can you maintain the peace here?"

"I can direct this circus in my sleep."

"I don't want to hurt anyone. Sorcha, there must be another way." Vir sunk beneath bubbles in the claw foot tub and shielded his eyes against the candlelight. "It's as if I'm holding my stethoscope up to the entire city. That running water shut out the maddening jumble of voices and heartbeats, but just for a minute."

Sorcha placed a wet cloth over Vir's swollen eyelids. "Burning valerian incense will keep your thoughts or conversations confidential, but in a pinch, an open faucet is just as effective. Assume that nothing in your mind is private until you learn to control your boundaries and block the eavesdroppers out."

"Are you sure it isn't just an excuse for a bubble bath?"

"Maybe a little of that too. Your hair is so much thicker and longer, I love it." The sensation of someone washing her hair had always been comforting, so Sorcha did the same for Vir. Her motives were selfish too. She couldn't stop touching him, anywhere and everywhere. Except for a few old photos, she had all but forgotten what she looked like before her change. "The spiders crawling under your skin will stop after you learn to feed."

"Does feeding mean what I think it means?" Vir slid farther down in the tub.

"It is not optional."

"Ah, tourists. Perfect choice for the first true meal." Draven cracked his knuckles as he strode back into the basement. "Gwyn, pay attention. Raimond is an excellent teacher. Then, tomorrow night we can go out."

"Ooo, I'd love to stroll the Quarter. It's been awhile."

"She certainly won't be able to sneak up on anyone unless you and your royal guard stay home." Raimond shut the door behind him, throwing each bolt with conviction.

"That, my friend, is highly unlikely. Just show her how to do it without making a mess please, like you did for Sorcha."

"You're funny—aren't you the one who lured Sorcha out in the fields to hunt without my permission? Great fun when she was a savage, but now that it's your progeny? Never mind. Let's get started."

"You're too kind, Raimond."

Gwyn was a perfect pupil, eager to satisfy her thirst with something tastier than aged blood wine, while Vir wouldn't take his eyes off the floor. If it were the fresh memories of pain and imprisonment, that would be understandable, but Sorcha suspected it was something more. Walking in circles, Vir covered his nose and mouth, cringing at every sound and smell of vampire feeding.

"Vir, she's had more than her share. You're starving." Sorcha gave him a gentle shove at the groggy victims.

Covering his face with his sleeve, he continued to pace, pausing every few moments to bend over and rest his hands on his knees.

Sorcha shrugged. "I couldn't have held back this long. Actually, I'm getting hungry now."

"Okay, Ashayle," Raimond said. "You can fight your nature for a while, but not forever. It's a very simple reality—feed or die."

"How about animal blood, or if I just keep drinking the wine?"

"You'll be so weak that someone else will have to open the bottle. Right now, especially now, you need strong, healthy human blood."

"Come on, it's not that bad." Draven drummed his fingers on the wall. "You don't have to kill anyone. Look how well my Gwyn did."

Gravel from the basement floor sprayed in every direction amid crashing bodies and flashing teeth. Ignoring all instructions, Vir dragged his first victim across the floor and slammed him into the wall, draining pints of blood before anyone could react.

Draven's initial instinct was to shield Gwyn, but he pitched in to pull the dying human to safety, most likely to appear heroic, not to save a precious life. Vir broke Raimond's grasp once before he was subdued, tearing a huge chunk of flesh from his victim's thigh first.

"That's enough!" Raimond used all his strength to haul the seething vampire into the stairwell. "Look at me. Stop—*arrête!*" Turning around as much as he dared, Raimond glared at his superior. "You still think he's a natural?"

"Well, he's a natural something." Draven licked blood off his fingers like a kid who had stuck his hand in cake frosting. "He sliced the guy's femoral artery." With a sigh he healed the gruesome injury. "What is everyone staring at? I'm starving. It would be a shame to waste—don't want to set a bad example or anything."

"You're an incredible ass. Take the women to the penthouse so I can clean up this disaster." Raimond propped the humans up against the farthest wall. "Sorcha, keep an eye on Vir."

All the warning signs were present after the basement incident, but Vir reached the kitchen before Sorcha grasped that something was still off. "Still a mess, aren't you?"

Vir staggered toward the counter, bouncing off marble corners and stumbling the length of the room. "I hate this. Can't do it." He intentionally smashed his head into the floor and walls. "I tried not to, but I lost control. That poor man. Am I a killer?"

"No, Draven healed him. He'll be slurping a beer in some dive on Bourbon in another hour." Sorcha didn't have the heart to tell him that all vampires were killers; it was only a matter of time. Efforts to slam the silverware drawer shut were unsuccessful, leaving her wrestling to stop Vir from slicing his wrists with a carving knife. "Do you seriously think you can kill yourself with this steel garbage?"

"I wish I were dead. I can't take it." His wail mixed with a moan, as if the last remainder of human emotion was finally escaping.

"Lover, this never should have happened. I shouldn't have left you here alone."

"What difference would that have made? Raimond does whatever he wants anyway." Vir's tone was flat, dead and resigned.

Sorcha slumped to the floor. *Wait a minute…*

Sorcha. Raimond hovered at the edge of the parlor, silently whispering in her mind, holding his finger to his lips.

The light bulb in Sorcha's head was blinding when it finally blinked on. "Vir, you have it wrong. Raimond didn't change you. I did." Out of the corner of her eye she saw the head of the family throw his hands in the air and shuffle out onto the balcony.

"I thought—wait—I'm your bloodline?" Vir leapt onto the counter. "Am I Rakshasa too?"

"I thought you knew. You have my blue eyes, so I'm pretty sure the legend is alive and well in you."

"I just assumed—all I saw was Raimond when I woke up. There was so much pain and thirst, I unloaded all of my anger on him."

"Everything was so sudden. When I left you were smiling and then the next day you were gone!" Sorcha looked up at Vir. "I had no time to think. You were a corpse in my arms."

"Did you even try anything else? Why bother with all the medical research if magic is so much more damn convenient?" Vir pointed at Sorcha. "Do not come up here, I'm warning you."

"I was weak. I couldn't face forever without you, so I made the decision. If you hate anyone, it should be me."

"I'll never hate you, angel. If your love is the reason that I'm still here then that makes it a little more tolerable. The thought of someone playing God with my life makes me furious."

"Raimond has spent every waking hour trying to help you, not kill you. If he was such a bastard, wouldn't he have let you die? That would have fixed all his problems."

"Good point, very rational." Vir hurled candlesticks through the kitchen window, sending slivers of stained glass ricocheting around the room. "It doesn't help."

Digging around the bottom of a drawer in the parlor, Sorcha triumphantly produced a pack of clove cigarettes, holding them as high as her fingertips reached. "It may take more than one, but these will smooth your ragged edges."

Sorcha watched Vir breathe smoke and struggle to sit still. Finally, he jumped up, zoomed to the balcony and froze at the sight of New Orleans sprawled out in front of him.

Not a great place for a newborn vampire with control issues.

"Vir, what are you staring at?"

"Not what—who. That's the chef from a little diner on Decatur, the first place I ever ate in this town."

Sorcha followed Vir's line of sight to the other side of Canal, where a husky man sat on the roof with his pipe.

"He's a force of nature. Took me weeks to try every local and signature dish on his menu. He tucked a foreign doctor under his wing, as if introducing me to this city was his personal responsibility. I don't want to kill him."

"Then let me teach you something a little less gory."

The chef was a treasure chest of positive, strong energy. Following detailed instructions, the newest vampire stole it out from under him in a matter of minutes.

"He appears perfectly fine."

"That's because he is. Maybe you gave him a headache, nothing more."

Vir leaned back and rubbed his eyes. "Amazing. I feel stronger but peaceful, like I could sleep for days."

Sorcha slid down the wall and Vir slumped in her arms. She stroked his hair while he slept, fixated on the dark outlines of the French Quarter roofs in the dead of night.

A whole new world is waiting for you, lover.

Chapter 63

DR. BOYFRIEND

CRAWLING ACROSS THE decrepit buildings undetected had been a chore, but only one location had a view of the highly guarded Banitierre balcony. Cole Victoire braced himself against the peeling shutters and crumbling brick while he juggled binoculars to his face. The vantage point was far enough away that even his vision required help.

A long line of cars had been dropping passengers at the Canal Street address all night. It remained to be seen whether the rumors on the street were true—that there had been a death in the family. Royal clans had a world's worth of lethal enemies.

Cole muttered to himself as he took a head count. "Let's see which one of these snobs is missing. Well hello, Julia, you uptight shrew, and Lily, daughter of a whore. Steven, present, accounted for, and still light in the loafers. There's the duke himself, and the blood slave who is way too chummy with her owners. Lovely Sorcha. I'm glad you aren't missing, blue vixen—what a waste that would be. Who else do we have here? Sorcha's nitwit boyfriend—wait a minute."

Shards of ancient brick and concrete clattered to the street four stories below. Cole froze in place, praying no one in the alley looked up to see where the debris fell from. Even the blind drunks had an active gossip network, and he didn't need the entire city knowing he was spying on the ruling family.

"Dr. Boyfriend looks a little different than I remember. Good grief, the change has been kind to you. Even though she's an ocean away, keeping this development from Danielle will be impossible. You, sir, will cause quite a commotion."

Chapter 64

FLAWED

VIR'S NIGHT ENDED much the same as every outing had for the past month, with trudging footsteps through the penthouse courtyard. Sorcha was the only one able to coax him out of his nightly depression. Tonight, getting them home safely took all her persuasive skills.

Sorcha stopped Vir at the base of the stairs to brush white dust off his shirt. He flicked her hand away before she could touch his face.

"I know you're angry." Vir wiped his chin with his sleeve. "Rolls off you in waves."

"We're all just worried."

"Who's we? Your family?"

"It's your family too," Sorcha said. "They've gone above and beyond for you. Lily's the one who suggested that we sit down at Café Du Monde and have coffee. Like old times."

"Abject disaster."

"She said to lick the powdered sugar, not smash the plate into your face."

"The whole Café saw Steven's signature look. What is that exactly, disdain or contempt?"

"You covered everyone in sugar, Vir."

"He talks to me like I'm a child." Vir flashed up a flight of stairs. "I know what you're thinking. Spit it out."

"You have no idea what I'm thinking." Sorcha waited on the landing, staring at his back. "Don't go to your room right away. Sit for a while—have a smoke."

"I just want to be alone, and please don't cry all night. I can hear you through the floor and it's like nails on a chalkboard."

"I'm sorry."

"Don't be sorry. Just stop already."

"You don't have to be so nasty."

"I don't want your pity."

Sorcha jammed her eyes shut to force back tears. "I'm only trying to help."

Vir spun around and caught hold of the banister, letting his fingers grasp the railing one at a time. "Haven't you helped me enough already?"

"Excuse me? Raimond said this would be difficult but—"

"Get lost or run back to Raimond—either way, shut up."

"Vir, why are you so screwy?"

"You killed me! You and your stupid obsession over a locket that you never even wear." Vir vaulted up another flight of steps and leaned back over the rail. "Didn't Raimond get it fixed for you? Or maybe you prefer his diamonds? The antiques and wine are sexy too."

Sorcha's eyes ignited in blazing red. She grabbed a clay planter, scrambled up the brick wall and hurled it at Vir's head.

Vir ducked and the pot whizzed past his ear. The explosion of dirt and pottery from the wall left mud dripping off his face.

"You deserve to be miserable." Sorcha dropped back to the courtyard floor. "Go to hell. Alone."

"Sorcha, wait!" Rayna chased her friend out a side door of the apartment building, dodging busy traffic on Canal Street. "You know men are idiots."

"Why are you following me?" Sorcha slowed down enough to let Rayna catch up before they entered foggy Jackson Square. "You shouldn't stay in the city. It's dangerous and every night is a debacle."

"You know why I'm here. You need me. I love you. Where else would I be?"

"Sorry I'm such a mess."

"Come back to Normandie with us. Let Vir deal with his own garbage—maybe grow up a little. Don't take this the wrong way, but it's painful to watch."

Slumping against the cool stone of the cathedral, Sorcha covered her eyes and tried not to cry.

"I'm sure Raimond will drag him back in time for this year's Gala." Rayna stepped into the shadows and cupped Sorcha's face in her hands. "Please, come home." She kissed her friend's lips cautiously.

"Rayna, I need to tell you something about the night Vir got sick."

"It can wait."

Across the street, Cole Victoire ducked into a shop doorway and muffled a laugh as he watched the two women and their uncommon embrace. He tipped his face to the sky and thrust a fist in the air.

"Ashayle, I'll have a word with you." Draven waited until Sorcha was safely off the property before he spoke.

"Why are you pestering me?" Vir rubbed dirt from his eyes. "I have nothing to say to you, freak."

The old building shuddered on its foundation when Draven pinned Vir against the wall by his neck. "Fight as hard as you like. That newborn strength is long gone. Now you're just like all the rest, hopelessly outmatched. Your lack of respect is troubling."

"My apologies. Royal freak. Shall I bow down to you?"

"Never mind me, I want to give you a little direction on how to treat the women of this family—one in particular. I've had enough of your tantrums. Enough!"

Vir's eyes rolled back as Draven slammed his head into the wall and let him slump to the floor.

"Sorcha is a world-class beauty. A loyal friend—your only one, though I've no idea what she sees in you. You think you have a right to treat her like garbage, because you were somehow wronged by the universe? Get over yourself, you imbecile. You're about to lose her, but way too selfish to notice. If you make her cry again, I will personally gouge your eyes out with an ice pick."

"You wanted Sorcha for yourself, didn't you?"

"I did once. Forgive me if I don't want to see her destroyed now." Draven kicked Vir's face before he stormed up the stairs into the heavy air of the penthouse balcony.

"Trying to knock my building down?" Raimond splashed whisky into two glasses and leaned on the iron railing.

Draven straightened the tabs of his collar. "I know he's your family, but that is one arrogant ass."

"Don't I know it. He's been like that since the day I met him."

"The way he acts—that sullen mood of his? A genetic flaw, but not severe enough for Dorjes to cast him aside. Everything else is on the money. I'll bet he was scheduled to be turned before all this business with Sorcha happened, and that's the only reason he's not a Rakshasa prince right now."

"If he doesn't snap out of it soon, I don't know if he and Sorcha have a future. She's amazingly positive and he's still dragging her to hell with him every night." Raimond gulped his whisky and grimaced. "At least the mangled body count has decreased."

"There's not one drop of artistry in that man. I've seen him feed and it's alarming. I don't like exposing Gwyn to all that negativity—being young is difficult enough. I may take her to Savannah for a few weeks before the Gala, just for a break."

"I dread bringing that train wreck into my home, but what choice do I have?"

"I can think of a few. Sorcha would probably object." Draven didn't bother to hide his vicious smile. "The next time you and I have a row, I'm taking the mansion. Not your title."

"Was it that awful this time around?"

"Infernal bastards in this city fight over anything and everything. If I have to listen to one more argument over the square footage of pickpocketing rights…don't know how you do it."

"Enjoy yourself in Savannah. Gwynevere is an exceptional young woman. So, it's true? She just washed up on the rocks of your island?"

"Recreational swimming between the atolls." Draven chuckled. "Thought it was a prank until I went to the beach and saw for myself."

"Sounds like fate to me, old friend."

"One more thing, Raimond. Maybe we should have discussed this sooner, but Sorcha has visions."

Raimond's hand froze before the whisky reached his lips. "Still?"

"Still. And what she sees very often comes true."

Chapter 65

IN MEMORIAM

SORCHA WALKED RAYNA home. Convincing her to go upstairs took time and creative lying, but eventually she found herself alone, staring at the hospital windows again.

Don't have much time before sunrise, and it's such a risk—bet no one has been in that room all night. Sorcha made a familiar climb up the wall and through the window to find Marion alone, dirty, with tears streaming down her cheeks.

"Okay, honey. I've got everything under control." *Damn hospital.*

Sorcha busied herself bathing and changing linen, keeping a sharp eye on the horizon. Noise at the door snapped her head around. She'd almost been caught once before by an orderly on early-morning rounds. That time she'd hidden in the tiny washroom, clinging to the ceiling like a spider. She did the same tonight, waiting silently for the visitor to leave.

"I know you're in here."

Oh no! Sorcha clamped her hand over her mouth.

The door swung open and Raimond glared at the ceiling. "Get down, now." He grabbed Sorcha's arm and yanked her to the floor.

"How did you know—"

"You've been sneaking in here for a while, haven't you?"

"Since the outbreak." Sorcha struggled to break his grip on her arm. "Ow—you're hurting me!"

"I suspected as much." Raimond pointed at Marion. "She shrieks each time she's wheeled past your picture in the hallway. You know, the one that reads 'In Memoriam'? Have you any clue how dangerous this is?"

"Do nurses still work here? Because you should have seen the state I found her in."

"I'll correct that with the staff, but you cannot—"

"You know I hate laziness."

Raimond shook Sorcha so hard it cracked bones in her spine. "You will not enter this building again. Do I make myself perfectly clear?"

"Yes, yes." Shocked at Raimond's violence, she collapsed against the wall when he finally released her. "I just wanted to help. Marion is so vulnerable and nobody cares."

"You didn't give her your blood, did you?" Raimond checked the patient's forehead for fever and squeezed her hand.

"No, never." Sorcha's eyes landed on the weapon hanging around Raimond's waist. "Em?"

"Good, because that would just put her through a world of torture. Some things even vampire blood can't fix."

"I'm just trying to help somebody. Anybody. That's all I've ever wanted to do and in my present state, I'm a complete failure."

"You're not. Have you considered working with me on my project?"

"Seems morbid and sad." Sorcha pointed to the dagger. "You brought that to confront me?"

"Can't be too careful these days, especially after your friend Alexa got that priest all riled up again." Raimond unsheathed the blade and showed Sorcha the initials *P L* inscribed on the hilt. "Gift from a Highland soldier. I used it to kill Faison."

"The metal is all swirly."

"Forged from Damascus steel," Raimond said. "It's a lost, ancient art."

Sorcha cringed away. "But it's stained."

"With the blood of freedom and a little French magic. In case of emergency, it's hidden under the false bottom of my desk drawer.

Lower left."

"I'll keep that in mind."

"Reconsider working with me." Raimond folded his hands around Sorcha's trembling fingers. "You'd help a lot of people in a way that nobody else can. Just give me one night to convince you."

The next evening, Sorcha followed Raimond to a stately home in the Garden District and soaked up his instructions.

"Listen with an open mind. Treat the body with medicine if you need to, but these patients are in agony from inner pain. Their mortal bodies are dying but they can't let go of the vessel, afraid an entire life of struggle will mean nothing. Listen to their stories—what they've seen and done—who've they've loved and who they've lost. Your consciousness is forever a safe place for their treasures. Take their pain with your eyes, just as you harvest power from those you find intriguing."

"Doctor, thank you so much for coming. I pray that you can help." The housekeeper invited them over the threshold and up the stairs. The open bedroom door revealed a frail man, dwarfed by his four-poster bed.

"*Monsieur*, I'm Dr. Banitierre." Raimond encouraged Sorcha to pick up the patient's hand.

"You're lovely dear." Bony fingers squeezed lightly as she sat on the bed. "What's your name?"

"Sorcha."

"Irish?"

"Irish and English." She took his hand in both of hers under the gentle breeze of the ceiling fan.

"Do you have pain?" Raimond pulled up a chair. "I have medicine."

"No doctor, nothing hurts anymore." The patient wheezed as he whispered. "I'm just so, so tired and ready to go—almost. I'm the last one of my line. No one will remember me."

"Tell us anything, everything...whatever you want to keep alive forever." Raimond nodded to Sorcha. "Start from the beginning."

The man's death was painless for him but excruciating for Sorcha. She absorbed his thoughts, triumphs and tragedies. She pulled back in horror at the worst memories, yet leaned forward to absorb the heroism and the love story.

I'm not saving a life, but I'm granting peace at the end of one. Well-deserved peace and absolution.

Sorcha collapsed on a garden bench after it was over. "That hurt."

"But you've given an immeasurable gift. Do you think Vir could be convinced to join us?" Raimond asked.

"I don't know. His passion is healing. Or it was, when he was still human. How do I sell this?"

"Talk to him, plead with him. You're both strong, but as a couple, you're a force more incredible than anything I've been able to offer." Raimond held Sorcha's knuckles to his lips and then his forehead. "Please, just try."

Chapter 66

THE KEY

VIR STAGGERED BACK to his room to hide any evidence of his fight with the prince. His face would heal quickly and nobody needed to see it, especially Sorcha. He lunged to turn on the faucet before he fell to pieces.

Lose her? No—that's impossible. I can't lose her.

Hiding inside running water was the only chance to keep his thoughts private. He'd learned to block most vampires from his mind, but Sorcha made him. It might never be possible to shut her out completely.

"Oh God, Sorcha." Vir leaned his forehead against the mirror.

I've hurt her so deeply. What the hell is wrong with me? I actually complained that her crying hurt my ears? Can't believe those words ever came out of my mouth. Norman is a wretched bastard, but I'm an insensitive ass and I may actually owe him one.

Vir splashed water on his face, washing away blood, dirt and sugar to reveal vanishing damage. *What if I've already lost her?* He gagged again, but nothing came up. *Nobody would blame her for leaving.* She wouldn't be alone for long. Plenty of other men were interested and some women too. Vampires didn't waste much time being subtle.

Without Sorcha there's no reason for me to go on. I'll be a cursed killer with zero reasons to exist.

Vir's depression had a life of its own. Some nights were worse than others, and on the bad ones, the vortex spiraled into drowning torture. *I have to find a way to beat it. I'll win her back. I'm not giving up.* He peeled the bloody clothes from his body and stuffed them in the garbage. *That was less of a fight and more of a beat down.*

Running bathwater couldn't drown out the sounds of Draven and Gwynevere engaging in their daily sexual workout.

I haven't made love to Sorcha since—weeks or months—before I turned. How could I have lost track, especially with the constant reminder from downstairs? I need somewhere private to reconnect with Sorcha, to romance her and find the key to unlock the love we used to share.

"Wait a minute." Vir grabbed a towel, and wrapped it around his waist. "I've seen the key. I know exactly what to do, and who to ask for help."

"So, you value my fashion advice all of a sudden?" Steven slouched in a chair, watching the tailor conduct Vir's fitting. "Anything would be an improvement over your usual, dreadful choices."

"I need a new look and a fresh start." Vir turned to inspect the details. "Besides, none of my old stuff fits anymore."

"And this is going to help you mend things with Sorcha, how? You've acted like a complete piece of shit. We've all begged her to dump you."

"So far, she hasn't, though I may have pushed my luck."

"You?" Steven fanned his face with both hands. "I'm stunned."

"Everything will work out. I'm planning to apologize."

"And you think a pair of denim trousers and a new shirt is going to heal all the pain and embarrassment you've inflicted?"

"Clothes won't fix that, but I will. I love her too much. You've made it abundantly clear that you disapprove." Vir stared at Steven in the reflection of the mirror. "Were you able to get the reservation or not?"

"I am the miracle worker." Steven smirked and tossed over the prize. "Tomorrow night, dusk 'til dawn."

"Thank you, thank you." Vir twirled the familiar metal key on his fingers.

"To be clear, I'm doing this for Sorcha, not for you. Remember, the building is old, so try not to demolish it. Things may feel, you know, different," Steven warned. "If you don't understand, you will soon. And feed before you meet up with her, unless you want all this scheming to be for nothing."

Vir and Steven parted ways at the tailor's front door, both shadowed by security. Steven headed out to his favorite hunting grounds while Vir returned to the penthouse, new clothes slung casually over his shoulder. He narrowly missed crashing into Gwyn as she stumbled through the door.

"Sorry, I assumed nobody would be home at this hour." Vir's jawed twitched at the angry bruises on her wrists and neck. "What the hell is Draven doing to you? I'm going to have a word with him."

"Wait!" Gwyn chased him down the hall.

"Is that his idea of intimacy, hurting you?" Vir kicked the bedroom door open. "Where is he?"

"Don't know, out doing royal whatever. Come on, you haven't had any fun with all your new power?"

"None at all. That's the problem."

"You and Sorcha? I thought—" Gwyn bit the inside of her cheek. "You two are so in love."

"I've been…unavailable to her since I turned, emotionally and physically. Hideous, with no excuse. But I have a plan to get us back on track."

"I know we're the same age, but can I give you some advice?"

Vir rested a hand on his chest. "I desperately need it."

"Why do you wait so long to feed? Only my opinion, of course, but you push it off later and later every night until you lose control."

"I still hate that I have to do it." Vir sunk onto the sofa, dropping the garment bag in a heap. "In the end, my hunger wins out. An epic struggle, every time."

"Then you get depressed."

"It's as if tentacles are dragging me under water. It's pitch black and I can never escape."

"You need to break that cycle." Gwyn retrieved Vir's bag and laid it over the chair. "Or you'll lose Sorcha. Have you ever considered, I don't know, embracing what you are?"

Vir closed his eyes and shook his head. "I've wanted to be a doctor since I was a kid. Becoming a demon was not in my career plan."

"I hear Raimond is an amazing doctor."

"He spent decades learning that kind of self-control."

"So what if it takes years? You have all the time in the world."

"Thank you." Vir squinted at Gwyn, really seeing her warm smile for the first time. "That's the most encouragement anyone has given me since I opened my eyes in that basement."

"We have a bond no one else shares, you know? We died and were reborn on the same day—twins."

"Can I ask you for just one more favor, sister?" Vir spun the key in his fingers. "I need you to deliver something for me."

Sorcha touched up her lipstick and pulled a crumpled note out of her coat pocket.

Dearest Sorcha,

Meet me at our river bench, where it all began. Nine PM sharp.

Love always,

Vir

Her chest still fluttered when she saw his handwriting, just as his doctor's signature had given her butterflies so long ago in Nepal. The cryptic note had been delivered by Gwyn this afternoon. *Something must be up. That girl couldn't hide her goofy grin, although she made a gallant effort.*

Turning left out of the back alley, Sorcha walked toward the river. Her eyes caught the subtle movement of Raimond's security guards as they fanned out behind her. Protection from an entire platoon was probably unnecessary, but it did simplify things. She never thought twice about what she did or where she went. Driving her hands deep into her pockets, she strutted down the middle of the wharf that curved along the Mississippi.

Hope my mini-dress and tall black boots aren't inappropriate for this meeting. She fluffed the hair out of her collar and let the breeze tousle it into full waves around her head. Tonight, the familiar humidity and smell of river mud had been replaced by the invigorating, salty scent of the ocean.

The area around the bench looked oddly deserted for early evening. *It is nine o'clock. Vir's been acting so odd. Hope he didn't stand me up.*

"Angel."

She whirled around to see a figure in a black leather jacket, leaning against the railing.

"Vir?"

She almost didn't recognize her own boyfriend, but more than his new image caught her off guard. *That pure, Vir smile! I haven't seen it in months.* He looked casual, relaxed, almost happy.

"Come over here, beautiful." Vir held up his hand. "Please." Scattered rays of moonlight peeked out from behind clouds, making his skin glisten as if he were lit from inside.

"Everything all right?" Surprised that he remembered their quirky custom, Sorcha offered her palm to meet his. A jolt of energy shot down her spine as the electricity now jumped both directions instead of only coming from her. "Almost forgot about that."

"My fault, because I let you forget. I've been acting like a spoiled brat, among other things, and want to make amends."

"You don't have to apologize. I'm the one who—"

"Shhh." Vir placed his fingertip to Sorcha's lips, redirecting her eyes to meet his. "Yes, I do, and I need to make it up to you."

350

Molten eyes. Liquid brown with swirls of sapphire.

"Do you remember our first kiss in the hospital garden, when I asked you to forgive me?" Vir tipped Sorcha's chin upward, until they were separated only by a sliver of charged air. His lips brushed the skin of her cheek, working across her eyelids until he had covered her entire face. "I'm asking again. Forgive me, angel. I love you. I never stopped."

Months of suppressed emotion welled up as Sorcha flinched against the steel frame of his body. Lunging for each other, they collided in a frantic kiss.

"Bastard." Sorcha pulled back and hammered his chest with her fists. "You hurt me."

"I know I did." Vir absorbed her assault. Lifting Sorcha off her feet, he carried her to the river railing in three strong strides. Her wind-swept hair billowed around their next kiss like a cloud.

"I have a surprise for you." Vir gripped Sorcha's hand and steered her toward the city. He shot down murky alleys and walked brazenly through bars full of drunks and questionable clientele. Not one person made a move to challenge them, either looking away or following with their eyes only.

"I'm still angry." Sorcha's mind fought back, but her feet followed willingly. "Where are we going?"

"You'll see." Vir didn't look back.

This is just the tip of the iceberg. When he learns how to control and wield his power, he'll be unstoppable. Right now, he's pretty damn sexy. Sorcha slowed for a few steps, distracted by a figure camouflaged in the shadows. This one didn't shrink away. *Who is that?*

"Close your eyes," Vir commanded. The tumbling of a familiar lock was followed by the unmistakable scent of incense and strains of eerie chanting.

Sounds and smells of delicious sin. "I know where we are!"

Vir sped halfway up the stairs before Sorcha caught him. Tossing both their jackets aside, he searched the bar until he found a bottle of port. Sinking into the velvet sofa, the faint ringing of the bells sent them back in time.

"Right there." Vir pointed to a shiny mirror. "When you showed yourself to me, I was so in awe of your strength."

"Now you're just as strong, if not more."

"I need to learn how to use my power, not let it consume me and ruin us. The first step is to make things right. I brought you here because it's one of my cherished memories and I thought we deserved some simple happiness."

"You're not much of a talker anymore."

"I'm working on it."

Finishing off her wine, Sorcha straddled Vir's lap and stroked his face with her fingertips. "So, can tonight be as good as our first time?"

"Or better?" Vir ran his hands up her thighs and under her emerald dress, hooking his fingers into lace panties. "Hope these aren't your favorites."

"They're brand new."

"Buy more." Vir tossed the shredded underwear aside. He unzipped Sorcha's dress and helped her slip it off. "No bra?"

Sorcha removed his shirt with trembling fingers, teasing his skin in between each button. "Sometimes, I don't bother. Complaining?"

"Hell, no." Vir eagerly took her nipple in his mouth, flicking with the tip of his tongue. Instead of interrupting his momentum, he embedded the next request into Sorcha's head. *Leave those boots on.*

Take those pants off.

He squirmed out of his trousers before carrying her deeper into the red suite, careening off walls as they ravaged each other.

Careful—it's an old building.

"I was warned not to wreck the place." Vir lowered her into a lush pile of pillows. "Sorcha, you are so beautiful."

"What are you waiting for?" Sorcha had only admired Vir's new body from afar until now. The close-up view was nothing short of spectacular.

"Spread your legs." Vir leaned back.

"I remember what you like." Sorcha arched her back and placed one high-heeled boot next to each of his hips.

In the blink of an eye, he was on top of her, gripping her chin, forcing her face straight ahead. "Don't close your eyes. Look at me, watch me when I take you." He crushed his hand over Sorcha's mouth at the precise moment that she screamed in exquisite pain.

Rolling over and under each other, their bodies fell into rhythm. Sorcha knew Vir was close to finishing by the quivering of his muscles. Forcing herself to keep her eyes open, she grabbed the furniture behind her and braced for the final push. He surprised her again.

"Ow!" Vir had bitten Sorcha before, playfully, but there was nothing lighthearted about it this time. He sunk fangs into her neck and tasted her blood for the first time as a vampire. The act of teeth piercing flesh pushed Sorcha to the brink of her own climax.

"Do it, Sorcha. Bite me, complete the circle."

Entwined in each other's bodies, they kept up the slow, maddening pace while she made up her mind. Finding the perfect spot on his neck, Sorcha bit tenderly and then sucked hard, swallowing enough blood to launch her over the edge. Vir's eyes flew open as he rode the waves of pleasure, his guttural growls smothered in pillows.

As if the sex wasn't mind-blowing enough, their first pure vampire encounter had come with one extra perk. Sorcha thought her imagination had gone crazy.

"Vir, our hands." Sorcha placed her palm on the back of his hand and watched as their fingers laced and flesh melted together at the edges.

"That's new."

"After I swallowed your blood, every inch of our skin that touched, blended and got blurry. Not just our hands—"

"So, we truly are a part of each other now." Vir exhaled, content to lie still, tangled and fuzzy. "Sorcha, I said some things."

"Don't worry—"

"Stop." Vir pressed his fingers to Sorcha's lips. "I hurt you and I regret it, every stupid word. Forgive me."

Chapter 67

Hands Full

THE GALA OF the Equinox was spectacular and dazzling, minus the stress of the previous year's festivities. Now that Sorcha was an established family member, the only ceremony pending was a private gathering to witness Vir's signature in the official coven registry. Sipping wine in Raimond's private library, they waited in silence for Prince Norman to arrive. Even though Vir's attitude and overall behavior had improved, the family still whispered around him, unsure what was safe to discuss and what might ignite his temper.

After an awkward delay, Draven entered with a formal nod. "Good evening, Sorcha. Vir." His voice dripped with distaste. "Well, you two appear to have mended things." His eyes lingered on Sorcha's bare shoulder where Vir's hand rested and their skin visibly melted together.

"I appreciate all your help, Prince Norman," Vir said, making more than the customary eye contact before looking away.

"Let's get this done, shall we? I left my Gwynevere downstairs in questionable company." Draven swept his hand over the ancient book, fanning it open to the correct page. "As you can see, Dr. Ashayle, your name is already printed below that of your maker." Glancing toward the corner, he continued. "Raimond, I assume you informed our newest associate of the rules and responsibilities that go along with membership in this coven?"

"I have," Raimond answered.

"Ashayle, do you understand and accept all that has been told to you?"

"Yes, Your Highness."

"Excellent. Sign it." Draven held out a pen and watched as the ink of Vir's sweeping cursive dried under Sorcha's.

With official business concluded, the somber mood lifted and the house band played to a full dance floor all night. In between royal obligations, Draven spent his evening dancing with Gwyn and introducing her to all in attendance as the new love of his life.

"I'm sure the next big announcement will be their engagement," Sorcha said.

"Ever been to a vampire wedding?" Vir asked.

"Nope, but I'm sure it'll be a production. Everything is. Is it true Gwyn has no living ancestors?"

"She has no memory of her parents, only bits and pieces of time spent at orphanages."

Sorcha traced a finger across her eyebrow. "Her features almost look Egyptian."

"Because of her, Draven isn't threatening to kill me anymore trying to get to you." Vir nuzzled Sorcha's neck. "Have I told you yet how exquisite you are tonight?"

"Yes, but you can tell me as often as you like." Sorcha was thrilled that he approved of the outfit Steven whipped up. She wasn't used to wearing light colors or pastels, but this gown was exceptional. Ice blue with delicate sapphire scrollwork, the floor-skimming, strapless gown was the perfect frame for her heirloom diamonds.

Though obligated to serve samples of her blood to party guests, Rayna made herself available to dance with Vir, Raimond, Steven and Draven. The prince never wasted an opportunity to tango with Rayna.

"I'm not crazy about the idea of all these strangers drinking from our friends downstairs. It seems dangerous, especially for her." Vir nodded to Rayna's slender form on the patio. "Some of these misfits are getting off on it."

"That's always made me squirm. She seems to take it in stride, though." Sorcha raised the walls in her mind. *Rayna's stuck by me through this whole nightmare, even though the night Vir got sick, I was ready to break away from her. If she knows, she's never let on, and I sure can't go through with it now. She waited, she comforted me when Vir all but discarded me, and what did she get in return? I chose him over her. Again.*

"Angel?" Vir touched her elbow. "Where did you go just now?"

"Em, daydreaming." Sorcha scanned the crowd. "Think our skin mingling frightens people?"

"Maybe a little. I've noticed a few stares."

"Every time I turn around, creepy Cole Victoire is leering at me." Sorcha pulled down the walls in her mind. *He's burning holes in both of us—probably still angry that his tart of a girlfriend was banished to Europe. Too bad he didn't go with her.*

"I've got this."

"No!" Sorcha hissed as Vir stepped past her.

"We've never formally met." Vir held out his hand to Cole in greeting. "Dr. Vir Ashayle."

After a double take and a furtive glance at Sorcha, the bald man returned the handshake. "Cole Victoire."

"Can I help you?" Vir asked. "You appear to be searching for something or someone."

"No, I'm quite satisfied. Beautiful party—what could I possibly need?"

"Good to meet you then, sir. Enjoy the rest of your night." Vir stood his ground.

"I plan to." Cole squared his shoulders and winked at Sorcha. "Welcome to the society, Vir Ashayle. You have your hands full."

Raimond assigned Vir a room in a wing of the main house. A glorified closet painted a more accurate description, but the strict rules of conduct had loosened. Afternoon refreshments in Sorcha's sitting room became a ritual.

"Rayna, I don't mean to harp, but I don't see why you have to cater to strangers at these parties." Vir poured himself a second cup of coffee.

"I don't even think twice about it." Rayna sipped from her china.

"We're aware," Sorcha said. "That's what makes it a security nightmare."

"Stop worrying. Last night I met a new fella with an Australian accent." Rayna smiled wistfully. "So charming, but it made me homesick."

"Who?" Vir asked.

"Don't remember his name." Rayna yawned.

"Lady Sorcha." Penny bustled in with a cardboard container. "Duke Raimond sent over a box of your personal items found in storage at Sisters of the Peace. He's offered to save anything you like in the vault with your diamonds."

"I completely forgot about this box. I'm not sure I can handle..." Sorcha looked helplessly at Rayna and Vir. "It's my mum's stuff."

"We'll help, don't worry." Rayna tapped dust off the lid. "Heavens, these look like love letters to your mother."

"And World Series tickets." Sorcha fought back tears.

Vir opened a velvet box. "Captain's bars from your dad's navy uniform and quite a few British military medals."

"Sorcha, have you seen these pictures?" Rayna untied the ribbon on a stack of black and white photographs.

Delicately separating the old papers, Sorcha was sure she'd never noticed the collection before. "This one looks like Dad in front of a castle." She held it up for her friends to examine.

"I visited the Highlands often during medical school. That structure might date back to medieval Scotland." Vir looked at several more pictures. "Why is this one familiar?"

"I think that's the full-size version of the wedding picture in my locket."

"I see handwriting on the back. What does it say?" Rayna asked.

"Aldenridge, 1914." Sorcha shrugged. "Aldenridge? Never heard of it."

"I can see the castle in the background." Vir placed the photo on the table, spun it with his fingers and slid it to Sorcha. "I'll bet your parents got married in a chapel on your father's family estate."

Sorcha's dingy cardboard box looked out of place next to the treasures in Raimond's vault. She assumed her diamonds were kept in a safe, but a hulking iron door ushered her into a labyrinth of subterranean rooms.

Might as well be a tomb. In contrast to the witch sentry and magic password system of the mansion's underground tunnel, security on the vault was a conventional combination lock. *Lame.*

"Don't worry, it's more secure that it looks." Raimond stepped out from the shadows. "Trick lock."

Sorcha's eyes scanned shelf after shelf of ornate boxes along with racks of wine and scotch. "Is everything here yours?"

"Not all of it. I encourage coven members to safeguard their human heritage. Most of what's stored here is similar to what you have. Pictures, letters, jewelry and war memorabilia." Raimond threw open a walk-in armoire, displaying frayed clothing. "Here's what passed as my uniform during the French Revolution, complete with the bullet holes."

"You were killed in these clothes? I remember you said 1789. Was it Bastille Day?"

"That's the correct year." Raimond scratched his chin. "I was shot two days before the storming of the Bastille, during a minor skirmish in the Tuileries Garden."

Sorcha opened her mouth and closed it again.

"Oddly, I was the only one shot during that incident. It was almost like someone, maybe foreigners, targeted me."

Sorcha slumped against the wall.

"Too morbid? Let's see what else we have. Those belong to Draven." Raimond pointed farther back on the rack. "His favorite Bavarian ball gowns from the last few centuries."

Lavish fabric, perfectly preserved in colors ranging from icy white to the richest jewel tones. Sorcha regained her composure and touched the lace hem of an ivory garment.

"His great-grandmother's wedding gown."

"Some family he was born into."

"He's complicated." Raimond blew invisible dust off his fingers. "Steven says he invited you and Vir to his summer party. Planning to go?"

"Guess I have no choice."

"Things must be bad if Vir wants to hang around with Steven."

"He's hungry and bored. Between you and me, I'd rather stay here."

"With Rayna?" Raimond asked quietly.

"Well, with everyone, I mean, not just…"

"Your best friend has been through some difficult times since I recruited her. She always winds up as someone's second choice."

"It seems like a terrible trap." *Does he know about us?*

"There are options open to her. So far she's never shown the desire to follow a different path."

Thoughts blurred behind Sorcha's eyes as she slammed her mind shut. *How long has he known?*

"Calm down, Sorcha. Keep yourself safe. I'll either be here or at the hospital if you need me and I'll keep an eye on Rayna." Raimond picked up her hand and brushed a kiss across her knuckles. "By the way, I've changed the password on the tunnel gate and I'm not doing it again until after Christmas."

Sorcha wrapped her arms around her chest. "Why not?"

"Those witches make it so complicated. Wailing, fire, blood—more blood. Much too much drama."

"Well, what's the password?"

"I'm telling you, Steven, Lily and Jules. That's it." Raimond pointed to her head. "Keep it locked up." *Ouragon.*

"What the heck does it mean?"

"Hurricane. How about some French lessons in your spare time?"

Chapter 68

ALGIERS

IVORI AND ZELIA flopped on a front-porch glider, exhausted from lugging boxes and furniture into an old house on Algiers Point.

"I don't know how I let you talk me into moving way over here, Ivori." Zelia mopped her forehead with a sleeve. "This place needs a lot of work."

"You know the situation in town is more volatile every day. At least we can get a little breeze off the river, plus I need a life."

"Can we actually live together? We've never been best friends."

"Being friends isn't necessary." Ivori looked down her nose. "Having things in common, such as enemies, is essential."

"I agree, we tempted fate living under the roof of the church for so long."

"You and I both believe something is up with Banitierre. He's a great doctor, but it's a meticulously crafted front."

"I was so devastated when we lost Sorcha, but I should have been suspicious, even back in Nepal." Zelia inspected her fingernails. "If he knows we aren't exactly who we say we are, all the more reason for us to get some distance."

"How 'bout Ashayle? Are we supposed to believe that he and Sorcha just—poof—without a trace?" Ivori pulled her hair free, one clip at a time. "Hell no."

"You seem positive about the connection. Hope it's more than the theatrics in your blood."

"Don't go knockin' my heritage now. It's why I own this house. All the boys in my family went to Paris for a fine education. But the women, we stayed here and studied other subjects."

"Even I know about your great, great—"

"Add one more great," Ivori said.

"The quadroon grandmother. She was one of the elite," Zelia said.

"Legendary, minus that taboo nonsense people gossip about. She was a force of nature—set the Journes free." Ivori pointed to a second-floor window. "That bedroom belonged to her, and every matriarch since."

"I haven't seen your hair down before. I mean, ever." Zelia stared hard at Ivori's fingers, twirling smooth waves. "Is it really…?"

"Mahogany?"

"And purple?"

"Another Journe gift." Ivori gave the glider a nudge with her heel. "Don't roll your eyes, Zel."

"I'm one hundred percent Roussel witch. Will your family spirits allow me to live here?"

"You'll be safer than in the convent. I wanted to get the hell out of there the minute we got off that ship."

"Pfft, that trip was cursed, and I think the hex is still alive and slithering around the hospital. Especially with that St. James girl showing up every other week."

"You know what you need Zelia? A man. When was the last time you—"

"Stop right there. Roommates, remember, not friends. And wipe that smirk off your face."

"I can't see my face." Ivori leaned back and crossed her legs. She planned to confirm her beliefs before dropping any more bombshells on Zelia. Sorcha and Vir were alive or walking among the living, at least. She'd seen them both, but only for a split second. What they were—that she needed to find out.

Chapter 69

ST. PETER

STEVEN TURNED A key and the Cord's engine roared to life in Normandie Hall's driveway.

"Shotgun!" Vir jumped into the automobile's passenger seat.

"What, no canoodling tonight?" Steven glanced at Sorcha's frown in the rearview mirror.

"Have I told you how much I admire your driving skills?" Vir asked.

"Oh, Dr. A likes my driving now? Will wonders never cease."

"Step on it. I want to be safely in the Marigny in time for a quick hunt."

"Yes, sir, doctor sir." Steven nailed the gas pedal. "Maybe not Marigny, though. I have a surprise. Sorcha girl, where have you always wanted to live?"

Taking the scenic route, the coffin nose sedan cruised along the Mississippi River and into New Orleans, snaking around turns and slowing to allow its passengers to peek down alleys and through the open doors of neighborhood bars. The car was brand new, but after sixty miles of Louisiana mud, the nasty chrome grill made it look like a monster ready to devour anything in its path.

"What do you think of this address?" Steven pulled up to a curb in the middle of the block.

"*Rue St. Pierre.*" Sorcha remembered the first time she saw the red buildings surrounding Jackson Square and wondered who was lucky enough to live there. That was a lifetime ago, before she set sail across the Pacific as a terrified, young girl. She whistled her approval as she stepped out and looked up at the tiered balconies overflowing with luscious plants. "These apartments are impossible to come by."

"Well, it's only a sublet, but my friends from Hattiesburg owed me a favor. We have the place until October. Four solid months of location, location, location. Come on, let's check the inside."

A petite human maid greeted them at the door and invited each vampire in by name. Sorcha took Steven's outstretched hand and followed him down a long corridor that ended in a spiral staircase.

"This is spectacular." Vir gaped at the high ceiling and French doors that soared to meet it. "When was it built?"

"Eighteen hundred...something." Steven showed off the third-floor bedrooms, simple and elegant, each set up to take full advantage of the river breeze. "Not ideal for those easily damaged by the sun, but there's a secret."

A closet door concealed the gateway to a night walker's playground. Elegant wall panels concealed a tight stairway that spun below street level. The basement featured an expansive gallery with individual rooms arranged around the common area. The spaces above ground were for appearances, while the cozy subterranean nooks were designed for everything else.

"Vir, look up." Sorcha flopped across the huge bed, swiveling her head to admire stone walls draped with velvet and illuminated by soft lights. The drama didn't stop with the fabric. "The designer was a genius."

"Mirrors, whatever will we use those for?" Vir crushed her body into silk sheets.

"Not now, you nut—everyone's right outside the door." Sorcha giggled. "Thought you were starving?"

Vir rolled to the side, still stroking her hair and tugging at the hem of her shirt.

"A stroll and a quick bite." Sorcha made a break for the door. "Then we'll test out every angle of these mirrors."

They found the Quarter just as they left it. Time seemed to stand still as perpetually sagging buildings were held up by invisible forces.

Damn, I missed this place.

Watching Vir feed in any environment had become a sight to behold. While most made socially acceptable work of drinking and sending their clueless victims on their way, he had a different approach—and finish. Only complete anonymity and the element of surprise allowed him to be brutal enough to satisfy his cravings. Vir's attack mimicked the lightning strike of a viper, right down to the razor-sharp fangs. His swift recoil included repairing the victim and covering his tracks in one seamless motion. The unfortunate human was abandoned in a heap, wherever it fell.

Lethal, unforgiving, powerfully erotic—and he knows it.

The weeks that followed flew by in a haze of blood and booze, chocolate and smoke. Steven worked his connections on the street, filling the underground lounge with a mind-bending cloud every night.

While cloves relaxed Sorcha and took the edge off any lingering jitters, whatever contraband was packed in the little pipes made her lose inhibition and heightened her senses. *Why Steven smokes, I'll never know.*

For Vir, the illicit substances gave him tunnel vision to the bedroom. "Shhh…" He placed a chocolate square in Sorcha's mouth. "Where's your sense of adventure?"

"We're upstairs, anybody could see—not sure how comfortable I am with this." She tried her best to resist lips trailing down her neck. *Where does he get these ideas?*

"It's nothing the eyes of this city haven't beheld." Vir twirled her to face him, brushing a delicate silk strap off her shoulder. "On the other hand, nobody but me has glimpsed you, angel. Think I'll tempt fate and show you off."

Stifling a groan, Sorcha let him guide her backwards, to the inky blackness of the third-floor balcony. *Between his tongue and his fingers, I can't—damn it.*

Spinning her around, he guided her hands, one to each side of the door frame. "Hold on—admire your view while I admire mine."

Danielle flattened her back against a stone pillar. With her hair jammed under a hat, she'd trolled the city in dirty shapeless rags, waiting until the darkest hours to drink blood no other vampire would touch and no human would ever miss. She still feared for her life, even though Lock assured her safety. Jealousy and anger boiled in her chest, but she couldn't tear herself away from Sorcha's hands braced against the door or the slip draping off one shoulder while her body moved to another vampire's rhythm.

"I hate her guts."

Danielle registered every graphic detail in the upstairs window. Gauzy curtains waving in the breeze hid Vir's body from view, but she knew he was there. She saw his hand clamped around Sorcha's throat and flashes of brown skin against her alabaster flesh.

"I hate her. With every fiber of my being—I despise her."

Other than Lock, nobody knew she was back in Louisiana. Not Nicholas, not even Cole.

"Here I am, again, in the gutter. Spent my human life drowning in it—I'll be damned if I'm stuck here for eternity."

Sensing a change in Sorcha's gaze, Danielle darted behind the concrete post, peering cautiously around it at the silhouettes in the window.

"What the devil is she looking at?"

She craned her neck to search empty darkness.

The vampire princess in her tower screamed, but no sound shattered the heavy silence of Jackson Square. Vir's hand clamped over Sorcha's mouth, stifling the cry as he drove his fangs into her neck.

"Goddamn it." Danielle ripped into the flesh of her own forearm to stay quiet. "Can't stomach anymore of this."

One last glance upward gave her a clear view of a barely dressed

Vir, his satiated lover cradled like a feather in his arms and his piercing eyes fixed on the dark horizon. Stumbling away in a fog of rage, Danielle's escape ended when a chilling voice stopped her in her tracks.

"Do you want them to get away with it?"

"What?" Danielle didn't dare turn back.

"I've been listening to you, babbling to yourself. You want to make those damn Banitierres pay?"

"I do." She whirled around. "But who, exactly, are you?

"I'm an Allemand. Friend to your family and an enemy of theirs, Ms. Victoire."

"You know who I am?" Danielle cringed, expecting the Royal Guard to swoop in at any second.

"Calm down ragamuffin, I won't give away your secret. I can help you get revenge though, if you're willing to join forces with an old witch."

"What's in it for you? I have no money."

"You aren't the only one tired of their extravagances. They may be the reigning family, but their actions this summer have been a disgrace and their foreign blood makes the entire region unstable."

"What's the plan?"

The witch flashed a crooked smile. "Bring me an article of Lady Sorcha's clothing—something substantial. I've conjured a spell lethal enough to throw a wrench in the mighty Banitierre holiday plans."

"I can get that bitch back?"

"Her, and her snake of a lover too, if you desire."

"Oh, I desire it—more than you know."

"I'll be in touch. Stay hidden, and keep quiet." The witch slipped into the pre-dawn shadows.

"Sorcha, you stuck-up little bitch and pathetic excuse for a vampire." Danielle looked up at the glowing window. "I'll have what's yours and if I kill you in the process, so be it. When my allies and I are finished, you'll never know what hit you."

Lock ordered two shots and kicked a bar stool out for his brother. "Where have you been, mate?"

"All the bars in New Orleans, and you choose this hell hole."

"It's called keeping a low profile, Chapal. If you weren't such a butcher, we would still be welcome in the high-class establishments." Lock sipped cheap whisky and grimaced. "I can't chance being seen with you."

"You're pathetic—know that? Word on the street is Ashayle got himself turned."

"Ah yes, an impressive specimen too, as was the original intention. Have you ever considered his value as family?"

"Father would want him dead now and you know it. He'll never be pure."

"You're really hung up on the purity of blood." Lock grabbed the drink out of Chapal's hand. "What about me? Am I any less your brother because I'm from Australia?"

"This has nothing to do with you."

Not yet—until it does. Lock rubbed his throat and returned his brother's icy stare. "Have I mentioned that Ashayle is bigger than you? Significantly."

"And I'm older and smarter." Chapal wrangled his drink back. "Human or vampire—he's a dead man. Did you get into that Equinox event up the Mississippi?"

"I did. The menu was exceptional, reminded me of home. And that mansion..." Lock kissed his fingers. "Magnificent."

"Why didn't you get rid of Ashayle that night?"

"The Banitierres are guarded like the crown jewels."

Chapal snorted. "I think you were too busy having fun."

"And what's wrong with that?" Lock asked.

"We're Dorje. We don't do fun. What's our next move?"

"The St. Peter party," Lock mumbled into his glass. "I'll talk my way in."

"That place has a revolving door. I can get in too." Chapal ordered another shot.

"Are you sure, brother? You might accidentally enjoy it."

"You've failed to complete our mission multiple times. Father is facing enemy threats back home."

"He's got his army and all the tigers," Lock said. "Nobody would dare."

"The region is more unstable than you think. The hell with being recognized. We need to put this filthy town in our rear-view mirror."

Lock sucked air through his teeth. "Fine by me." *That's a lie. I've got plenty more to do here, with or without him.*

"Does this place have a trough for a urinal?" Chapal turned his back as the restroom door swung open.

"And a mirror above it." Lock suppressed a smile. *I do love this city.*

"I've had enough. Meet me on the levee at three, after all the lightweights have called it a night."

Lock waited for his brother to leave before he flagged down the bartender.

"Another, mister?" The young man flicked a lock of orange hair out of his eyes with the back of his tattooed hand.

"How about you just leave the bottle?"

"Mister, that's against our policy." The young man smiled faintly as he slipped into Lock's stare. "But I'll make an exception."

"Thanks, mate." Lock tucked the bottle under his arm and tossed cash on the bar. "Join me outside and maybe I'll take you to the wildest party you've ever seen."

"I live here. I've seen it all."

"I'll go out on a limb and say you haven't. Not yet anyway." Lock smirked. *I predict he changes his mind.*

The usual cast of characters filtered along the street below, drinks in hand, coveted strings of beads around their necks.

This city has opened my eyes. I want it, need it. I'm not going back across the Pacific to that lonely, boring and suffocating life. It may take some backdoor deals and sacrifice, but if I play it right, I can have my piece of paradise. Chapal—he's going to be tricky.

A tap on his shoulder brought Lock back to Bourbon. His eyes followed ink up the bartender's arm, as he took a swig from the whisky bottle. "You've changed clothes."

"Does your wild party invitation still stand, Daddy?"

Chapter 70

POISON

THE REASON FOR the Banitierres' privilege of living in the historic building became clear to everyone as time wore on. Steven tended to the jungle of tropical plants on the gallery and talked to each one as if it were going to grow a mouth and chat back. His reputation as a gardener was well deserved. The flowers were magnificent, filling the rooms with divine scent only sweltering nights in a deep, Southern garden offered.

Every year the trendy crowd found a fresh location to indulge their darkest urges. By summer's end, the party beneath St. Peter had become local legend, a continuous orgy with a parade of victims that would have made the devil himself stand and applaud.

Sorcha and Vir participated on the fringes of the debauchery, but other family members dabbled in every vice imaginable. Steven and Lily both took advantage of the nameless and faceless prey that offered themselves up for service. Even straight-laced Julia took a handsome stranger to her bed on occasion.

Draven visited, but while he thrived in the carnival atmosphere he never let Gwynevere out of his sight. "Darling, stay right next to me while I attend to business." The prince zipped into Steven's private corner.

Steven grabbed his hands back from his companion, shoving pipes and rolling papers in his pocket.

"Terribly sorry to rattle you." Draven forced a smile. "Such a wonderful party, so well attended and a masterful use of space. Would you mind if I had a look around?"

"Of course, Your Highness. I'm sure no one would mind if you...used their room. You and Gwyn, I mean."

"Thank you, kindly. And your guest? We've not been properly introduced."

"I apologize." Steven coughed and clapped his chest. "This is Lock... Just Lock."

"No last name? How very scandalous. So you're aware, he arrived with a tattooed local." Draven looked the stranger up and down. "This younger generation. Carry on, then."

After a moment in Sorcha and Vir's bedroom, Draven cursed and dragged Gwyn toward the stairs.

"What is it? What just happened?" Gwyn forced a grin and waved at the partygoers. "Draven, I thought we were sneaking a look at the rooms?"

"Did you feel someone or something rush past you?"

"No, I was admiring all the fabric. Weren't the mirrors just..."

Draven sniffed a chalice in her hand and recoiled. "Is that cup from their chamber?"

"I didn't steal it. They have a whole bar set up in the corner."

Draven clenched his jaw as he scanned the crowd. "I smell silver sage."

"Poison? Who else was in there?"

"No idea." Draven channeled all his power to his girlfriend's eyes. "Don't let your fear show. There's one exit from this dungeon. If it gets blocked, we may never get out."

"What about Vir?" Gwyn started to shake.

"We'll warn him, but let me handle it." Draven beckoned from the edge of the lounge. "Ashayle, may I have a word with you?"

"Are you going to beat me up again?" Carrying a half-empty bottle of scotch, Vir dragged his feet behind the prince to a smoky alcove. "Sister."

Gwyn nodded.

"Can you give it a rest with the damn booze?" Draven snapped the bottle from Vir's hand and tossed it onto a chair behind him. "Listen, I'm going to give you some advice. Please try to put our past differences aside and take what I have to say seriously."

"O…kay?" Vir said.

"I'm all for fun and living the high life. Hell, I'm famous for it, but this," Draven motioned in a circle behind him, "has gone way too far. Take Sorcha and leave."

"Tonight?"

"This place is far from a secret, and some of the characters you've invited in? Let's just say I wouldn't close one eye with these criminals under the same roof."

"Where do I take her?"

"To the penthouse. Do the right thing and take her home to Raimond."

Vir stared at his feet. "Sometimes, I think he hates me."

"Sometimes, I hate you too. Get over it. Relationships and dynamics between vampires change constantly. Raimond will be overjoyed, I promise."

"Go, brother," Gwyn whispered.

Vir's invitation for a short walk led Sorcha past her favorite statue. The sky began to brighten before she was ready to go. He took her hand and without hesitation walked to the penthouse on Canal Street.

"Did something happen?" Sorcha asked.

"It's just time." Vir led the way up familiar stairs to the penthouse.

"You're home!" Raimond hugged Sorcha, let her go, hugged her again and clapped Vir on the shoulder. "I'm thrilled to see you too. Truly, I am."

Over the next few weeks the Banitierres drifted back to the nest, and their leader welcomed each one with open arms. Sorcha was positive he wanted to know what had gone on under that St. Peter apartment, but he never asked and none of them offered any details. In the days after her departure, as memories became clearer, she realized that the culture there had gone from fun, to toxic, to incredibly dangerous. Whatever motivated Vir to leave must have been stronger than the deep hold that scene had on them. He never offered an explanation and, like Raimond, she never asked.

Chapter 71

REVELATION

IN THE FIRST week of October, Raimond sent for Rayna. Sorcha hadn't communicated with her in months. No letters, no phone calls, nothing.

"How is she?"

"Healthy, but sad," Raimond said. "I didn't think bringing her here during the summer was a good move."

"Definitely not the place for a human girl, or any girl."

"Don't beat yourself up. That party experience is all part of growing up. Far as I can tell, everyone came home safely and that's all that matters." Raimond stroked Sorcha's shoulder. "I assume you and Vir are planning to attend my dinner at Karen's? I reserved the hall with your favorite mural."

"Wouldn't miss it. That emerald room is the jewel of the French Quarter."

"Do me a favor and let Rayna tag along. Cheer her up with a night out."

The autumn equinox fell late in the year, leaving only a few weeks between the annual protection ceremony and the Masquerade Ball. Raimond's formal dinner party kicked off the Halloween season. Family members were invited, along with dignitaries from local covens. Some were solid allies, while others danced in the fringe of uncertainty. Rayna spent the night bouncing between friends she hadn't seen since the dawn of spring.

Reminds me of Bon Voyage night. Sorcha leaned on Vir's shoulder and spun a delicate flower in its crystal vase on the bar. *The menu was a little different.*

"Well, well, Dr. Ashayle." Cole appeared and extended his hand. "It's been since the Equinox, if I'm not mistaken?"

Vir curled his lips and declined the greeting.

"I trust all's well after the summer fun. You're quite famous, you know?"

"What do you want, Victoire?"

"See you've trotted out the little blood slave tonight. Available for all?" Cole pointed around the room. "Or private use only?"

"Excuse me?" Vir's menacing tone muted the merry chatter.

"Your precious Sorcha's love toy on the side?"

Vir stepped away from the bar, his eyes darting over a sea of stunned faces.

Cole tapped a finger on his cheek. "Terribly sorry—I thought you knew."

Rayna shot Sorcha a horrified look.

"That'll be enough, Victoire. Out." Raimond shoved Cole and intercepted Vir as he lunged for the bald man's throat. "Come with me, Ashayle. Everybody, let's go."

Cole tore half the bannister out of the wall before security tossed him down the stairs. "I saw you girls in the shadows of the cathedral. Secret's out!"

"Excuse me, barman." Draven dropped a large bill in the tip jar. "Forget the glasses—hand over that whole bottle of whisky, would you?"

Vir pinched the bridge of his nose and staggered into a chamber off the main dining room. "What the hell is he talking about?"

"Vir, he's a lia—"

"Stop Rayna—it's true." Sorcha's voice rang so clear, she shocked herself.

"What?" Vir waved everyone away.

"I said yes. Rayna and I were lovers." Fear knifed Sorcha's chest as she turned to see a room of frozen stares and one blond prince about to explode with excitement. *Great.*

"I knew it," Draven whispered.

"Shhh!" Gwyn pulled him back.

"You. You knew?" Vir glared at Draven. "Of course you did."

"Instinctive guess," Draven said, "What Gwyn? I just meant—fine, I'll stop."

Sorcha shut out all the voices and spoke directly to Vir. "It's been over since before you died, before I changed you."

"Oh, that makes it all better."

"I thought I'd never see you again. Then, I didn't think you'd accept me. I judged you and couldn't have been more wrong. You embraced me unconditionally and I chose you. The night you got sick, I was at Normandie." Sorcha shot Rayna an apologetic look. "Choosing you."

"Oh." Vir repeated.

"Oh? That's your best answer?" Draven asked.

"Shut up." Gwynevere shoved Draven into a chair. He responded with a zipping motion across his lips.

"I care for her deeply—I don't regret anything we did. But I love you, Vir."

"So, you two lied to me all this time?" Vir turned his back. "Sorcha, you make some lousy decisions."

"Whoa, hold on." Steven stomped to the center of the room. "You're blaming her? Seriously fool, she saved you."

"You were in on it, too?" Vir stood nose to nose with Steven. "I'm not surprised—deviant."

"And I thought you'd evolved, Dr. Hypocrite." Steven slammed his drink down hard enough to crack crystal.

Rayna snapped her fingers in Vir's face. "Imagine what it felt like to be Sorcha, and see you dying."

"I don't care what it felt like to be her. I'm busy with how shitty it feels to be me you lying, cheating little—"

"Don't you dare speak to her like that!" Sorcha pulled Rayna back. "Ever."

"How I wish Sorcha didn't turn you." Steven jabbed his finger in Vir's face.

"Gentlemen, enough. Ashayle, I won't tolerate the language." Raimond stepped in. "And Rayna, you know better than to get in the middle."

"Vir, I'd light a candle at your grave." Steven ducked past Raimond. "Chant fake prayers and dance a jig every week if I never had to hear you whine again."

"Steven, let it go." Julia tried to drag him away.

"You've never been grateful a day in your life, spoiled bitch." Steven's fist shot out and connected with Vir's jaw.

Vir staggered back, dabbing the blood off his lip with the back of his hand. "I'm the bitch?" He leapt at Steven.

"I said enough!" Raimond ripped the vampires apart and slammed both to the ground. "I'll snap your necks. Any time you want to help, Draven."

"You seem to have things well in hand." The prince remained seated.

Vir used furniture to haul himself upright, spreading his arms out to the audience. "Any more shocking news tonight?"

"I may have something." Draven popped up. "I'm sorry, Gwyn— really."

"Oh, here we go," Raimond sighed.

"First let me say, Rayna, you're quite the little trollop."

"Draven!" Raimond, Gwyn and Sorcha shouted at him in unison.

"Gwyn, you do know she was with me for years, right?"

"I never thought you were the virgin prince." Gwyn crossed her arms. "Sure you've had plenty of girlfriends. Relic."

Raimond struggled to keep his composure. "The future Mrs. Norman."

"Lovely. Thank you, darling." Draven offered Vir whisky. "Remember all the times I said you were scrawny and pitiful?"

"Uplifting memories." Vir grabbed the bottle. "What's your startling revelation?"

"I've always maintained that the weakest link in the universe is a human in love. But you were far stronger than any of us realized." By the time Draven finished telling his theory of Vir's Rakshasa breeding, the news of Sorcha's sexual exploits had faded.

"You're saying that my parents were paid by some mountain vampire clan, who shapeshift into tigers—"

"Royal, mountain vampire clan," Draven corrected Vir. "You don't believe, after all you've seen?"

"It's just too despicable—the lying. Were they paid to create me?"

"Don't turn all sour. I'm sure they were happy together."

"I stayed with either Mother or Father." Vir's shoulders sagged. "Never both at the same time."

"Well, it only takes once."

Gwyn tugged Draven's sleeve. "Dear, I think you've said enough."

"Wait, let me get this straight." Sorcha rubbed her temples with her fingers. "The monsters were looking for Vir, but instead they killed me?"

"Not just any monsters. Dorjes." Draven nodded. "But in a nutshell, yes."

"So, all this time you've been throwing blame around," she zoomed at Vir, "this whole mess, everything you're so indignant about, is your fault. You—not me!"

"He didn't ask for it, Sorcha," Raimond said.

"Not as simple as wrong place, wrong time though, was it?" Sorcha clenched her fists. "And you had me believing that bloody rubbish all along."

"Where's Rayna?" Lily asked.

Steven scanned the room. "Gone."

"It's your fault." Sorcha pointed at Vir. "Jackass."

Raimond covered his ears. "I give up."

"Finally." Draven chuckled into his drink.

"I'll find her." Julia ran down the steps, with Vir, Lily and Raimond close behind.

The group of vampires in the private lounge shrunk to four.

"You were full of information tonight, Your Highness. Was this really the right time to spin that tale and pile on?" Steven flexed his fingers and winced. "I've never even seen a Dorje."

"They're so lethal, you may have and don't even know it." Draven sneered while Steven inspected his bruises. "I remember every minute of that train wreck you called a party. My guess is, you do not."

"I maintained full control." Steven plunged his hand into a glass of ice. "Years from now, people will be raving about my—"

"For the love of the devil and his daughters. Shut the hell up—" Draven blinked and fought back a laugh when Gwyn poured her drink over his head.

"Napkin?" Gwyn offered.

"No need." Draven plucked the lilac handkerchief from his breast pocket. "Lady Sorcha, your Irish accent was fierce tonight."

"And a fabulously sexy accent it was." Steven grinned.

"Pains me to admit he's right," Draven said. "Why you keep that hidden—"

"Enough, Prince Draven Norman, you're grating on my final nerve," Sorcha snapped.

Draven held his hands up in mock surrender.

"And you're treading on shaky ground too, Mister Steven Banitierre."

"I'm all weak in the knees." Steven patted his forehead. "Is it hot in here?"

"Jayz, you're a lunatic." Sorcha shoved Steven toward the main dining room. They both turned back to watch Draven twist a handful of Gwynevere's hair like a rope, pull her close and nuzzle her ear.

"Never thought I'd see the day," Steven said. "That man may truly be in love."

"Wait." Sorcha's eyes narrowed as she strained to hear snippets of conversation.

"Shame on you, eavesdropper." Steven leaned across the bar and grabbed a full bottle of tequila. "Anything dirty?"

"No, I heard something about poison and war." Sorcha grabbed the bottle before Steven could take a swig. "Do you think Draven has seen the Dorjes?"

"He's full of shit." Steven wrestled the tequila back. "What's with your throat?"

"It's burning." Sorcha pawed at her neck. "Do you see blood?"

"Not a drop. Girl, if you're having visions again, I'm officially worried."

Security congregated around the front door, in a standoff with a bald man.

"That guy doesn't know when to quit." Vir launched himself at Cole. For the third time that night, Raimond stopped him.

"Rayna went that way." Raimond pointed the group downriver, toward the Marigny. "Vir, you will not take your anger out on her."

Once they were gone, Raimond turned his attention back to the Victoire leader. "You must have a death wish. This is your final warning—do not mess with my family again." He dragged Cole down the street by his neck and ended the encounter by driving the heel of his boot into the man's face. As he walked away, the duke threw a last glance back to Cole's limp body in the alley and the vagrant who sifted through his pockets. "Serves you right, bastard. I hope that homeless boy steals every cent."

After Raimond disappeared, the tattered figure stopped rummaging and crouched down to whisper in the beaten man's ear.

"Wake up, Cole. It's me, Danielle."

Chapter 72

NO PROTECTION

THE CEREMONY OF protection was held in the same underground location as the previous year, although this time the crowd entered through the floor of a dingy shed on a vacant piece of land between Poydras Street and Loyola Avenue. The ancient witch who frightened Sorcha presided over the gathering again. *She may have been ugly, but she wasn't wrong. Vir was in mortal danger and he never got the luxury of choosing his own destiny.*

Despite long afternoons in conversation with Gwyn, Vir had been moody and withdrawn since the fiasco at Karen's.

Sorcha believed that he wasn't angry at her anymore, or jealous of Rayna. She would have been able to feel it in his touch, scarce as that was. Still, tonight he seemed extra twitchy and uncomfortable. "What's wrong with you?"

"This place, this room is crushing me. Can't stand it," Vir answered, the split second before he ran.

Where are you going? Sorcha narrowly missed knocking over several annoyed vampires as she bolted after him. "Sorry, sorry—excuse me." *Move!* She barely kept up with Vir as he flew into the night. *Damn, he's fast.*

"Had to get some air." Vir slammed to a stop at the riverbank.

"What spooked you?"

"Being in a chapel with all those demons felt dreadfully wrong.

You believe that hocus pocus?"

"Some of it," Sorcha said. "That old bat scares me, but she's from a respected family and she's been right about a few key points. I don't like that we're missing the protection spell."

"Can't we do it tomorrow?"

"It had to be tonight—Equinox and all."

"You can go back. I just—" Vir sunk onto a concrete bench. "Last year at this time, I never could have imagined what's happened to us."

"Wasn't your choice."

"And it wasn't yours either. No more apologizing or fighting. No blame. Gwyn is right, both she and I were born because someone loved us too much to let go." Vir slipped his jacket around Sorcha's shoulders. "My heart aches for you angel, and the hell you went through."

"The truth is, if we stayed human, we'd both be dead," Sorcha said. "Well, maybe not you."

"I wouldn't be human. Always thought I imagined things, but Rakshasa have been following me since I was a child. Watching and waiting. My number was almost up." A frown shadowed Vir's face. "I just wanted to be a doctor. This is rotten."

"Indeed, it is. I think you should talk to Raimond. He's pretty good at solving problems."

"You mean his project? It's all about death."

"It's so much more," Sorcha said. "You should give it a chance."

"I'll consider it."

"Tell me the truth—are you still angry about Rayna?"

"I think the human me would have been destroyed, but now, honestly? I'm impressed and intrigued. Where's my shy, innocent nurse from New York?"

"I'm still right here."

"If you recommend Raimond's special venture, then I'm in." Vir pulled her into his chest and rubbed his cheek on her hair.

Sorcha snuggled into his arms. "You asked me, a long time ago, to free you. Are you free, lover?"

"Almost."

The first glimmers of dawn were alive on the horizon before Raimond found Vir and Sorcha huddled on the bench. "You two need to come home."

"We missed the protection ceremony," Sorcha whispered.

Raimond rested his hand on her shoulder. "I know."

"Can we go back?" Sorcha grabbed his wrist. "Maybe talk to the witch?"

Raimond tipped his head back and stared at the sky. "Not until next year."

Chapter 73

ENGAGEMENT

ZELIA AND IVORI jammed into a tiny attic on Iberville Street.

"Hurry up, the view's perfect from here."

"Who are we spying on?" Zelia asked.

"Them." Ivori pointed to a wave of well-dressed people converging on the club entrance.

"Whoa." Zelia whistled softly. "This is the Masquerade Ball."

"What tipped you off—the masks?"

Zelia slapped her knee. "So funny."

"But it's not just any costume party. It's the vampire ball."

"That's a whole lot of vampires, even for the French Quarter. What are we looking for?"

"See anyone you recognize?" Ivori observed Zelia scanning the crowd. "Focus on the tall guy next to the gate."

"Can't see his face, obviously, but he's well built under that tuxedo. Turn around handsome, let me get a better look. Ho…ly."

"Shhh, Zelia!" Ivori pressed a finger to her lips.

"That's Ashayle."

"You see who's with him?"

Both watched the couple linger in a kiss. The glamourous woman grabbed a drink from the roving waiter, plucked a lemon slice off the frosted rim and tossed it over her shoulder.

Zelia leaned over the sill. "Oh my God—Sorcha. We can't let her go in that club. Those bloodsuckers will kill her."

Ivori hauled her roommate back. "Think. She's not in danger from the vampires because she is one. They both are. Banitierre too."

"They look like themselves, but different. Ashayle is a giant. Sorcha was beautiful but she always played it down...*that* lady could be a movie star."

"I should have figured it out sooner." Ivori scrunched up her face. "She had the eyes."

"I'm afraid to ask," Zelia groaned.

"I saw the flicker in her eyes more than once. Black silhouette of the crypts. All foggy."

Zelia rubbed goose bumps that sprung out on her arms. "Okay, what now?"

"I did all the detective work. What else do you want from me?" Ivori crawled to the stairs. "Let's go, I feel like we're not alone in this attic."

"I'm not done watching them." Zelia pointed to the shadows of the club entrance.

The Banitierre family paraded down the stone alley arm in arm, not as close as they had once been, but the tension was well hidden from outsiders. They chattered with energy, still flying high from Martin's latest performance.

"What did we ever do before him?" Rayna giggled and cuddled with Steven. Both kept their distance from Vir.

"He's finally accepted that Sorcha doesn't wear wings and a halo," Julia said.

"I'm sure Barwick wishes she were still available." Vir patted Sorcha's head.

"Stop it." Sorcha punched Vir in the arm and stopped to take a modest bow. "I must be psychic. I knew Draven and Gwyn's engagement would be the next big announcement."

"That is going to be some wedding," Steven said.

"That's some ring." Lily wiggled her fingers. "Did you see the size of it?"

"Family heirloom, I'm sure," Julia added.

"A blood red ruby." Sorcha raised her hand. "Who else thinks it's real blood?"

"I bet they get married on Draven's island. Take it from me—it's a paradise," Rayna said. "For her, not for me."

"What's wrong?" Vir watched Sorcha scan rooftops and dark windows the second they emerged on the street.

"I feel eyes on me. Anyone else feel watched?" Sorcha looked from person to person. "Apparently not."

"Honey, you're just remembering last year with Danielle," Steven said.

"That bitch is gone, and good riddance." Sorcha brushed her palms together. "Let's take the long way home."

Sorcha and Vir walked the slowest and lingered for a kiss in front of their apartment building.

"Adorable as you two are," Julia tapped her foot in the foyer, "I'd like to lock up."

A stooped woman crept up and tugged Sorcha's sleeve. "You're the angel lady. The one who showed me kindness, a long time ago."

Julia reappeared. "Get inside. Sun's almost up."

"We have an hour at least, Julia." Sorcha recognized the homeless lady. "Ma'am, are you hungry?"

"Not this time." The woman shuffled her feet on the Canal Street banquette. "People say you're a nurse. My granddaughter…"

"Is she sick?" Sorcha saw a dirty little face peeking around the woman's skirt, clutching a bundle wrapped in a bloody shirt. "Or bleeding?"

"No, it's her pet bunny. The pharmacy lady takes care of animals sometimes, but her shop is closed."

"I can help." Vir stepped up and the woman flinched back.

"My boyfriend's a doctor," Sorcha said. "He'll be gentle, I promise."

"No doctor man wastes time on a little girl's pet."

"I have all the time in the world." Vir held his palms out. "Please, let me help."

"The bunny got caught in some wire down by the river…poor thing almost drowned." The old woman grasped one of Vir's fingers for a split second. "Please."

Julia grabbed a handful of Vir's shirt and stared hard at Sorcha. "This is a bad idea."

"I was halfway upstairs—" Lily marched into the corridor and froze at the sight of a child covered in blood. Her eyes snapped to Vir. "What did you do?"

"Really? You blame me?" Vir's shoulders slumped.

"Sorry, I just." Lily tugged on her earring. "I assumed."

"He's a talented doctor." Sorcha herded everyone into the building. "There's a barber shop in our lobby. Plenty of supplies and enough light to examine the rabbit in there."

Lily squeezed Vir's hand and turned her attention to the little girl. "Come on, honey. No more tears. What's your name?"

"Anna."

"And your bunny's name?" Vir tenderly lifted the furry creature from her arms.

"Easter."

"Let's see what I can do for Easter. Sorcha, can you grab some bandages and warm water?" Vir arranged a towel on the sleek counter and placed the bloody rabbit on its side. He stroked the black and white fur until the animal relaxed. "Also, a tweezer, if you can find one."

"What the hell is taking so long?" Steven dragged Rayna through the lobby door and stopped short. "I leave you alone for five minutes and strangers are bleeding on the furniture?"

"Whisht." Sorcha glared at Steven. "Vir's working."

"Should I get Raimond?" Steven asked.

All four girls answered together. "No!"

Steven held his hands up in and the lobby went silent while Vir examined the bunny's injured paw, dabbing blood and dirt from his fur with steady hands. Draven and Gwyn arrived in time to see him extract a sliver of metal wire from the wound. The group let out a collective breath when the animal perked one floppy ear up and looked straight at his doctor.

"You're very welcome, Easter." Vir applied iodine and a bandage before setting the rabbit back on his feet.

"He's all better?" Anna asked.

"Come see for yourself." Vir pulled the little girl onto his lap.

Draven silently shifted his weight. "That guy holding a child frightens me."

"Not me." Gwyn shook her head. "It's glorious."

"Look at his cute nose twitching up and down." Vir took Anna's tiny hand and helped her pet Easter. "That's how you know he's happy."

"Thank you, doctor." The old woman wrung her hands. "I have nothing to pay you with now, but I owe you a favor."

"Nonsense, I'm glad to help. If there's any redness or swelling, bring him back to us."

Sorcha wrapped the bunny in a clean towel, and handed him to Anna. Rayna helped them to the door.

Draven rubbed his chin. "Must say I'm both surprised and impressed."

"I'm not at all surprised." Gwyn hugged Vir. "But very proud of my brother."

"I've told all of you how gifted Vir is," Sorcha said.

"Carried on, endlessly." Steven stared into the dark street.

Sorcha took a deep breath. "That was proof."

"You were perfect with little Anna." Lily kissed Vir on the cheek. "She's your friend for life."

"That twisted wire was not an easy fix." Julia patted Vir's shoulder. "Raimond told me you were exceptional. He wasn't kidding."

"Oh, come on! Not you too, Jules." Steven planted his hands on his hips. "He took a splinter out of a rodent."

"You're so negative." Lily waved Steven off.

"I'm what?" Steven flashed into the middle of the room. "I radiate positivity."

"Not when you're making that face." Draven pointed to Steven. "Have you seen yourself?"

"Oh great." Steven grabbed his throat and feigned retching. "Now I'm the bad man, and Vir's the bunny savior?"

"Dramatic." Rayna waved her hands over her head. "As always."

Steven rooted around in a corner coat rack until he found an umbrella and waved the pointy end at the group.

"What are you planning to do with that?" Sorcha fought to keep from laughing.

"In case I need to vomit." Steven covered his face with the umbrella, gagged and stormed into the courtyard.

"Is he gone?" Lily giggled.

"That was priceless." Gwyn looked at Draven and shook her head.

Julia doubled over in silent laughter.

"You guys are making him resent me more," Vir said.

"No." Sorcha laid her hand over Vir's heart. "They finally believe in you."

"Sorry to disappoint—not gone." Steven zoomed back into the lobby and tossed the umbrella over his shoulder. "Dr. A, have you told Raimond you aren't joining us at Normandie tomorrow night?"

"Not yet."

"Ooo, I don't envy you." Steven pointed at Vir. "He will not be happy."

The minute they arrived in the penthouse, everyone scattered.

Julia dragged Rayna down the hall. "She needs some sleep."

"Lily, let's go for a smoke." Steven grabbed her hand and

disappeared back into the stairs.

"Did I leave my cape at the club?" Sorcha's heart sank as she brushed her bare shoulders.

"I'll send Penny for it tomorrow," Vir slid his arm around her. "I'm sure it's in the coat room."

"All right, maybe I'll take a bath." Sorcha slipped out of his grip, swallowed her guilt and trudged to her room. Staying in town for Halloween was Vir's idea—not hers. *How did I forget that cape?*

"Goddamn it, Ashayle!"

Sorcha cringed at Raimond's tirade.

"Sir, I just—"

"How many times do I have to explain? What part of not safe don't you comprehend?"

"Raimond." Draven's voice cut through the uproar. "May I make a suggestion?"

Sorcha retraced her steps and met Julia and Rayna in the hallway. All three peeked into the parlor. They saw Steven and Lily do the same from the kitchen.

"Gwyn and I have just gotten engaged." Draven implored Raimond to sit down. "I'm not throwing my usual Halloween bash. This year, it's an intimate gathering that I wish you'd attend."

Raimond collapsed into his favorite chair. "I'm listening."

"I know you have a ritual and your annual toast." Draven sat down across from Raimond. "What was Emily's favorite flower?"

"Lily of the Valley."

"I'll have a truckload delivered tomorrow. We'll all celebrate her memory together on the hotel rooftop."

"Not many are planning to take refuge at Normandie this year." Raimond stared at the ceiling. "Security was flawless last night."

"Then stay. Let Gwyn celebrate with her brother." Draven offered his hand. "The courtyard and ballroom are available for your brass band soiree the next night."

"Ben and Vera will be thrilled to play host at the plantation."

Raimond smirked at his family's silent applause from every corner before he shook Draven's hand. "Deal."

Vir slumped onto the kitchen counter in relief.

"You." Raimond pointed at Vir. "Be ready to start work on Monday night."

Chapter 74

ONE NIGHT MORE

DR. BANITIERRE'S OFFICIAL practice was with the Sisters of the Peace, but his personal project, the one closest to his heart, took place at the location of every mortal's darkest hour.

"Listen carefully. The smallest voice often carries the most powerful message." Vir repeated Raimond's words of advice before he saw his first patient. Sorcha became his nurse again. Back to the beginning.

"Remember, the miracle and the strength of this enchanted place doesn't lie in the rowdy bars or the glitzy clubs." Sorcha led Vir far from the mansions and hotels to the fringes of New Orleans. "Our city's backbone is the rich history of the people, the quiet ones, heroes and villains alike. They're the lonely souls, and with each death we lose a piece of history that exists only in their memory."

"Sounds like you're quoting from scripture."

"I kind of am." Sorcha opened the black doctor's bag. "Raimond wrote it in a letter to us, so we'd never forget."

The patients were mostly human, the type who talked very little and trusted strangers even less. Some were wracked with pain while others remained stuck in emotional purgatory. The common thread was that they were all dying. Whether alone or surrounded by others, everyone crossed that bridge as a solitary traveler. Vir carried drugs potent enough to halt any physical suffering, but he and Sorcha were there for something more elusive.

As patients unburdened their memories, the couple gained years of wisdom, but agony and heartbreak were the undeniable price of life experience.

After the first evening, Vir climbed the levee and collapsed on the grassy swell. "I can barely move."

"I think that means we've done our job. We gave those souls peace to fly. We opened the window."

"That's an elegant way to say it." Vir tucked a lock of Sorcha's hair behind her ear.

"Learned that from my Mum. Always open the window."

New Orleans turned chilly in December, but the air was dry and still, as if waiting for something to awaken.

"One more night in the city, Vir, for fun. I'm ready for some happiness." Sorcha grabbed his hands. "You know how much I love Christmas."

"Then we need to get to Normandie." Steven wrapped a scarf around his throat. "Raimond is depending on us to finish decorating."

Vir ignored him. "Sorcha, we need some private time. This new job is rewarding, exhausting and all-consuming. There's a distance between us that I don't like."

"When we get home, it's all about you and me." She arranged Vir's hair over his collar. Their relationship was still strained, but different than after their first fight. This aftermath was a deeper scar—far more difficult to repair. "We need to take care of each other."

"Sorcha, wear your cape—it's chilly out there," Lily said.

"Who found this anyway? I thought I'd lost it forever."

Julia shrugged. "Someone dropped it off at the door."

"I'm just glad to have it back." Sorcha swung the navy cloak around her shoulders.

"Gwyn!" Vir shouted down the hall of the third floor. "Are you coming?"

"Yes, yes." Gwyn appeared from her suite. "Draven had to go out of town on some damn business. He'll meet us tomorrow at the plantation. Will Raimond be able to wrap things up tonight?"

"He's signing off to his staff right now." Vir held the door open. "Christmas at the hospital is the loneliest day of the year."

"You've both worked so hard." Gwyn slipped her arms around Vir and Sorcha. "You deserve to celebrate."

The evening flew by in a merry flurry of drinking and shopping. If anyone assumed that vampires didn't obsess over Christmas gifts, they were terribly mistaken.

"Finished. Everything will be delivered to the penthouse in the morning." Steven brushed his palms together. "Sorcha, why are you dawdling?"

"What I wouldn't give for a normal breakfast." Sorcha pressed her nose against the glass window of a diner. "To sit right there at the counter with my family and eat Eggs Benedict."

"With bacon," Julia said.

Lily rubbed her belly. "I miss grits."

"I crave fresh fruit," Gwyn added.

Steven stared at the pies in the display case. "And crepes for dessert."

"Sounds heavenly." Vir kissed the top of Sorcha's head. "So simple, yet so impossible."

"Think about Normandie." Sorcha brushed Vir's face with the back of her hand. She relaxed to let their skin and minds mingle. *Can you see us, waltzing in the ballroom?*

Everything sparkling white, even the Christmas decorations. Vir raised one eyebrow. "There are things in your mind that make no sense. It's like another language."

"Ooo." Sorcha planted a kiss on Vir's lips. "Don't you go rummaging 'round in there now, Dr. Vir Ashayle."

"Only when I'm invited." Vir held her face in his hands. "And I love the happy Irish accent."

"Are those Mardi Gras beads in the branches?" Sorcha focused on the trees in Jackson Square.

"Only if the beads have feathers and chirp like maniacs." Vir paused to stare at the glittering birds. "They sound sinister."

"Hardly." Sorcha pushed Vir down the slate path. "One last walk past the cathedral? It's breathtaking with the chandeliers and the candles…twinkling through the stained glass."

"That's the accent." Vir buried his face in her hair. "Like chimes in the breeze."

"All summer I watched these windows. From the corner of our gallery, I could see inside." Sorcha hesitated before she told her secret. "Spying on the weddings."

"I was only in there once. I lit a candle for you, and got you back."

"Now you have me forever. We're finally on the right track, I think. Made quite a detour, but the people we help—maybe that's what the universe had planned for us all along."

"Sure feels right. I'm happier right now than I've ever been."

"I want to peek inside." Sorcha planted a kiss on Vir's cheek and pulled him toward the alley alongside the massive church.

The little family of vampires stood on their toes and climbed on each other's shoulders to see through the tall windows.

"Don't touch this glass, you'll get a nasty shock," Julia warned.

"Look, it must be a rehearsal for the Christmas show," Gwyn said over her shoulder.

"We've been hearing about this pageant from our patients," Vir said. "It's sad in a way, but a great memory for so many people."

Steven nodded. "Some elaborate decorations in this place. I'm counting…eleven or twelve Christmas trees."

"How many shepherds are there supposed to be?" Lily asked.

"I don't know, but there are more than three wise men too." Gwyn craned her neck to see around Steven. "All these kids are so cute."

"Sorcha, can you see the baby? I'll boost you up." Vir turned around to the dark alley. "Sorcha? Where are you?"

Cole peered through his car window and across Jackson Square. "I don't know, Danielle. I have a sick feeling about this. Don't get me wrong, I'm glad you're home, but you should be lying low, not concocting revenge plans."

"I have contingencies for everything. Nothing can go wrong."

"Witches and curses are unpredictable."

"Don't you trust me?" Danielle asked.

"If Norman finds you, you're dead."

"He won't. Our spies say he's safely in Savannah. Go to your meeting in Galveston, you'll find it interesting. I'll handle things on this end."

"I would ask you what things, but I think I'd rather not know."

"You'd be correct." Danielle slapped her hand on the car roof, stepped back and watched him disappear down Decatur Street. "See you across the bridge."

The changing weather was perfect for what she had planned. Climbing the steps leading to the top of the levee, she watched fog roll off the river. It swallowed up buildings and street lights one at a time, like a hungry monster. "I can't wait to see the look on Cole's face when I hand him the keys to his precious city. He's going to owe me—big."

"Aren't you forgetting someone?"

Danielle nearly jumped out of her skin. "Lock—don't sneak up on me. I'm still a fugitive, remember?"

"Not for long, if all goes well."

"Don't get the wrong idea. I know I owe you for helping me get back into the country…"

"But?"

Danielle scowled. "Why exactly are you and your brother helping us?"

"Does it matter?" Lock kept his eyes on the cathedral. "Our

agreement still stands? Steven Banitierre will be mine to dispose of?"

"We're planning a battle, not choreographing a musical."

"Point taken. But remember, without our men your family stands zero chance of winning."

"I'm well aware." Danielle followed the man's eyes back to the square. "Shouldn't you be at the Galveston meeting?"

"I'll be there, distracting your boss and making him think this was all his idea."

"Perfect. Now let's see how good these witches really are." Danielle flipped up the hood of her cloak and sauntered across the square to wait for show time.

Chapter 75

TAKEN

"SORCHA? DID ANYONE see where she went?" Vir's shouts became more frantic as he searched the dark alley. "Sorcha!"

"Vir, she's—oh shit," Gwyn groaned.

"What?" Vir's heart sunk as he saw Gwyn's full lips pressed into a thin line. "Where is she?"

Gwyn pointed toward the cathedral window.

Vir stepped onto the ledge and peeked inside. "She can't be. Holy shit—she's in the church. Steven! Get your ass over here."

"You two look like you've seen a ghost—whoa." Steven gaped at Sorcha standing at the back of the chapel's center aisle. "How's that even possible?"

"Look at her eyes," Gwyn said.

Sorcha's attention locked onto the railing in front of the altar. Julia and Lily gestured toward the children from windows across the cathedral. The members of the pageant didn't know they were in danger from the pretty lady with the blue eyes, until she tore their teacher's throat open with her fangs. Church doors slammed shut, each sealed with wicked flames.

"Did you think you were safe here, Sister? You were wrong." Sorcha tossed the woman aside and turned to the petrified kids.

"We have to stop her. Steven, help me." Vir ran at full speed to the front of the cathedral. "Maybe we can get in the same way she did."

"Don't! I wouldn't touch that—" Steven zoomed up behind him, a fraction of a second too late.

Vir grabbed the brass handles of St. Louis's main doors. A blaze of black flame propelled him across the square with enough force to smash the iron fence into rubble. Screaming in pain, he cradled his burned hands as Steven beat on the door with a twisted piece of iron.

"Sorcha, don't!" Gwyn's anguished wails echoed from around corner. "Vir! Where are you?"

"I'm here," Vir said. "Don't touch the glass."

"Your hands."

"They're healing. Don't look."

Leaning on each other, they watched Sorcha walk down the aisle, fire licking at her heels like a pack of snakes.

"She's going to kill those kids."

"That's not her, not my Sorcha." Vir fought the desperation crushing his heart.

Oblivious to the scene outside, Sorcha grabbed a little shepherd, sunk her fangs into the soft skin of his neck and drank long and deep. She dropped the limp body and turned her blood-streaked face to the group huddled around the manger.

"Scared now? You should be." Crouching down as if she were a tiger about to pounce, Sorcha screamed at the top of her lungs and leapt toward the children. Christmas trees and church pews exploded with blue flames, closing off any chance of escape.

"She's possessed, she has to be. She would never," Gwyn said.

"The baby. Sorcha stop, please!" Vir threw himself against the glass, absorbing the shocks until he collapsed in the alley.

Sorcha leaned over the manger and drooled, stroking the infant dressed as baby Jesus until the cape slipped off her shoulders. As the garment fluttered to the tiles, blue fire dimmed and retreated, curling back along its original path, sucking Sorcha out of the church and spitting her through the doors into the square. The entire episode had taken mere minutes but left behind scorched wood, smoldering Christmas trees, an unconscious child, and a dead woman.

Converging on Sorcha's motionless body, Steven, Lily and Julia tried to wake her.

"We have to get out of here." Julia spun around. "I hear sirens already."

"Where's Vir?" Lily's eyes darted between her friends. "And Gwyn? We can't leave them behind."

"Vir's hands got burned down to bones." Steven tucked his fingers into his sleeves. "Last I saw him, he was staggering back to the alley."

"Lily, go find Raimond. Steven, take her back to the penthouse." Julia scooped Sorcha into his arms. "This place will be crawling with crazy people in minutes. I don't know if anyone will believe traumatized children, but we can't take any more chances. Move!"

"What are you going to do?" Lily blocked Julia's path.

"Find Gwyn and Vir. And if I'm lucky, the criminals responsible for what happened here."

"Step on it, Nick." Danielle jumped into the front seat. "This massacre is going to cause hysteria." The witches' curse had been successful. Her well-laid plan worked perfectly—almost.

"On the word of those little kids? They don't even know what they saw." Nicholas whipped the van around tight corners and out of the cramped French Quarter. "Cole approved this plan?"

"I'll explain it all to him when we get across the lake. Just drive."

"How did you overpower a guy like that?" Nicholas nodded toward Vir.

"Didn't have to. He knocked himself out—burned the hell out of his hands. That made snapping his neck unnecessary." Danielle chuckled to herself. "But way too fun to pass up."

"You really needed to take Prince Norman's woman?"

"She wouldn't stop screaming—she saw me. I had no choice." Danielle sneered at Gwyn's body in the corner of the van. A twist with no contingency.

"Where are we going?"

"Take Highway 11 across the lake. Cole has a safe house there with the perfect basement."

"Perfect for what? If you want to kill them, just do it now."

"What's your rush, Nick?"

"I don't want to get caught with these two in the car—that's what."

"Killing them would be way too easy. I'm aiming higher."

"Good grief, Dani. The man doesn't want you. What are you going to do—rape him?"

"No, stupid. There's got to be a weakness in their security. I don't care if I have to rip his mind apart. I'll find it."

"And then what?" Nicholas eyes strayed from the narrow bridge and landed on Danielle.

"Geez—watch the road!" Danielle grabbed the dashboard. "I'm going to destroy the Banitierres. Every last one of them. That is, if you don't kill us first."

Chapter 76

PRAY

RAIMOND FLEW INTO the penthouse, tossing a stethoscope and black bag aside. His normally stoic face twisted in fear. "What the hell happened?"

"Sorcha was in the cathedral. Inside. Walking down the aisle."

"Yes, Lily told me that already, Steven. I want to know why and how." Raimond lightly patted Sorcha's face. "Honey, please come back to us."

"She looked possessed. Fire trailed behind her. Doors slammed, Christmas trees exploded." Steven's chest rattled with a wheeze. "Don't you think if I had clue why I'd have tried to stop it?"

"I'm sorry. Didn't mean to imply...." Raimond closed his eyes and let his neck sag. "Did strangers touch her? Anything out of the ordinary?

"No, nothing. We went shopping in the normal places. We were at the Warehouse Club, but Jeffrey mixed our drinks," Lily said. "Everyone we talked to, we knew personally."

"I smell smoke. Was she burned?"

"No, but Vir was, horribly. He wasn't healing." Steven looked at his own hands and cringed.

"By what?"

"The church door. I warned that idiot not to touch it, but he was crazed," Steven said.

"Where is Vir?" Raimond looked around the room.

"Missing." Julia burst through the balcony door.

"What do you mean? He was in the alley, slamming into the windows," Lily said.

"Vanished, as in gone. Gwyn too." Julia shifted her troubled stare to Raimond. "I think they were kidnapped."

"How did you come up with that, Jules?"

"There was so much chaos and screaming, people started peeking out of their apartments. One boy finally admitted he saw two hooded figures attack them."

"They overpowered both of them?" Raimond asked. "Where the hell was Draven?"

"Away on business. He's supposed to meet us at Normandie tomorrow night," Lily said.

Raimond cradled Sorcha's limp body in his arms.

"The boy said that one of the kidnappers, the smaller of the two, broke a dark-haired man's neck and they moved fast."

"Vampires?"

"Definitely, Raimond," Julia said.

"I'll use these last hours of darkness to look for them. Can't just leave town without searching. And Jules, we do need to leave," Raimond emphasized.

"I agree. If people think they saw vampires in their church, biting children—"

"Are you kidding me?" Raimond froze.

Julia shot an exasperated look around the room. "Sorcha killed a Sister and bit a child in the Christmas pageant. She was lifting the baby from the manger when the fire went out."

With gentle movements Raimond transferred Sorcha into Steven's arms before he stood. "Did she kill any kids?"

"I don't think so," Julia said. "But if they remember what they saw, people will go on a rampage."

"Everyone spends the day in the basement, locked in the safe room." Raimond peeled his white coat off and tossed it aside. "At dusk, cars will be waiting at the curb. Get in and don't look back. I'll

404

meet you at Normandie Hall."

"Lily, grab some blankets and extra clothes for Sorcha." Julia tossed a quilt across the parlor. "It may be safe downstairs, but it's far from comfortable."

"Take care of her, Steven." Raimond stopped and lifted Sorcha's limp hand to his lips. "She's going to need our support when she wakes up to this nightmare."

"What about Draven?" Julia asked.

"Pray that I find his fiancée."

"Pray to who, Raimond?"

"Anyone who'll listen."

Normandie Hall was oddly dark for the week before Christmas. All the holiday lights had been extinguished when word of the tragedy reached the plantation.

"So wait a minute, Raimond. You lost Vir and my fiancée? Are you f—" Draven raked his hands through his hair. "That's my future wife who's missing!"

Raimond shut the double parlor doors for privacy. "Don't forget my family member."

"Do we even know what happened? Has Sorcha woken up yet?"

"No, and I'd appreciate it if you don't scream at her when she does. She's traumatized already. Driving her into a frenzy won't help us get answers."

"Are you aware there's a mob in the city, searching door to door with torches?"

"I've heard. We need to make ourselves scarce for a while."

Draven scoffed. "You think?"

Chapter 77

SAFE HOUSE

"WAKE UP, DOCTOR." Danielle slapped the wounded vampire's face and waved a cup of blood under his nose. "Rise and shine."

The scent jolted Vir back to consciousness. "What the hell did you do to my neck?"

"Vampire tranquilizer. Don't worry, you won't have any permanent damage. Whatever happened to your hands though, that's nasty."

"Gold handcuffs?" Vir's eyes rolled back as he rattled chains holding him to the wall.

"Added incentive for you to stay put. You were born stronger than me, but a little gold levels the playing field."

"Who are you?"

"Oh, come on—you know I'm Danielle. I almost killed you once before." She took a long sip of blood and held it out for Vir. "Hungry?"

Vir lunged for the glass, falling just inches short.

"Ignore her."

"Gwyn?" Vir's eyes darted around the basement prison. "Why are you here?"

"Bitch wouldn't shut up." Danielle shrugged.

Vir lunged again, fangs slashing the air at the end of his chains. "That's my sister, you piece of trash. Whatever you want, she has no part of it."

"Ooo—temper, temper. Conserve your energy. You'll need it."

"For what?"

"I'll tell you when you wake up." Danielle crushed Vir's skull with a metal pipe.

"Think about what you're doing." Gwyn choked back sobs. "Hurting our family can't be worth it."

"Shut up, stupid shrew, before I knock you out too." Danielle waved the weapon at Gwyn. "Don't worry, I think about your precious family all the time."

"Take your time." Raimond handed Sorcha a glass of wine and watched as she sipped. "I know sometimes you see...or rather, tell us what you see."

"How did I get to Normandie?" Sorcha ran her fingers along the collar of her shirt. "The last thing I remember was watching kids sing in the cathedral."

"That's it?" Draven flew across the room. "I can't believe you forget going inside."

"In where?"

"The church—you walked into the damn church, you—"

Raimond flashed in front of Draven. "I warned you to take it easy."

"I don't know what you're talking about. Where's Vir?"

Draven forced himself to step back. "Sorcha. Nobody has seen him since before Christmas."

"What?" Sorcha clutched at a sudden crushing pain in her head. "Raimond, when is Christmas?"

"A week ago, honey. You've been unconscious for two weeks."

"You're lying. I mean, how—so long?"

"You must remember something. Please, think hard. Sorry I was rude. Gwynevere is missing too." Draven slipped onto the bed next to Sorcha and stroked her hand. "Whoever's behind all this, they're hurting them. Can't you feel it?"

"Everything hurts." Sorcha looked at her hand and then at Draven, before wiggling out of his grasp. "What happened to me?"

At first, she didn't believe the story Raimond told and when she did, it made her gag. "I bit a baby?"

"You drank from a child, but you didn't kill him." Raimond shoved an ice bucket under her chin as she started to wretch. "You didn't even bite the infant."

"We know it wasn't your fault," Draven said. "Foul play, no doubt. If you can recall anything, it may be the break we need. Have you had any visions?"

"I don't see anything. I swear I'll tell you if anything changes. Can I talk to Rayna or Steven?"

"Let's give her a break." Raimond opened the bedroom door, summoning her friends from the hallway.

"About time," Steven snapped.

"We'll be downstairs if you need us. Rayna, try and get her to drink," Raimond said. "She's weak, but maybe she can hold down your blood."

"Steven?" Sorcha groaned. "Steven, my head is splitting."

"I'm here now." Steven brushed past the older vampires. "Darlin', what are you wearing?"

"I—I have no idea, but it's so soft."

"Looks like one of Raimond's old linen shirts. Keep this shawl on—it's a little see-through."

Draven gritted his teeth as Steven pushed him into the hall and clicked the bedroom door shut. "Sorcha was our last chance."

"If you'll agree to watch things here," Raimond said, "I want to go back to town and search. I have a few more sources to try."

"Going to the city is—"

"Risky, I know." Raimond reached for Sorcha's bedroom doorknob, stopped and let his hand drop. "I'll stay hidden."

"Go. I've got things under control. How much trouble could these little cretins give me?" Draven asked.

"You'd be surprised."

"Just find them. Find Gwyn." Draven slumped against the wall. "Please. I'll pay your sources a king's ransom."

Chapter 78

LAST RESORT

A TERSE PHONE call forced Zelia to leave her patients. At the same request, Ivori abandoned her lunch. The nurses met in the basement.

"What's going on?" Ivori asked. "Are we in trouble?"

"How should I know? We got the same message."

"Seemed more like a command." Zelia picked her way around grimy puddles on the floor. "Who in the world asks nurses to report to the boiler room?"

"That would be me, ladies."

"Dr. Banitierre?" Ivori steadied herself against the wall. "Wh—what can we do for you, sir?"

"Well, first of all, you can come clean about who you really are." Raimond looked back and forth, dangling a file folder in each hand. "No? Nobody? All right. I have your employee records right here. Ivori Journe and Zelia Pavet—or shall I say Roussel?" Their names rolled off his tongue in a thick French accent.

Slumped shoulders and silence was their reply.

"Did either of you think you had me fooled? Ivori, the heiress to a voodoo legacy and Zelia—I employ half your ancestors to conjure spells and raise shields to protect my own family."

"I know, sir, but I don't practice," Zelia answered.

"And you, Ms. Journe?"

"Oh, I practice. I just prefer not to advertise it to my Catholic bosses."

"All fine and good. Now, get over yourselves and help me save some lives."

"Is someone injured down here?"

Raimond ignored Zelia's question. "I assume you both know—think you know—what I am?"

"Vampire?" Ivori whispered, slinking behind Zelia.

Raimond tipped his head back and willed his appearance to change. Dark veins raced across his skin and his eyes ignited to burning red as he curled back his lips to show off impressive fangs.

Zelia and Ivori both flinched and stifled screams.

Before they could turn, Raimond was behind them, wagging his finger. "Don't even think about running. I don't know if you have any loyalty left for me, but Sorcha and Vir need your help. I'm certain you won't let them down."

"Sir, we saw them, outside that new club," Zelia said.

"They were supposed to be dead." Ivori pointed her skinny finger. "You—you said so, Dr. Banitierre."

"Well they are, technically."

"Oh, come on! They walked out of that party like celebrities." Zelia clapped her hands on her hips. "Did you do this to them?"

"No, I did not. I don't have time to explain the details. They're both members of my family and in grave danger. A few weeks ago, Sorcha fell victim to a spell." Raimond picked his words. "Things got a little out of hand."

"Oh no, somebody crashed the pageant rehearsal at St. Louis, killed a Sister and bit a child. People are saying it was vampires, but the little ones are still too traumatized to talk." Zelia squeezed her eyes shut. "It was her."

"Do you know people here are hunting for vampires all night, every night?"

"Yes, Ms. Journe. The fragile balance of our coexistence with humans has been disturbed."

"So that was Sorcha—good God. Where's Vir?"

"That's the thing," Raimond answered. "During all the chaos, Vir and his sister were kidnapped and are still missing. Most likely they're being tortured, and the criminals may not stop at that."

"He has a sister?" Ivori asked.

"In a manner of speaking. You don't know her, but she's unmistakable—olive skin and black hair down to her waist. Her name is Gwynevere and she's engaged to my...friend."

"Is Sorcha safe?" Zelia asked.

"She's at my country home. She's fine for now, but if Vir dies..."

"I want to see her." Zelia inched closer to Raimond.

"Well." Raimond ran his hands through his hair. "If we get out of this mess, I'll have no objection to that."

"What do you want us to do?"

"Use your families. Work your connections. Some witch or priestess out there must know what happened. Secrets don't last long in this town, and Gwyn is a high-profile hostage."

"And if we learn anything?"

"I'll be here, or close by. You two are my last hope."

Zelia and Ivori backed out of the boiler room, sprinting down the hall and up the stairs until they reached the safety of sunlight.

"What now, Zel?"

"I'm going into the Quarter to see what I can dig up."

"I need to go all the way out to Plaquemines." Ivori glanced at her watch. "It's noon now. Let's meet at midnight, at the Algiers house."

"Got it. Listen, I know Banitierre is counting on us, but be careful—don't trust anyone you don't know."

"Don't worry," Ivori smirked. "I barely trust my own flesh and blood."

Raimond paced the floor of the muggy chamber. He exhaled and rubbed his hands over his face. *Can't just spin my wheels down here—those nurses will be gone for hours.*

It was a risk, but a calculated one. Raimond held his ear to the door before he cracked it open.

Silence.

He inhaled and read only the scent of mold and decay.

Perfect. No humans.

Flashing down the passage, he slipped into the janitor's office. Raimond made certain nobody else was on the line before he dialed the phone.

A formal voice answered after three rings. "Normandie Hall."

"DeLynch, it's Raimond. How are things there?"

"It's been rough, sir, but we're holding up."

"Is Julia available?"

"Yes, sir. Miss Julia, the—"

"Raimond, where are you?"

"At the hospital, in the cheerful cellar."

"The zealots are out in force. What if you get trapped down there?"

"Nobody's seen me." *Except a witch in denial and a voodoo starlet.* "I have the sewers as an escape plan, if necessary."

"That's revolting."

"I've survived worse, Jules, and so have you. How's Sorcha?"

"In excruciating pain most of the time. Then she just passes out. Is that a reflection of Vir's condition?"

"Most likely—and Draven?"

"He's a mess too," Julia said. "Emotionally and physically."

"The curse of knowing too much."

"He seems to be shrinking, if that's even possible."

"I'm sure Gwyn's captor isn't feeding her much," Raimond mumbled. "Do they speak to each other at all?"

"Mostly they just sit and stare. Have you turned up anything useful?"

"I have operatives out working for me. Fingers crossed."

"If you need to run, just do it."

"There must be an answer to this problem. What am I missing, Jules?"

"I have no idea, just come ho—"

Raimond stared at the phone as the line went dead.

Chapter 79

AXE

VIR STRUGGLED TO swallow. *How long have I been like this? Sorcha. Wait, no, she isn't here. Gwyn is with me. Gwyn needs help.*

"Take it easy. Stop fighting, brother."

"Gwyn!"

"Shhh, that dreadful girl is just outside the door."

"Have they hurt you?"

"As long as I don't touch these bars, I'm fine."

Vir squinted at Gwyn's hands. "Where's your engagement ring?"

"They must have taken it, the miserable thieves. Have to get that back, somehow. It's Draven's grandmother's ring."

"Did they say anything about their motives?"

"No, nothing."

"There's got to be a way to get you out of this hell." Vir groaned as he shifted his wrists in the brutal cuffs.

"Someone will find us. Draven won't leave any stone unturned, I'm sure of it. Shhh, they're coming back." Gwyn slid herself into the center of the cage, hugging her knees and hiding her face.

"Well, well. You're awake again, Doctor." Danielle planted her hands on her hips.

"Why do you hate me?" Vir asked.

"I don't. I hate your girlfriend."

"And why, exactly, is that?"

"Because she's stuck up and entitled."

"You're doing all this because you're jealous of Sorcha?"

"Doesn't matter." Danielle jabbed her finger into Vir's forehead. "You're stuck with me now."

"There's no reason for you to hurt Gwyn."

"She's meaningless. I'll sell her to the highest bidder. I'm far more interested in you."

"What the hell do you want?" Venom dripped from Vir's fangs.

"A little taste of you. So many dirty rumors." Danielle leered at Vir's shredded clothes. "But I'll settle for the password to your mansion, instead."

"You're insane. Even if I knew, I'd never tell you."

"Maybe you need to think about it a little longer." Danielle surveyed an array of gold weapons hanging on the wall. "Eventually you'll both starve and slip into a coma, but in the meantime…" She plucked a dagger from the rack and jammed it under Vir's chin, drawing a thin line of blood down his neck and across his stomach. She stopped the blade just below his waist.

"Danielle!" Nicholas screeched from the corner. "If you're going to dismember him, I'm out of here."

"Don't worry, Nick. As much gory fun as that would be, it would be a crying shame. Such a perfect specimen."

"Don't—touch—me," Vir hissed.

"As you wish." Danielle turned away and her face went ugly. Spinning back, she plunged the blade through Vir's thigh and twisted it until blood shot up like a geyser.

Vir's shriek shattered the basement windows.

Nicholas grabbed his partner and dragged her down the hall, slamming the dungeon door behind them. "Get yourself together! Figure out what you want from these two before their royal rescue party shows up."

"Sorry." Danielle licked Vir's blood off her lips. "That was a little silly."

"Try reckless or insanely stupid. Stay here." Nicholas zipped in and out of the torture chamber. "I pulled the knife out of that jerk's leg.

Can't take the screaming."

"I'm completely in control now. Can you feed him?" Danielle held out a flask of blood. "Just a couple swallows."

"Dani, I'll do anything for you, but you stabbed him and now you want me to feed him. You know you're sick, right?"

"I'm not great at this mind reading stuff but I do know that if he's unconscious and not thinking, I can't read anything."

Nicholas rested his hands on his knees before he snatched the flask from Danielle and charged down the hall.

"Pour it down his throat if you have to," Danielle called after him, rubbing her palms together. "Wait—stop! I have a better idea."

Nicholas leaned his forehead on the steel door. "We're gonna' die."

"No, I'm going to give you a city, a sparkly one. Make the girl do it."

"What if she drinks the blood and attacks us?"

"I'll be ready with gold aimed at his heart."

Nicholas followed her instructions.

Grabbing the flask, Gwyn zoomed to Vir's side. She touched his battered face gingerly. "Wake up, brother—wake up and drink. That's it, slowly."

"Clean him up."

"What?" Gwyn looked at the bucket in Danielle's hand, up at her captor and back at the bucket.

"Never mind, I'll do it." Danielle tossed the pail of ice water over Vir's head as he screamed in shock. "Welcome back, you look so much prettier."

Vir ground his teeth. "Let my sister go."

"Sure, tell me the password for Normandie Hall's back door."

"Raimond doesn't trust me with family secrets."

"Come on, you and Sorcha must have used that tunnel entrance dozens of times—sneaking in and out for your little trysts."

"She never spoke any password."

"Think hard. Maybe you screwed your little slut in the mud and didn't want to track evidence through the front door?"

Vir raised his burning stare to Danielle's face.

416

"Ooo, what would the uppity staff think? I can frolic in the mud too."

The shackles snapped Vir's lunge short.

"Nick, get that girl out of the way."

"Vir! Block her out, don't listen to—" Gwyn howled as she was dragged across the floor by her hair.

"Come on, Doc, it'll be fun. You and me in the middle of that ballroom floor."

Nicholas snapped his fangs and stared at the stone wall.

Danielle toyed with the buttons on her shirt. "We could sell tickets."

"Go to hell."

"One time inside me and you'll forget that pitiful little nurse." Danielle lifted her skirt and straddled Vir's legs. "How about I do all the work?"

Vir flew at Danielle, knocking her on her back. "Not if you were the last female on earth." He spat in her face. "Revolting whore."

The basement fell into crushing silence.

"Goddamn it—goddamn you." Wiping her face with the back of her shaking hands, Danielle grabbed a battle axe from the wall and held the gold tipped blade against Vir's neck until blood oozed around it. "I'd love to do this, but I've got something better." Whirling around, she swung the weapon with deadly accuracy, leaving Nicholas holding Gwyn's severed head.

Vir's fury exploded like a bomb through the basement. His screams drowned out Nicholas' shrieks as the head tumbled across the floor.

"Gwynevere!" Vir's mind exploded in a cacophony of terror and pain, crushing him from the inside out. "My sister!"

"What the hell did you do? We have to go, we have to run." Nicholas frantically tried to scrape Gwyn's blood from his hands. "Now!"

"Wait."

"For what? Do you have a death wish? You just killed the prince's damn wife."

"Fiancée."

Nicholas clawed his forehead with his fingernails. "You think that'll make him any less furious?"

"Vir's defenses are down." Danielle concentrated on the quaking body. "I'm hearing gibberish."

"I don't care, Dani, let's go!"

"No, one more minute. I'll tear it out of him."

"Dani, you know I love—" Nicholas clapped his hand over his mouth. "One minute—then I'm leaving you in this dump."

Danielle crawled across puddles seeping through the floor. "There are things in your mind—random words that belong to Sorcha."

"I don't know anything—I swear!" Vir couldn't clamp his eyelids shut hard enough to keep blood from spraying through. "Get out of my head!"

Danielle groaned and licked her lips. "Ouragon. That's the key to the fortress. Now, I'm going to destroy your family."

"Just kill me," Vir whispered.

"Nah, too easy. I'm leaving you here to rot. It's far worse than actually dying."

Vir didn't bother to fight as Danielle patted his cheek and zoomed to the door.

"Thank you for your assistance, Dr. Ashayle." The red glint of the ruby on her finger was the last thing he saw.

Chapter 80

LOCKDOWN

DRAVEN SLAMMED THE parlor doors open and stumbled across the tiled foyer. "Sor—Sorcha!" Clutching his chest, he leapt up the staircase. "Sorcha…"

Vampires who cracked their doors open for the turmoil, retreated at the sight of the prince careening off walls and knocking crystal off tables.

Steven stood his ground in the hallway. "She's sleeping."

"Move, boy." Draven barged into the bedroom.

"I'm awake." Sorcha braced herself against the headboard. "What's wrong?"

"Are you still in pain?"

"It's excruciating." Sorcha slid out of bed. "Why?"

"I don't feel anything. Nothing."

"Maybe they let her go?"

"No, I think—she's gone." Draven reeled and crashed through the balcony doors.

"What do you mean gone?"

Draven dropped to his knees. "Those animals killed my beautiful lady."

"No—no, I'm sure that can't be," Sorcha said.

"Do you still sense Vir? Your heart feels his pain?"

"It feels like a scalding rock in my chest. I can't even imagine what he's going through."

"Then he's still alive, because I only feel emptiness. Raimond didn't find Gwyn in time."

Sorcha reached to comfort him but snapped her fingers away from his raw waves of grief.

"I have to leave."

"No." Sorcha jumped onto the balcony, gritted her teeth and absorbed ice bullets of agony as she dug her nails into Draven's flesh. "Don't you dare give up on them."

"It's over. I can't save anyone." Draven peeled her fingers from his arm, one at a time. "My royal guards will keep you safe enough." He launched himself off the balcony and into the swirling night sky.

"Damn you, Draven!"

"Shhh—stop screaming." Steven whipped the handkerchief from his pocket and held it against Sorcha's shredded knees.

"What do I do now?" Sorcha staggered into the room and tore at her hair with shaking hands. "Wait around to die inside?"

Julia secured storm shutters across the shattered French doors. "We all stay put until Raimond comes home. Sorcha, I don't know what happened with Gwyn, but Raimond is looking for Vir. You have to trust in that."

"We're doing absolutely nothing to save him. Why are we just sitting here?"

"Because I've seen what humans do when they're scared." Julia rested her hand on Sorcha's shoulder. "We can't go wandering the countryside."

Things must be bad. Julia's never done anything remotely comforting since I've met her. "This is because of me, what I did. All this blood is on my hands."

"It wasn't your fault. You know it—everyone else knows it." Steven whipped the drapes shut. "That wind is howling right through here."

"I'm sure Draven blames me."

"No, he doesn't and he isn't here anyway." Julia rammed a bureau in front of the billowing curtains.

"What are you doing?"

"Putting the house on lockdown and the guards on full alert. Rayna, instruct the donors. Nobody goes in or out."

"You're scaring everyone," Steven said.

"This is serious. Stay away from the windows."

Sorcha ignored the panic and twirled her locket on its chain. "I have no pictures of Vir. None."

"When all this is over we'll have one taken—a portrait fit for a king and queen," Steven said.

"I know you two don't get along." Sorcha stared at her fingers.

"We're on the same side. He loves you, I love you. Nothing else matters."

"How about in the ballroom, dancing? That's my favorite memory."

"You got it." Steven crushed her to his chest.

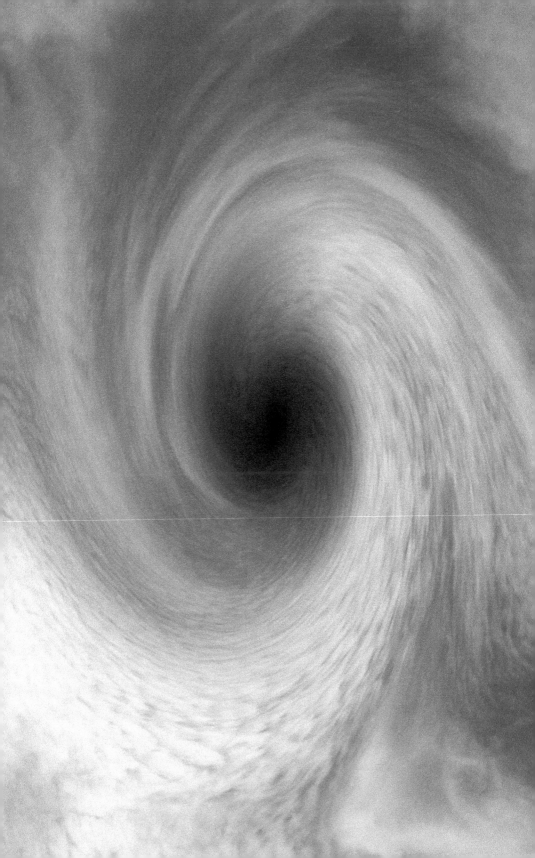

Chapter 81

OURAGON

DANIELLE CRAWLED ACROSS Nicholas' lap and rolled down the window. "Stop the car."

"Are you crazy? The wind nearly blew us off this rickety bridge already."

Danielle flailed her hands at the oncoming car. "Cole! Stop, it's us!"

Cole shouted over the wind. "Thought we were meeting at the safe house?"

"We're done there." Danielle brushed damp hair off her face. "I—we—got what we needed."

"Did you kidnap them in that?" Cole pointed at the dented van.

Nicholas' expression went blank. "You know about the kidnapping?"

"How could I not know, genius? The entire city is whipped into a frenzy. Humans are hunting for vampires and the vampires are hunting for you. Ditch the damn van."

"Where?"

"Push it in the lake. Geez, do I need to do everything?" Danielle dragged Nicholas out of the front seat and heaved the van through the fence into the roiling water. She slid into Cole's car and shook the rain out of her hair.

"What did you two find out?" Cole asked.

Danielle smirked and crossed her arms. "I got the password."

"The password for…?"

"The tunnel entrance to Normandie Hall."

"Impressive." Cole's eyes flicked to the rearview mirror. "Nicholas, what are you not telling me? Speak up!"

"Danielle killed the girl, boss," Nicholas blurted out.

The car swerved and ricocheted off the guardrail before Cole regained control. "You did what?"

Danielle braced herself against the door. "I didn't plan it. It just happened."

Cole let go of the steering wheel and grabbed her by the throat. "Killing the prince's fiancée just—? Do you know what kind of war you've brought down on us?"

"Then, let's take the fight to them. I can get you and your army—us—into that mansion before anyone sounds the alarm," Danielle wheezed.

Nicholas crawled across the seat and twisted Cole's neck until he released Danielle.

"Get your hands off me!" Cole hit the brakes and slammed Nicholas into the roof of the car. "Have you lost your mind?"

"I got us the keys to the city. Your city, Cole." Danielle's eyes darted between the men.

"Fine. Great." Cole nailed the gas pedal. "You should never have taken that girl. Was she part of the meticulous plan?"

"No, I improvised," Danielle answered.

Shaking his head, Cole let several minutes pass in silence. "So, what's the password?"

"Ouragon."

"What the hell is that?" Nicholas muttered.

"Very clever, Raimond." Cole twirled his finger around his head.

Nicholas leaned forward. "So, you just say Oura…whatever and the door opens?"

Danielle rubbed the red marks on her throat. "Nope, you write it on a chalkboard. Then, your body passes through the gate."

"You got all this from the girl?"

"Vir told me."

Cole chuckled. "He told you?"

"She tortured him for days. She almost cut off his—"

"That's enough, Nick. I stole it from him." She tapped her finger against her forehead. "Get it?"

"Where's Vir now?" Cole asked.

"Killed him too."

Nicholas grabbed his head. "Dani—you didn't!"

"Yes, I did. Who cares?" Danielle slammed her mind shut. "Nobody will be alive to avenge him." *And nobody needs to know I didn't finish the job either. I'm keeping the doctor for myself—my own private victory celebration.*

"That mansion is a fortress. How do you plan to get our bumbling crew past the Royal Guard?" Nicholas asked.

"The element of surprise." Cole stared through the windshield at the darkening clouds. "This storm is the perfect cover for our little invasion. I have allies lined up, local clans, and the Rakshasa army Danielle's friend Lock brought to the table. We may have to divvy the city up block by block, but New Orleans will soon be ruled by Victoires."

Nicholas slumped back into his seat. "That's a lot of people to trust with a secret."

"I packed for you." Ivori shoved a partially zipped satchel at her friend as they collided on the Algiers Point street corner.

"Slow down, I thought we were meeting at the house?"

"We need to move, Zelia. Look at the sky. If we don't catch this ferry, there may not be another one for days."

The women sprinted to the dock, hopping on board just as the captain blew the whistle and gunned the massive engines into the wind.

"This storm was supposed to be a dud."

"Forecast changed. You should have seen the flooding out in Plaquemines already." Ivori wrapped a scarf around her head and glanced up at the swirling clouds. "May be a direct hit."

"At this time of year?"

"And nobody's ready for it."

"Timing couldn't be worse." Zelia braced herself as the ferry lurched. "Did you learn anything while you were out there?"

"Sure did—how about you?"

"Yep, and none of it's good. We need to talk to Banitierre."

The nurses slipped through the back door at Sisters of the Peace, barely escaping the first raindrops hitting the pavement with the force of miniature bombs.

"Dr. Banitierre, you down here?" Zelia stood stone still in the basement. "Ivori, what if he left already?"

"I didn't leave." Raimond held his hands up as Ivori and Zelia jumped. "What did you uncover?"

"Witches are behind it, all of it—not Roussels." Zelia cleared her throat. "They used her own power against her."

"There are plenty of bad apples who'd love to see my coven out of power."

"When Sorcha put her cape on, the curse was activated. Then it slipped off her shoulders."

"And the fire went out and she got thrown into the square." Raimond walked in circles. "Blasted cape."

"Just in time, before she killed the baby," Ivori said. "The Allemand coven cast the spell—"

"What was that name?"

"Allemand?" Ivori hesitated. "But they partnered with a vampire."

"I still think those mercenaries conspired to kill me."

"Doctor?" Ivori leaned forward.

"I'll deal with the Allemands later. We suspected Vir and Gwyn were abducted by rivals, but that's tremendously brazen." Raimond ran his hands through his hair. "Who would do something so reckless?"

"Do you know anyone named Danielle?" Zelia asked.

"Victoire? Danielle Victoire?" Raimond roared. "She's not even supposed to be on this continent. I'm sorry, I didn't mean to scare you—I'm just..."

Ivori shuffled backward. "This Danielle, she planned to take Vir but not Gwyn. No witches in this city are stupid enough to kidnap a royal."

"What in the world does that little tramp want with Vir, besides the obvious motivation of hurting Sorcha?" Raimond drummed his fingers on the wall.

"Why would she ever have a problem with Sorcha? She's a saint."

"Jealousy, Zelia, plain and simple."

"My aunt gave me an idea of where they may be." Ivori rubbed her arms. "Gwyn apparently wears a big ring?"

Raimond's head snapped around. "An heirloom ruby. Why?"

"It's traceable," Ivori said. "The energy signature it gives off is coming from a house across the lake."

"Give me the address. That's where they are." Raimond patted his pockets frantically until he located a set of keys.

Ivori stepped in front of her boss. "Wait, there's something else. My family said this whole scheme had something to do with a password?"

"There's no way..." Raimond braced himself against the doorframe. "That's bad—I never changed it—Lord, they're all there."

"Who, sir, who's where?" Zelia shook her head.

"Ladies, I'm going to ask you for a favor, a dangerous one."

"We want to help Sorcha, whatever it takes."

"Then follow the signature of that ruby ring. Find Vir and Gwyn. Can either of you drive a hearse?"

Zelia caught the keys in mid-air. "Where are you going?"

"Normandie Hall, to save my family from those Victoire animals." Raimond shoved a box of bottles at Ivori. "Take this, you'll need it."

"What the—what is it?"

427

"Blood, Ivori. Feed it to the vampires so they don't feed on you."

"Ugh, terrific."

"Bring them back to the city. They'll know where to go." Raimond zoomed to the phone.

"Sir, the lines are—" Zelia ducked when he threw the silent receiver across the basement.

"Be careful, both of you. Use all the sense and magic you have. This is deadly business."

Raimond burst out into the rain, searching for a vehicle to borrow or steal. He fixated on a sleek sedan parked by the curb and tapped on the window.

"Mister, can I get some help?" Hunching his back against the wind-blown rain, he waited as the driver cranked down the heavy window. "I'm a doctor here. Wondered if I could borrow your car."

"No way man, you can't..." The driver focused on Raimond's eyes. "Sure, take it—anything I can do to help the hospital."

"Thanks, buddy. Actually, you can do one more thing for me."

"Name it."

Raimond scrawled a number on a scrap of paper and handed it to the stranger as they traded places. "Find a phone that works and call this number. Let it ring until someone picks up. Tell them to seal the tunnel using whatever means necessary. Tell them the duke is on his way."

"You got it."

Raimond slammed his foot on the gas, sending the car hurtling toward Normandie Hall. "Hope I'm not too late."

"Zelia, stop!"

"You're dragging your feet." Zelia cinched the raincoat tighter around her waist.

"My family made me promise not to get involved in vampire

battles," Ivori said.

"Don't you think my coven made me promise the same thing?"

"Could have guessed that. Quarter politics."

"I know you've played all disapproving with Sorcha, but I'm pretty sure it was an act."

"She wasn't a complete saint, you know."

Zelia whirled around. "Did she deserve to be slaughtered?"

"Of course not."

"You damn near fed Vir out of your palm during that miserable voyage because he would've let himself starve." Zelia pointed at Ivori with both hands. "So, I'm betting you won't walk away and let them die now."

"All right, why the hell are we standing out here in this storm? I'm soaked to the skin already."

Zelia grinned as they climbed into the musty hearse and navigated the deserted streets to Lake Ponchartrain.

Chapter 82

FLOOD

A SINGLE CANDLE still burned in the basement where Vir faded in and out of consciousness. His spirit watched from the ceiling, flawless, undamaged and perfect down to the last carnal detail as his vampire body battled to give up.

Just want to die—then I'll be with my sister. Not sure I can kill myself, even if I want to. Can't really starve to death. I'd be a withered skeleton, still technically alive for anyone with a few drops of blood to offer.

"Gwyn…" Vir leaned toward what was left of her body and drifted back into a stupor.

Sorry I didn't—couldn't—save you. I've lost everything to death. First Sorcha, then myself and now you, sister, except this time it's final.

If I give up, what happens to all those people whose last words I witnessed? I promised not to let their memories die. Gave them my word. Sorcha heard their dying stories too, but Danielle is planning to destroy the whole family.

Can't let that happen—Sorcha is my life, my only love. I have to get out of here. If someone kills me, so be it. Whatever's on the other side of this hellish existence, I'll go there with a clear conscience.

Hope this works. Vir turned his attention to the gold cuffs. *Hope it grows back.* He set his fangs into the flesh of his left wrist.

Why is this so damn difficult? I can see my bones but I can't bite off my own hand fast enough to beat this curse. Just gnaw the edges enough to pull it through.

Vir screamed as his flesh peeled back and a bloody stump

resembling a hand slid free.

"Zelia, I definitely heard something." Ivori flipped her collar up and stepped out of the hearse. "But all these houses look abandoned."

"That wind almost blew us off the bridge, so we're not leaving until we search every one. Do you see a faint light in that basement?"

Ivori squinted into the dark. "The fact that any house even has a basement in this flood zone is—"

Zelia pounded her fist on the steering wheel. "Too suspicious to be coincidence."

"Don't park too close. Turn this jalopy around in case we need to get out in a hurry."

Zelia aimed the car at the river before she turned off the ignition. "You scared, Ivori?"

"Hell, yes. Hungry, tortured vampires? Don't expect Vir to remember us. He's different now—a killer."

"Don't forget that box of blood. We give it to them and we'll be safe, like Banitierre said."

"Still can't reach her." Vir stretched as far as his chains allowed, his bloody fingertips falling just short. Gwyn's body started to disintegrate the moment she died. All that remained was ash and a few clumps of hair.

"If you're still here sister, say something." *I swear this house is shaking. What the hell is going on out there?* Vir made a futile attempt to dislodge the remaining shackle before he looked down again. Water leaked through the basement walls. *I'm not drowning in this tomb.* He tore into

431

his other hand with his fangs.

"Dr. Ashayle, Vir! What are you doing?"

Vir spun to face two strangers peeking through the doorway. Covered in dirt and his own blood, he looked like a monster.

"Oh Lord, his eyes!" Ivori stumbled back, barely holding on to the precious cargo. "And I see bones. Is that even...?"

"It's him, I think, what's left." Zelia peered into the flickering light at his burned flesh. Her shaking hands held out an open bottle. "For you."

Vir finished it in a single gulp. "More."

Zelia slid the entire box to Vir and watched as he bit off the corks, drained three more bottles and seemed to grow larger in front of their eyes. "Save some for your sister."

"That's my sister." Vir pointed to a puddle of muck. "Gwyn's dead."

Zelia's hand flew over her mouth. "I have to unlock that handcuff—where's the key?"

Fortified by the blood, Vir tore the manacle from the wall in one violent motion.

"Please don't kill us."

"Give me a break, Ivori. I'm not going to eat you." Vir dropped to his knees next to Gwyn's remains. There was nothing left to save, she wore no jewelry except her ring, and that was long gone. "She was beautiful, you know? Kind and loyal, a rare friend."

"I am so sorry. What happened?" Zelia asked.

"They killed her because of me."

"Who?"

"Danielle Victoire. She murdered my sister because I wouldn't give in to her. I spit in her face."

Ivori recognized the name. "Dr. Banitierre mentioned her."

"Where's Raimond, and where's Sorcha?"

"He sent us to find you. He went to Normandie Hall. He said Sorcha was there—everyone was there."

"Danielle stole the damn password, which I knew, but I shouldn't have known." Vir pounded his fists into his face. "She ripped it out through my eyes."

"Dr. Banitierre told us to bring you two back to the city."

"It's only me now." Vir flexed his hand, tossed the broken the cuff aside and grabbed a weapon off the floor. "Where the hell are we anyway?"

"Slidell." Grabbing the remaining bottles, Zelia and Ivori followed Vir's flash up the stairs.

"You're a vampire, why do you need an axe?"

"Not just any axe—this one. I'm getting payback." Vir grabbed a phone off the wall and dialed a set of numbers, over and over. "Had a dial tone for a second, now nothing. Can't even warn my family. They're sitting ducks."

"Whoa." Zelia stopped short on the porch. "The lake is at the door already."

"And almost at the car." Ivori pushed past her friend and stopped on the first step. "Too much current, we'll be swept away."

"Hold onto me." Clenching his teeth against the pain in his hands, Vir muscled through the rushing water with both women clinging to his arms. "We need to get to the west bank of the river. Normandie is about sixty miles away."

Zelia flipped the ignition and engine roared to life. "There are waves lapping at that bridge."

"Just keep driving. Don't stop or we're finished." Ivori steadied herself against the dashboard and turned around. "Vir, she's not there anymore."

Vir let the curtain on the hearse's window fall back into position. "It's the last place Gwyn was alive. Feels like I'm abandoning her."

"I don't know where vampire souls go when they die, but I can tell you for sure that nobody was in that house when we left."

"How did you two get involved in this mess anyway?"

"First tell me what happened to your hands." Ivori passed him a bottle from the front seat. "Then I'll explain everything."

"Nail that gas pedal to the floor, Zelia," Vir said. "The Victoires have a tremendous head start."

Chapter 83

AMBUSH

"DANIELLE, I THOUGHT you said we were going to waltz right through this tunnel?"

"Stop whining, Nick. A little water won't kill you."

"Yes, but you might—you and this idiotic plan."

"Shut up." Cole cringed as he waded into the blackness. "Pay attention to what you're doing, Nicholas. You'll be thanking her when you're living like royalty in the Quarter—if I allow it."

"Where's your stupid Kettly?" Danielle asked.

"Why's she *my* Kettly?" Nicholas shrugged at Cole's icy stare. "She's afraid of the mud. Said she'd meet us upstairs."

"You both remember the password, right? I'll go first. If it works, copy what I do exactly—one at a time." Danielle steadied her hand and printed on the chalkboard. All three Victoires passed through the iron gate before the dragon lady burst through the wall.

"You people can't come in here!"

"Yes, we can, you miserable crone. We just did." Danielle struck a match on the stone wall and ignited three torches. "Time to let the troops in the fancy front door."

Nicholas watched Cole barge past him and disappear up the stairs. "Dani—we don't have to do this. We can still get away."

"We're almost there." Danielle shoved the torch into his hand and kissed his lips. "See you on the other side, Nick."

"Take his advice, little demon," the dragon lady said, "or your final death will be in this house."

Danielle took a last look at the gate and jammed her finger in the witch's face. "Go back in your box, old woman, and kiss your job good-bye." Flashing up the stairs, she kicked open every door until she found the donor residence.

"What the hell?" Humans converged on the stranger. "Who are you?"

"How did you get down here?"

"You're not a member of our family. You—you're that…"

"Yeah, I'm her and I'm not here for a drink. Your family is dead." Danielle grabbed a bottle filled with kerosene from her bag and lit the fuse. "Run or die."

She dashed up the stairs seconds before the tunnel exploded into a raging inferno.

Julia paced the floor of Sorcha's bedroom, rubbing her eyes and twisting her fingers.

"What's the problem with DeLynch? That phone has been ringing for…bloody wires must be crossed." Steven slammed his fist on the table and collapsed in a coughing fit.

"Steven, you're wheezing." Sorcha and Lily helped him to a chair. "I know about your childhood asthma but I don't get this."

"Raimond can't figure me out either."

"Why now? Nobody sprayed perfume and I haven't seen a flower in weeks."

"Staff must be cooking. Something's burning." Lily grabbed a decanter. "We need a refill and I'll answer that damn phone." Before she had one foot out the bedroom door, a gold dagger pierced her heart.

The grand home turned into a war zone in the blink of an eye.

"Lily!" Sorcha caught the wobbling girl and sunk to the floor.

Steven grasped the dagger's hilt and yanked. "Not budging."

"I can't stop the bleeding!" Sorcha gritted her teeth and held pressure on the wound. Her skin sizzled with Lily's, where the gold pierced her chest.

Julia leapt past all of them and charged into the hall, forcing the intruders away from her family.

"You can't save Lily." Rayna pounded on Steven's shoulders and tore at his hair as he threw all his weight against the dagger over and over. "Listen to me!"

Steven crawled over Lily's body to kiss her forehead and stroke her hair. "My sweet girl."

"You're just giving up?" Sorcha grabbed Steven's shirt with her bloody fists.

Ben burst into the room dragging Vera behind him. "Mr. Steven, what's your plan? They're killing everyone."

"Fight back." Rayna climbed over Lily's shrinking corpse. "Avenge her!"

Sorcha squeezed Lily's hand and recoiled when it crumbled into black ash.

"She's gone, dear." Vera's eyes darted to flames licking through the shattered french doors. "We will be too, if we don't get out of this firetrap."

Steven swayed to his feet, eyes flashing from the pallor of grief to black orbs of anger. "Grab any weapon you can. Blades, fireplace tools or..." Tearing a picture off the wall he snapped the frame into pieces, handing out four jagged spikes. "Won't kill 'em, but you can slow a few down."

"Where are the gold stakes?" Vera tugged on the one in Lily's chest. It wiggled but stayed stuck. "Can't wait for this one."

"Raimond's library." Steven poked his head through the doorway, reached back and hauled Sorcha along by her arm. "Fangs out, follow me."

"Vera and I aren't kids, but don't underestimate us." Ben grabbed Rayna and brought up the rear of the line. "We've seen a few fights."

"Perfect." Steven barged into the library and ripped a panel off the wall, revealing a secret compartment. "Have you fired guns before?"

"I prefer the crossbow." Vera pointed to the back of the closet. "Hand it over."

"But…" Sorcha lingered in the blazing hallway and watched Julia force her attackers toward the foyer, using elegant decorations as weapons. "Steven…"

Through the wall of fire, Sorcha watched jagged shards of crystal flay two strangers' throats.

Julia wiped sticky blood on her shirt and crouched to meet the next attacker. "Who are you?"

"I'd like to know that too, you murdering bastards." Sorcha charged to the edge of the flames, looking for a way through.

"Go back, Sorcha." Julia ducked, but couldn't dodge a blow that snapped her head back.

"Stupid bitches. What does it matter who I am?" The man feinted left and right as Julia tore a light fixture free and twirled it in her fingers like a baton. "Brass? Why bother?"

"Look out!" Sorcha gestured wildly as the man pulled a gold dagger from his belt.

Julia's palms trailed woodwork as she inched along the wall. She glanced down at flickering under a bedroom door, waved her makeshift dagger at her enemy's eyes and took half a step back. "Antique brass."

"Clumsy wench." The attacker grabbed the shank and Julia whipped him around, smashing his wrist into the doorframe and sending the gold clattering down the hall.

"Steven, Julia needs us!" Sorcha dashed to the library and back to the edge of the inferno.

Julia invited the growling man to charge again. "Sorcha, duck, now!" Bracing her back against the wall, she jumped as high as she could and kicked his chest with both feet. The bedroom door splintered with the impact of his body. Flames exploded into the fresh oxygen and erupted both directions down the hall.

Steven dragged Sorcha away by her ankles. "You alive over there,

Julia?"

Julia rubbed her singed eyebrows and slithered along the floor, searching for carpet fringe and the end of the hall. A wry smile crossed her lips when her fingertips sizzled on the gold dagger. She turned back, and gave her friends a thumbs-up through a fleeting window in the fire.

"We'll meet her downstairs." Steven jammed a stake in Sorcha's hand. "She can handle herself."

Raimond's car careened to a stop on the flooded driveway. "Shit." Fire illuminated the grand lawn full of rag-tag soldiers watching his house burn. He sliced two men's throats as soon as his feet hit the mud. Fragments of familiar voices floated over the chaos. "Steven!"

Screams of protest were cut short by an explosion. Raimond ducked and daggered another soldier. "Sorcha!"

"I trust you've had fun so far."

Raimond heard that deep voice, loud and clear. Scrambling up the lawn, he could see through the smoky French doors enough to recognize Cole. The bald man stepped onto the landing and spread his arms in mock welcome to someone.

"Aren't you glad to see me, little Paris vagrant?"

"Julia." Raimond reached the veranda and was yanked back. He twisted the attacker's neck until it snapped and kicked his way free. "Jules!"

"This is your foolish operation?" Julia's voice answered. "Raimond will destroy you."

"Look around. No Raimond."

"I'm here! Jules!" Raimond screamed into the roar.

"Raimond?" Julia dropped into a fighting stance.

"You're delusional, and you're going to need that." Cole lunged for Julia's throat.

She swung the gold blade and split his chin to the bone.

"After tonight, your snobby family and this mansion will be history." Cole smiled and tasted his own blood.

Julia jumped back and crouched.

Cole's gaze didn't waver as he hurtled straight ahead.

Julia jabbed at his torso and missed. Holding onto the dagger took all her strength as he slammed her to the floor.

Raimond took cover behind a massive white column as a flurry of arrows speared the walls of the house. He heard Cole's cackle when he wrestled the blade from Julia's hands, tossed it over his shoulder and forced her knees apart.

"Enough." Raimond grabbed every arrow within reach and lunged for the front door. A girl blocked his path, recognized him and panicked.

"You're a Victoire." Raimond grabbed her throat.

"I'm Kettly. I'm sorry."

"How many are there?" Raimond yanked her face to his. "How many soldiers?"

"So many. Strangers. Witches." Kettly sobbed. "Please don't kill me."

"What witches?"

"Allemands." Kettly clawed at his grip. "Please, Duke."

"That bloody name keeps popping up." Raimond flung her aside, screamed a jumble of curses and kicked the door open. His blazing eyes zeroed in on Julia and Cole.

"Kill me." Julia hissed and spit out Cole's blood that dribbled from his chin.

"Fun first."

"Now—in my burning house?"

"Frustrating little tease." Cole flicked his tongue up her cheek, ignoring the rising sounds of battle below.

Julia dug into the carpet with her heels, flailing her hands until she found the wooden bannister of the landing. She tore a railing from the floor and drove the spike into his ear.

"Fight Jules!" Raimond reeled as skilled sentries inside the house tore into him with fangs and gold. "Fight hard!"

Cole's blood-curdling scream jumped an octave when Julia's knee connected with his groin. She flung him off and kept stabbing while her eyes scanned for the lethal dagger. She reached toward the glint of gold until Cole's hand shot up and clamped onto her throat. Her second attempt to grab gold ended when Cole's vise grip demolished her right wrist.

"Die, freak." Julia threw all her strength into a final assault on his chest with her left hand. She kicked his twitching body to the side and scrambled across the blood-soaked carpet for the stairs.

"Jules!" Raimond's voice finally defeated the fire's chaos.

"Raimond, I knew I heard you."

"Behind you—"

Julia wheeled in time to see Cole pull the wood from his chest. He tossed the gold blade in the air and grabbed it with his fist. "Now you pay."

"Don't you dare, Victoire!" Raimond roared.

The blade sliced Julia's skin and pierced her heart. Laughing in her face as she wobbled, Cole used one finger to push her off the balcony. Her body slammed to the tiles in front of Raimond.

"The others…" Julia's eyes landed on Raimond's face. "Steven was alive last time I saw him…Lily didn't make it. Sorcha tried so hard to help me."

"I've got you, Jules," Raimond said.

"All turning dark." Julia's hands clutched her bloody chest. "Can't feel anything, Raimond…I'm sorry."

"Jules." Raimond wrapped her in his arms before life left her eyes forever. Fury rippled under his skin and turned it black. "Victoire scum, you die tonight."

"We have to find Julia." Steven tumbled down the back stairs.

"Cover your mouth with this." Sorcha pulled the shawl off her shoulders and forced it over his face. When they emerged on the first floor of the mansion, fire was crawling up the drapes and racing across the ceiling. "This smoke is thick!"

"Don't breathe, stay close to the floor."

"How are we going to put this out, Steven?"

"We aren't—"

"But—"

"We need to concentrate on keeping our family alive. Hold onto Rayna and don't let her go."

Sorcha clamped Rayna's hand in hers like a vise and dragged her through both parlors.

"Shhh—both of you." Steven put his finger to his lips and pointed to the scene unfolding in the foyer.

Sorcha's jaw dropped when she saw the bloody tiles.

Cole skipped the stairs and leaped, landing between Julia's body and Raimond. "Any tips for me on ruling New Orleans, sir?"

"You may have wrecked my house, but you aren't taking my city or my family."

Cole nodded to the shrinking corpse. "Lovely lady."

Raimond struck first, smashing Cole into the solid columns that circled the foyer. Dropping to the ground, both men circled again, looking for an opening. Cole vaulted into the chandelier.

"You're hiding in my antiques now?"

He snapped a piece of metal from the fixture and hurled it past Raimond.

"Come down and fight like a man, Victoire."

"More family." Cole pointed to the ballroom.

"Stay there!" Raimond tried to stop the sobbing vampires, but they bolted for the front door and were slashed in half on the veranda.

Cole fell from the chandelier and landed on Raimond, yanking him backwards with a gold blade to his throat. "Say goodbye."

Raimond. Ignoring her instructions, Sorcha dropped Rayna's hand.

441

Raimond. She grabbed the revolver from Steven's waistband and zoomed in front of the fighting masters. *Raimond.* Before Cole flinched, she shot him point blank in the forehead.

Raimond gathered Sorcha in his arms. "That was dangerous."

"But—"

"And incredibly brave, but we need to get out of here. Where are the rest?"

"Ben and Vera jumped out a window." Steven carried Rayna into the clearer air of the foyer. "She won't last much longer in here."

"Rayna, stay alive. I have an important job for you." Raimond ripped into his own wrist and forced it into her mouth. "Do you know where the family book is?"

Rayna nodded in between swallows.

"Get it, leave through the original tunnels. There won't be any fire back there. Run until you reach the trees." Raimond clamped Rayna's face in his hands. "Do not—under any circumstances—come back in this house. Understand?"

"Yes, sir!" Rayna bolted into the smoke.

"Who else is left?" Raimond asked.

"I don't see how anyone could be alive upstairs. It's a furnace." Steven dodged embers from the roof. "Raimond, we couldn't save Lily. Our perfect Lily..."

"We—I lost Julia too." Raimond grabbed Steven's shoulders and shook him hard. "We'll recover, we're survivors."

"Not so fast." Danielle appeared behind Sorcha, pressing a blade to her throat. "One move and I end her. Actually, she's dead either way."

I'm tasting blood—my blood.

The front door exploded, cutting Danielle's victory laugh short.

Nobody recognized Vir until he slammed Danielle through the wall. He crawled into the rubble of the foyer. "Angel, are you hurt?"

"You're alive. I didn't think..." Sorcha staggered toward Vir's scarred hand. *I need to be in his arms.*

"Sorcha, don't move!" Steven waved frantically from the parlor.

What now?

The chandelier crashed to the floor between Sorcha and Vir. Fire and water rained down through a gaping hole to the black sky. Normandie Hall was collapsing around them.

"Behind you, angel."

Stepping back from the wreckage, Sorcha drove her elbow into Danielle's throat. *Sweet.*

"Finish it, Sorcha—choking her isn't enough this time." Raimond wrestled crystal and metal on his way across the foyer.

A figure burst out of the rubble. His gold blade opened a gash on Raimond's cheek.

"Cole?" Sorcha staggered back into the staircase. "I shot you, bastard."

Cole sneered and dug the warped bullet out of his skull. "Harmless lead, darling."

Raimond cleared the rest of the debris and inserted himself between Sorcha and Cole.

"Follow the plan, everybody." Cole snapped his fingers, never breaking eye contact with Raimond.

Danielle scampered into the smoke with Vir right behind her, the gold axe still in his hands.

"Sorcha, take care of Vir." Raimond pointed to the ballroom, his eyes never wavering from Cole. "Steven and I will handle this clown."

Windows in the upper gallery exploded from the heat. Fire roared across the pristine ceiling, turning everything it touched black. Vir caught Danielle and pinned her to the wall by her neck. "Not so funny from the other side, is it?"

"My plan incinerated your house and killed most of your family. I call that a success."

"You aren't going to call it anything." Vir slashed her throat open with his fangs and shoved the girl at Sorcha.

"Em, what are you doing?" Sorcha deflected Danielle into the fireplace mantle. "Just end her—don't mess around."

"Oh, I plan to—business first."

Danielle gurgled and vomited blood as she crawled to the middle of the floor, flipping onto her back amid burning paint and wood. "Come on, Doctor. I know you want it—center of the ballroom. Remember?"

"What the hell is she talking about?" Sorcha asked. "Vir?"

"That's it." Vir flew at Danielle, crushing her to the floor with the axe slicing into her neck. "Give me my sister's ring back."

"My ring now. Stole it fair and square."

"You want to play fair?" Vir yanked Danielle's clenched fist between them. "Take Gwyn's ring off."

Danielle's laugh was a weak gurgle. "Never."

Vir locked eyes with Sorcha as he clamped his teeth onto Danielle's hand and bit down. He twisted her arm back and dragged her, screaming, across the entire ballroom before his fangs severed her fingers.

"Sorcha, catch."

The engagement ring hit Sorcha in the face as mangled fingers flew past her head. Her hands fumbled for the ruby as she watched Vir's eyes go from blue to red and then to pure black.

The grandfather clock chimed then skipped a beat.

Danielle tore into Vir with her fangs, shredding the weakest skin on his hands and arms. She spat burned flesh onto her shirt. "Nick, where are you!"

Vir discarded the clunky axe and reverted to his natural, brutal strength.

"Vir, don't!" Sorcha's mind spun. *My hellion power, my Rakshasa blood.* "This isn't you."

"Sorcha, she killed my sister—my innocent, beautiful sister."

"Nick!"

"He can't help you." Vir slammed his hand into Danielle's throat. He crushed the cartilage with his fingers and tossed it over his shoulder like trash. "You're done."

The clock chimed again and choked.

Vir tore past jagged ribs and wrenched Danielle's spine through the wound in her neck, one vertebrae at a time. He held it in front of her face like a trophy. "Can't move—can't talk, but I know you're in there." Vir forced her eyelids open. "You and your heart can burn together."

"Oh no—Vir." Sorcha flew to him. "My Vir."

"I'm sorry if that was too..." He held his hands up. Bloody tar dripped on the white floor. "She was a murderer. Mercifully, Gwyn never saw it coming."

"Don't apologize. Danielle deserved it and more—look what she did to us—to you." Sorcha cradled Vir's wrist in her hands.

"It's healing."

"Not fast enough. Let's find the others and get out."

"Is Draven even here?"

"He left after he felt Gwyn die. He loved her, Vir."

"I did too, but leaving you is unforgivable."

Chapter 84

BETRAYED

THE DORJE BROTHERS hung back as the armies clashed, watching a small basement fire spread to engulf the entire mansion.

"That's a shame, really."

"Again, Lock? Whining about the brother you'll never know?"

"Actually, I was referring to the house, but don't you have a shred of affection or loyalty for Sorcha? She's purely your bloodline."

"She was in the way." Chapal tested the sharpness of a sword with his finger, drawing black blood.

"She was innocent." Lock's eyes exploded in blue fire. "You were out of control."

Chapal stood toe to toe with his brother. He smeared his own blood on his face as warrior paint. "I've no interest in that weak child. Honor above all, even family."

"You're a damn fool." Lock whirled away. "You've underestimated Vir this entire time—Sorcha too."

"They're in the ballroom. Looks like your friend Danielle didn't make it. Time for our signature finish."

"Chapal, just wait. Let the fire do the dirty work. We don't need more death on our hands."

"I'll do it then, since you're so sentimental." Chapal took a step toward the battle.

"Would be more of a signature finish with our tigers. Did you send

Father that message?"

"Weeks ago. Don't know what's taking so long, but we can't wait." Chapal gripped a dagger. "Lock, do you have my back or what?"

"Yes, brother, of course." Lock bit his tongue and ducked behind an old oak. Hair stood up on his neck as he peered through the twisted branches. "Chap—" The warning died in his throat.

Chapal dropped to the grass, swiveling his head around to Lock's position. A nod and hand signal from his brother assured him it was safe to stand tall in the clearing.

From a gazebo in the trees a crossbow glinted, held steady by a tiny hand in tasseled gloves.

"I can't take this back." Lock raked his hair with both hands before pounding a fist into his chest. "Forgive me, brother."

The bolt found its mark, slicing through Chapal's back and lodging in his heart. The vampire dropped his weapons, grasping the tip of gold protruding from his chest. He twisted and fell, his wild eyes searching for answers and finding nothing but fire and rain.

Lock cringed in his hiding place, unable to look away as the shooter stepped from behind a vine-covered trellis. Vera, a little old lady he met once, had just killed a Rakshasa prince. "Bloody impressive, and she'll kill me next." Lock bolted for Normandie Hall. He circled, looking for an entry point, repelled by flames at every turn. "Sorcha, Vir—damn it, Steven! Don't you dare die. I'm guilty of murdering my brother already."

Chapter 85

THE SWORD

VIR AND SORCHA didn't have to inhale black smoke, but seeing through it proved next to impossible. They stumbled into the foyer to search for Raimond. The roar of the fire was too deafening to yell over.

He would never have left without us—must be here somewhere.

Upstairs. Vir pointed to the second-floor landing. *They're fighting.*

Let me look first—you're really hurt. Sorcha hugged the wall of the curved staircase to avoid the flames. *I see them. Raimond needs our help.* She was a step from the landing when the grand stairs gave way, leaving her dangling above an inferno by one hand.

Vir dove away to avoid crashing debris. *Angel, hang on.* He took a running start and leapt through the flames, scaling the walls like a spider and hauling her onto the landing. *Can't stay here long.*

The battle was visible through the fire. Steven wrestled Nicholas, while Cole and Raimond were a blur of fangs and blood. Neither Banitierre had the upper hand.

Sorcha, you go to Steven. Raimond is trapped.

Take some of my blood—you're a mess.

No time—this is almost over. Vir untangled himself from her arms and slithered along the wall, out of Cole's sightline.

Sorcha waited for his nod and they made their moves simultaneously. Vir's weak body managed to knock Cole off balance, allowing Raimond time to free himself from a fallen timber. Sorcha broke up the jumble that was Steven and Nicholas, identifying the enemy vampire by his long hair and driving her fingers into his eye until it burst.

"Evil bitch!" Nicholas retreated to the threshold of the burning hallway. "Where's my Danielle?"

"In pieces. I enjoyed every second of ripping her apart," Vir answered. "What are you going to do about it?"

Sorcha grabbed Steven as he teetered on the edge of the landing.

Raimond slammed into Cole with all his force, knocking the man on his face. "I win." He slashed flesh and snapped ribs like twigs, sinking fangs into Cole's back until he tasted his heart. Raimond shredded it and tossed the bloody, black tissue into the fire.

"Now, let's get out!" Raimond spun, looking for an escape.

There was no time to react—no time for warnings. The final attack surprised everyone.

Nicholas burst onto the landing with his clothes in flames, screaming loud enough to pierce the roar of the inferno. Running with a gold sword in front of him, he launched himself at his enemies.

Vir defended Raimond the only way he knew how, by throwing himself in front of the blade. The weapon sliced through his shoulder and didn't stop until it emerged from Raimond's back.

Nicholas let go of the handle but his fingers didn't move, as if the sword were still in his grasp. "Oh, shit." He bolted through a jagged hole in the wall.

Sorcha shrieked out loud or inside her head. It didn't matter. All she heard was her own horror.

Steven zoomed to the edge of the landing.

"Stop, Steven." Raimond strained to lift his head. "Don't leave her."

"Vir—Raimond?" Sorcha didn't know which one to help first.

"You're still wearing my old shirt."

"Raimond?" Sorcha cringed when she touched his fiery skin. "Tell me what to do."

"Pull Vir off the sword. It's just a flesh wound, he'll live."

"This is all my fault." Vir pushed Sorcha away.

"What the hell are you talking about?" Raimond asked.

"Password—stolen." Vir reached for Sorcha's face, but his hand fell short.

"I never told…" Sorcha's tears rolled down her face.

"I must have taken it from your thoughts," Vir mumbled. "Didn't know."

"Just as much my fault. Much more. I should have known better." Raimond ripped into Vir's shoulder with his fangs. "Pull, Sorcha. Hard!"

Vir's remaining skin and tendons tore free, leaving him writhing on the floor. "Sorry, sorry, sorry."

"Let us help you, Raimond." Sorcha and Steven grasped the hilt and pulled the sword with all their strength. The blade didn't budge.

"Can't save me—the gold is in my heart."

"Nicholas is dead." Steven's eyes plunged to murderous black. "If it's the last thing I do."

"Steven!" Raimond struggled to sit up. "Please don't, it's not worth it."

"I have no choice."

Sorcha grabbed for Steven and missed, as he dove through a hole in the flames and disappeared. "What now?"

"Save Vir." Raimond crumpled to the floor. "He's your life now, your future."

"But I need you." Sorcha sobbed as she ran her hand over Raimond's cheek. "How can I—I can't…."

"You have to. Julia's gone." Raimond's voice cracked. "You're my heiress. Lead my family."

"Tell me how—please." Sorcha frantically tried to dislodge the dagger again.

"Find Rayna. Send her and the book to Draven. You and Vir run as far away as possible."

"Run where, Raimond? This can't be real."

"Don't blame yourselves or each other for anything that happened here. It'll be your downfall." Raimond's hand trembled as he touched the locket around her neck. "You'll know where to go."

Sorcha stood and spun around. "How could Steven leave me?"

"Don't be angry. He's avenging me." Raimond grabbed for her hand and fell short. "Promise you'll protect each other at all costs."

Sorcha froze in a sea of flames.

"That window—" Raimond pointed to the stained glass over the stairs. "Your escape route. Promise me!"

"I promise." Sorcha's knees buckled as memories of that magical window flashed through her mind. *The Gala, my blood signature, our beautiful waltz.*

"Damn it, Sorcha!" Raimond's fangs sprang from his mouth for the last time. "*Sortez!*"

Sorcha recoiled from Raimond's rage and the vicious force of the fire that scorched her skin. She squinted through dense smoke at Vir staggering on the landing. *Trust me, lover.* She only had a few strides to accelerate, so she made the most of them. She hurtled into him, clamped her arms around his chest and spun in midair, absorbing the brunt of the impact with her own body.

The force of her leap shattered colored glass and kept them airborne until they skidded to a stop at the tree line. She looked back at Normandie Hall in time to see fire explode from the window. Pouring rain did nothing to douse flames that licked the sky and disappeared into swirling clouds.

Raimond's home is gone—my home. "Raimond!" She clawed at her chest and stumbled back toward the blaze.

Rayna darted from behind the trees and blocked her path. Rain washed ash from her skin in streaks.

"I can't leave him in there."

"Nobody's alive in that hell." Rayna grabbed Sorcha's sleeve, and tore the thin fabric off her shoulder. She pointed at a crumpled form in the grass. "Vir needs you or you'll lose him too."

Vir's mangled and burned body was almost unrecognizable, but he was alive and staring at the sky. "Angel?"

Sorcha sunk to the soggy ground and cradled him in her lap. "Whisht, don't move. Rayna, can you feed him? Please."

She offered her wrist without hesitation.

"I know I've hurt you so many times." Sorcha touched Rayna's cheek. "I pushed you away when I shouldn't have, yet you're still here for me."

"Always for you—and Vir too. I would have done whatever you needed."

"Drink, Vir, come on." *For me. Do it for me, lover.*

"I would even give you a baby."

Sorcha's jaw dropped.

"You used to talk to me, remember?" Rayna said. "Occasionally, Vir did too."

"Ancient history." Sorcha rested her forehead in Vir's burned hair.

"You wanted children. So did he."

"Well, forget whatever we said." Flames from the destroyed mansion reflected in Sorcha's eyes. "Those lives are gone now."

Faint strength slithered beneath Vir's skin.

"That's enough, Rayna. Can't have you passing out on me."

"*Mais chère*, we can help too."

Heartbeats.

Sorcha snapped her head around at the unexpected voice, fangs out, ready to fight again.

Two shaky young women stood in the deluge, holding wine bottles. "Zelia? It can't be... Ivori?"

"They rescued him." Rayna dabbed blood from Vir's face. "Raimond sent them. He trusted them."

"Zelia." Sorcha clutched Vir's body to her chest and broke down. "I'm so sorry—I'm..."

"No, no don't cry—sorry for what?" Zelia wrapped Sorcha in her arms.

"I left you—let you believe I was—"

452

"You had no choice, but I'm damn glad to see you now."

"Should I give Vir more wine? It helped him back at the house."

"Yes, please." Sorcha met Ivori's gaze as she discarded the cork. "Thank you for saving him."

Vir gulped from the bottle. Rain washed blood and grime from his skin, as it began to heal and knit together. Sapphire blue flickered behind his lashes.

"Welcome back, lover."

"You folks need to get moving." Another strange voice rang out from the trees.

Vampire.

"Jayz, who's there now?" Sorcha slid in the mud and struggled to her feet as a man stepped from the shadows.

"Sorcha, I won't hurt you. I'm a friend. Danielle and Cole may be dead, but the Victoires have reinforcements looking to finish what they started."

"Okay—friend." Sorcha sunk to one knee and muscled herself back up. "What's your name?"

"I'm Lock." The stranger took Sorcha by the shoulders and stood her upright. "You need to drink, you can barely stand."

"I'm perfectly fine. Don't touch me."

"His blood will lead Victoire mercenaries right to you. There's a price on your heads." Lock pointed to Vir's injuries. "Wrap his hands, cover them—something."

"They're not healing like they should be. I don't..." Sorcha shivered. "Why?"

"I burned them, Sorcha—on the door to the cathedral when I was trying to get to you." Vir's voice was weak, but it was coming back.

"He nearly chewed one hand off to escape shackles. He'd already started on the other when we found him." Zelia swept a blanket around Sorcha's bare shoulders.

"What else did that Danielle bitch do to him?" Sorcha asked.

"Go now." Lock shoved Zelia in the direction of the hearse. "I'll find Steven."

"Steven got out?" Sorcha helped Vir balance on his unsteady legs.

"Fled over the roof, chasing a one-eyed vampire. Shouldn't be hard to catch up," Lock said.

Sorcha strained to see through the torrent. *He's so familiar.* "How do you know me and my family?"

"I don't just know your family, Sorcha. I am your family."

"I'm demanding your last name. Now!"

"Dorje."

Lock vanished before Sorcha could react.

"I'll try my blood directly on the wounds before we bandage them." Sorcha mulled Lock's answer over in her mind as she lifted Vir into the backseat. *Did he say Dorje? That's Vir's family.*

"Cheerful choice of vehicle." Rayna wrung the water out of her hair.

"It's fast, dry and safe for vampire travel," Ivori said.

Zelia gunned the engine. "Where are we headed?"

"Good question. I know where we're going, I'm just not sure how we're getting there." Sorcha ran her hand along the chain around her neck, clicked open her locket and found a tiny piece of Crescent stationary. "Zelia, can you find Nashville?"

"Alexa will be thrilled, *chère*. She never stopped searching for you."

Chapter 86

ALDENRIDGE

CONTAINERS OF WAR supplies provided the perfect cover to smuggle vampires into Great Britain.

Vir rested his head on Sorcha's shoulder. "Can't believe you kept Alexa's note all this time."

"She's the first person I met after I left New York. She had a hard time saying good-bye tonight, and I didn't fiddle around in her mind. Doesn't work on her anyway."

"She saved us, and all the memories we promised to protect."

"It's an enormous responsibility, isn't it?" Sorcha asked.

"But a tremendous strength—maybe the only reason we've survived." Vir winced as the doors slammed shut. "I've never flown before."

"Me either. I'm sure we're missing some of the thrill stuck down here in the cargo hold, but you need to rest."

"This is my fault." Vir turned his face away. "I ruined us."

"It was an accident." Sorcha pretended she didn't see the bloody tear run down his cheek. "Raimond made me promise we wouldn't blame ourselves. I'm keeping my word."

"I'll try. That's all I can promise."

"It's enough for now." Sorcha held his shaking body as close as he allowed.

"You won't let anyone bust this box open in the middle of the day?"

"I will not. Close your eyes and sleep, my love." Sorcha switched off the tiny flashlight and felt Vir's body shudder before he passed out.

He doesn't melt anymore.

They were both still traumatized from the last time they blended flesh, and shared one innocent word. A password.

We crashed an empire.

Sorcha yearned for sleep too, but her mind wouldn't turn off. She glanced at Vir, relieved to see him unconscious and free from guilt. He looked different, younger and deceivingly innocent in the borrowed black clothing. Fashion wasn't a priority at the moment, but hiding was essential, plus everything they owned was gone.

Pull yourself together.

Tears threatened again. The losses were almost too much to bear.

Think about the good times with him, not the murders or the sickness, the violence or the depression. Think first kiss. Our second kiss in the orchid grove was magical too. The first time we made love, you were so gentle—so fierce.

Sorcha pictured sparkling Normandie Hall, Vir in his tuxedo and her in her formal gown and diamonds, gliding across the ballroom floor like a fairytale couple.

You can waltz with the best.

And I remember you asked to be set free. Still working on that.

Takeoff made her queasy. Sorcha clasped her locket out of blind habit. It was the only possession that didn't go up in smoke. She traced her fingertips over Vir's face and through his hair.

Raimond said you're my future.

It must have been excruciating for the proud duke to step aside and watch their love affair play out, but he did it with incredible grace.

In the end, you offered your life to defend Raimond. It was your instinct— brave and true to you name.

But Raimond still died. Sorcha couldn't stop the tears from flowing this time.

My dear friend, I miss him already.

Plenty of others would miss his presence as well. The Sisters of the

Peace were going to have to adjust to new leadership. Dr. Banitierre had been the driving force behind their success since before anyone could recall.

I don't know how Zelia can return to life as normal and work at that hospital. I always knew she was a strong woman, but she turned out to be nothing short of incredible.

Ivori was never my biggest fan, but she came through too, when the chips were down. The Journe home was heavily damaged in the storm, and she committed to helping them rebuild. *She says she's done being a nurse and I believe it.*

Ivori had been seduced by the family business.

If I—I mean we—ever go back home... No—when we go back, we'll need both of them. The witch and the voodoo priestess—two powerful and connected allies.

Rayna knew her job was to keep the Banitierre records safe. *She's grieving and alone.*

Draven's island was Rayna's destination, but the prince had disappeared and covered his tracks well. Maybe he knew what happened to Normandie by now. Maybe he was too far gone.

I know his grief—yours too, lover. Sorcha brushed the hair from Vir's eyes as a weak smile slipped across his face.

Your sister, his fiancée—she's been avenged but nothing can bring Gwyn back. Then there's Vir's mysterious family member who helped us escape.

If Lock was Vir's relative, he was hers too. *I never considered myself a Dorje, but I am.*

Nobody knew Sorcha and Vir's destination except Alexa, who had made their arrangements. It was safer that way. They needed time, years maybe, to recover—somewhere to hide and make plans to take back control of New Orleans.

"You're awake." Sorcha brushed Vir's lips with hers. He was alive but cold—colder than even a vampire should be. "We're almost there."

"I'm getting better. Promise I won't always be so pathetic."

"Don't speak—drink the last of the wine."

"You take it. You need your strength too."

"We'll share it then." Sorcha swallowed a mouthful and offered the rest to Vir. "Remember our plan and the signal?" The plane wobbled as the tires made contact with the runway.

"Yes, angel. Three knocks on the lid and it's safe for you to get out. Just you."

"That's right." Neither of them moved a muscle as their accommodations were unloaded, dragged and bounced for what felt like eternity. "Here we go."

Three knocks.

Sorcha climbed out of the car into the grey light of impending Highland dawn.

"This is it. This is the place." She had stared at a photograph of Aldenridge Manor for most of her life, but never thought she'd see it in person. Most likely she was conceived here, on her parent's wedding night, and now she was back seeking shelter, the final smoldering ember of not one but two proud families.

Talk about full circle.

The crumbling castle was regal in her old age, inviting, enveloping and gloriously dark. Even the creak of the front door sounded like a cryptic hello, drawing Sorcha across the threshold and into the abandoned foyer.

This is my home. I can feel it.

She winced as she took Vir's hand in hers, feeling bones through his paper-thin skin.

He's still so fragile.

"Come in, my love. We've made it—we can both heal here."

"Is that fireplace big enough?" Vir nodded to the stone eyes and jagged teeth of a lion in full roar.

"I guess my family had...unique taste." Sliding her arm under Vir's shoulders for balance, Sorcha guided him through the mouth of the beast, to a hidden staircase. It was as if she had walked the worn passageways for years—following in the footsteps of phantoms. She instinctively pushed on a specific stone. A door swung open revealing a cavernous hall.

"Is this a wine cellar?" Vir asked. "That would be a miracle."

"Anywhere away from the sun will be fine with me." Finding a lamp with oil in it was another surprise. "Enough wine for you?"

"It's a damn good start."

Sorcha's head snapped around to the corridor behind her.

What was that? This place is supposed to be abandoned—but that hum. It's not vampire, but not entirely human either. If it's vagrants, we'll be eating them.

The crash of bottles on the stone floor stole her attention.

"The wine—angel, it's not just wine. This is blood!" Vir dove to the floor, licking his fingers as he grabbed for another bottle.

"Why the hell is there blood wine in an abandoned castle?"

Now I really hear someone in this damn cellar.

And then Sorcha saw it above her. The movement—the glint of gold in the lamplight—a deadly threat.

No, no, this can't be happening—after all we've survived.

Lying on the floor, guzzling blood to feed his damaged body, Vir never saw the killer coming.

Blind instinct propelled Sorcha's body in front of his as a shield.

I can't lose him too. I won't. Everything's been ripped away—my home, my mum, Raimond.

"Stop! Please—please don't." She summoned her last shred of power to change.

Hope I can scare him off. I know I can't fight anymore.

An attacker lunged, gold dagger in hand, skidding across the pool of wine and blood.

Heartbeat.

"Please, sir, we don't want to fight. I thought this was my home."

Did I really lead Vir into another ambush? He trusted me and I let him down—again.

"It's my house—mine. How did you demons even get in here?" The man drove the gold into Sorcha's chest.

This guy is too strong.

Her last ounces of strength kept the dagger from traveling deep enough to end her, but in her soul, she knew it was done. Then, the man looked at her.

Heartbeat.

"You—you look like…no, it can't be. Adelaide is dead."

The attacker's lapse gave Sorcha a glimmer of hope. Gold burned through her hands as she directed the razor-sharp weapon away from her heart. "Wait, what did you just say?"

Heartbeat!

"Sorcha? Good God in heaven—are you my Sorcha?"

That face, his face. It's different. Mangled—but I recognize it.

"Dad?"

Acknowledgments

Writing these acknowledgments is scary because I don't want to miss an essential contributor…but here we go!

First, I want to thank my husband Scott for being my grandest cheerleader and sharing in every bit of blessed craziness it took to finish this project.

I want to thank all the friends, family and fellow writers who made my dream of publishing *Monsters & Angels* come true: Jordan Rosenfeld, my first editor without whom this novel would still be an unfinished, messy manuscript; Katie Bartholomew Anderson for your analysis, editing and encouragement; Racquel Kechagias, my critique partner, for your precious insight and love of Raimond; Kat Mancos, for your comments and support; Magali Frechette, my cover designer who saw my vision and hit it out of the park; Courtney McDermott, my proofreader; Ray Laskowitz, for your New Orleanian wisdom; Linda and Stefan Bright, for so many years of spectacular images; Lynn Cozza, the genuine Dragon Lady; Christina Mercer, Suzanne, Crystal, Brooke, and Marissa, my earliest readers who loved the story enough to carry me past my doubts; Karen Andrus for her French Quarter insider tips: John Andrus, for driving me to Commander's Palace; Diane Bartholomew, for her legendary quotes; Bruce and Ryan Bartholomew, for asking me questions that made me think; New Orleans, the city, the people, for the power of your collective spirit.

And finally, the cast of *Monsters & Angels*. You inspired me, grabbed my hand, led me on an extravagant journey, and brought me home richer than when I left.

Merci beacoup!

About the Author

Anne Marie has been an equestrienne, chorale singer, candy-striper, EMT, and baseball fan. Roaming the back roads of New Jersey with her family, she found great respect for antiques, historical locations and the stories they hold. Her current list of favorite pastimes include coffee, bourbon, and *Les Misérables*—which requires more bourbon. She has been known to attend sporting events just for the flyover. The boat she and her husband christened Glory Days is her escape from the chaos of everyday life.

The inspiration for Anne Marie's debut novel, *Monsters & Angels*, is her fascination with vampires and her passion for everything New Orleans. When she isn't writing, she can be found working nights with the critical care team in a busy trauma center.

CPSIA information can be obtained
at www.ICGtesting.com
Printed in the USA
FFHW021826301218
50007140-54747FF